SIEGE

Simon Kernick is one of Britain's most exciting thriller writers. He arrived on the crime writing scene with his highly acclaimed debut novel *The Business of Dying*, which introduced Dennis Milne, a corrupt cop moonlighting as a hitman. His big breakthrough came with his novel *Relentless*, which was selected by Richard and Judy for their Recommended Summer Reads promotion and rapidly went on to become the bestselling thriller of 2007.

Simon's research is what makes his thrillers so authentic. He talks both on and off the record to members of the Met's Special Branch and the Anti-Terrorist Branch and the Serious and Organised Crime Agency, so he gets to hear first hand what actually happens in the dark and murky underbelly of UK crime.

To find out more about his thrillers, please visit
www.simonkernick.com and
www.facebook.com/SimonKernick

D1419837

Featuring Dennis Milne

THE BUSINESS OF DYING
Featuring DS Dennis Milne, full-time cop,
part-time assassin.

'Taut, gripping, disturbing - a most assured and
original debut'
Daily Mail

A GOOD DAY TO DIE
Exiled cop Dennis Milne returns to London to hunt down
the murderers of a close friend.

'Great plots, great characters, great action'
Lee Child

THE PAYBACK
Two cops with pasts that haunt them, and a present
that could see them both dead. They are about to meet.
And when they do, it's payback time.

'It delights, excites and stimulates, and the only
reason you consume it so quickly is because
it's so damn good'
GQ

SIMON KERNICK
SIEGE

arrow books

Published by Arrow Books 2012

2 4 6 8 10 9 7 5 3 1

First published in Great Britain in 2012 by
Bantam Press an imprint of Transworld Publishers

Arrow Books
The Random House Group Limited
20 Vauxhall Bridge Road, London, SW1 2SA

www.randomhouse.co.uk

Addresses for companies within The Random House Group Limited can
be found at: www.randomhouse.co.uk/offices.htm

The Random House Group Limited Reg. No. 954009

A CIP catalogue record for this book is
available from the British Library

Penguin Random House is committed to a sustainable future for
our business, our readers and our planet. This book is made from
Forest Stewardship Council® certified paper.

Typeset in Palatino (11/15pt) by
SX Composing DTP, Rayleigh, Essex

Printed in Great Britain by Clays Ltd, St Ives plc

For the boys: Matthew, Danny,
and my godson Jack.

Thursday Morning

1

They killed her as soon as she opened the front door.

It was all very easy. Bull was dressed in a navy blue Royal Mail cap and sweater, with a blue shirt underneath, looking just like any ordinary postman, and he was carrying a mid-sized empty box with the Amazon logo on the side in front of him, so the girl didn't suspect a thing.

Fox was standing just out of sight. He was dressed similarly to Bull, and was wearing a backpack. He also had a semi-automatic pistol with a suppressor attached down by his side, so that no one walking past the front gate would see it. Not that they would have been able to see much anyway, with the huge laurel hedge in the way. He brought the pistol up as the girl came into view, and before she had a chance to acknowledge his presence, he pulled the trigger, shooting her in the temple at point blank range. The

3

gun kicked in his hand, but thanks to the suppressor the noise it made was little more than a loud pop. The girl fell back against the doorframe, blood pouring down the side of her face, and Bull dropped the empty box and caught her under the arms as her legs gave way.

Moving past him, Fox produced a balaclava from his back pocket and pulled it over his head as he walked through the cluttered hallway, the still-smoking gun outstretched in front of him. He was making for the back of the house where he could hear the noise of a family breakfast time. Behind him he could hear Bull dragging the dead girl into the hallway and closing the front door.

'Who is it, Magda?' a male voice called out from the kitchen.

'Nobody move,' said Fox, striding into the room as if he owned the place, which right then he pretty much did.

A well-built middle-aged man in a shirt and tie sat at the table holding a mug of tea. Opposite him were a boy and a girl in different school uniforms. The kids were twins but they didn't look much alike. The boy was tall for fifteen, with the same broad shoulders as his father, and a shock of boyband blond hair, while the girl was small and dumpy, and looked much younger. All three of them stared at Fox with shocked expressions.

'I'm afraid Magda's dead,' said Fox, pointing the

gun at the father, his hand perfectly steady. 'Now, everyone needs to cooperate, or they die too. And that means stay absolutely still.'

Nobody moved a muscle.

Bull joined him in the room. He was wearing his balaclava now and he stood near the doorway, waiting for orders. As the name suggested, Bull was a big guy. He was also dim-witted and did what he was told without question, which was why he'd been chosen for this particular job. That and the fact that he didn't seem to possess any obvious compassion for or empathy with his fellow human beings. Fox glanced at him and noticed there was a dark smear on his shirt collar where Magda had bled on him.

'Please,' said the father, meeting Fox's gaze and keeping his voice calm for the sake of the children, 'take what you want and leave. We haven't got much.'

Fox glared at him. The father had been a police sergeant for seventeen years before being invalided out when he'd been stabbed on duty three years earlier, and he was therefore used to being in control of confrontations, which made him potentially dangerous. Fox's finger tightened on the trigger. 'Don't say another word or I'll put a bullet in your gut. Understand? Nod once for yes.'

The father nodded once, slowly placing his mug on the table and giving his two children a look of reassurance.

'Stand up, turn round and face the wall.'

'Don't hurt my dad,' said the boy, who Fox knew was called Oliver. His voice was deep and irritatingly confident.

'No one gets hurt if you all do as you're told.' Fox's tone was cold but even. He knew it was essential that he didn't give off any sign of weakness, but also that he didn't do anything to panic the prisoners. It was all a very delicate balancing act. For the moment, they had to be kept alive.

'We're not going to offer any resistance,' said the father, getting up and facing the window. 'But can you tell me what this is all about?'

'No.'

'We're just an ordinary family.'

Well, you're not, thought Fox, otherwise we wouldn't be here. But he didn't say that. Instead he said, 'Because it's early in the morning, I'm going to pretend that you're still only half-awake and didn't hear me the first time. If you talk again, I will shoot you. I'd prefer to have three of you alive, but I can just as easily manage with two.'

That was when the father belatedly seemed to realize that he was dealing with professionals and fell silent once again.

Fox slipped the backpack off and threw it to Bull, who unzipped it and pulled out plastic flexi-cuffs and ankle restraints. With Fox covering him, he went over to the father, pulled his hands roughly behind his back and started to put on the cuffs.

This was the dangerous part. If the father was going to try anything, it would be now.

'I'm not pointing the gun at you any more,' Fox told him, moving his gun arm a few feet to the left, 'I'm pointing it at your son's head. Remember that.'

The father stiffened, and seemed about to say something, then settled for a simple nod.

'Where's your phone?'

'In my pocket.'

'Thank you. If you'd be kind enough to get it, Bull.'

Bull nodded, fastened the father's ankles, then did a quick search of his pockets, coming up with an iPhone 4 which he handed to Fox.

'What's the code to unlock it?'

The father told him. Fox pocketed the phone and wrote the number down on the inside of his forearm.

'Right, kids, your turn. Up against the wall, next to your dad. We're going to put restraints on you as well.'

The father started to look round, wanting to say something, but was sensible enough to hold his tongue.

For a few seconds the twins didn't move. The girl – Fox had been told her name was India – was staring down at the table, as if by doing so she could make this whole thing go away, while Oliver was breathing heavily and clenching and unclenching his fists. He got up first, giving Fox a defiant look, before going over to stand to the right of his dad. Fox admired his guts. It took something to pull a face at a man who's pointing a gun at you, especially when you're only fifteen. India was a different story. She remained glued to her seat, and Bull had to lift her to her feet and shove her bodily against the wall.

When all three had been restrained and were standing in a forlorn row with their backs to him, Fox took out the father's iPhone and took a photo of them. Then he told them to turn round and took another one. India was looking weepy; the father was looking scared but in a manly, lantern-jawed way; Oliver was still glaring from beneath his blond hair, as if he was some brave superhero who'd been caught unawares by the dastardly villain and was now plotting his revenge. Well, too late for that, boy, thought Fox. You had your chance.

He got them to turn round again so they were facing away from him, and handed the gun to Bull. 'Cover them,' he said. 'Anyone moves, shoot them in the leg.' Fox knew he wouldn't have to do it, but it was worth ramming home the penalty for non-compliance. Subtlety really isn't a useful trait in hostage-taking.

Pulling off his balaclava, Fox went back out towards the front door, stepping over Magda's body, which Bull had propped up against the wall, walked out of the house and down to where he'd parked the van.

The street was fairly quiet. It was an affluent area of detached 1950s homes built when space wasn't so much of an issue in the outer London suburbs, and Fox guessed that people minded their own business here. He saw an overweight man in a suit get into his car, a new-looking Lexus, thirty yards up the street. The man didn't see him. He looked tired and stressed. A sheep, thought Fox contemptuously. Not living, just existing. Unaware of everything outside his own little suburban world. Well, today would be different. Today, this man, like millions of others, would take notice of the world outside his door because today the world was coming to them all with a vengeance.

Fox backed the van through the gates and up the gravel driveway, stopping just outside the front door. He opened the van's rear doors and went back inside the house.

'OK, we're all going for a short drive,' he announced as he entered the kitchen, pleased to see that nobody had moved.

'Can you tell us where we're going?' asked the father, without turning round.

'Unfortunately not, but I can confirm that your stay will be temporary. By this evening you'll be released, and this will all be an unpleasant memory.'

As he finished speaking, he pulled the Taser from his backpack, clipped on the cartridge, and let the father have it with the two electrodes. He went down with an almighty crash, and the kids both jumped.

'What are you doing to my dad?' yelled Oliver.

'Keeping him quiet for a moment,' said Fox calmly.

One of the keys to successful hostage-taking is never allowing your hostage to get used to the situation, and the best way to achieve this is by delivering constant shocks. Which Fox then did for a second time by stepping forward and punching Oliver on the side of the head.

The boy clearly hadn't been expecting the blow. He stumbled and almost fell, but Fox grabbed him by the collar of his school blazer and dragged him out into the hallway as he fought to keep his balance in the ankle restraints. At the same time, Bull wrapped one of his huge arms round a now near-hysterical India's neck and, shoving the gun in her back, brought her out behind.

Oliver gasped when he saw Magda's corpse. Her head was slumped to one side and her mouth was slightly open, her bottom lip and tongue jutting out, as if she was pulling a face. Her eyes were closed, and her blonde hair looked like it had been dipped in blood. 'She's dead,' he said with the first hint of a wail.

Before he could say another word, Fox kicked his legs from under him and forced him to the floor, so that his and Magda's shoulders were almost touching. Bull forced India down next to Magda on the other side, pushing the end of the suppressor into her forehead to help things along. She'd stopped crying now but still looked suitably distraught.

Fox pulled out the father's iPhone for a second time and took two photos of the three of them together, then switched the setting to video as Bull slowly moved the gun from one child to the other. The message was obvious.

When that was done, Fox put hoods on the kids, securing them in place with duct tape, and led them out one by one to the van. He made them lie next to each other on the floor, checking their pockets to make sure they weren't carrying mobiles before locking the van doors. He also switched off the father's iPhone. Like every criminal worth his salt, Fox knew how easy it was to trace mobiles, and it was essential that the journey this one made should never be known to the security services.

Finally he turned to Bull. 'You know what to do,' he said slowly. 'It's time.'

Bull nodded, and the two of them went back inside.

The father was still lying on the floor, the shock from the Taser having made a serious if temporary mess of his nervous system, but he was a big guy and he was already beginning to recover.

While Fox watched, Bull sat down on his chest, his knees pinning the father's arms down, and pushed the end of the suppressor into his face. The father's eyes widened in alarm and he tried to move his head, but he was still largely incapacitated. Bull glanced up at Fox, like a dog waiting for its master's command.

Fox gave an affirmative nod, and Bull pulled the trigger.

It had never been the plan to take the father along

Simon Kernick

with them. There was just too much risk of him trying to be a hero, and, anyway, the kids were far more useful to them than he was.

'Now you're one of us,' he said as Bull got slowly to his feet.

Bull smiled. He looked pleased.

Fox took the gun from him, slipping it into the back of his trousers, and checked his watch as they went back through the house.

07.51. So far the whole thing, from the first knock at the door, had lasted six minutes. Bang on schedule.

But as they walked back to the front of the van, Fox ran into the first complication of the day. An old lady with a mad head of white hair like the silent one in the Marx brothers was walking a couple of rat-like dogs past the open gates. She had that perpetually suspicious demeanour of a neighbourhood watch coordinator, and straight away she slowed down and clocked him and Bull with a long stare that said (a) she'd not seen them round these parts before, and (b) because of this she was noting all their physical details just in case they were up to no good.

She was going to have to die too.

Relying on the fact that he was a fairly ordinary-looking white man in his mid thirties and therefore not all that threatening for an old suburban lady, Fox smiled broadly. 'Excuse me,' he called out, striding down towards her, his gun hidden from view, 'I wonder if you can help us?'

His plan was simple. Pull her inside the gate, break her neck with one quick yank, and hide the body in the bushes. Then throttle the yappy little hounds.

The old lady stopped, but she was looking past Fox, who was still grinning from ear to ear, and towards the van and Bull. That was the flaw in the plan. Bull. He was sure the big oaf was trying not to look suspicious and coming across guilty as sin. Or worse still, giving the old bitch one of his dead-eyed glares.

Fox, though, was closing in on her. He kept talking, trying to allay her suspicions. 'We're meant to be delivering a washing machine, but there's no answer . . .'

Three more seconds and she'd be his.

But the old lady suddenly looked scared. 'I'm sorry I can't help,' she said quickly, and before he could put out a hand to grab her she turned on her heel and hurried beyond the gate, just as a UPS truck came past, slowing down to negotiate the parked cars on either side of the road.

Fox cursed and walked quickly back to the van.

'You didn't give her one of your looks, did you?' he said to Bull, getting in alongside him.

Bull shook his head, his expression defensive. 'I didn't look at her at all, Fox. Honest.' His voice was deep yet with an irritating childlike whine to it.

Fox sighed, knowing there was no point pursuing the matter, and he started the engine and pulled out of the drive.

The old lady was twenty yards away now with her back to them, her head cocked slightly as if she was listening out for signs of pursuit. It was almost light, way too risky for them to try anything now, so he drove off in the opposite direction, hoping that by the time she realized the significance of what she'd just seen it would be far too late for her, or anyone else, to do anything about it.

It started to rain, that cold November drizzle that goes right through to the bones, and as Fox looked up at the leaden grey sky he thought that it really was an awful day.

And for many people, not least the ones in the back of the van, it was soon going to get a whole lot worse.

Seven Hours Later

2

So she'd finally done it. Got engaged. She was twenty-eight years old – near enough an old woman in the eyes of her parents' generation. In fact, her mother had already had three children by the time she'd turned twenty-eight. But unlike her mother, who'd married young and stayed at home to raise her family, Elena Serenko had put everything into her career. In the ten years since she'd come to London from Poland she'd risen from a night receptionist in a rundown dump in Catford to the youngest duty manager at the 320-room Stanhope Hotel on Park Lane, one of the West End's most prestigious five-star establishments. Not a bad achievement for a girl from rural Krasnystaw.

And now, after all that, it looked like she would be leaving. Her boyfriend of eighteen months – sorry, fiancé – Rod was Australian, and he wanted them to go out there to live. He'd been on about it for months now. His family home was in a coastal town an hour south of Sydney, and she knew how much he missed the sunshine and the ocean. To be fair, after a decade in grey, drizzly London, Elena was tempted too. Australia seemed a long way to go and would leave her thousands of miles from her family and close friends. But she'd always wanted to travel, having been born with a sense of adventure, and she knew she'd always regret it if she didn't at least give life out there a go.

So when Rod had proposed to her out of the blue the previous evening in the lounge of the flat they shared, she'd replied with a delighted yes, because for all his faults (and, like all men, he had plenty) she truly loved him. He'd then dropped his second bombshell, saying he wanted to be home for Christmas. For good. With her.

But Christmas was only five weeks away, which meant she'd have to give in her notice within the next few days. She'd asked Rod for a couple of days to think about it, as it was all so sudden, and because of the man he was, he'd agreed. But as she walked across the Stanhope's grand lobby, instinctively checking that the flowers in the vases lining the walls were all fresh and properly arranged, Elena Serenko made up her mind. Just like that. She wasn't normally impulsive, but as soon as the decision was made she knew it was the right one. She was going to go and start a new life on the other side of the world.

The thought filled her with a mix of nervousness and excitement, and she vowed to call Rod and tell him the good news as soon as she had a spare moment. Right now, though, she had to deal with a more pressing issue. Mr Al-Jahabi.

Mr Al-Jahabi was one of the hotel's regulars, a wealthy Saudi who was often in London on business and who, along with his family, usually took several of the penthouse suites for the whole of August to escape the desert heat. As such, he was a hugely valued customer as well as a very large tipper. However, he also had a sex drive that, as far as Elena could tell, was off the scale. He engaged the services of prostitutes every night his wives weren't with him. This wasn't a problem in and of itself. A significant minority of single male guests at the Stanhope (and at most other hotels) entertained escorts in their rooms, and any attempt to stop the practice was always going to be doomed to failure. So if things were done discreetly, a blind eye could be turned. The problem with Mr Al-Jahabi was that prostitutes weren't always enough. On at least three occasions over the past year he'd made passes at female employees. On one of those occasions a chambermaid had actually alleged a sexual assault, and was prepared to go to the police until Mr Al-Jahabi paid her off with a £1,000 tip, or bribe, depending on how you wanted to look at it. The chambermaid, a Filipina girl, had left not long afterwards. This had been six months back and since then Mr Al-Jahabi had been behaving himself – or at least keeping matters under control.

That was until earlier that afternoon.

According to Colin, the duty manager on the seven a.m. to three p.m. shift, a maid had gone in to clean his room at just after one and had been confronted by a naked and aroused Mr Al-Jahabi who'd requested something called (in Colin's words) 'a happy finish'. The maid had run from the room and immediately complained to her boss, Mohammed the maintenance manager, who'd then informed Colin. According to Colin, he'd managed to calm the maid down, made sure that she wouldn't take things any further, said he'd sort it, and given her the rest of the day off.

Except he hadn't sorted it. Instead he'd made up some excuse about having to deal with a family who were refusing to leave their room, and had left it to Elena to speak to Mr Al-Jahabi, which was typical of Colin. No one wanted to upset Mr Al-Jahabi, for fear he'd take his extremely valuable custom elsewhere, citing them as the reason. But Elena knew she was going to have to raise the issue. She just wished she hadn't still got the vestiges of a painful hangover from the celebrations of the previous night. Five a.m. was no time to go to sleep when you were working the next day, even if you didn't start until three o'clock in the afternoon.

On her way up, Elena made a quick check of the

mezzanine floor to ensure that the ballroom had been cleaned properly after the three-day conference that had finished in there that morning (it had, and it looked immaculate), then slipped into the satellite kitchen behind it.

Like all big hotels, the Stanhope had a number of satellite kitchens situated at catering points in the building where food from the main kitchens on the ground floor could be reheated before being served to guests, thus ensuring that it was piping hot when it reached the table. The kitchen behind the ballroom contained a walk-in store cupboard which was a favourite among certain members of staff for taking a sneaky nap in, because there was a crawlspace beneath the bottom shelf where a person could lie out straight and not be seen. So popular was it that a few months earlier two Bangladeshi cleaners had even come to blows over which of them should sleep there, resulting in one ending up in hospital with a broken nose after the other had struck him with a family-sized tin of pineapple chunks. Since then there'd been talk of boarding the space up, but so far no one had got round to it, probably because pretty much everyone had put their head down there at one time or another, including Elena herself (though only once, and for barely ten minutes).

Feeling oddly mischievous, Elena tiptoed over to the store cupboard door and gently opened it, bending down in the near-darkness so she could see inside the space, although from the sound of gentle snoring she already knew there was someone in there.

She smiled. It was Clinton, the ancient maintenance man who'd been with the hotel for more than thirty years. He was on his back, his tool belt by his side, his ample belly inflating and deflating as he slept like a baby.

If it had been anyone else, Elena would have woken them up and given them a talking to, but Clinton was a hard worker, she was in a good mood, and he looked so damn peaceful down there she couldn't bring herself to do it. So she left him there, closing the door gently behind her.

The Stanhope had four penthouse suites on the tenth floor, all of them with private terraces and views across the greenery of Hyde Park. They cost an average of £4,000 a night – pocket change to a man like Mr Al-Jahabi, who'd already been in the largest and most expensive of them for the past week.

Aside from greeting him on occasion when he arrived at the hotel with his retinue, Elena had never had to talk to Mr Al-Jahabi before, and she wasn't looking forward to starting now. Steeling herself, she stopped outside his door, took a deep breath, and knocked.

For a few seconds there was no answer. She was just about to knock again when the door opened a few inches and a young woman, not much older than eighteen but already with the hardening look of some-one who does a job they despise, poked her head out.

'Oh,' she said, looking Elena up and down with an expression of vague distaste, 'I thought you were room service. We've ordered champagne.'

Swallowing her irritation, Elena introduced herself, giving the prostitute a cold look, and asked to speak to Mr Al-Jahabi.

'I'll just see if he's available,' the girl said, returning the cold look as she closed the door.

It was a good two minutes before it was opened again, this time revealing a portly Arab man in his fifties with a thick black moustache, wearing only a black linen gown. Knowing she couldn't have this discussion in the hallway, even though she'd have preferred to, Elena apologized for the intrusion and told him she'd like a private word.

He smiled, as if this was the most natural thing in the world, and ushered her into the spacious foyer. The doors to the different rooms were all closed, but Elena could hear giggling coming from the master bedroom.

'Take a seat, Miss . . .' he said, peering at Elena's nametag and pointing to a leather sofa in one corner. He stepped towards her. 'Is it Serenko?'

'Yes, it is,' she answered, taking a step backwards. Even in her heels, he still had a good couple of inches on her in height. 'And I'd prefer to stand, thanks. We've had a serious complaint from one of our staff.'

'Really? And what did they complain about?'

'Apparently, you exposed yourself and made suggestive comments. You're a very valued customer, Mr Al-Jahabi, but the Stanhope can't tolerate that kind of behaviour towards its staff.' You dirty old bastard, she felt like adding, but didn't. Elena could be remarkably self-controlled when she wanted to be.

Mr Al-Jahabi laughed, which was when Elena noticed that his eyes were a little unfocused, and that he was none too steady on his feet. It looked like the classic combination of alcohol and coke.

God, that was all she needed.

'She says what, exactly? That I showed her my dick? Why would I want to do that?'

'I'm not sure, Mr Al-Jahabi, but—'

'I got two beautiful girls in there. I don't need one of your maids.' He paused, eyeing her slyly through pinprick pupils. 'Still, if she looked like you, I might be tempted. How would you like to earn yourself some real money, Miss See-Renko?' He reached into the pocket of the gown, produced a huge wad of cash, and leaned in close to her again.

Elena could smell the booze on his breath and it made her feel sick. She needed to get out of here, and fast. And when she did she'd get straight on to Siobhan, the general manager, who was away on a course, and tell her that she wanted permission to throw this man out of the hotel right away, however much his custom was valued.

'I think you want to, don't you?' he leered, so close now that the material of his gown was brushing against her trouser suit. 'Maybe party with us in there for a little bit, huh? Snort some powder. You'd like that, I think.'

He began peeling off fifty-pound notes from the wad, each one worth more than half a duty manager's shift after tax. Nothing to a man like him. Elena could tell from the arrogant, drunken look on his face that he'd bought plenty of people in the past just by flashing a little bit of his wealth.

Instinctively, and without a moment's thought, she drove her knee into his groin. Hard.

Mr Al-Jahabi's eyes widened in total shock. Elena was shocked too. She'd never done anything like that before (aside from the time when she was nine and her older brother Kris had been trying to stuff a worm in her mouth), and for a long, surreal moment she watched as Mr Al-Jahabi crumpled to his knees, both hands on the affected area, a low groan coming out of his mouth. Then, coming to her senses, she turned and strode rapidly out of the suite, trying to come to terms with the fact that she'd just assaulted one of the Stanhope's highest-spending guests.

She stopped in the corridor, trying to calm herself down. Even if she told Siobhan the truth about what had happened, she couldn't see herself keeping her job. Al-Jahabi was rich. He had power. That was why he was able to get away with his behaviour. He'd demand revenge on her, and he'd get it. She'd never get a reference from the hotel, which would mean she wouldn't be able to get a decent job in Australia. It was so damn unfair, on what should have been one of the happiest days of her life, and it made her want to weep, but she forced herself to calm down. As her grandmother used to say, tears alone have never solved a problem.

Instead, she took a deep breath and started towards the lifts, wondering if the day could get any worse.

3

15.25

The Westfield Centre in Shepherd's Bush is London's largest and one of its newest shopping malls. It opened for business on 30 October 2008 and contains 255 stores spread over 150,000 square metres of retail space – equivalent to thirty football pitches.

An underground car park with 4,500 spaces is situated directly beneath the centre, and although there were still more than five weeks to go until Christmas, spaces were already few and far between as Dragon drove the white Ford Transit van on to the car park's upper level. By a stroke of luck he managed to find a space next to the pedestrian walkway, barely fifty metres from the Waitrose Customer Collection Point, and the entrance to the lifts. Out of the corner of his eye he saw a harassed-looking woman in expensive designer clothes unload two pre-school boys from her brand-new 4 × 4, and shove them into a double-pushchair. One of the boys was struggling in her grip, and the woman's expression was one of anger and frustration as she shouted at them, although she was too far away for Dragon to hear what she was saying.

He watched her for a moment, wondering what pleasure she derived from her material wealth. Very little, he suspected. That was the problem with these people. They led joyless, empty lives, and because they'd had it so damn easy they'd ended up becoming soft, fat and lazy.

In the back of the van, hidden from view behind a Tottenham Hotspur flag, were sixteen 47-kilo cylinders of propane gas piled on top of one another in groups of four. Wedged between the cylinders and the front seats of the van was a rucksack containing a specially modified mobile phone set to vibrate, a battery pack, and a 3-kilo lump of C4 plastic explosives. When a call was made to the phone, the vibrations would complete the electrical circuit, thereby setting off the detonator and igniting the C4, which in turn would ignite the propane gas, causing a huge fireball.

Casualties wouldn't be particularly high since the bomb would only hit those people passing by, either on their way to or coming back from the shops, and the blast wouldn't have the force to cause any damage within the centre itself. But that wasn't the point. The point was to cause panic and chaos among the civilians in the immediate area, and to stretch and divide the resources of the security services so that they'd be less quick to react when the main operation got under way.

Dragon watched the harassed woman as she wheeled her kids down the walkway, and he wondered if she, or they, would be among the casualties. He hoped not. He didn't like being able to put individual faces to the names of victims. But he'd always been a believer in fate. If your number was up, then it was up, and that was just the way it was. The world wasn't fair. It never had been, and despite the efforts of at least some of mankind, it never would be. All Dragon could do was protect himself, and he was sure he'd done that pretty effectively. The number plates on the van were false. He'd changed them en route here for another set of false plates so that the police wouldn't be able to use the ANPR system to trace the van's journey. He'd also changed his appearance for the numerous CCTV cameras that would be filming him as he moved through the building. His skin had turned a deep olive thanks to the tanning agent, coloured contact lenses had turned his eyes from grey to dark brown, and his hair was far longer and darker than usual. To counteract the facial recognition software available to the security forces, he'd also changed the shape of his face. His nose was bigger and more crooked, thanks to the highlighted putty base that had been added to it; padding had pushed his cheeks out, making them look fatter; and a prominent, raised birthmark the size of a fifty-pence piece had appeared on his upper cheek just below the left eye. If any witnesses were asked to describe him later, it would be the birthmark they remembered.

Success, he knew, could only come through intensive planning. They'd planned this whole thing down to the last detail, and Dragon was experiencing a heady mixture of confidence and excitement that was all too rare these days as he got out of the van and joined the thin but steady stream of shoppers heading into retail nirvana.

4

Nothing ever prepares you for it. The moment the consultant walks into the room and closes the door quietly behind him, and you see that look on his face. The grim resignation as he prepares to give you the news you've been waiting for, ever since he did the tests. And you know the news is bad. It's as if it's stalked, uninvited, into the room with him.

You pray to God Almighty. Just as you have done every night these past two weeks. Even though you haven't believed in years. Because before you've never had to think about death. It's always been an abstract, distant thing. Something that happens to other people. And it's not fair. It's not fucking fair, for Christ's sake. You're forty-five. Young, almost. You haven't smoked in years; you probably drink too much, but no worse than anyone else you know; you eat OK – too many ready meals, sure, but then who doesn't these days? – and you're definitely not overweight. If anything, you're too thin. You still go to the gym at least once, sometimes twice, occasionally even three times per week. You're fit. You're healthy.

But you're not. Because the consultant's face is still grim. He takes the deep breath, steadies himself, and—

'I'm afraid there's nothing we can do, Mr Dalston. Your particular cancer is inoperable.'

Strangely, you don't react. You just sit there, and now that the words have been spoken, you feel a sense of bleak calm. There is, at least, no more suspense.

The consultant, a dapper little Asian man called Mr Farouk who always wears brightly coloured bow ties, starts talking about chemotherapy and the opportunity it provides to prolong life, but you're not really listening. You only ask one question. The obvious one. The one we'd all ask straight away.

'How long?'

With chemotherapy, as long as two years, although Mr Farouk is quick to point out there are no guarantees, and that it might be considerably shorter. Possibly a year. But again, no guarantees.

'And without chemotherapy?'

He answers immediately. 'In my opinion, an absolute maximum of six months.'

'And there's no hope?' You have to ask, even though you know that Mr Farouk is one of the UK's foremost cancer experts, a man whose opinion you have paid serious money for, precisely because his word can be trusted. It's the survival instinct in you. Looking for that tiny chink of light.

'No,' he says quietly. 'I'm afraid not.'

And that's it. The death sentence has been passed.

In the end, Martin Dalston had decided against chemotherapy. He didn't see the point, mainly because the end result was always going to be the same. It felt too much like prolonging the agony. When he'd told his ex-wife and their son, who at seventeen was old enough to understand the consequences of his decision, they'd both tried to persuade him to reconsider. 'You never know, they might find a cure in that time,' had been Sue's rather optimistic argument. But Martin had read up enough about advanced liver cancer to know that that wasn't going to happen any time soon. He wanted to enjoy his last days, he told them, even though the words had sounded empty as soon as he'd spoken them. Sue had been remarried for two years, so those last days weren't really going to involve her, and though she'd been very sympathetic, Martin had the feeling she wouldn't spend too long mourning his passing.

Robert was different. Until he'd become a teenager, he and his father had been very close. They'd grown apart as the marriage had descended into its death spiral, with Robert regularly siding with his mother in their arguments, or ignoring both of them, and at times it had felt to Martin like he'd been at war with both his wife and son, while all the time trying to keep his business afloat. But the news of his cancer had brought them back together. They'd taken a week out to go to Spain, a fishing trip to the Ebro river, where they'd bonded over good food, good wine and good conversation. The break had been so successful that Martin had even started looking into the two of them doing a three-week road trip in Australia, taking in the Barrier Reef, the Outback and the Great Ocean Road.

And then the sickness had started: the intense bouts of abdominal pain; the chronic tiredness; the nausea; and, finally, the steadily accelerating weight loss. Martin knew he was fading. Given his views on treatment, he had only two alternatives. One: let the cancer take him at its own pace, with Robert there by his side helplessly watching him as he deteriorated. Or two: end matters himself.

Martin had never been a particularly brave man. He'd always avoided confrontation and, if truth be told, he'd avoided hard decisions too. But perhaps, he thought as he walked into the lobby of the Stanhope Hotel that afternoon, there was an inner steel in him after all. Because today was going to be the last day of his life and he felt remarkably calm about it.

He'd booked room 315 four days earlier. At first the receptionist had told him that the hotel couldn't guarantee a particular room, but then he'd explained that he wanted it because he and his wife had stayed there on the night of their wedding, and wanted to stay in it again for their twentieth anniversary.

Sadly, none of this was true. Martin had never stayed in the Stanhope with Sue. But even after all these years room 315 held hugely important memories, and it was ironic that the thing he was most worried about as he approached the desk was that the hotel had accidentally hired it to someone else.

But they hadn't, and because it was after two p.m., it was ready for him.

The pretty young receptionist smiled and wished him a pleasant stay in lightly accented English, and he thanked her with a smile of his own, and said he would, before heading for the lifts, hoping she wouldn't notice the fact that he'd brought very little luggage.

For the first time, he felt guilty about doing what he was about to do in a public place like a hotel room, where his body would inevitably be discovered by an unfortunate member of staff. He could, he supposed, have done it in the poky little flat he called home, but somehow that seemed far too much like a lonely end. There was, he had to admit, something comforting about having other people near him when he went, even if they were strangers.

When he got to the door to 315, he stopped as the memories came flooding back. Memories of the only time he'd truly been in love – indeed, truly happy – and he felt an intense wave of emotion wash over him. This had been their place. Thousands of people had stayed in the room in the twenty-two years since, but it would always be their place. He thought of her now, all those thousands of miles away, and wondered if she was even still alive. In the past few weeks he'd seriously considered making contact to let her know what had happened to him, but in the end he'd held back. There was too much scope for disappointment. Carrie Wilson was the past, and it was far better simply to have her as a lingering, beautiful memory.

He opened the door and stepped inside, ready to relive it all again for the very last time.

5

The rendezvous was an empty warehouse on the sprawling Park Royal industrial estate just north of the A40 that had been hired on a three-month lease by an untraceable offshore company registered in the United Arab Emirates.

Fox was the first to arrive, at 15.40. It took him the best part of five minutes to get through the complex set of locks they'd added to maximize security. Once he was inside and had disabled the state-of-the-art, supposedly tamper-proof burglar alarm system, he relocked the doors and did a quick sweep of the main loading bay area with a bug finder. He was pretty sure that no one would have been able to get in without them knowing about it, and even surer that there'd been no leak in the cell, but he was also the kind of man who left nothing to chance. It was why he'd survived as long as he had.

Once he was satisfied that the place was clean, he put a call in to Bull using one of the three mobiles he was carrying. He'd left Bull with the kids at a rented house three miles away that morning.

Bull answered with a simple 'yeah' on the second ring, and Fox was pleased that he was keeping the phone so close to hand, and that he was answering it in the way he'd been instructed, giving nothing away. Bull wasn't the sharpest tool in the box, and Fox had had to spend a lot of time prepping him about his role today, which was one of the most important of all of them.

'It's me,' said Fox, pacing the warehouse floor. 'Everything all right?'

'All good. I just checked up on them now.'

He sounded alert enough, and Fox was sure he wouldn't hesitate to do what needed to be done when the time came. But he wanted to make sure Bull remembered the timings. The timings were everything today.

'You remember what time you've got to be at the final rendezvous, don't you?'

'Course I do. We've been through it enough times. Twenty-three hundred.'

'Not a minute later. Give yourself plenty of time, but don't leave before you get final confirmation.'

Bull said he understood. He didn't sound the least bit annoyed at being asked the same question by Fox for the hundredth time in the past three days. He sounded keen and eager to please. This was the biggest day in his whole life and he knew it.

Fox ended the call and switched off the phone.

There was an office at the end of a narrow corridor leading from the loading bay, and he unlocked the door and went inside, switching on the lights. At the far end of the room, hidden behind a pile of boxes, was a large padlocked crate. As he did every time he came here, Fox checked the contents, making sure that nothing had been tampered with.

The weaponry for the operation originated from the former Yugoslav republic of Kosovo. It consisted of eight AK-47 assault rifles, six Glock 17 pistols with suppressors, grenades, body armour, and 25 kilos of C4 explosive, along with detonators and thousands of rounds of ammunition. It had been bought from a group of former members of the Kosovo Liberation Army in a deal arranged by the client, before being smuggled into the EU in the hidden compartment of a lorry usually reserved for illegal immigrants.

Because of the levels of security at British ports, and the use of sniffer dogs to detect explosives, it had been considered safest to avoid bringing the consignment into the country using the lorry. Instead, the crate had been dropped at a safe house in Antwerp. A contact of the handler there knew a Belgian fishing boat captain who occasionally did hashish runs into the UK. For a fee, the captain had agreed to transport the weapons and land them using a RIB on an isolated stretch of beach north of Peterhead in Scotland. From there, the crate had been collected by Fox and several other members of the team, and driven to London.

Because the C4 had still been in powder form, Fox had delivered it separately to a lock-up in Forest Gate, along with the detonators, where it had been collected by the people whose job it was to turn it into bombs. Fox had no idea of their identities, he'd simply dropped off the tub containing the C4. Then, two weeks later, he'd received an anonymous text telling him to go back to the lock-up, where six identical black North Face backpacks and a small trolley suitcase were waiting for him, all of them now converted into deadly weapons.

Fox didn't bother re-padlocking the crate since they'd be needing the contents soon enough. Instead, he pulled out one of the Kevlar vests, grabbed a set of stained navy-blue decorator's overalls from a built-in cupboard next to the door, and got changed, packing the civilian clothes he'd come here in, and which he'd be needing later, into a backpack. Although he wore gloves throughout the process, he wasn't too worried about leaving any DNA behind. A local cleaning company had been hired to come in the following day and give the whole place a full industrial steam clean, which would remove all traces of his presence here.

Fox could feel the excitement building in him now. This was it. The culmination of months of planning. Success, and the whole world was his. Failure, and it would be his last day on earth.

Death or glory. The choice was that stark. It reminded him of his time in the army, in those all too rare moments when he'd seen action. It was that feeling of being totally and utterly alive. He loved the thrill of violence, always had. And today, for the first time in far too long, he was going to get the chance to experience that thrill on a grand scale.

Down the corridor, he heard the sound of the rear loading doors opening, and he smiled.

The others were beginning to arrive.

6

Cat Manolis paced the hotel room, wondering if it was work or the interminably heavy London traffic that was delaying her lover.

Their affair had started innocently enough. The occasional shared smile as they passed each other in the corridor at work, or in the gym beneath the building, where they both worked out; the first conversation on the treadmill at 7.30 one morning; the knowing look he'd given her. Even then it had been weeks before he'd asked her out for a coffee. Everything had had to be so secret. It was the same old thing. He was trapped in a loveless marriage, a handsome, charismatic man in need of female attention, possessed of the kind of power that was always such an aphrodisiac, even to a woman barely half his age.

They'd met for coffee one Saturday morning in a pretty little café on the South Bank. He'd made an excuse to his wife, telling her he had to come into town, and they'd spent a snatched couple of hours together. They'd walked along the banks of the Thames, and Cat had put her arm through his as they talked. She'd told him about her upbringing in Nice, how she'd been the only child of a father who was long gone by the time she was born, and a mother who'd never forgiven her for it, as if she was somehow to blame for his fecklessness. How she'd gone off the rails (although she refused to give him too many details about how low she'd fallen) before pulling herself together and marrying a man who was the love of her life, only to lose him a week before her twenty-fourth birthday. It was grief, then, that had brought her to London five years earlier.

He'd seemed genuinely touched by her story and had told her his own more familiar one: how he'd been with the same woman since university, how they'd once been in love, and how, over the thirty years and three children since, their love had faded to nothing more than a hollow husk, leaving him desperate to be free of the marriage.

'I care for you very much,' he'd said gently when it was time for them to part. He'd looked into her eyes as he spoke so she'd know his words were heartfelt.

They'd kissed passionately. It had been something that was always going to happen, and it seemed to last for a long, long time.

When they'd finally broken apart, they'd promised to meet again as soon as circumstances allowed.

43

Since then they'd had three separate trysts – all involving coffee, followed by a walk, though never in the same place – and all the time they'd been moving towards this day. When they would finally sleep together for the first time. Michael had wanted to consummate their relationship at Cat's apartment, but she'd explained that it would be impractical given that she shared her place with three other women, so they'd settled for the far more romantic destination of the Stanhope on Park Lane.

Cat was dressed seductively in a simple sleeveless black dress that finished just above the knee, sheer black hold-up stockings, and black court shoes with four-inch heels. Usually she dressed far more modestly and, as she stopped and looked at herself in the room's full-length mirror, she felt a frisson of excitement. She looked good. There was no doubt about it. Michael would melt when he saw her.

If, of course, he turned up.

She looked at her watch. It was five to four. He was almost half an hour late. And he hadn't even called. She couldn't call him either. She was under strict instructions never to call him. Too easy to get found out, he'd said, and then that'll be it for both of us.

Trying to hide her concern, she poured a glass of Evian from the mini-bar and took a long sip, contemplating breaking the law and annoying Michael at the same time by lighting a cigarette.

If she had to wait, then she might as well make the most of it.

7

'If we want to survive, then we have to operate like a well-oiled machine. That means obeying orders when they're given.

'Innocent people are going to die. There's no getting around that. But that's not our problem. They're collateral damage in a war. Nothing more, nothing less. At no point can you forget that, or suddenly develop an attack of conscience, because if you hesitate about pulling the trigger, or refuse, then the penalty's immediate death. No exceptions. We can't afford for the machine to break down. If it does, we're all dead, or worse still, in the hands of the enemy, which means the rest of our natural lives in prison. And I'm not going to let that happen. Are we clear on that?'

Fox looked in turn at each of the four men facing him, watching for any signs of doubt in their eyes, but none of them gave anything away. All of them had worked for him in the recent past, and they had three things in common. One: extensive military experience in a combat role. Two: no spouses or dependants. And three, and most important of all: they were all disaffected individuals who harboured a rage against the many perceived injustices in the world – a rage that had manifested itself in the heady mix of violent extremism. There were other motives at play too which explained why they'd chosen to become involved – money, boredom, a desire to once again see real action – but it was the rage that was the most important, because it would be this that drove them to do what was needed today.

There were two he considered totally reliable. One was Dragon, the ex-sapper he'd picked to drive the van bomb to the Westfield. He was currently on the run from prison, where he was being held on remand on a number of explosives charges. He'd run down and killed a ten-year-old boy in a hijacked car during the course of his escape, as well as seriously injuring a prison officer, and he was facing the rest of his life inside if he was recaptured. The other was Leopard, a short, wiry former marine who'd once come top of his group in the SAS selection trials, only to be turned down because apparently he didn't have the right mental attitude. Leopard had ended up being court-martialled in Afghanistan for breaking the British Army's ultra-strict rules of engagement by carrying out an unauthorized kill on two members of a Taliban mortar team. He'd served more than two years inside on manslaughter charges – just, in his mind, for doing his job – and the burning anger he felt at his treatment was authentic.

Tiger, a typically Aryan Dane who'd received extensive shrapnel injuries while serving in Afghanistan and walked with an aggressive limp, also had plenty of ruthlessness, but Fox was a lot less sure of his reliability. A one-time member of a neo-Nazi group, Tiger had grown up with an almost psychotic hatred of Jews, and after his experience in Afghanistan had added Muslims to his list of sworn enemies, along with politicians and, as far as Fox could tell, pretty much everyone else who didn't agree with him. He was also a violent sadist and bully who'd stripped and tied up his ex-girlfriend the previous year and burned her repeatedly with cigarette butts. He'd only avoided jail because she dropped the charges against him after threats to her life. The other men didn't know about this, or they probably wouldn't have agreed to work with him.

And then there was Bear, the so-called 'man with the face'. Of all the men involved in the operation, Fox trusted Bear the least. And yet he owed him the most. Bear had once saved his life when they were serving together in Al-Amarah back in 2005 by spotting an IED half-buried in an irrigation ditch just as the platoon was passing by on patrol. Fox had been closest to it and would have taken the brunt of the blast, but Bear had shouted a warning and jumped on his back, sending them both sprawling into the dirt just as it was detonated by the insurgents. Fox had been temporarily deafened by the blast but was otherwise unhurt. Bear had been less lucky. A jagged, burning piece of shrapnel the size of a baseball had struck him on the side of the face. Alerted by his screams, and the sizzling, Fox had managed to pull it free, burning his fingers through his gloves in the process. Although the heat had cauterized the wound, the shrapnel had burned away most of the flesh just beneath the eye to the jaw line, leaving him permanently disfigured, and bitterly resentful of the politicians he'd always blamed for it.

Bear had worked with Fox since those army days, and Fox knew that he was a proven killer, but he was still concerned that, when it came down to it, Bear wouldn't be able to murder an innocent person in cold blood.

They caught each other's eyes, and Bear gave him a long, hard look to demonstrate that he knew what was expected of him.

Fox acknowledged it with a nod before turning to the sixth man in the room, standing next to him. 'Now, I'm going to hand you over to Wolf, who you've all met before. I just want to reiterate that he's the client's representative, and in overall command of the operation on the ground, while I'm acting as his second in command. You refer to him, as you refer to me, and each other, by codename rather than rank, and never, at any point, use real names. Understood?'

The men nodded, and Wolf took a step forward. He was a short, squat man, well into his forties, with dark skin and a pockmarked face which, combined with his lacquered, dyed-black hair, gave him more than a passing resemblance to the former Panamanian dictator, General Noriega. He cleared his throat loudly and let the cigarette he'd been smoking fall to the warehouse floor.

'In the next fifteen minutes, you are all going to be half a million dollars richer,' he announced in a clear, strong Arabic accent.

Fox saw all eyes light up at this. After all, whatever their political affiliations, this was what they were really here for.

'As soon as I give the word, the money will be sent to your nominated bank accounts. The remainder, one and a half million dollars, will be paid at nine o'clock tomorrow morning, on successful completion of the job. Before I give the word for the first instalment, however, I need proof that we are all committed.'

Wolf reached into his overalls pocket and produced a mobile phone, which he held up for everyone to see.

'We all know about the decoy bomb in the Westfield Shopping Centre car park that Dragon delivered. The man who presses the call button on this phone will detonate it. I understand that we'll be able to hear the explosion in here, as we're only a mile away.' He paused for a moment, watching them carefully through hooded eyes. 'So, my friends, who wants to make the call?'

Dragon spoke up. 'I drove the van, I'll do it.' He put out a hand.

He looked like he'd do it too, thought Fox. So did Tiger, the psychotic Dane, who was standing there with an expression of utter boredom on his face. He'd have done it as casually as blowing his own nose. Leopard wore an impassive expression. He'd do it too, if he had to.

Bear, though, was sweating.

Wolf noticed it too, Fox could tell.

Bear lowered his eyes, like a kid who doesn't know the answer to a question. He was trying not to draw attention to himself, but it didn't work. Bear was a big man with a ruined face. He was always going to stand out.

Wolf lobbed the phone over to him. 'You do it.'

Bear caught it instinctively in one gloved hand, looked at it, then looked at Fox, the expression in his eyes demanding 'you owe me, help me out here'.

But Fox couldn't. There would be no favouritism on his part.

The warehouse was utterly silent.

Bear took a deep, very loud breath, his finger hovering over the call button.

Fox's voice cut across the room. 'We said no hesitation.'

He and Bear stared at each other as if locked in a silent battle of wills.

Fox began counting the seconds in his head. One. Two. He saw Wolf slip a pistol from his waistband and hold it down by his side. Bear was unarmed. All of them were except him and Wolf.

Three.

Wolf's gloved finger tensed on the trigger.

Four.

Bear pressed the call button in one swift decisive movement.

The silence in the room was absolute.

And then they heard it. A dull but unmistakeable thud coming from the south.

Fox straightened up and took a deep breath. There was no going back now. The operation had begun.

8

16.05

The man called Scope heard it in the cramped flat he'd been renting for the past month. A faint but distinctive boom. It was a sound that would always remind him of heat and death. He ignored it. After all, he was in the middle of a big, sprawling city where the unnatural noises of constant human activity were always coming at him from one direction or the other. He guessed it was probably just a crane dropping its load on one of the many building sites that dotted this surprisingly drab part of west London. It was all a far cry from the peace and tranquillity of home – a place he hadn't seen in far too long.

Thankfully, he was almost done here. One last job and then he would be gone.

He finished dressing and looked at himself in the mirror. The face that stared back at him was lined and gaunt, with hollow cheekbones and skin that was dark and weather-beaten from the sun. He'd been handsome once, or so he'd been told by more than one woman who wasn't his mother. But no longer. He'd lost a lot of weight this past year. Now he bore the haunted look of a man who'd seen and done far too much and there was a hardness in his flint-grey eyes that was impossible to disguise.

Still, he was going to have to try.

He produced a pair of horn-rimmed glasses from the breast pocket of his cheap black suit – the type a mid-ranking hotel manager would wear – and put them on, adopting a polite, almost obsequious expression. 'Good afternoon, sir,' he said, addressing the mirror with a respectful, customer-oriented smile. 'May I have a word? It's about a small discrepancy on your latest bill.'

Not perfect, but it would have to do.

Turning away, he picked up the tools he was going to need from the pockmarked coffee table, all small and easily concealable, and secreted them about his person. Finally, he slipped the hotel nametag introducing him as 'Mr Cotelli, Manager' into his breast pocket and headed for the front door of the rental flat.

A woman's scream from somewhere down the hall outside stopped him as he turned the handle.

More memories tore across his vision. Recent ones. The converted farmhouse at the end of the track. The naked girl tied to the bed, bleeding. The boyfriend with his long, tangled hair and sunken, cokehead cheeks. On his knees, narrow eyes focused on the barrel of the pistol. The interrogation. The answers. The pleading.

Then the thunderous blast of the gun around the filthy room and the bullet blowing the boy's brains all over the bare wall. And the girl's desperate screams starting all over again, because she was convinced that Scope was going to kill her next.

He shivered, waiting for the memory to pass, surprised by the strength of the guilt he felt.

'Pull yourself together,' he said aloud to himself. 'It's nearly over.'

He opened the door and stepped out into the hallway. A man's drunken shouting had replaced the scream. It was coming from the flat at the end. In the time he'd been here, the guy and his old lady had been constantly yelling and shrieking at each other, and more than once he'd considered going round there and telling – or getting – them to shut the hell up. But he'd always resisted. There was no point drawing attention to himself, which was why he'd chosen a dump like this in the first place, and thankfully he wasn't going to have to put up with it for much longer.

Holding this particular thought at the front of his mind, he made his way down to the street and, conscious of the wail of sirens starting up from pretty much every direction, hailed the first passing cab and asked the driver to take him to the Stanhope Hotel.

'Then you'll have to come back to Oz with me, won't you?'

She wanted to tell him then that she'd made her mind up to go with him, but decided to break the news when they were sharing a glass of wine after she'd finished her shift and everything had calmed down. 'I don't want to leave under a cloud. It wouldn't be right.'

'Look, you did the right thing. Don't worry about it. If they try to sack you over it, we'll sue the bastards.'

'Do you think I should call Siobhan and let her know what's happened?' she asked, mounting the fire exit steps.

Rod sighed. 'I would, babe. Otherwise it'll look like you're trying to hide something. But don't worry, all right? You're going to be fine. We both are.'

She had a sudden, overwhelming urge to go home. To walk out of the hotel and forget the whole bloody job with all its hassles and moaning guests and head back to their little flat and jump straight into his arms. Rod had taken the day off after their late one the previous night – as a self-employed plumber, he could get away with it – and he'd tried to get Elena to do the same. She should have done too. She hadn't had a day off sick during her whole time at the Stanhope, which given the levels of absenteeism in the hospitality industry almost certainly put her in a minority of one. Instead she'd done the right thing – and now it was going to cost her her job. Siobhan was a supportive

GM, and the two of them had always got on well, but Elena couldn't see her boss siding with her over this one.

'Shit,' said Rod down the phone, interrupting her thoughts.

Elena frowned. 'What is it?'

'They're saying on the TV that there's been an explosion at the Westfield. It sounds like it might be a bomb. Have you heard anything over there?'

The Westfield was barely a mile from where they lived, and she and Rod had been shopping there the other week.

'No, nothing. But I haven't been past a TV in the last twenty minutes. Has anyone been hurt?'

'I don't think they know yet. It's only just happened, but they're saying it's in the underground car park. Blimey, it's all going on today, isn't it? Maybe you ought to come home. Call Siobhan and tell her you've been traumatized by your experience with that Arab bloke and get back here for a bit of R and R.'

Elena sighed. 'I'll be fine. Maybe I'll take tomorrow off, but I'm the only DM on today so I need to stay put.'

As she spoke, she heard someone talking on the steps above her. Looking up, she saw a young room service waiter on the phone by the third-floor doors. His tray was on the floor in front of him. She'd never met Armin before, but she'd have bet a week's wages it was him.

'I've got to go,' she told Rod. 'I'll talk to you later, OK?'

Without waiting for an answer, Elena ended the call and marched up to the waiter.

He quickly ended his own call and replaced the phone in his pocket.

'Armin,' she snapped, reading his nametag. 'Where have you been? Rooms 422 and 608 haven't received their food orders.' She looked down at the full tray at his feet. 'I assume that's them.'

Armin was lean and wiry, and would have been quite good-looking if it hadn't been for the pinched, aggressive expression he wore. He looked her up and down dismissively. 'Sorry,' he said in heavily accented English, sounding like he didn't mean it. 'I got held up.'

'You left the kitchen more than twenty minutes ago. How held up can you be?'

'I was on the phone.'

'Who to?'

He hesitated before answering. 'A friend.'

Elena considered herself a fair boss, and one who didn't lose her temper easily, but Armin's bizarrely unapologetic attitude was infuriating her. 'You shouldn't be calling your friends in office hours. Especially when you're in the middle of delivering room service orders. What were you thinking about? Don't you want this job? Because there are plenty of people out there who do.'

She stopped, realizing that she'd raised her voice, something she'd always been taught to avoid doing since all it showed was that you were losing control of the situation.

Armin looked her right in the eye, and there was such naked rage in his expression that she took a step back. 'I said I was sorry,' he said quietly. 'I'll deliver the order now.' He picked up the tray and continued up the stairs, leaving Elena staring after him.

She took a deep breath and ran a hand over her face. The confrontation, short as it was, had really shaken her. Partly it was because she was still in shock from what had happened earlier, but it was more than that. It was because she could tell from the way he'd spoken that he despised her. Yet she'd never even met him before.

Beginning to wonder whether it might actually be quite a good idea to pull a sickie, as Rod had suggested, she turned and started back down the stairs, determined to have a word with Rav and get him to sack Armin the moment his shift was finished.

10

16.17

They left the warehouse in a white Transit van with Andrews Maintenance Services written on the side, beneath which was an out-of-service 0207 number. The van had been bought with cash at an auction in Kent two weeks earlier and it was completely clean. Fox was driving, with Wolf in the passenger seat next to him, while the other four were hidden away in the back behind a grimy curtain, along with the bulk of the weaponry.

As Fox turned on to the A40 heading eastbound he could see a pall of smoke over the buildings to the south-east, where the bomb had struck. By the time they reached East Acton and the Westway flyover a steady stream of emergency services vehicles – police, fire and ambulance – were approaching from the other direction. Fox counted seventeen of them altogether in the space of three minutes, and there'd be others coming from different directions as well, severely stretching their resources, as had been the plan.

They turned off the A40 just before the start of the flyover, heading south on the A3220, then taking a left on to Holland Park Avenue, where the traffic suddenly became more clogged. An ambulance drove down the middle of the road coming towards them, its blue lights flashing, and Fox was forced to mount the pavement to let it through.

The atmosphere in the van was tense, and Fox could hear the men shuffling about in the back. Everyone was jumpy. Not just because of what they were about to do but because all of them, except him, had snorted a generous line of speed before they'd left the warehouse. The drug would keep them awake and alert, and lower their inhibitions, making it easier for them to kill people when the time came. It would also dull their natural fear. But for Fox, who'd never taken illicit drugs in his life and wasn't prepared to start now, two cups of strong coffee had had to suffice.

Wolf's phone rang. He answered it, identified himself by codename, then paused while he listened to the person on the other end of the phone. 'You know what to do,' he said at last, and ended the call, exchanging looks with Fox.

Fox tightened his fingers round the steering wheel. It was time to put the next stage of the plan into action.

11

The First Great Western from Bristol Temple Meads crawled snake-like into Paddington Station, two minutes behind schedule.

The young man was one of the first to his feet, picking up his rucksack from the floor in front of him. He hauled it over his shoulders, making sure the detonation cord was out of sight but within easy reach, and headed for the exit door at the end of the carriage, stopping to let out a couple of other passengers en route, wondering idly whether or not he was saving their lives by doing so or merely prolonging them for a few minutes. Most of his fellow passengers were business people heading back to town from their meetings in the provinces, or middle-aged theatregoers. He saw no children, God be praised. The young man was ready to do what he had to do, but he had no desire for kids to be caught up in it. He was, after all, a soldier not a butcher.

There was a bottleneck forming as the tiny corridor between carriages became thronged with passengers, and he was forced to stop next to the luggage rack, only feet from the trolley suitcase containing five kilos of explosives rigged up to a battery pack and mobile phone. No one had noticed him bringing it on earlier, and by the time anyone realized that it had been left behind it would be too late. He tried not to look at it, but couldn't help giving it a glance out of the corner of his eye, wondering what damage it would do, and to whom, when it exploded.

The train came to a stop, its brakes emitting a long metallic shriek, and the doors opened. Immediately, the bottleneck eased as the passengers exited one at a time. When it came to the young man's turn, he took a quick look up the platform at the wall of people pouring down the platform towards him from the rear coaches, then stepped down and joined them.

This was it. The time. He'd been building up to it for months now. Ever since the cowardly dogs of NATO had declared war on his country and tried to divide its peoples so that they could steal the oil that was rightfully theirs. And now he'd received the honour of being one of the few chosen to strike back.

The young man had been travelling on the train's third carriage, and when he was level with the beginning of the first carriage, and some twenty yards from the ticket barriers, where already the passengers were slowing up as a new bottleneck formed, he took his phone from his pocket and speed-dialled the number on the screen.

The sound of the explosion was deafening. Even though he'd steeled himself against it, and was wearing noise-suppressing headphones, he was still pushed forward and fell to one knee.

For a long time, no one moved. This was the moment of shock, when everyone's senses were so scrambled they didn't know how to react. And then the screams started.

Slipping the phone back into his jacket pocket, he got to his feet and took a first look at the mayhem behind him.

Thick black smoke and claws of flame billowed out of a huge hole in the side of the train. There were a lot of people lying unmoving on the platform, while others were on their hands and knees, clutching at injuries. He couldn't tell how many because his view was blocked by people – some trying to help, others simply milling about with shocked, terrified expressions, and a few sensible ones making a dash towards the exits and safety.

The young man took no pleasure from the scene, but he felt no guilt either. This was war. And in war, there were always civilian casualties. The British had been committing atrocities against his people with their warplanes and missiles for months now, and the people all around him supported their government's actions with their votes and their tax money. All he was doing was restoring some balance.

The station staff had opened the ticket gates now and were yelling at people to get away from the source of the explosion, while a couple of over-whelmed-looking police officers shouted for people to leave the station but to stay calm, even though their own faces seemed to radiate panic.

Immediately, there was a rush for the exits. People were yelling and screaming, some leaping over the turnstiles rather than waiting to go through them, one man even trying to scale the roof of a shop selling ties. On the public address system an announcement started up, playing on a loop: 'All passengers must evacuate the station now. Please follow the instructions of staff. All passengers must evacuate the station now.'

The young man knew where they were being sent. It was common knowledge that the meeting point in the event of a fire or related emergency was on the slip road next to the taxi rank on the southern side of the station. He also knew that having reached what they thought was a place of safety, most people would then stay put, wanting to be near enough to the unfolding drama so that they didn't miss anything.

Which was exactly what he wanted them to do.

When it came to his turn, he hurried through the turnstile, following the barked commands of the police officers as they ushered him to the right, towards the exit.

His last walk on Planet Earth.

It wasn't particularly inspiring, taking in the giant overhead signs carrying the arrival and departure times of the trains, the information centre, the bland-looking shops . . . all temples of a western consumerism he despised.

He wouldn't miss this place. A far better one awaited him, as it awaited all good warriors.

He thought of his childhood. Playing football in the street outside his home with his brother Khalid and his friends; Friday lunch with the whole family, when everyone would be laughing and happy; his grandma bringing him and his brother candies hidden in the folds of her skirts. He missed Grandma, who'd been gone almost ten years. He missed his father, who'd been gone four. And he missed Khalid – dear, handsome Khalid – who'd been incinerated by a NATO missile fired by some coward hundreds of miles away as he fought against the mercenaries and traitors trying to divide and destroy his country. He hoped to see them all in paradise, God willing. Soon now.

Very soon.

A crowd of people were waiting on the slip road outside the station, many of them already on their phones telling others about what they'd just seen and heard, while a far smaller number of station staff in fluorescent jackets tried to keep them adequately marshalled.

The young man reached round behind his back and

gently tugged the detonation cord free from his rucksack. His whole body throbbed with anticipation. His palms were lined with sweat, and he could hear nothing except the steady drumming of his heart. For the first time, perhaps in his life, his whole world was in perfect focus.

The crowd seemed to part naturally, allowing him to move inside it. One of the staff urged him to keep moving.

But he didn't. He slowed right down. He was in the middle of it now, only feet away from a man talking loudly into a phone pressed hard against his ear. But he hardly saw the man. He hardly saw any of them. It was as if he was watching them through a rain-drenched windscreen.

This was it. The time.

He stood up ramrod straight, the detonation cord gripped firmly in his hand.

Someone saw him. A middle-aged woman with bleached blonde hair. No more than five feet away. She cried out. One single, howled word: 'Jesus!'

The man on the phone looked round and seemed to realize what was going on. Instinctively he moved towards the young man, his hand outstretched.

But he was too late. The young man was ready.

'For God and my people!' he cried out, and yanked the detonation cord with all his strength, embracing the eruption of noise and light as he was torn to pieces.

12

The van was just passing Notting Hill Gate tube station when Fox heard the faint boom of the explosion through the open window.

That'll be the train bomb, he thought.

He took a quick breath as the enormity of what he was involved in was brought home to him. In the van, everyone was quiet. Even Wolf had stopped drumming his fingers on the dashboard – something he'd been doing for most of the journey – as he waited for what they knew would happen next.

They were moving faster now, the traffic easing up, probably because they were heading away from the earlier blast at the Westfield and the numbers of emergency vehicles moving towards it had temporarily thinned out. The new explosion would stretch them even further, and trigger the first real signs of panic in the capital. It was, thought Fox, incredibly easy in the digital age, where information was only a second away, to sow fear and chaos among the population with only the most basic weaponry.

Two minutes later, just as they came towards Lancaster Gate, they heard the second blast.

Wolf nodded slowly and rubbed his pockmarked face. Fox had never met the man who'd just turned himself into a walking bomb but he knew he was one of Wolf's protégés. He watched as Wolf reached for his phone and dialled a number.

'It's out of service,' he said. 'He's gone.'

'I can just imagine what it's like in Scotland Yard's control room now,' said Fox. He had nothing but disdain for the politically correct leadership of the Metropolitan Police and their bosses the politicians, all of whom would be in a state of wide-eyed confusion now as they realized how truly powerless they were in the greater scheme of things.

'It's time to rain down some more havoc,' Wolf responded, putting the phone on loudspeaker as he dialled another number.

After a good minute a woman's voice came on the line, her tone harassed. '*Evening Standard*, Julie Peters.'

'In the last five minutes two bombs have exploded at Paddington railway station,' Wolf announced, using his heavy Middle Eastern accent to maximum effect. 'One on the First Great Western train from Bristol, the other a martyrdom operation by a young

mujahideen warrior on the concourse. These bombings, and the bombing at the Westfield Shopping
Centre, were carried out by the Pan-Arab Army of
God in direct retaliation for Britain's involvement in
the NATO attacks on Arab nations and their occupation of Muslim lands. There are four more bombs
planted on trains coming into Waterloo, St Pancras,
Fenchurch Street and Liverpool Street. We give you
this warning to show that we are prepared to
negotiate.'

'And what is it you want?' asked Julie Peters
breathlessly, but Wolf had already ended the call. He
switched off the phone and removed the SIM card,
which he flung out of the open window. By the time it
was found it would be of no use whatsoever.

Fox knew that Wolf had given the *Evening Standard*
reporter enough information about the bombings to
confirm that he was involved in them, so his warning
would be taken seriously, and a vague warning of
multiple potential targets would stretch resources to
the absolute limit.

And it would be all for nothing. There were no
more bombs on trains. They weren't needed.

Their real target was somewhere else entirely.

13

'What was that, Mom?'

'I don't know, honey,' said Abby Levinson, giving her son a reassuring smile as they walked back towards the hotel. 'Probably nothing.'

But the heavy bang had unnerved her. She looked across at her father, who was walking next to the road on the other side of Ethan, and now it was his turn to give her a reassuring look – the sort of look he'd been giving her all her life. As always, he was a strong, calming presence.

'Definitely nothing,' he said, ruffling Ethan's hair. 'You always hear stuff like this in big cities. New York's much noisier than London.'

'Is New York nicer?' asked Ethan.

His grandpa laughed. 'I'm biased. I grew up there. But I like both. Although maybe we should have come to London at a different time of year.'

He pushed his hat down over his head as a gust of wind threatened to send it flying. It was beginning to rain again, and Abby contemplated pulling out her umbrella for the last fifty yards of the journey, before deciding against it and increasing her pace.

It had been a fun, if exhausting, day. A visit to the London Dungeon, lunch at McDonald's, the London Eye, and finally the Aquarium. Ethan had had a great time, and in the end, that was what counted. It had been almost a year to the day since his father left the family home to supposedly 'find himself', having concluded that, actually, parenthood and its attendant responsibilities wasn't for him, and Ethan had taken his absence hard. This trip, combining the Thanks-giving holiday with his seventh birthday, was a way of taking his mind off his father and having some fun. Although Abby had to admit she was amazed at how expensive London was. And how grey and cold. She should have expected it, of course. After all, the UK had never been known for its fine weather. But maybe she'd just got too used to Florida's blue skies and its warm sunshine on her back. Tomorrow she was going to do some Christmas shopping in the West End on her own – a little bit of much-needed 'me' time before they flew home on Saturday morning – while her dad took Ethan to the Natural History Museum. The two of them loved spending time together, and it was important that Ethan had a strong male role model in his life now that Daniel was gone.

The second bang stopped her dead in her tracks. It was louder than the first. Other passers-by had stopped too, and they were now looking in the direction the noise had come from. One man looked at her and raised his eyebrows, before turning away.

'And what do you think *that* was, Mom?'

Abby didn't answer her son. She was watching a thin plume of smoke rising up through the rain and gathering dusk, somewhere beyond the other side of Hyde Park. She suddenly felt very vulnerable out here in the cold and gloom of this sprawling foreign city far from home.

A police car raced through the traffic past Marble Arch with sirens blaring. It was heading in the direction of the smoke.

'Whatever it is, it's nothing to do with us,' Ethan's grandpa replied over the noise of the siren. 'And I'm getting wet out here. Come on, let's get inside.'

He put a protective arm round both their shoulders, steering them towards home, and even though he was barely as tall as her and almost seventy-five years old, his touch made her feel a little safer.

Trying hard not to grip her son's hand too hard, Abby hurried past the tall concierge – a guy who'd smiled mischievously at her every time she'd seen him before but who was now frowning anxiously – and into the warmth and security of the Stanhope Hotel.

14

Newly promoted Deputy Assistant Commissioner Arley Dale was bored and restless. She was chairing a meeting between community leaders and senior officers from Operation Trident, the unit that dealt with so-called black on black gun crime in the city. The meeting had dragged on for close to two hours now and absolutely nothing of any substance had been achieved. The community leaders were demanding action after a series of shootings in Brixton over the previous six months, while the Trident officers were demanding more cooperation from the community itself, and everyone seemed to be going round in circles, mouthing the same old platitudes. Arley, who had a reputation for banging heads together and getting things done, had tried her best to move things along but had now all but given up. She knew they had to have these meetings so that the Met could demonstrate its new, more caring attitude to minority groups, but as a DAC in one of the biggest police forces in the world she genuinely believed there were better ways of allocating her time.

She was also distracted. Twenty minutes earlier, her secretary, Ann, had interrupted the meeting to inform her that there'd been an explosion in the underground car park of the Westfield Shopping Centre. There'd been no further details available at the time, and Arley had asked to be kept informed as they came in. If the explosion turned out to be suspicious, then as the most senior officer of the Met's Specialist Crime Directorate on duty she'd be heavily involved in implementing the Major Incident Plan in response.

The prospect of suddenly being flung into a major operation had Arley in two minds. On the one hand she relished getting her teeth into challenges, especially fast-moving ones, and it would be an excellent opportunity to prove her worth, having only been in the job less than a month. But on the other, she badly wanted to go home. She'd been away Monday and Tuesday on a residential course, had put in thirteen hours the previous day, and quite frankly, she was exhausted.

Surreptitiously, she looked at her watch as Genson Smith, a veteran Lambeth councillor with a longstanding grievance against the police, and a man who never tired of hearing his own voice, launched into another of his polemics. 4.35. If she could wrap this meeting up quickly she could be out of here by five and relaxing in a hot bath with a much-needed glass of Sauvignon Blanc by six.

The knock on the door interrupted her thoughts.

It was Ann, her secretary, again, and her expression was concerned. 'Ma'am, you're needed urgently.'

'I'm afraid I have to go,' Arley announced to the attendees, pleased at least to be leaving the room. 'I'll leave you in the capable hands of DCS Russell.'

Genson Smith looked extremely irritated, but Arley was out of the door before he could actually say anything.

'The explosion at the Westfield has been confirmed as a bomb,' said Ann when they were out in the corridor.

'What do we know about casualties?'

'So far we've got reports of six people injured, but no fatalities.'

'Thank God for that.'

'That's not all,' Ann continued.

Arley felt her heart sink.

'There have been two more explosions at Paddington Station. Initial reports say they're both bombs. The commissioner wants you in the control room right away.'

Arley had been with the Met for over twenty years. She was used to crises, and knew how to handle them. It was one of the reasons she'd risen so high. 'I'm on my way,' she said, knowing that the bath and the

Sauvignon Blanc were going to have to wait, but already feeling the adrenalin as it pumped through her system, shaking her out of the torpor of the meeting.

15

He wasn't going to come.

In her hotel room, Cat was about to light another cigarette and break the cardinal rule they'd set of never calling Michael on his mobile when there was a loud knock on the door.

She put down her glass of Evian and bounded over to open it.

It was Michael, his presence immediately filling the doorway. He was a big man with big, rugged features who'd worked hard to keep himself in shape, and even though he was in his early fifties, he wore the years easily.

He grinned and produced a bunch of flowers from behind his back, handing them to her.

'Darling, you shouldn't have done.' Smiling, she stepped aside to let him inside, taking in the scent of his Dior aftershave and a tang of single malt on his breath. 'But I'm glad you did.'

Michael took her in his arms and kissed her. 'I need you, Cat,' he whispered. 'God, I need you so, so badly.'

'You've got me,' she whispered back, feeling his hardness against her. 'And we've got all night.'

She twisted round and threw the flowers on the bed, and a second later they were kissing again. Outside, she could hear the blare of police sirens coming past the window.

They walked crab-like together towards the bed, his hand running up her leg to the stocking top, his breathing getting faster now as he became more and more aroused.

She felt his phone vibrate in his trouser pocket. He ignored it. So did she.

By the time it had stopped vibrating they were standing against the bottom of the bed, and his fingers were stroking the bare flesh of her inner thigh. Instinctively she opened her legs a little, and he gave a pleasing grunt of pleasure.

Almost immediately, his phone started up again.

'Damn,' he cursed, removing his hand from the folds of her dress. 'I'd better see what they want.' He gave Cat an apologetic look and turned away, putting the phone to his ear. 'What is it?' he demanded brusquely.

As he listened to what was being said, his shoulders slumped visibly.

Cat stepped away and reached under the pillow on her side of the bed as outside more sirens shrieked past.

'All right,' said Michael at last, 'I'll be there as soon as I can.' He ended the call and turned round with a frustrated sigh, his eyes dark with disappointment. 'I'm truly sorry about this, Cat, but there's been some kind of terrorist incident—'

'I know,' answered Cat, her voice perfectly calm as she brought the gun round from behind her back and pointed it right between his eyes.

16

Michael stared at her in utter disbelief. His phone fell to the floor. 'What on earth are you doing?' he asked.

Cat stared back coldly, her gun arm steady. 'Don't ask questions. Just do as I say.'

'But I've just told you, there's a major terrorist incident going on and—'

'And I told you, I know. There's been a bomb at the Westfield Shopping Centre, and two more at Paddington.'

Michael's eyes widened. 'God, how the hell—'

'Because I'm involved. Now sit down in the chair by the bed, and no more talking.'

She cocked the pistol, still keeping it trained between his eyes, and deliberately tightened her finger on the trigger.

'Now look here, Cat, I'm sure we can sort this out,'

he said, a patronizing expression on his face, as if he was confident that she could be reasoned with, which was typical of him. Michael Prior was a man used to getting his own way.

'There's nothing to sort out. I'm a soldier of the Pan-Arab Army of God and you are my prisoner.'

Michael sat down heavily in the tub chair next to the window, his face pale with shock.

'If you put the gun down, we can sort this out, I promise. It's not too late.'

Cat could hear the strain in his voice. 'And if you keep talking, I'll shoot you in the kneecap, and I won't miss. I've had extensive training with the Glock 17, and the suppressor does a very good job of keeping the noise down, so if I do pull the trigger no one's going to hear. My orders are to keep you alive, but no one's going to care if you can't walk.' She kept her voice totally calm, as she'd been trained to do, and it seemed to do the trick. Michael was visibly nervous now and beginning to sweat.

Keeping the gun on him, she reached into a Harrods bag she'd brought with her, pulled out two pairs of ankle restraints, and lobbed them over to him. 'Put these on – one hoop round each ankle, the other round each of the front chair legs. Make sure they're locked, then throw the keys on the bed.'

He caught them easily, but rather than put them on he made one last effort to salvage the situation. 'Come on, Cat,' he said, looking at her imploringly. 'We have something together, don't we? Something special. Let's not destroy it. I'm in love with you, darling. Remember that. I'm in love with you. You mean everything to me.'

Cat shook her head. What fools men could be sometimes, especially when they wanted sex. 'You make my skin crawl, Michael. I was given orders to draw you into a relationship, and that's exactly what I've done. Now put those restraints on before I lose patience.'

She watched the realization that he'd been utterly suckered finally sink in. He looked truly upset, which pleased her. She'd done her job well.

'You're making a big mistake, you know,' he blustered. 'If you go through with this, you won't see the outside of a prison for years.'

Once again her finger tightened on the trigger, and Michael must have seen the contempt in her face, because he finally did as he'd been told.

When he'd finished she came up behind him and made him put his hands behind his back and lean forward, towards the floor. 'The Glock's trained on your right shoulder blade, so don't try anything,' she said, putting a pair of old-fashioned handcuffs on his wrists and locking them with her free hand.

Michael was now completely helpless.

'But I've seen your background details,' he said, the confusion in his voice obvious as he watched her remove the ball gag from the Harrods bag. 'How could this have happened?'

She bent down close to his face, smiling coldly. 'The woman you employed does not exist. Catherine Manolis died in Nice in October 1985, aged twenty-three months. Her identity was stolen and used to apply for false identity documents. We tailored her to suit the job application, and no one spotted it.'

Michael sighed. 'So, everything you told me about your upbringing was rubbish. You're not a widow at all.'

'Oh yes,' she told him, her voice hardening, 'I'm definitely a widow. My husband was murdered last year defending his country against men like you. Except while he was fighting on the frontline you were sitting far away behind a desk giving orders.'

'But Cat, you must understand, I had nothing to do with that. I was—'

Before he could finish the sentence, she stuffed the ball gag into his mouth. Again he tried to protest, but she pushed the gun against his cheek and ordered him to bite down hard on the gag, and he did as he was told.

When she'd finished gagging him, she pulled out his mobile phone and switched it off. It would be switched on again later and moved to different places in the hotel to confuse any rescuers trying to locate him.

She then pulled out her own phone and speed-dialled a number. 'I have the prize,' she said, 'and it's ready to be opened.'

And Michael Prior truly was a prize. But then, a director of MI6 was always going to be.

17

16.40

Wolf put down his mobile and turned to Fox. As he did so, some of the hardness left his face, and for a moment he had that faraway look of the daydreamer.

Every man has a weakness, thought Fox, and, like a lot of men, Wolf's was the opposite sex. The woman on the other end of the line had him wrapped round her little finger, and that worried Fox because she was a wilful little bitch. He had the feeling that when the op began in earnest she might well cause problems.

He'd have to watch that.

'Cat's got him,' Wolf said as Fox turned the van out of the traffic chaos of Park Lane and down one of the side streets. 'The MI6 man is ours.'

'Good. She's done well.'

And she had too. To lure such a senior member of one of the largest intelligence agencies in the world into a honey-trap was no mean feat, and it had taken a lot of skill and planning. But then it seemed that Michael Prior's weakness was women too.

Fox drove the van round the back of the Stanhope Hotel, parking on double yellow lines a few yards short of the delivery entrance. The journey had taken them eight minutes longer than anticipated, and Fox could almost feel the adrenalin surging round the interior as each of them prepared for the assault. Wolf had pulled back the curtain separating the front cab from the back, and Fox could see the others now. Each of them was quiet and focused. Everyone was waiting to begin.

Wolf put his mobile on loudspeaker and made a call to Panther, their inside man in the Stanhope.

Panther was Cat's brother, Armin. Both Fox and Wolf had met him on a number of occasions as they endeavoured to find out everything they could about the hotel. He was an unpleasant little bastard with a bad attitude who resented the fact that he might have to take orders from Fox, a foreigner he neither knew nor respected, but in the three weeks he'd been working at the Stanhope as a room service waiter he'd been an invaluable source of information.

It had been no problem getting him the job. Big hotels are notorious for their lack of background checks. He possessed good-quality fake papers supplied by his embassy, entitling him to work in the UK, and the fact that he had no experience, and virtually nothing on his CV to indicate what he'd been doing for the past few years, was clearly of no consequence. What mattered to the hotel's management was that he had a valid work permit and, more importantly, was prepared to work hard for the frankly appalling wages on offer.

Panther answered immediately. 'What kept you?' he hissed into the phone. 'I've been waiting by the back door for the last fifteen minutes. If anyone spots me—'

'We're here now,' Wolf told him. 'What's the situation in there?'

'Everything's good. The kitchens are beginning to get busy. About twenty to twenty-five staff inside.'

'What's the security on the gate like? Can you see?'

'Just the usual guy, Kwame. He's sat down reading the paper. I can see him now.'

Wolf and Fox exchanged glances, then Fox turned to the men in the back. They were all sat up straight in anticipation, cocking their weapons.

'OK, get the back door open,' ordered Wolf. 'We're coming in.'

'Right,' Fox said, 'we all know what we're doing. This is crowd control, not a shooting fest. We want them scared but not panicking. But if anyone resists or makes a bolt for it, take them down. If any of you still have mobiles on you, turn them off now and do not use them for the duration of the op. From now on, all communications are face to face. Got that?'

Every man grunted his agreement.

Fox pulled the van away from the kerb and into an archway that led through to a rear courtyard where the Stanhope received all its deliveries. As the van approached the single-bar security gate, Kwame put his paper down and got up from the chair. He was only a young guy – twenty-five, twenty-six – with the kind of round boyish face that was never going to cause anyone any trouble.

As he walked up to the driver's-side window, Fox pulled a gun from the seat pocket beside him and pointed it at his face. 'Open the gate.'

Kwame nodded rapidly and immediately put a code into a keypad on the gatepost that lifted the gate automatically, before shoving his hands in the air just so no one was in any doubt that he was being cooperative.

Not that it made any difference. Fox held his gun arm ramrod straight and shot him in the eye, the bullet's retort echoing round the archway, before accelerating into the courtyard.

Panther had already opened the double doors that led through to the kitchens, and it looked like he was talking animatedly to someone behind him.

Fox swung the van round in a wide semi-circle and backed it up to where Panther stood in the open doorway, looking over to where Kwame's body lay unmoving on the ground. Anyone passing along the street outside would see it, but it no longer mattered.

They'd arrived, and soon the whole world would know about what they were doing.

He cut the engine, removed the cap and glasses disguise he'd been wearing, and pulled on a balaclava. Then, grabbing his AK-47 and backpack from behind the seat, he leapt out of the van along with the others, feeling a tremendous exhilaration.

It was time for war.

18

The Stanhope's main kitchen was situated on the ground floor, directly below the main ballroom on the mezzanine floor, yet well out of sight of the lobby. It was reached through a soundproofed door marked STAFF ONLY, and as soon as Elena was through it she was assailed by the smell and noise of preparations for the evening food service.

Her mood hadn't improved much. Having mollified the guests who'd originally complained about the late arrival of their room service orders with complimentary champagne, she'd just been informed by reception that there were two more similar complaints, including one from a VIP guest who'd been waiting almost an hour for a steak burger and fries. There were always occasional delays in delivering orders in a hotel the size of the Stanhope, but they tended to be rare. A cluster of five was almost unheard of and Elena had decided to get it sorted out once and for all with the catering manager. If it turned out that Armin was the one responsible, she'd march him off the premises herself then and there.

She spotted a familiar face – Faisal, the Jordanian line cook, who was stirring a giant steaming pot – and he gave her a big grin and an exaggerated tip of his chef's hat. 'Miss Serenko. Looking beautiful as always. How are you?'

'Why thank you, Faisal,' replied Elena, feeling better immediately. 'I'm fine, thanks. Have you seen Rav? I need a word with him.'

'I think he's out the back telling off one of the employees.' He arched a thick grey eyebrow and was about to say something else when there was a loud commotion and a series of barked shouts coming from behind the door that led to the kitchen's main storage and delivery area.

As everyone turned towards it, another sound rang out. One that was unmistakeable.

A gunshot.

No one moved. It was just too unexpected for anyone to react.

And then the door opened and Elena let out a shocked gasp as Rav stumbled through it. Dressed smartly, as always, in a navy suit, he was clutching his stomach, where a dark red stain was visibly spreading across the white of his shirt. His face registered complete surprise – a surprise that was reflected in every other face in the kitchen.

Two more shots rang out in quick succession and Rav's face appeared to explode, showering one of the stainless steel work surfaces with blood. As he collapsed, another figure filled the doorway. It was Armin, the room service waiter Elena had had the confrontation with barely half an hour earlier, and he was holding a smoking handgun out in front of him.

A young pot washer Elena vaguely recognized was standing a few feet away from Armin, and he leapt at him, going for his gun. But Armin was quicker. He swung round and opened fire, his bullets sending the pot washer crashing backwards.

More men strode into the room, one after another, dressed identically in balaclavas and dark clothing. All were carrying assault rifles.

'Everyone down on the floor now!' screamed the first of the men, pointing his rifle straight at Elena's chest.

For an interminably long, slow moment, she was completely mesmerized by the scene in front of her; then Faisal grabbed her by the collar of her jacket and pulled her to the floor.

A second later the noise of automatic rifle fire from more than one weapon erupted around the kitchen, and as Elena hit the floor, shoulder blades first, she heard Faisal cry out and saw him stumble past her before collapsing to his knees. He swayed unsteadily in that position as more bullets tore up his back like angry geysers, and then he pitched over sideways, landing on Elena's feet, already dead.

The whole thing had lasted barely ten seconds, and it had taken Elena a good portion of that time to come to terms with what was going on; but now that she had, she experienced an icy, stomach-wrenching terror followed immediately by a desperate desire to survive. Knowing she had to get out of the line of fire, she kicked Faisal's body off her and scrambled on her hands and knees behind one of the kitchen units as another burst of rifle fire reverberated around the room, the bullets ricocheting like pinballs off the stainless steel work surfaces.

Leaning back against the unit, the fear coming at her in ferocious waves, she realized she was trapped. It was a good ten feet to the door that led back into the lobby, most of it over exposed ground. She'd never make it. She was going to die, helpless and without the people she loved – Rod, her mother, her sister – by her side.

In a hotel kitchen that smelled of fat, for God's sake.

Elena caught the eye of another member of staff, a young Irishman called Aidan she'd seen working in the kitchens a few times before. She remembered him because he looked more like an artist or a singer than a cook. He had raffish curly hair and a cool beard, and sad but very beautiful blue eyes. Even though she loved Rod, she'd always found Aidan attractive in an exotic way, as if he was a box full of secrets. He was squatting down on his haunches next to a unit a few feet away, looking scared but calm. He tried to give her a reassuring look.

But there was nothing to be reassured about. They could either run and be cut down by the guns or wait here and die.

The shooting had stopped. Somehow, Elena found the silence even more terrifying than the noise because she had no idea what was going to happen next.

She heard more shouting coming from the gunmen, telling people to get down and stay down, followed by footsteps coming closer.

She held her breath and pushed back against the metal, hoping it would somehow open up to conceal her, praying for God's help.

The footsteps stopped. Out of the corner of her eye she could see a pair of scuffed black shoes, only feet away. On her side of the unit.

Slowly, experiencing a cold dread that seemed to turn her whole body to jelly, she looked up.

Armin stared back at her coldly, no feeling at all in his dark eyes, the barrel of the gun close enough to her face that she could feel its heat.

Then he looked beyond her towards Aidan.

Aidan looked at Armin calmly and there was defiance in his deep blue eyes. 'There's no need,' he said, his voice steady.

The gun kicked violently as Armin pulled the trigger, hitting Aidan in the head. He gasped once and toppled silently to the floor, his blood splattering the tiles. Then he lay still in a foetal position as his face was slowly overrun by a curtain of red.

Seeing him go like that – his life, his dreams, his secrets, snuffed out in an instant – was such a huge shock that Elena hardly noticed Armin turn his gaze back to her.

He looked down at her, and he was smiling as his finger tightened on the trigger.

Surprisingly, like Aidan, she felt perfectly calm. If this was her time, so be it. She thought of Rod. Of the life they could have had together . . . the sun, the sea, children, because she'd always wanted children. A boy and a girl.

And then one of the balaclava-clad gunmen appeared. 'What's going on?' he demanded in a Middle Eastern accent.

'That one tried to run away,' Armin lied, motioning dismissively towards Aidan's body. 'And this one's the manager.'

The masked gunman looked down at Elena. 'All right, on your feet. You're coming with us.' He leaned down and grabbed her by the hair, yanking her roughly to her feet, which was when she saw that there were five other gunmen dotted around the room.

God, Elena thought, beginning to panic again. What the hell is going on?

Simon Kernick

'Grab anyone that's still alive and bring them through,' the man holding her shouted. 'Fox – you, Panther and Leopard are the vanguard. Now, let's take the rest of this place. And remember, hold your fire and only shoot when you have to. We want to keep as many people alive as possible.'

With that he shoved the rifle in Elena's side and dragged her towards the door that led through to the rest of the hotel.

19

The plan called for the utmost speed when taking control of the building.

Already things had got out of hand with the assault on the kitchen. Fox had told the men to fire some warning shots to encourage the staff to comply, but the inside man, Panther, had gone crazy, shooting dead at least three people and panicking the others, several of whom had tried to escape. The result had been more people shot down by other members of the team. The Dane, Tiger, had been pretty liberal with the bullets as well, the sadistic bastard. Fox knew it was time to restore discipline, otherwise they'd provoke an early assault from the security forces, which would mess up everything.

As Wolf took hold of the hotel manager, an attractive blonde in a smart trouser suit, and began barking out orders, Fox grabbed Panther by the collar

Simon Kernick

of his waiter's uniform. He thrust his face in close to the other man. 'No more unauthorized shooting, or you die too. Understand?'

Panther's eyes blazed with anger, but Fox was undaunted. The little shit could glare all he wanted. He might be Wolf's fellow countryman, but he still had to know who was boss.

'Understand?'

Panther nodded, and Fox motioned for him and the ex-marine Leopard to follow as he ran through the door that led into the lobby, holding his AK-47 out in front of him. He'd set his stopwatch the second the first shot had been fired, and as he came out into the hotel's immense lobby it read sixty-two seconds.

The kitchen was supposedly soundproofed, but as Fox moved into the lobby the first guests were already hurrying towards the main doors, while the door staff, decked out in their ridiculous tasselled uniforms and peaked caps, had come inside to see what the commotion was. As soon as they saw Fox in his balaclava with the AK and the other two coming in behind him they started bolting for the exits.

'Everyone on the floor!' Fox yelled. 'Now!'

Almost all of them obeyed, but one guy, a businessman in a suit, who'd almost made it to the doors, clearly decided to take the risk and keep going. There was no way Fox could let him go. It would be a show of weakness, and he was too pumped up for that anyway. He'd always found something exhilarating about shooting people – it was the hunter in him – and it was the reason he'd joined the army. He was no indiscriminate killer, he always needed a reason; but give him one and he never hesitated. Flipping the AK to his shoulder, he took aim and, as the man's hand reached out to push open the glass door, he fired a single burst of automatic weapon fire into his back. The force drove the target into the door with an angry thud. There was the sound of breaking glass, and a second later he collapsed.

Fox looked round the room. 'Anyone else try anything, they die too.'

No one did. They lay still, faces squashed into the expensive-looking burgundy carpet. There'd be no further resistance here.

Fox motioned for Panther to stand guard over their new hostages, hoping he wouldn't decide to start shooting them, and took Leopard through the adjacent corridor and into the main bar and restaurant area, where there was now outright panic. People were running around looking desperately for a way out. Unfortunately for them, although there was a bank of windows looking on to Park Lane and Hyde Park beyond, their only obvious means of exit was through the main lobby of the hotel. It was one of the reasons they'd picked the Stanhope as a target. It was easy to corral their prey.

At this time of the afternoon there were also exactly the right numbers. Fox estimated that there were about fifty people in all in the restaurant and bar, a manageable mix of afternoon teas, business drinks and the first of the after-work crowd. An hour later and there'd have been too many; an hour earlier, too few. Like everything else about the op, they'd planned the timing of the assault carefully. Publicity-wise, five p.m. GMT was perfect. Their audience would be eating breakfast in LA, getting ready for lunch in New York, heading home from work in Europe, and sitting down to dinner all across the Arab world. Even in Pakistan, India and beyond people would be up and tuning in to what was happening on a billion television sets.

Soon the whole world would know about them. It was an intoxicating thought.

Once again, Fox yelled at everyone to get down on the floor, putting a burst of fire into the ceiling to encourage them.

There were a few screams, and everyone hit the deck. They really had little choice.

When they were done, Fox walked into the room and began his prepared speech, delivered in a non-specific eastern European accent he'd been working on for the past few months. He spoke loudly, but with a deliberate calmness. 'Please do not be alarmed. You've been taken hostage by the Pan-Arab Army of God. As long as you cooperate, no harm will come to you, and you will be released when our demands are met.'

entrance to the hotel. A few of the sick bastards were even using their phones to film the scene. It seemed to Fox that everyone was a voyeur these days, preferring either to film or watch events rather than help shape them. It was one of the key differences between them and him.

He knew it wouldn't be long before the first police arrived on the scene. Fortunately, they were unlikely to be armed, since less than seven per cent of officers in the Met were authorized to carry guns, and even if one of the mobile armed response vehicles did turn up, they were trained to act with extreme caution and wouldn't attempt to penetrate the building at this stage.

Still, the ground floor was going to need securing quickly.

The ballroom was the perfect location for holding the hostages. It was a cavernous place with no windows or natural light, and like the main restaurant and bar area, there was only one way in or out, making escape impossible and severely limiting the scope of an assault by the security services to free them. Once again, it was why they'd chosen the Stanhope – and proof, thought Fox, of the effectiveness of good surveillance.

The hostages themselves were largely calm and quiet as they were shepherded over to the far end of the room and made to sit down. There were about eighty altogether, and all adults, which made things a little easier. After the earlier shootings, no one was asking any questions or trying to engage in amateur negotiation. A couple of the kitchen staff had minor injuries, but none were seriously wounded. All the seriously wounded were still in the kitchen, and they were going to have to be finished off since there were neither the resources nor, to be frank, the desire to do anything to save them.

When everyone was sitting down and four of the men had formed a guard around them, Wolf approached the group, still holding the blonde hotel manager by the collar of her jacket. He forced her to her knees in front of him and stood legs apart, chest puffed out, looking every inch the man in charge, as he delivered his own speech to the assembled hostages, which was pretty much a rehash of Fox's but with an added harangue about the crimes of the West, and the UK in particular, against the Muslim world. He finished by ordering everyone to turn off their mobile phones and put them on the floor where they could be seen.

There was a flurry of activity as the hostages complied, after which they sat staring intently at the floor as Wolf moved his AK in a lazy arc from one hostage to another.

The first part of the operation was complete. The hotel was under their control and the hostages subdued.

Fox looked at his watch. The time was 16.55.

20

Elena gasped as the man holding her, who she assumed was the leader, pulled her to her feet.

His grip hurt, but she was getting used to it now. In fact she'd calmed down a great deal, even though it gutted her to have to leave behind her mobile phone on the floor. She'd always been a practical sort of girl, one who preferred to get on with things, and right now she knew she had to deal with the current situation and do her best to stay alive. And that meant cooperating. These men might be animals – to kill Rav, Faisal, Aidan and the others in cold blood like they'd done, they had to be – but for the moment at least they'd stopped shooting.

The man the leader had addressed earlier as Fox took the rucksack from his back and placed it in the middle of the hostages. He opened it up, fiddled about inside for a few seconds, then removed what looked like a roll of cable, which he trailed across the floor over to one of the other gunmen. She saw that there was a press-down lever attached to the roll, which the other gunman put his foot on. She'd seen something similar once on a TV programme about the Beslan siege, and her heart lurched as she realized that it was a detonation device and that the rucksack contained a bomb that would probably kill them all if it exploded.

Elena didn't resist as the leader marched her across the ballroom floor and into the satellite kitchen. They were followed by Fox, who'd collected rucksacks from two of the other gunmen.

As soon as they were inside, the leader told her to face the wall, with her hands in the air.

She felt a spasm of pure terror. Were they going to shoot her?

But then the two men started peppering her with questions. Where were the master key cards to the rooms kept? What was the password for the hotel's electronic guest register? Where was the CCTV camera control room?

Elena answered each question honestly, but when the leader asked her how to disable the hotel's sprinkler system, she hesitated. There could be only one reason why they'd want to know this: so that if it came to it they could set the place on fire. Her mind went back to the Mumbai sieges of 2008, the flames and thick black smoke billowing out from the upper windows of the grand old buildings. She'd felt so sorry for all the people involved in those horrifying events but never for one moment had she expected to find herself in the middle of something similar. It just didn't happen in somewhere like London.

'Answer me,' demanded the leader, 'or I'll shoot you through the kneecap.'

'There's a box on the wall in the storage room on the ground floor,' she said quickly, too scared to lie with a gun pointed at her. 'There's a lever inside that you pull down to disconnect it manually.'

'And is the box locked?'

She nodded. 'Yes. So's the storage room. The keys to both are in the safe.'

'I'll take her down there with me,' said Fox. 'I need to secure the downstairs area.'

'Make sure she doesn't escape,' replied the leader. 'We need her.'

'I know that. She won't try anything.' He looked over at Elena. 'Will you?'

Elena looked back at him and shook her head emphatically.

Fox took her by the arm, his touch a lot gentler than the leader's, and led her towards the door.

As she was ushered out of the room, Elena glanced briefly back towards the store cupboard door. She wondered if Clinton the handyman was still in there, and if he was, whether they'd find him. Armin had obviously told them about the satellite kitchen and its potential as an HQ, but she wasn't sure he'd know about the secret sleeping spot, since the staff who did know about it tended to keep the knowledge to themselves. She hoped not. She liked Clinton. She wanted him to live.

Fox didn't speak as he hurried her down the staircase. He kept the assault rifle down by his side and if she'd been incredibly brave she could have tried to take it from him, but there was a concentrated intensity and confidence about him that scared Elena almost as much as the aggression of the others did, and she knew she'd never succeed.

As they strode across the lobby, she saw the body of the businessman lying just inside the main doors. It was dark outside now, but there were two figures standing just beyond the doors, and she could tell by their fluorescent jackets that they were police officers. They were both looking at the body, and one was talking into his radio. As soon as they saw Fox they took a step back.

Fox told her to get down as he raised the assault rifle to his shoulder in an easy, fluid motion, which made her think that perhaps he had a military background.

She fell to her knees, putting her head in her hands and shutting her eyes, as a heavy burst of automatic weapon fire filled the air. He pulled her up again and, as she opened her eyes, she saw that the bullets had peppered the glass of several of the doors close to where the policemen had been, but that neither of them had been hit. She wondered whether he'd deliberately missed them, and if so, why.

'OK, let's go,' he said, hauling Elena to her feet. 'I want the front doors locked. Have you got the keys on you?'

'No, they're kept in the main safe,' she said, knowing there was no point lying since Armin would have already told them most of what they needed to know about the workings of the Stanhope.

'And you know the combination.'

It was a statement rather than a question, and again she told the truth. 'Yes.'

'I want all the master key cards too. The ones that'll open every room, including the suites.'

'I can get them.'

He looked at her closely for a moment, and she saw that beneath the balaclava he had pale blue eyes. This surprised her. Because these people claimed to be representing an organization called the Pan-Arab Army of God she'd assumed they'd all be Arabs. Yet Fox was clearly white. He spoke with a vague eastern European accent, so perhaps he was a Muslim from the south.

'I got engaged today,' she said quickly.

He didn't answer. Instead, he tightened his grip on her arm and walked across the lobby, stopping beside one of the leather sofas to deposit a rucksack beneath the glass coffee table in front of it, before continuing over to the door that led behind the main reception desk. With Fox following closely behind, Elena walked round the back of the desk and into the CCTV control room where the main safe was kept, relieved that no one was hiding behind the door. She hadn't seen Walter, the duty security guard, or Katrina, the nineteen-year-old Slovakian receptionist, upstairs in the ballroom and hoped that they'd managed to make a break for the doors in the few short minutes when the lobby had been unguarded. Katrina was such a sweet girl and didn't deserve to get caught up in something like this. But then, of course, none of them did.

While she opened the safe and took out the keys, she watched Fox out of the corner of her eye as he took a package from another of his rucksacks. He leaned down and carefully placed it beside the desk and out of sight before standing back up and reviewing the bank of screens on the wall.

'Why isn't this camera working?' he said, pointing to the only blank screen.

Elena frowned. The hotel's CCTV system was generally reliable. It had to be in a place like this where people were free to come and go as they pleased. 'I don't know,' she answered. 'It must be faulty.'

'Where is it?'

She came forward to take a closer look. 'Up on the top floor. Where the suites are.'

He nodded slowly, then took the key cards and told

her to turn off all the lights in the front section of the lobby, which she did manually from behind the reception counter. Finally, he ordered her to lock the hotel's front doors.

That was the hard part. Being so close to freedom. Being able to see the two police officers she'd seen earlier as they ushered the crowds of onlookers away from the front courtyard; and beyond them people driving past in their cars on Park Lane, utterly oblivious to what was going on in this place. And then the line of trees that bordered Hyde Park, a place where she and Rod loved to walk on summer evenings.

People looked at her, some pointing, as she went from one door to the other, stepping over the body of the dead man, ignoring the sickly smell of faeces as she imprisoned herself, the gunmen and the hotel guests inside. She paused for a moment and looked at her faint reflection in the glass. The stress had stretched and twisted her face, and the blood splatters on her usually impeccable uniform stood out. Immediately her thoughts turned to escape. The outside was so, so near. All she had to do was fling open one of the doors, run for her life in a zigzag motion, keeping low like they did in the movies, and she'd be free.

But behind her, in the glass door, she could see the gunman, Fox, and she knew she'd never make it.

'Is your fiancé here?' he asked her suddenly.

She wondered if he was going to let her go, and felt a surge of hope mixed with guilt. She knew it would be wrong to leave the guests and staff here alone with these animals, but she also knew that, given the choice, she still would. 'No,' she said, moving key in hand to the next door. 'He doesn't work in the hotel.'

'That's one piece of good news. For you, anyway.'

'I suppose so.'

'If you do exactly as you're told, you'll be back with him by the end of the night.'

'Why are you doing this?' she asked, angry suddenly. 'You talk about being part of some Army of God, but what exactly do you hope to achieve?'

'Keep locking those doors,' he snapped back. 'The less you know about any of us, the better it'll be for you, I promise.'

Elena did as she was told, annoyed with herself for losing her temper.

Behind her, Fox was speaking again, his tone conversational. 'Politicians will always tell you that violence solves nothing. You watch them on the TV; that's what they say every time. That violence is counter-productive and that if you want something you have to act within the law.' He laughed harshly. 'Let me tell you something: that's bullshit. Violence gets your voice heard. It makes people listen to you. It makes them react. It brings them to the negotiating table. It makes them fear you. In the end, it always gets you what you want.'

Elena put her key in the last door and twisted it. There was no prospect of escape for anyone now. 'So how much more violence are you intending to commit?'

'That depends on the government.'

'They won't negotiate. They never do. Even I know that.'

'They negotiate a lot more than you think.'

Elena looked down at the body at her feet. The man was about thirty, with thinning hair and glasses that were now broken. Just an ordinary person, like the rest of them. 'They won't let you get away with murder,' she said, her voice shaking.

'Well, you'd better hope they do,' said Fox, taking her by the arm and leading her away from the door. 'Otherwise none of us are getting out of here.'

21

Ten floors above Fox and Elena, the man called Scope watched as police cars stopped on either side of the hotel, acting in unison as they blocked the traffic in both directions, creating a car-free zone right in front of the main entrance.

They were out of their vehicles in seconds, moving very fast for cops, who in Scope's experience tended to amble everywhere unless they were slap bang in the middle of an emergency. These men were gesticulating and shouting orders, moving people away from the hotel, while at the same time putting out traffic cones and scene-of-crime tape. Another police car pulled up slightly behind the others, and three guys got out. They went round the back of the car and opened the boot, pulling out what looked like MP5 sub-machine guns. Proper firepower.

Something big was going on, and for a moment

Scope thought it might have something to do with what he'd done here, except he was sure it couldn't be. He'd worked efficiently and there'd been no noise. Mr Miller's corner suite only backed on to one other room, and when he'd put his ear to the wall all he could hear was the sound of loud dance music.

No, whatever this was, it was way bigger than him. Already he could see more police cars, along with a fire engine and two ambulances, driving into Hyde Park and taking up position a hundred yards distant like some kind of wagon train, while in the sky overhead a helicopter with search beam made tight circles.

He wondered what the hell was happening. Up here on the top floor of the Stanhope you were above everything and insulated by silence. It was the perfect spot for his work. But the problem was, he had to get out, and soon. And with all these police around it wasn't going to be easy.

He briefly inspected the wound on his left forearm, the result of a mistake that could have ended in disaster. He'd dressed it using the first aid kit from the bathroom, and added antiseptic, but the teeth marks were deep, and the blood was still staining the dressing a deep red. It might be even more serious if it turned out the guy responsible for it was HIV-positive, but right then he was more concerned about his blood leaving potentially incriminating DNA traces behind.

Simon Kernick

Turning away from the window, Scope returned to the bathroom and applied a roll of fresh dressing over the top of the first. There was a cut about an inch long just above his left eye, and although the plaster he'd covered it with was still sticking, the area around the edges was beginning to darken and swell. It looked conspicuous, and that was bad, but there was nothing he could do about that.

He took a deep breath, buttoned up his jacket so that it covered the telltale red flecks on his shirt, then walked back through the suite's lounge, stepping round the bodies. Finally he removed the manager's badge and left the room, slipping off his gloves as he started down the corridor.

22

Martin Dalston took another long sip from his glass of Pinot Noir and placed it on the bedside table next to the three bottles of pills neatly arranged in a row, and the two envelopes containing the letters to his ex-wife and his son. He then lit his second cigarette of the afternoon. His second cigarette, in fact, of the last twenty-two years. It didn't taste too good, and it was making him cough, but to be honest, he no longer cared.

He looked at the rope with noose attached that he'd hung from the large picture hook on the opposite wall. In hindsight, he wished he hadn't put it there since it was constantly in his field of vision – an annoying reminder of what was coming to him – but there'd been nowhere else suitable, and even so, he still wasn't sure the hook would take his skinny ten stones.

Typically for a man who'd always liked to keep his options open, Martin had chosen two different ways to die. Hanging was the quick method, although, thanks to the height of the hook, it would mean him keeping his legs bent and off the floor as the rope either throttled him or broke his neck, something that would require the kind of self-discipline he wasn't at all sure he possessed. The slow, more painless method was the drugs – a combination of barbiturates, oxazepam and aspirin that he'd been assured would send him gently to sleep.

The disadvantage of an overdose was that it would give him time to think about what he was doing, therefore opening up the possibility of a change of mind. At least if it was quick he'd have no choice in the matter. His preference would have been a gun, but this was England, so that was impossible. So, after much thinking, he'd come up with a simple plan: take the pills, lie back on the bed, and keep the rope in sight as he drifted off, so that he'd always know how painful the alternative was.

His coughing subsided, and he took another deep drag on the cigarette, trying hard to enjoy it. Strangely, he'd been looking forward to this afternoon. He'd always been prone to melancholy. Dreaming of happier days, and viewing them through the inevitable rose-tinted glasses. So to have the opportunity to relive blow-by-beautiful-blow the happiest two weeks of his life, and to savour all the things that could have happened if he'd followed his dreams and made a life with Carrie Wilson, rather than taking the sensible option and marrying Sue, was a guilty pleasure indeed.

But so far his reminiscing had been disturbed by the constant noise of sirens going past the window in both directions. A few minutes earlier there'd been a lot of shouting inside the hotel; he even thought he'd heard some shots, although he wasn't entirely sure. As he lay back on the bed the sound of the sirens grew louder, and they now seemed to be stopping directly outside the hotel.

He thought about getting up to see what all the fuss was about, but quickly dismissed the idea. The world outside the door to room 315 was no longer relevant, especially when he had a date with a young, gorgeous Carrie Wilson, with the gap-toothed smile he'd missed so much.

He picked up the wine glass and took another long sip of the Pinot Noir.

Soon it would be time to start taking the first of the pills.

23

Room 1600, the Operations Control Centre on the sixteenth floor of the New Scotland Yard building, was bedlam. Of the twenty or so officers and staff crowded inside, many of them talking on phones, DAC Arley Dale was the most senior, and she had the Herculean task of coordinating the evacuation of the entire London transportation system, as well as all major public buildings, in response to the bombs at Westfield and Paddington Station. No one knew where the next bomb would strike, or how far to extend the evacuation, and now matters had been further complicated by multiple reports of an attack on the Stanhope Hotel in Park Lane.

Arley knew she had to clear some of the people out of the room if she was to impose a semblance of order on the situation. She remembered all too well the criticism levelled at the Met following the shooting of

Jean Charles de Menezes. Huge mistakes had been made in this very control room because there were too many people inside, many of whom didn't seem to know what the others were doing. But the scale of this operation, coupled with the volume of information being sent through to them from the Central Control Room at Hendon, where all phone traffic relating to the attacks had been directed, was making things next to impossible. They'd already had a reported sixty claims of responsibility for the bombs as well as separate bomb threats for a total of thirty-seven locations within London, including four in the City of London financial district, and right then Arley was wrestling with the decision of whether or not to extend the evacuations to all prominent buildings within the Square Mile.

A bank of TV screens showing real-time CCTV footage of central London took up the whole of the wall, and they recorded vividly the problems the police faced. All the major roads, including the A40 and Marylebone Road, both of which were needed by the emergency services, were gridlocked. On a screen somewhere in the middle, a thick pall of smoke could be seen above Paddington Station. The latest reliable report said that there were already thirteen dead and as many as sixty injured at Paddington, while the number of injured had risen to nine at Westfield, although thankfully there were still no fatalities. But for Arley, what it all meant was that there was no point taking risks with public safety.

'We need to make a decision on the Gherkin, ma'am,' said a young male officer manning one of the phones. 'We've just had a second bomb threat against it.'

'Evacuate it,' she answered, raising her voice above the noise. 'In fact, evacuate every building we get a threat against.' Arley wasn't at all sure she had the authority to make this decision, but there was no time to worry about that now. The important thing, she knew, was to keep making decisions. 'And let's clear this bloody place out. Anyone who does not have to be in here, get out. Now.'

'Ma'am, I've got the head of Westminster Council on the line,' said someone else. 'He wants to speak to you urgently.'

'Find out what he wants and I'll call him back.' The last thing she wanted to do was waste time talking to someone from the council.

A female officer stood up at the end of the room, a phone cradled in her shoulder. 'I've got Brian Walton of London Transport on the line. He wants to know if they can keep a bus service running from zones three through to six.'

'Have we had any specific threats against buses?'

'I don't know.'

'If there haven't been any, he can. If there have, he can't. Find out and let him know.' She had to delegate as many tasks as she could to keep her head above water amid the chaos that was all around her. 'And can we try and get some cameras on the scene at the Stanhope Hotel? I want to see what's going on there.'

'Ma'am?' Her secretary, Ann, was tapping her on the shoulder. 'You're wanted in the commissioner's office. DCS Stevens is going to take over in here.'

Arley snapped out a few more orders, repeated her demand that anyone who shouldn't be in the room must leave, then went out into the corridor. Like most police officers, she craved the excitement of a crisis, and she had a cool enough head to cope with one, which was the main reason she'd travelled as far as she had in the Met. More than one colleague had hinted that it might also be down to the fact that she was a woman, but her bosses knew better than that.

Chief Commissioner Derek Phillips was one of the good guys, a copper's copper with the best interests of the people beneath him at heart, but Arley sometimes wondered if he had the necessary decisiveness to deal with a major incident. It wasn't just that he looked more like a comfortably off accountant than a police officer; his stewardship of the recent student protests in London, when the students had been allowed to go on the rampage virtually unhindered, had seen him become a hostage to events rather than the person in control of them.

He was standing behind his immense glass desk

when Arley walked in, the backdrop of a murky London skyline stretched out behind him. 'Thanks for coming so promptly,' he said, without gesturing for her to take a seat. 'How are things in 1600?'

'We're under the cosh, sir. Do you have any more information on the Stanhope attack?'

'Apparently a group of gunmen have broken into the building and are taking hostages. There are unconfirmed reports of casualties, and we do know that shots were fired from inside the hotel at the first officers on the scene. That was about twenty minutes ago. But so far the picture of what's actually going on is very patchy. Chris Matthews, the chief inspector down at Paddington Green, is on the scene. He's put a cordon in place and set up an RP in Hyde Park, but he's being hampered by all the gridlock round there. It looks like everyone's trying to leave the city at once.'

'I can't say I blame them. We're getting a lot of claims of responsibility for what's happening, but nothing's confirmed. Whoever it is is clearly well organized.'

'I've just been on to Hendon. They say one call stands out. It was made to the *Evening Standard* at 4.34 p.m., just after the Paddington bombs had gone off. It came from a mobile in the western Hyde Park area, which is a good three-quarters of a mile from the scene.'

'So there's no way the caller could have known

about the bombs unless he was responsible for them?'

'Exactly. It was too quick and too assured to have been a hoax. The caller claimed to be from an organization called the Pan-Arab Army of God. They're not on our list of proscribed organizations and no one at Counter Terrorism Command seems to have heard of them, so we're guessing they're new boys. It's possible they're being sponsored by an unfriendly Arab government because the caller said something about the attacks being in retaliation for British and NATO interference in Arab and other Muslim countries. He also claimed that there were bombs at a number of London's other mainline railway stations. Have you had any other reports of bombs going off?'

Arley shook her head. 'Plenty of scares, but nothing else.'

'Thank God for that. We're stretched enough as it is.'

The commissioner looked shaken by the afternoon's events, which wasn't good. Arley was shaken too, but she knew how to keep a lid on her emotions, and she was hoping that Commissioner Phillips did too. Trying to remain as businesslike as possible, she filled him in on the evacuation plans she was putting in place.

'You're doing a good job,' he told her, sounding like he meant it. 'But I need you out in the field. It looks like it's turning into a siege situation at the Stanhope. The PM's been informed and he's convening a meeting of COBRA for six p.m. In the meantime, we have to respond fast. We're using the usual structure. I'm Gold Commander. Assistant Commissioner Jacobs is Silver. We'll both be based here. I want you as Bronze, running things on site at the Stanhope. I've asked Paddington Green to requisition a suitable building you can use as an HQ, and we're sending over a mobile incident room as well, but in the meantime you're just going to have to make do with whatever's available at the scene.'

Arley was pleased to be Bronze Commander, though a little awed by the size of the task ahead. 'I'll get down there as soon as I can but you know what the traffic's like. It may take me some time.'

'We haven't got time. There's a helicopter waiting on the roof. It'll take you there now.'

The phone on Commissioner Phillips' desk rang. He picked up the receiver, listened, then replaced it. His expression was grim. 'That was Hendon. They've just had a call from a wounded kitchen worker inside the building. He told them that there are at least half a dozen masked gunmen in the building, and that there are three people dead. And that's just in the kitchen. They were still talking to him when there was the sound of gunfire and he was cut off. It sounded like he was shot.'

Arley nodded slowly. This was a situation that already appeared to be running out of control. 'If we've got gunmen firing indiscriminately, it sounds as though it's going to have to be handed over to the military sooner rather than later.'

'That's why I want you on the scene. Get going, and good luck.'

Arley took a deep breath. She was going to need it.

24

Fox stood over the body of the kitchen worker, his AK-47 still smoking, and shook his head angrily. He hadn't wanted to kill him but the guy had been on the phone to the emergency services, doubtless giving them important information as to the number of gunmen, as well as letting them know there were multiple casualties.

Beside him, Dragon, the man who'd left the bomb at the Westfield, sighed. A former sapper, he was the explosives expert, and Fox had brought him with him to help secure the rear of the hotel, having taken the pretty hotel manager back to the ballroom and the other hostages.

'What did that prick think he was doing going on a shooting fest like that?' said Dragon in his deep Welsh accent. He was referring to the actions of Panther, the inside man at the hotel, and his words matched Fox's own thoughts. 'It's stuff like that that brings on an early assault.'

'I'll speak to Wolf. Get him to keep an eye on him.'

'He needs more than that. He's dangerous. Fucking Arabs. You can't trust them.'

'It's *fucking* Arabs who are paying our wages,' Fox reminded him. 'Come on. We need to get this area locked down. If Special Forces do launch an assault on us, it'll be through here.'

He went over to the main kitchen window and looked out. They'd killed the lights so that no one from outside could see what they were doing, but it didn't look like there was anyone watching them. The building at the other end of the courtyard, a vacant office block with no windows looking back towards the hotel, blocked the view from the road. The only way of seeing or getting in was through the archway beneath the office block where the body of the security guard Fox had shot earlier still lay. The street beyond it looked empty. Fox assumed that the police would still be evacuating the area around the Stanhope so for the moment it was safe to work.

The rear of the hotel was their most vulnerable point. If there was an attack, Special Forces would come in through the kitchen and fan out into the building. He and Wolf didn't have the manpower to put guards down here so it was essential to make entry as difficult for them as possible.

Dragon had brought one of the rucksack bombs

with him, and while he prepared it in one of the wheelie bins in the delivery area, Fox locked all the external doors using the manager's keys and booby-trapped each of them with a grenade – a simple enough procedure that involved taping down the grenade's lever before loosely attaching it to the door-frame and removing the pin.

They worked quickly and in silence, having practised these manoeuvres time and again in training, and though Fox tried to empty his mind of all thought so that he could focus on the job at hand, he couldn't help feeling a sense of satisfaction at the way this op had been planned. Even with the complications caused by the earlier uncontrolled shooting in the kitchen, they were still very much on top of things.

Six minutes later, having wheeled the bin out into the courtyard and placed it against the wall among half a dozen others, they were done. It was 17.22, and still the street beyond the archway was empty.

'Jesus, I don't know how I got involved in something as risky as this,' said Dragon, picking up one of the backpacks they'd brought inside the building when they'd first arrived.

Fox grinned at him. He liked Dragon. The guy was no-nonsense. 'Because you're on the run and wanted for murder. You don't have a lot of options.'

'But I've just basically helped seal myself in a building with half the Met outside. I didn't even walk into a trap. I made it for myself.'

'It's all part of the plan,' said Fox, picking up the other rucksack and hauling it over his shoulder. 'Cause maximum chaos, maximum embarrassment to the government and the establishment, and then, pfff! We disappear into the ether, two million dollars richer.'

Dragon grunted. 'That's the theory, anyway.'

He pulled off his balaclava and dabbed his brow with a tissue. Like the rest of them he was wearing black camouflage paint on his face, and with his dark contact lenses and longer hair he looked far removed from the handsome, raffish surfer-boy who'd appeared in the police mugshots when he broke out of prison, leaving an injured prison guard and a dead kid behind.

'If it wasn't risky, you wouldn't be getting paid two million,' Fox told him, stepping over one of the bodies and heading for the door, keen to get on.

They walked back through the darkness of the lobby, keeping close to the wall so they couldn't be seen by anyone outside, then went round the back of reception.

Ultimately, the most important part of the plan was not just getting into the hotel, it was getting out afterwards without getting caught, and they had a plan for that as well.

Using the password he'd been given by the hotel manager, Fox logged into the guest reservation database on one of the tabletop PCs. He pulled a piece of paper from his pocket containing a list of fake IDs and which operatives they applied to, and while Dragon watched he matched their names to empty rooms, making a note of the number of each one as he did so.

'How the hell did you manage to get into the system so easily?' Dragon asked him when he'd finished.

'The manager told me. It's amazing what people will tell you when you've got a gun to their head.'

'That's the blonde girl in the suit, right? The good-looking one.'

'That's right.'

'Ah man, that's a pity. I'm assuming we're going to have to make sure she doesn't tell the authorities that she gave you the password to their computer system.'

Fox nodded, thinking about what she'd told him earlier, about getting engaged. She seemed a nice girl. 'You're right,' he said, logging out and standing up. 'She's going to have to die.'

25

Elena sat on the ballroom floor along with the other hostages while four of the gunmen, including Armin, stood in a semi-circle guarding them. Usually the ballroom was full of noise and drunken laughter. Now it was like some kind of vast tomb. No one spoke. No one even seemed to want to move. They were all too shocked by what had happened.

What scared Elena the most was how well organized the gunmen were. They seemed to know exactly what they were doing, and they were so damn calm. Especially the one called Fox, the white man who'd dragged her round the lobby while he set traps and disabled both the lifts and the sprinkler system. She'd just seen him come back up, along with one of the other gunmen, carrying more bags. They'd gone straight into the satellite kitchen, which they seemed to be using as some kind of HQ.

She wondered what it was they really wanted, and what they were trying to prove. She was sure they had to be on some sort of suicide mission. Why else would they disable the sprinkler system unless they planned to set the hotel ablaze?

It angered her that they'd chosen to murder people because it meant they couldn't be reasoned with. Armin the waiter had killed Aidan in cold blood, just, it seemed, because he could, while Fox had set up bombs and shot at the police in between making conversation with her as if it was the most natural thing in the world.

When she was a young girl, Elena's grandmother had often told her stories about life under Nazi occupation, stories that had scared and upset her but which had always seemed strangely compelling. How the SS and Gestapo treated the Poles as sub-human; how they executed people for the smallest of infringements, often in public; how they would round up whole villages – men, women, even children and babies – and slaughter them just because someone in another village had killed a German soldier. And Elena had asked her grandmother how they could have committed such evil deeds.

'Because they were cruel,' she'd answered, as if this were reason enough. 'Because they were cruel.'

Just like the gunmen in the ballroom now.

The door to the satellite kitchen opened suddenly and the leader and Fox came out. They strode over to

the other terrorists, one after another, and spoke to
them in hushed tones.

Then the leader approached Elena and, without
warning, yanked her to her feet by her arm. 'You're
coming with us,' he snapped in his thick Middle
Eastern accent.

'Where?' she asked before she could stop herself.

'Don't ask questions, bitch. Move.' Grabbing her by
the collar, he shoved the barrel of his assault rifle into
her back and made her walk towards the exit. 'Take us
to room 316. Use the staircase.'

Elena did as she was told, conscious that three more
gunmen, including Armin and Fox, were also coming
with her.

As they reached the emergency staircase she could
hear the occasional shouting of panicked guests, and
the noise of footsteps on the stairs, and she prayed no
one would come running down here, see her, and
think they were safe. She'd seen Fox disable the lifts
earlier, and right now the staircase was the only way
out.

The third-floor corridor was completely silent as
Elena led the gunmen through. She wondered how
many people were hiding terrified behind their doors.
The hotel was currently booked to over eighty per
cent capacity, so there would be quite a few of them.

'Which side's room 316?'

She pointed right.

'In a few minutes' time you're going to tell the

people on this floor to come out of their rooms and line up outside. But first I want you to see exactly what, and who, you're dealing with.'

Elena felt a growing sense of dread as they stopped outside room 316 and Wolf knocked four times on the door.

A second later it was opened from the inside by a young woman about Elena's age, with black hair and olive skin. She was barefoot and wearing a figure-hugging black dress that finished above the knee. She looked completely normal, except for one thing: she was holding a pistol with a long cigar-shaped silencer attached to it.

She was also smiling at the leader. 'Welcome,' she said in lightly accented English.

Elena looked past her and saw a grey-haired man tied to the tub chair beside the bed, with his back to the window. He had a gag in his mouth and he looked pale and terrified.

They filed into the room and she saw the woman and Armin exchange small smiles. They obviously knew each other, and for some reason the thought filled Elena with rage. Armin was an animal, and she wished she'd called Rav and got him kicked out of the hotel when she'd had the chance.

The leader ordered Elena to stand against the far wall. He then walked over to the man in the chair and, pulling a pistol from his waistband, shoved the gun against his forehead. 'Hello, Mr Prior,' he said. 'I trust you're comfortable.' He turned to Armin. 'Get everything set up. I want this recorded and put online straight away in case they switch us off.'

Elena watched as Armin pulled a laptop out of the rucksack he was carrying and connected it via a cable to a camera. At the same time, the leader removed what looked like a large belt with pouches along its entire length. Then she saw the wires poking out of the pouches and the old-style battery-operated alarm clock in the middle.

Elena knew next to nothing about explosives, but even she could see that this was a bomb.

The leader looped the belt over their prisoner and the chair so that the bomb was resting across his chest with the alarm clock dead centre, while the woman who'd answered the door pulled on a balaclava and went over to join him.

As Armin lifted the camera and began filming, the woman put the barrel of her pistol against the man's temple. He sat still, his eyes wide, sweat forming on his forehead. She spoke directly into the camera, her voice confident and educated. 'The man sitting here is Michael Prior, a director of MI6. His job is to oversee the surveillance, arrest, torture and imprisonment of Muslims all over the world, and both he and his government are responsible for the ongoing slaughter of Arab and Muslim civilians. We, as members of the Pan-Arab Army of God, have taken him into our custody, along with a number of other British citizens,

and we demand that the British government immediately cease all its current military, political and
economic operations against Muslim and Arab
countries.' She pushed the gun barrel harder against
the man's temple, forcing his head to one side. 'Unless
our demands are met in full, he will be executed
tonight, at midnight GMT, and this building will go
up in flames, along with everyone in it.'

Elena felt her heart sink as the woman stopped
speaking, and Armin lowered the camera and started
typing on the laptop.

'OK,' he said after a few moments. 'We've got the
footage online.'

This was the cue for the leader to start giving orders
again. He told the woman to take the laptop and go
downstairs to the ballroom to reinforce the others.
Then he ordered the rest of the men out into the
corridor.

Finally, he grabbed Elena roughly by the arm. 'We
need more hostages,' he said, bringing his face close
to hers. 'And you're going to get them for us.'

26

It was all going so damn wrong, thought Martin
Dalston as he lay behind the double bed, trying to
keep as still as possible.

One minute he'd been sipping the Pinot Noir and
remembering the sound of Carrie Wilson's laughter,
the pills still firmly in their containers, the next he'd
heard the commotion coming from the room next
door, followed by people talking just outside his door.
He'd tried to ignore it, determined not to be
disturbed, but then he'd heard a woman with a Polish
accent introducing herself as the Stanhope's duty
manager, her voice shaking as she spoke. She was
saying that the hotel had been taken over by a group
called the Pan-Arab Army of God, that they had
master key cards to all the bedrooms, and that everyone had to come out of their rooms, otherwise they
would be shot immediately.

The whole thing seemed so surreal that at first he'd thought it was some bizarre joke, but then he'd ventured over to the window and peered out, which was when he saw the flashing lights of dozens and dozens of emergency vehicles blocking the road in both directions. That was when he'd knelt down behind the bed.

'Please, please,' the manager kept saying, her voice fading then coming back into earshot as she paced up and down the corridor, 'do as you've been told and you won't be hurt.' She sounded very scared.

Martin was scared too. Terrified. Irrationally so, really, given that within the next few hours he'd fully intended to kill himself anyway. But the thing was, he wanted to die at a time and by a method of his own choosing, with happy memories filling his consciousness. Not at the hands of terrorists.

He could hear the sound of doors opening further down the corridor, barked orders, and the nervous whispers of frightened people. A young child was crying, and Martin felt his stomach knot. God, what on earth was happening? He knew if he didn't go out he risked being shot. Dying on his knees in a pool of his own blood. Even so, he didn't move, maintaining his position behind the bed, hoping that the terrorists were lying about having key cards, or that they'd rounded up enough people and therefore wouldn't bother searching all the rooms.

The noise in the corridor faded, and Martin felt his

hopes rise. 'You wouldn't believe this, Carrie,' he whispered to himself. 'All this happening outside our room.'

He had a sudden urge to speak to her then. Just one last time. To reminisce with her about those two fantastic weeks all those years ago. To find out what she was up to now. Whether she had children or not. How her life had turned out. He wished he'd found her contact details so he could ask some of the questions he so desperately wanted answered before he went to his grave.

'Please, this is your last chance to come out of the rooms.' The manager's voice was coming back down the corridor, loud and clear. And getting closer.

Martin remained absolutely still. There was no way he was going out. He suddenly felt brave. Braver than he'd felt in all his adult life. Even more so than on that day when he received the news about the spread of the cancer, when he'd held himself together so well.

He could hear muffled voices right outside the door.

And then it began to open, and he could hear movement.

God, they were inside his room.

He held his breath. But the wine, the stress and the ever-present cancer were making him feel nauseous.

With his eyes tightly shut, he felt rather than heard the man stop at the end of the bed, and he knew he'd been seen.

He heard the sound of a gun being cocked, loud in the silence of the room, and he gritted his teeth, waiting for it all to be over.

'Open your eyes.'

The words were delivered calmly in an eastern European accent that, for some reason, didn't sound quite right. Martin gasped and looked up into the eyes of a masked man in a balaclava and dark overalls, pointing a rifle down at him.

The man turned towards the door. 'See, I told you there'd be more of them hiding.'

'Kill him,' ordered a voice in a foreign accent, its tone terrifyingly casual, as if he, Martin Dalston – a man who'd lived, loved, had children and fought against a terrible illness – was completely worthless. Someone – something – simply to be disposed of as quickly and efficiently as possible.

But the gunman didn't fire. Instead, Martin could see him watching him beneath the mask.

'We need more hostages,' said the gunman. 'And if we shoot too many guests, we'll make the security forces jumpy.'

'As you wish,' grunted the other man dismissively.

The gunman flicked his gun upwards and Martin got to his feet unsteadily, unsure whether to feel relief, gloom or terror.

He could now see the other gunman. He was small and dark, heavily built, also dressed in black. Beside him was the hotel manager. She was tall and pretty, with blonde hair and a kind face. She was staring, horrified, at the noose hanging from the picture hook.

Their eyes met briefly, and Martin experienced a deep sense of humiliation as his carefully made and deeply personal plans were exposed to the world.

And then he was being pushed into the corridor along with the manager and maybe a dozen guests of varying ages, including the crying child, who was no more than ten. There were four gunmen in all, all masked, and the leader – the man who'd ordered his killing – didn't look happy at all.

'There must be more people on this floor,' he snapped, grabbing the manager and pointing his gun at her.

'Most of the rooms are taken,' she answered quickly, 'but it doesn't mean that they're occupied. A lot of our guests will be out.'

'There should be more.' The leader turned to two of the other gunmen, one of whom was Armin. 'You have your key cards. Clear the rooms one by one. Take people alive unless they resist. If they try to fight back, kill them.'

He turned away and, as the little girl's sobs grew louder, began herding the rest of them towards the exit doors.

27

For more than ten minutes after leaving the suite on the top floor of the Stanhope Scope had tried to get out of the building. The lifts were all out of order, and when he'd started down the fire exit stairs he'd run into one of the hotel staff, a room service waiter, coming the other way. The kid had hurriedly told him that there was some sort of terrorist attack going on. He didn't have too many details, other than that he'd seen some dead bodies and at least two men with assault rifles.

Just my luck, Scope had thought. To get caught up in the middle of a major incident and trapped in a place I have no choice but to get the hell out of. But he'd learned long ago that there was no point complaining about the hand you've been dealt. You just had to play it.

The kid had said he was going up to the restaurant

on the ninth floor, which was currently closed, where apparently there were some good hiding places. He'd suggested Scope join him, but Scope had declined, figuring he'd take his chances. But he'd only got a couple of floors down when he'd heard a burst of automatic gunfire coming from somewhere in the belly of the building, followed a few seconds later by people coming up the staircase far below. At that point he'd decided that, given that he was only armed with a knife, maybe discretion was the better part of valour. At least until he knew what he was up against.

He'd returned to the suite and put on the TV. Sure enough, Sky News was showing live footage of the front of the hotel, and the scrolling headline was reporting the presence of armed men inside and gunfire coming from the main lobby. There were also reports of bombs having gone off in two locations in London, and that a full-scale evacuation of the whole public transport system was under way. It sounded as if it had all been going on while Scope was up in the suite, but so far details were still pretty sketchy.

The point was, he was trapped. And the bodies in the suite were already beginning to smell. He thought about his options for a couple of minutes, before concluding that he only had two: stay where he was and sit it out until the cavalry arrived, or try to make a break for it.

Scope didn't have much experience of how the police worked in scenarios like this. It was possible, of course, that they'd send in the SAS, but if the real-life cop shows were any indicator they preferred to adopt a softly-softly approach and negotiate, and this meant that there was no guarantee they'd enter the hotel before the gunmen torched the place, or shot the shit out of it.

Which meant he had only one option.

He drew the knife, kept it down by his side, and made his way back to the fire exit stairs, passing the next-door suite whose occupants were still playing loud music. He considered warning them about what was going on in the hotel, but knew that to do so would attract unwanted attention to himself. They probably knew about it by now anyway.

This time when he reached the staircase he couldn't hear anything. He paused for a few moments, then started down the stairs, moving almost silently as he listened hard for any sound that might signal danger. The creak of a door; an intake of breath; the click of a hammer being cocked on a gun. He knew that it was unlikely anyone would be lying in wait for him, but he also knew from bitter experience that you can never be too careful.

And then, when he was between the sixth and fifth floors, he heard it. An exit door opening and a shouted command, delivered with the confidence that in a situation like this could only belong to someone holding a gun: 'Move.' This was immediately followed by the sound of people coming up the stairs in his direction. He could hear their frightened whispering, interspersed with angry shouts from more than one gunman.

Scope carried on down to the fifth floor and slipped through the exit door into the empty corridor, closing it behind him. Leaning back against the wall, he watched through the frosted glass as a masked man carrying an AK-47 came into view. The man had his back to Scope and was barking orders at a procession of stunned-looking hotel guests of all ages who were following him up the stairs. Another masked man, also carrying an AK, brought up the rear.

Scope pressed himself up against the wall, clutching his knife tightly, just in case one of the gunmen decided to come through the door looking for more hostages. But neither of them did, and their voices faded away as they continued towards the upper floors.

Scope gave them two minutes, then slipped back into the stairwell and continued his descent.

28

'We ought to leave,' whispered Abby Levinson, squeezing her son's hand and holding him close.

Her dad shook his head emphatically. 'No. We stay where we are.'

'But you heard what the manager was saying. They'll shoot us if we stay in our rooms.'

'They'll shoot us if we leave.' He looked at her imploringly. 'We're Jewish, and they're Arab extremists with guns. We're the enemy. At least if we stay in here, we have a chance.'

'Why do they want to kill us?' asked Ethan quietly, his voice barely a whisper.

'Because they're bad men,' said his grandpa, putting a reassuring hand on his shoulder, before turning back to Abby. 'There are hundreds of rooms in this hotel. They won't be able to search all of them.' He leaned forward and cupped her face in his hands.

'Have I ever lied to you? Have I ever given you reason not to trust me?'

'No.' And he hadn't. Dad had always been there for her, right from as far back as she could remember. He was the hard-working businessman who'd provided such a happy home for her and her three sisters while they were growing up; the rock that had held the whole family together when her mother died; and now the man whose love, and words of wisdom, had done so much to help her get over the sudden and brutal break-up of her marriage.

'Then please,' he continued, 'do as I say.'

He might have been getting more frail these past few years, but right then he exuded strength and purpose.

'OK,' she whispered. 'We'll do as you say.' She squeezed Ethan that bit harder. 'It's going to be all right, baby. Mom and Grandpa are here for you.'

Breaking away from them, her father picked up the tub chair in the corner of the room and manoeuvred it towards the door. Abby helped him and they tried to prop it under the handle so it wouldn't open from the outside, but the back of the chair fell a good couple of inches short.

Abby froze. She could hear footfalls outside in the corridor coming closer. Her father heard them too and he mouthed at her to take Ethan and go into the bathroom. Picking up a glass vase from the desk, he stood behind the door. Abby motioned for him to come with her, and took hold of his arm, but he shooed her away. 'Go,' he mouthed, pulling the same stern expression he'd pulled when she was a child and had done something wrong. It was a look that brooked no dissent.

The footfalls had stopped.

Slowly, silently, Abby crept away from the door, putting a finger to her mouth to warn Ethan to stay quiet, and led him into the bathroom.

Ethan looked up at her with wide, frightened eyes as she closed the bathroom door, and she gave him as reassuring a look as she could muster. She looked round, taking in the bath and the walk-in shower area, and caught her breath. There was nowhere to hide.

Then she heard a key card being inserted in the door to their room and the handle turning. Her heart pounding, she put a hand over Ethan's mouth.

The door was opening now, and she could hear the tub chair scuffing against the carpet as it was pushed out of the way. Unable to resist, she peeked round the bathroom door and saw her father holding the vase in both hands above his head. Suddenly, for all the aura of strength he projected, he looked so damned small and vulnerable – an old man fighting the battles of far younger men. She knew she had to help him.

And yet she didn't move.

The door continued to open.

And that was when she noticed it: the narrow gap

between the door and the doorframe widening at the hinges. Whoever was on the other side would be able to see her father standing inside. She opened her mouth to say something, willing her father to turn round so she could warn him somehow, knowing that as soon as she spoke she'd give them all away—

The shots exploded in the room – two of them, one after the other – and her dad fell back, dropping the vase and crashing into the bedside table. He managed to turn her way, a look of surprise crossing his face, and then his legs went from under him and he collapsed to the carpet with a dull thud, exposing the two holes in the woodwork behind him where the bullets had come tearing through.

'Grandpa!' cried Ethan, struggling out of his mother's grip.

'No, Ethan, stop!'

Abby tried to pull him back into the bathroom, desperate for him not to give them away. But it was too late. He broke away from her and ran towards his grandpa, just as the door was flung open and a man in a balaclava, dressed in what looked like a hotel waiter's uniform, came into the room. He was carrying a powerful-looking pistol. Behind him the door clicked shut, trapping them inside.

'You hurt my grandpa!' Ethan shouted, moving towards him.

The man raised his gun. 'Stop him or I'll shoot the little bastard.'

Abby grabbed Ethan and pulled him to her, with all the strength she could muster. 'I've got him. Don't shoot. Please.'

'Shut the boy in the toilet,' he said. 'Or I'll kill him now.' His pistol was pointed at Ethan's head.

Ethan had stopped struggling but she could tell he was sobbing behind the hand she'd placed over his mouth. Her father lay in front of them, his head almost at her feet. He'd been hit in the upper body, and blood was soaking through his shirt, but he still seemed to be breathing.

'Come on, Ethan,' she whispered. 'We've got to go into the bathroom.'

'Not you. Just him. Get him in there now.'

Something had changed in the gunman's voice. It took her a moment to realize what it was.

Whatever was going to happen to her, she didn't want her son to see it, so she pulled him inside the bathroom, then bent down and whispered in his ear. 'I want you to stay in here until I call you, OK? Please. Otherwise he'll hurt me.'

It was emotional blackmail of the worst kind, but what choice did she have? She shut the door and turned to face the gunman.

He stood in the middle of the room, his pistol aimed at her chest. 'Turn round and lift up your dress, or you and the brat die together.'

29

In the stairwell, Scope was level with the third floor when he heard two gunshots, followed by a woman's scream. He stopped and listened. He knew he ought to keep going. He only had a knife, but he'd never been one to walk away from someone in obvious danger. It just wasn't in his DNA.

Trying not to think too hard about what he was doing, he opened the stairwell door and stepped into the corridor, looking both ways. To his left, he could hear voices coming from behind one of the doors. It sounded like a man was barking orders and a woman was pleading with him.

Scope strode over to the door, and put his ear to it. The man had a foreign accent, the woman sounded agitated, and there was another noise – a kid, quite young by the sound of him, crying.

Sliding the homemade lock-picking device he'd

brought with him – a credit card with an angled divot cut in its bottom edge – out of his pocket, Scope pushed it into the narrow gap between the door and the frame and lowered it carefully on to the lock. He'd been practising opening doors this way for the past month, but it was hard to do it without making a noise, and he tensed as he gave the door a firm shove, the click of the bolt being released sounding loud in his ears.

Scope pushed the door open, holding his knife by the blade in case he needed to throw it fast.

An old man lay on his back on the floor next to a double bed. His white shirt was stained red where he'd been shot, and a thin trail of blood ran down from the corner of his mouth on to the carpet. At the far end of the room stood the gunman. But unlike the other gunmen Scope had seen, this one was dressed in hotel uniform. He had his back to Scope, and it was clear he hadn't heard the door opening. He was pointing a pistol down at a dark-haired woman who was on her knees just inside the entrance to the ensuite bathroom, with her arms round a child. Scope's view of the boy was obscured by the gunman's legs but he could see that he and the woman were shaking as they prepared for the end.

'You had your chance, whore. Now you die.'

'Kill me, but please let my son go,' the woman was saying, her voice surprisingly clear.

Scope took a long, silent step into the room.

156

The woman saw him then, her expression changing before she could stop it.

The gunman started to turn round and Scope charged him, ending his run in a flying headlong dive that sent him and the gunman crashing into the far wall. The gunman gasped, surprise rapidly giving way to anger, and he struggled violently as Scope grabbed his gun hand by the wrist and yanked it upwards so that the barrel was pointing up in the air. The gun went off, the bullet ricocheting off the ceiling, and the noise made Scope's ears ring. Eyes blazing with rage, the gunman drove his head forward, trying to slam it into Scope's face, but Scope turned, thrusting his shoulder out to deflect the blow, at the same time bringing up his knife hand and driving the blade deep into the gunman's side, between the sixth and seventh ribs, so that it pierced his heart.

Once again the room erupted in noise as the gunman's finger involuntarily squeezed the trigger, sending two more bullets into the ceiling. Scope stabbed him a second time, then a third, ignoring the ringing in his ears, and the stinging heat on his face from where the bullets had passed close by, waiting until the gunman's body relaxed in his arms before letting him slip to the floor.

Behind him the bedroom door swung open. Scope wheeled round in time to see a second gunman enter, this one dressed in dark overalls and carrying an AK-47. He was saying something, but Scope couldn't catch it above the ringing in his ears. It was clear by the way the AK was down by his side that he wasn't expecting to see his friend dead.

When he saw the scene of carnage in front of him he hesitated for a split second, and Scope threw the knife just as the guy raised his gun to fire. At the same time he ducked down and weaved away.

The knife hit the guy in the chest, blade first, embedding itself about an inch in, and though the force of the blow made him take a step back, he didn't fall. Instead, with the knife sticking out of his chest, he raised the AK to fire, which was when Scope realized that he was wearing body armour underneath the overalls.

But Scope was fast. Jumping over the old man's body, he drove himself into the gunman, grabbing his AK by the stock as the gunman opened up with a burst of automatic fire. The kick from the barrel sent shockwaves up Scope's arm, but he managed to push it out of the way so that the bullets flew high and wide, then he fell on the gunman, keeping him close, so that the AK was squeezed between them.

The problem was that this particular gunman was a lot bigger and stronger than the other one. With a roar, he threw Scope off, sending him crashing back into the tub chair by the door. But Scope held on to the rifle with both hands, knowing that as soon as he let go of it he was a dead man.

The gunman knew it too, and he yanked on the AK in a sudden, powerful movement, trying to twist it out of Scope's hands. But Scope clung on, letting himself be taken by the momentum for a couple of seconds so that his adversary thought he had the upper hand. Then, without warning, he dug his heels into the carpet, forcing the gunman to fall into him, before wrapping a leg round one of his ankles and tripping him up.

The gunman fell on to the bed, relinquishing his grip on the AK in the process, and swung round to face Scope, at the same time pulling the knife from his chest.

Scope didn't have time to turn the gun round and fire. Instead he slammed the stock of the AK into the gunman's face.

The gunman howled in pain as his nose exploded, splattering blood all over his balaclava. But he still managed to leap back up from the bed and thrust the knife at Scope, who had to jump backwards to dodge its arc.

The gunman's head was now exposed, though, and Scope came forward fast and drove the butt of the AK into his face a second time. This time, however, there was real power behind the blow, and it drove the gunman's head back against the wall with such force that part of the stock broke off.

Scope came in close, using the AK as a club to hit him again and again until the stock fell apart in his hands and the gunman slid silently down the wall, leaving a long smear of blood on the paintwork, his damaged head slumped forward as more blood dripped from the holes in the balaclava.

For a couple of seconds Scope didn't move as the adrenalin that was surging through him began to subside. He put his hands on his knees and took some deep breaths before retrieving his knife and turning back towards the woman and the boy.

That was when he saw that the woman had been hit.

She was sitting back against the bathroom doorframe clutching her leg just above the knee, her face contorted with pain as blood seeped through her fingers. The boy was holding on to her, sobbing and asking if she was going to be all right. At least that was what Scope thought he was saying because he still couldn't hear much above the intense ringing in his ears.

He went over and knelt beside her, gently prising open her fingers so he could see the wound. Blood leaked out steadily from a five-pence-sized hole three inches above the kneecap, and as he probed round the back of her leg he felt a larger, more ragged hole where the bullet had exited, and this was bleeding more heavily. Scope knew that the ammo used in the AK-47 could cause extensive tissue damage, but from the close positioning of the two holes it looked like this could be a relatively superficial hit.

'You're going to be OK,' he said, looking into her eyes. 'I'm going to dress the wound.'

She nodded tightly, her eyes focusing on him, and he was relieved to see that she didn't appear to have gone into shock yet. 'I understand,' she said through gritted teeth.

Grabbing a hand towel from the bathroom, he tied it round her leg to soak up the blood and restrict its flow, careful not to make the knot too tight. As he did so, he took in her appearance for the first time. She was in her late thirties, good-looking but rail-thin, with well-coiffured, shoulder-length black hair, dark oval eyes, and skin that should have looked tanned but was now an anaemic grey thanks to the shock of her ordeal.

Scope knew he had to get this woman and her son out of the hotel fast, but he also knew that, once outside, they'd tell the authorities what he'd done, which would attract a lot of unwelcome attention. He didn't want anyone linking him with what had happened in the suite upstairs.

He looked at the boy, who couldn't have been more than seven years old, and who was staring at Scope curiously. He had the same colourings as his mother, and the same dark oval eyes, but his face was rounder and he had a dimple on his chin that somehow made him look even more vulnerable than he was.

Scope turned to the woman. 'We've got to go.' His fight with the gunmen had made a hell of a lot of noise and it wouldn't be long before more of them turned up to investigate.

'It hurts,' she whispered, closing her eyes.

'The wound's not as bad as it looks. I promise you. Now, stay awake for me, OK?'

She nodded weakly.

'She's been shot,' said the boy, his voice high and panicked. 'People who get shot always die, don't they?'

'No, most survive,' Scope told him firmly.

'How do you know?'

'I just do.'

'Is Grandpa dead?'

Scope didn't have to look at the body of the old man. He'd seen enough dead people in his time to be certain of the answer. 'I'm afraid he is. I'm sorry.'

'The bad man killed him. He was trying to protect us.'

Scope spoke slowly, his tone reassuring. 'That's because he loved you, but the bad man's dead too. He won't be able to hurt anyone again, ever.'

The boy's dark eyes burned angrily. 'I'm glad you killed him.'

'How did the bad man get in here?'

'He had a key.'

So they had key cards to the rooms. Masters probably. It showed a level of planning that was worrying.

Scope got up and took the pistol from the man in the waiter's uniform. It was a Glock 17. He ejected the magazine and checked the number of bullets. Three.

He gave the guy a quick pat down but he wasn't carrying any spare ammo, and the 7.62 × 39mm bullets his friend was using in the AK wouldn't be any use. He took both their key cards and went back to where the woman was lying.

Her eyes were closing as Scope picked her up in his arms as gently as he could. 'What's your name?' he asked her.

'Abby.'

'We're going to get help, Abby. I want you to stay with us, OK?'

'OK,' she groaned in response.

'And what's your name, son?'

'Ethan,' said the boy.

'I want you to follow me and your mum, Ethan, and try to make as little noise as possible. Like you're trying to sneak up on someone. You think you can do that?'

The boy nodded. 'But what about Grandpa? I don't want to leave him here.'

'We've got to for the moment, but the police'll be coming back in for him very soon.'

'Do you promise?'

'I promise. Now don't say another word, OK?'

'OK.'

Conscious of the fact that if they were ambushed he wouldn't have a chance of fighting back, Scope carried Abby out of the room, Ethan following. It was completely silent in the corridor as he made his way over to the emergency staircase, trying not to think too much about what he was doing. That had always been his credo in the military. Never think too much. If you do, you're likely to get scared. And when you're scared, you're ineffective.

He took a brief look through the door's frosted glass, saw nothing on the other side, and led Ethan into the stairwell.

They'd just started down when Scope heard someone hurrying down the stairs a few floors above them. It might just have been a frightened guest, but there was also a good chance it was another of the gunmen, especially as the pace of the steps suggested confidence rather than panic.

Gesturing for Ethan to follow, he hurried down the steps to the second floor, opened the exit door and turned right down the corridor, trying to put as much distance as possible between them and the emergency staircase.

As soon as they'd turned the corner, Scope stopped outside the nearest room and carefully placed Abby on the floor, propping her up against the wall, while he fished in his pocket for one of the hotel key cards. Her face was contorted in pain but at least she was staying quiet.

He inserted the key card, and while Ethan held the door open, Scope lifted his mother up again and took her inside.

The room was empty, and in the semi-darkness

Scope saw that the bed hadn't been slept in. As he placed Abby on it, he noticed that the blood from her wound had seeped through the towel.

Clearly now in shock, she asked him where they were.

'In one of the other rooms. We should be safe here for now.'

'But we need to get outside.'

'I know. But right now, it's too dangerous.'

He moved away from the bed, switched on the lights, and pushed a chair across the door, positioning it so that the back was just beneath the handle, then got another towel from the bathroom to replace the first. As he wrapped the towel round Abby's leg, applying gentle pressure on the wound, and placed a cushion under her leg to elevate it, he noticed her staring up at him.

'Who are you?' she asked him. 'The way you dealt with those men back there . . .'

Scope returned her stare. 'I'm the man who's keeping you alive,' he answered.

30

A cold wind blew over Park Lane and, with impeccable timing, an icy drizzle began to fall as DAC Arley Dale stood at the police rendezvous point – a marked Land Rover Freelander 2 from Traffic parked in the middle of the road twenty yards west of the hotel. Two mobile incident rooms were en route from different locations but both were stuck in traffic. With her was Chief Inspector Chris Matthews of Paddington Green Station, who'd been coordinating the initial response to the crisis.

Matthews was bald and underweight and looked like he ran marathons every day. He had the kind of severe face that scares criminals, children, and probably a lot of other people too, but Arley had the feeling that if you pressed the right buttons you'd see a much softer side. He was highly competent too, and right then, that was by far the most important thing.

'I've got the inner cordon in place all round the hotel,' Matthews explained, 'but I'm short of CO19 officers.'

'They'll be here soon. We've got them coming from all over. But I also want a central and an outer cordon set up, so we can get civilians and camera crews as far back as possible. Ideally, I don't want any of them within a four-hundred-metre radius of the hotel, not when there are gunmen inside.'

'I haven't got the manpower at the moment, ma'am. All my spare resources are carrying out an evacuation of the surrounding buildings.'

Arley nodded, squinting against the drizzle, as she looked around. More officers were arriving all the time, some of them milling around, not quite sure what they were meant to be doing. This was always a problem in a fast-moving incident like this one. Everyone knew what had to be done: secure the area, move the public away, and establish control. Organizing it, however, when the whole of central London was gridlocked was a different story altogether, and though Matthews was trying hard, he was up against it.

'Evening all,' came a voice behind them. 'DCI John Cheney, Counter Terrorism Command.'

Arley and Matthews both turned round and were confronted with a tall, good-looking man in his mid forties with broad shoulders and a full head of natural blond hair that had been flattened by the rain. He was dressed in a suit and long raincoat, and looked every inch a copper, even down to the sardonic, knowing smile.

'I've been sent here to give what assistance I can,' said Cheney, as he and Matthews shook hands. 'My speciality's foreign terror groups.'

He turned to Arley and she gave him a thin smile. 'Hello, John.'

'You two know each other?' asked Matthews.

'From a long time back,' said Arley, shaking hands formally.

And it had been a long time. Getting close to twenty years. She'd still been a uniformed constable and he'd been a handsome young DC at the same station. Arley was engaged to someone else at the time, but even so, for a few short weeks she and John Cheney had embarked on a passionate affair that had lasted right up until the point she found out that he was sleeping with at least two other women. At the time, Arley had been truly gutted. She'd been infatuated, prepared to break off her engagement to be with Cheney, but, having had her fingers burned, she'd turned her back on him, and in the years since they'd seen each other only a handful of times at official functions.

Seeing him now, she felt nothing. It had all been too long ago. Getting straight down to business, Arley gave him a brief rundown of events so far.

'Have we had any claims of responsibility?' he asked in the familiar gravelly voice she'd always been sure he put on.

'We think they may be from an organization called the Pan-Arab Army of God. Have you come across them before?'

Cheney shook his head. 'Never heard of them.'

Arley rolled her eyes. 'That's useful.'

'It's also no great surprise. These terrorist groups chop and change their names and personnel all the time. New ones are always appearing. Have they made any demands yet?'

'Other than the phone call to the *Standard*, we haven't heard a word from them.'

'We're still getting the occasional bursts of gun-fire coming from inside,' put in Matthews. 'But not enough to suggest they're killing hostages indiscriminately.'

'Well, that's one thing I suppose. Do we even want to know if they want to negotiate?'

Arley looked up towards the hotel. 'They've been in there an hour, and they're making no move to get out or to blow the place up, and they said something in the call to the *Standard* about being prepared to negotiate, so I'm guessing they must want to talk at some point. But to be brutally honest, we haven't got a clue what they're up to in there.'

'We need to listen in to them,' Cheney said. 'I've got contacts over at GCHQ. I can get on to them and see if they can set something up remotely.'

'That'd be a help,' said Arley, who'd been so caught up in the immediacy of events that it hadn't yet occurred to her to use the technology of GCHQ, the government's central listening station, to gather information on the terrorists.

At that moment, Chris Matthews' mobile rang, and as he took the call Arley thought that the sooner they had a secure phone service at the scene, the better. Mobiles were far too easy to hack into, and the last thing they needed was some journalist, or worse still one of the terrorists, listening to them rather than the other way round.

'The first of the incident rooms is here,' Matthews told her, shouting above the shrieking of a police siren as a riot van pulled into the top of Park Lane.

Not before time, thought Arley, as the rain began to come down even harder.

31

The Stanhope's Park View Restaurant was on the ninth floor of the hotel and had floor-to-ceiling windows right across its western side, which looked out on to a spacious roof terrace that was used for dining in summer, and beyond that to the green, tree-lined expanse of Hyde Park.

Elena usually loved this view, and when she was on night shift she liked to walk out on to the terrace after the restaurant had closed and smoke a cigarette while looking out across the lights and noise of London, enjoying the sense of being a part of something huge yet somehow intimate at the same time.

Tonight, though, all the blinds were drawn, and tables and chairs had been piled up against the windows by her and the other hostages to create a space in the middle of the floor. They were sitting in that space now, a frightened, confused, largely silent

171

group of about twenty people bolstered in number by a group of guests and staff members who'd been discovered hiding in the adjoining kitchen. In the middle of the group, only a few feet from where Elena sat, was a rucksack bomb similar to the one she'd seen Fox preparing in the hotel lobby. She wondered why they'd been brought up here, a long way from the other hostages in the ballroom.

There were two gunmen in the restaurant: the man who seemed to be the leader, who she now knew was called Wolf, and his sidekick, the man who'd accompanied her to the lobby earlier, Fox. Both of them were holding assault rifles, and Wolf's foot was on the pedal connected by wires to the rucksack bomb. They'd even set up a portable TV next to them so they could use the news channels to keep tabs on what was going on outside. At that moment they were conversing in hushed tones, while keeping a close eye on the hostages.

On the way up, Elena had tried to speak to Fox, to establish some kind of rapport, but he'd told her to shut up, and the tension in his tone had persuaded her that it wasn't a good idea to carry on talking.

There were three young children among the hostages, two girls of about six and eight and a boy of about twelve who was dressed in his school uniform and who'd been one of those hiding in the kitchen, along with his parents. Elena guessed they'd come here for an early evening meal, maybe for a special occasion of some sort. Both the boy and one of the little girls were sobbing quietly – a sound that wrenched at Elena's heart. She loved children and had nieces and nephews of a similar age. It sickened her that these innocents were caught up in this nightmare.

Before she'd had a chance to think about what she was doing, she stood up.

Wolf and Fox immediately turned her way, and Wolf raised his gun. 'Sit down,' he ordered.

'Please,' she said, still standing, 'let the children and their mothers go. There'll still be plenty of us left behind.'

'Sit down.'

'But they've done nothing to you. Please. Have some heart.'

Wolf took three steps forward and put the rifle to his shoulder.

For a terrible second, Elena thought he was going to shoot her, even though she'd been banking on the fact that, as the most senior member of the Stanhope's staff on duty, she was a lot more useful to them alive.

'I'll tell you one more time: sit down.'

Reluctantly, and with anger coursing through her, she did as she was told, noticing that most of the other hostages were staring at her.

Wolf lowered the gun, and Elena saw him glance at the three young children in turn. 'If you all cooperate, and if your government cares enough about you,' he said at last, 'then you will all be freed. But in the meantime you will suffer the way so many of the world's people have suffered at your hands. You will be given no food or water, and you will not be allowed to leave the room. You will only speak when spoken to by one of us. Anyone who speaks out of turn from now on will be shot immediately.' He glared at Elena. 'Including you. Do you understand?'

There were a few nods and murmurs. Elena didn't say anything. She held Wolf's gaze, unsure why she was being so brave, or foolish, by constantly drawing attention to herself.

'Do you understand?' he demanded, enunciating the words slowly and carefully as he stared straight at Elena.

She nodded, hating him. 'Yes.'

'Good. Are there any guests staying in the suites?'

For a split second she thought about lying. Mr Al-Jahabi might have been a pervert but she had no desire to put him through this. In the end, though, it wasn't worth the risk, either for her or the other guests. 'Yes. Two of them are occupied, the Garden and the Deco.'

Wolf turned away. Elena looked round at the other hostages, and saw the fear in their faces. She caught the eye of the man next to her. It was one of the guests from the third floor. The man who'd had the rope in his room. He looked thin and pale, and Elena gave him a supportive smile, trying to forget the fact that he'd been planning to commit suicide in her hotel – an act she considered incredibly selfish, given that it would have been one of her staff members who had to deal with the aftermath. He smiled back weakly, and it was clear to her that he knew what she was thinking and was ashamed.

She turned away, and thought of Rod. He would almost certainly have heard what was happening at the hotel and would be terribly worried. For the first time she wondered whether she'd ever see him again. It made her feel sick to think that this could be it for her – the end.

She took a deep breath, keeping the panic at bay. She did have a future, she told herself. She was going to go to Australia with Rod, get married and have a family. But first she was going to have to get out of here, and that meant escaping. But how? She looked round the silent restaurant, feeling the sense of despair emanating from the other hostages. Wolf's foot was back on that damned pedal. It seemed an impossible task.

But Elena had long ago learned that if you tried hard enough, nothing was impossible. And she had to make herself believe that now.

32

Fox looked round the restaurant at the group of hostages sitting silently on the floor, a smaller and more manageable number than downstairs, then tensed as Wolf put a gloved hand on his shoulder.

'What do you think about releasing the children?' he hissed.

This was something Fox had given plenty of thought to. 'It'll make us look merciful, and therefore worth negotiating with,' he answered, casting a dispassionate eye across the room. 'We're playing to the Arab world as well as the West, and right now we just look like a bunch of killers. If we sow some doubt among the enemy, we'll delay their assault until we're ready for it.'

'But we need more hostages to replace them. We don't have enough up here as it is. What's keeping those two downstairs? Go and get them. I'll be all right here.'

Fox used the emergency staircase to get back to the third floor, moving quickly. He wasn't keen to leave Wolf on his own with the hostages for too long. Although they didn't look like they were capable of mounting any kind of organized resistance, he knew that you only needed one gutsy one, and for Wolf's attention to be diverted for a split second, and they'd be facing disaster.

When he came out into the third-floor corridor, it was silent. Too silent. There was no activity at all, and no sign of either of the men, or any of the people they were meant to be rounding up. Fox knew he couldn't have missed them. There was no other way up to the restaurant, with the exception of the lifts, and he'd put all of them out of action earlier.

He looked up and down the empty corridor, his finger tensing on the trigger of his AK-47 as his concern grew.

That was when he heard it. A scraping sound coming from inside one of the nearby rooms, as if someone was scratching at the door with their fingernails.

He walked slowly towards the source of the noise, stopping at the room from where it was coming.

A small dark patch was spreading out from under the door, only just visible against the burgundy of the carpet, and Fox could hear another sound now, alongside the scratching. The tight, gurgling breaths of a man drowning in his own blood.

Keeping his finger on the AK's trigger, he slipped the key card from the pocket of his overalls, pushed it in the reader and, in one rapid movement, kicked open the door.

It only flew back a foot because it was being blocked by a man lying across it like a human draught excluder. It was one of his own men, the ex-marine Leopard, and his balaclava-clad head had been smashed to a bloody pulp. Blood bubbles formed in his open mouth like petals as he tried to breathe.

Fox kicked the door again, harder this time, shunting the body back a few inches, repeating the process until it opened completely. Stepping over Leopard's body, he went inside and immediately saw Panther, propped up against the wall on the other side of the room near the bathroom door, still in his waiter's uniform. His head was slumped forward, his shirt drenched in blood.

Fox felt someone touch him and looked down sharply. Leopard had lifted one of his gloved hands, and the material had briefly touched his leg.

He sighed. Leopard had been a good soldier, but he was no use to him now. He pushed the barrel of the AK against his ruined head and pulled the trigger.

The hand dropped down with a leaden thud, and the rasping breaths stopped.

Fox looked round the room. Leopard's AK was lying on the bed, its stock smashed so badly that the trigger guard was hanging off, rendering the weapon useless. Near the bed on the floor the body of an old man lay on its side. He'd been shot, but there was no way, given his build and the damage done to Leopard and Panther, that he was the one responsible for their deaths.

Holding his rifle out in front of him, Fox checked the bathroom and the corner cupboard but they were both empty.

There were a few kids' toys on the floor – Transformers and a model truck – and a black leather handbag sitting on the table on the far side of the bed. Stepping over the toys, Fox picked up the handbag and looked inside, quickly locating an American driving licence in the name of Abigail Ruth Levinson. She looked skinny and petite in the photo, which made Fox pretty sure she wasn't the killer either, and since it definitely wasn't someone who still played with Transformers and Tonka toys, someone else was involved. Someone who clearly knew what he was doing.

His hand brushed against something in the handbag, and he pulled out a clear plastic bag containing what looked like stubby blue pens. He looked more closely and saw that the pens contained insulin. So, she was a diabetic, and one who had to inject herself as well. Which meant she'd be needing them again at some point soon.

He slipped the package into the pocket of his overalls and threw the bag on the floor. It was

Simon Kernick

possible that Abigail and the boy were not known to the killer, and therefore no longer with him, but if they were, and he had her insulin, then it might prove useful at some point.

However, in the end, that was scant consolation. Already two of their number were dead, and the Glock that Panther had been carrying was missing.

Fox sighed. Whichever way he chose to look at it, they now had a real problem on their hands.

33

Scope might have learned first aid during his days in the military, but he was no doctor, and although the wound didn't look that serious, he couldn't tell for certain.

It took him close to five minutes to get through to the emergency services on the hotel room phone. He told the woman on the other end about what was happening in the hotel, keeping out the details of his own involvement, and explained that he was with a woman with a gunshot wound to the leg that needed urgent treatment.

The operator asked him a lot of questions about the injuries, and told him how to stabilize the bleeding.

'I know all that, and I've done everything I can.'

'Is the patient conscious?'

Scope glanced at the bed where Abby lay on her back, smiling weakly at Ethan, who was crouched next to her, holding her hand and wiping her fore-head with a damp cloth, which was what Scope had told him to do, hoping that it might provide him with a distraction and make him feel useful. 'Yes, she is.'

'That's good. Help will be on its way soon.'

'Help's already here. I can see it out of the window. What I need to know is when it's actually going to come in here.'

'As you can appreciate, the situation is still very unstable, and the paramedics will need clearance from the police.'

Scope didn't bother asking when that was likely to be. He could tell from the operator's voice that she wasn't expecting a change in the situation any time soon. It felt very much like the security forces were preparing themselves for the long haul, which wasn't good news for either Abby or her son.

'Remain in your room, try to barricade the door if you can, and wait until help arrives,' the operator continued. 'Help will come, I promise. Now, I'm going to put you through to one of my colleagues in the police, who'd like to ask you some questions. Can you hold?'

Scope said he could, hoping that the police officer would have more than platitudes to offer him.

But he didn't. The cop sounded young, and he asked Scope a lot of questions about what was going on. How the attackers had got in, what their numbers were, that kind of thing. Scope told him the truth. He didn't know a great deal about what had happened, other than that there appeared to be quite a few gunmen, and that the one he'd heard speaking had what sounded like a Middle Eastern accent. The cop, who sounded way too interested for Scope's liking and therefore probably had something to do with the intelligence services, then started asking him more personal questions. What was his name? What was he doing in the hotel? Where was he in the building at that moment?

Scope was a good liar. He always had been. His dad had always said he'd have made a great salesman. He told the cop his name was John, that he'd been having a drink in the restaurant upstairs and wasn't a guest, and that he was hiding in one of the rooms on the second floor. 'Listen,' he said at last. 'If anyone's looking at the hotel switchboard, they'll see that someone in this room's on the phone, so I'm going to hang up now. But you need to get here fast. There are a lot of dead and injured.'

'We're going to be with you as soon as we can,' said the cop with the reassuring calmness that tends to come easily to those who aren't in the line of fire. 'In the meantime, stay where you are. And if you're discovered by any of the gunmen, on no account offer any resistance.'

A bit too late for that, thought Scope, ending the call.

The room's TV was on Sky News with the volume

turned right down, the news ticker running along the bottom of the screen continuing to announce that there'd been a series of terrorist bombs at locations across central London, and now a suspected terrorist attack on the Stanhope Hotel involving a mass hostage-taking by an unknown number of gunmen. A reporter in a trench coat standing in Hyde Park with the Stanhope as a distant backdrop spoke silently into the camera, looking suitably grim-faced. A moment later the camera panned up towards the hotel, focusing on a glass-fronted upper section of the building where the blinds had all been pulled down. The camera panned in closer but it was impossible to see inside, and after a few seconds they cut back to the reporter.

'When are they going to come and get my mom?' asked Ethan quietly.

'Soon,' said Scope, looking down at the Glock in his hand. Three bullets. That was all he had. Enough for an emergency, nothing else. He knew they were going to have to wait to be rescued. Breaking out would be next to impossible with a young kid and a wounded woman.

'When's soon?'

'As soon as they can get inside. They need to stop the bad men first.'

'Why don't you shoot them? You've got a gun.' Ethan looked at him with wide, innocent eyes that pleaded for answers.

'I haven't got enough bullets,' Scope told him, knowing it was best to be honest.

'It's going to be OK.' Abby's voice was strained, but some strength was returning to it as she reached out and stroked Ethan's cheek.

Scope pushed the gun into the back of his trousers and went over to the bed. She looked pale and listless, and he could see that she was in a lot of pain.

'How are you feeling?'

'I feel numb, and it hurts . . .' She stopped, and Scope could tell that she was making an effort to keep things together for Ethan's sake. 'But I'm OK. When do you think the police will have us out of here?'

'I don't know. It could be a while.'

'Then I've got a bit of a problem. I'm a Type One diabetic, and the insulin's back in my room.' She looked apologetic. 'I forgot about it in all the commotion.'

Scope nodded slowly. 'When do you need to inject yourself again?'

'When I next eat. Ideally, it should be about seven thirty, but I could hold on a while after that.'

'Will the gunshot wound affect the timing?'

'I don't think so.'

'Don't worry,' Scope told her, 'I'll go back to your room and get it, but if you're OK, I'll leave it a little while until things have calmed down. The terrorists will have discovered the two I killed by now, and they're not going to be pleased.'

'Of course.' She smiled weakly. 'Thank you for doing this for us.'

'It's fine. I'll make sure you and your son stay safe, I promise.'

But even as he spoke the words he wondered if he wasn't making a big mistake by playing the Good Samaritan.

34

A service lift, the only one they'd kept in operation, linked the hotel's main kitchen to the two satellite kitchens on the mezzanine and ninth floors, and Fox travelled up on it now, along with the Welsh sapper Dragon and the Dane, Tiger, who he'd collected from the ballroom. He'd told them what had happened to the other two men. Neither man was too sad to see the back of Panther, but they'd both known and trained with Leopard, and his death had unnerved them, as had the fact that his killer was still somewhere in the hotel.

'The plan's flexible enough to deal with eventualities like this,' said Fox as they came out of the lift on the ninth floor and moved into the kitchen next to the Park View Restaurant. 'We'll find him.'

Dragon and Tiger were professional enough not to argue with this, but Wolf didn't react in quite the same way when Fox gave him the bad news.

'What do you mean, they're dead?' he hissed, the shock clear in his eyes.

'Someone killed them both,' repeated Fox. 'He used a knife on Panther and beat Leopard to death with his own rifle, smashing it in the process. Whoever it is, he definitely knows what he's doing.'

'And what about the MI6 man?'

'I haven't had a chance to check. I wanted to let you know what had happened straight away. I'll go down there in a minute, but I'm sure there's no problem. No one except us knows he's there.'

'Do that. We don't want to lose him.' Wolf shook his head in disbelief. 'Has anyone told Cat about her brother?'

'No, I thought that was best left to you.'

Wolf rubbed at his pockmarked face through the balaclava. 'This is very bad news. I knew Panther well. He was a good man.'

Which was something he definitely hadn't been, Fox thought. 'I'm not happy either. Leopard was one of mine. But right now we've got a much bigger problem. There's someone in the hotel not connected to us who knows how to kill people, and he's armed with Panther's Glock.'

'Could it be the police or the SAS?'

Fox shook his head. 'No. If it was the SAS, I'd be dead now. Chances are we all would. This is a guest. It has to be.'

'Everything's OK in the ballroom?'

'Everything's fine in there, and everyone's accounted for. Also, Panther and Leopard weren't carrying grenades, so the only thing missing is the Glock.'

Wolf said nothing for a minute, but Fox could see his fingers tighten on his AK as he struggled for control. 'OK,' he said at last. 'We need to clear the top floor and secure it. Then I'll tell Cat what has happened to her brother.'

Leaving Dragon and Tiger guarding the hostages, Wolf and Fox used the emergency staircase to walk the one floor up to where the Stanhope's suites were situated.

As soon as they were through the staircase doors, the opulence hit them. There were no thinning carpets up here. Expensive Persian rugs covered the polished mahogany floor, while paintings lined the walls and fresh flowers and exotic plants sprang from china vases, giving the corridor the sweet smell of summer.

Fox despised the fact that the wealthy thought they were above everyone else just because they had money. He hated the fact that they expected others to do their dirty work for them. When he and his fellow soldiers had been stuck in a barracks in the flea-ridden hellhole of Al-Amarah in Iraq, being used for target practice by those Shia lunatics from the Mahdi Army, the rich hadn't given a shit about them. Instead they'd continued spending their millions while Fox fought to protect them. And when he'd come back from the war, having given ten hard years' service to his country, having lost friends to IEDs and sniper fire, having survived the bloodshed and the murderous heat, what had they, or the politicians, or any of the bastards, done for him?

Nothing.

There'd been no jobs above minimum wage. There'd been no occupational training, even though it had been promised to every soldier leaving the army. And because he was single, and not an asylum seeker or a teenage mother, they'd put him at the very bottom of the housing list. Fox knew of two men who'd wilted under the strain and committed suicide; another had been sectioned after trying to kill his own mother. But not Fox. He hadn't wilted. He'd shown ambition, setting up a firm providing security to private companies in Iraq and Afghanistan. He'd done well financially, selling his company at a decent profit to a bigger outfit and remaining onboard as a consultant.

But for Fox, there was far more to life than making money. He harboured a burning anger at the way his country had been sold down the river by politicians who'd opened the floodgates to millions of immigrants; who'd watered down their once great culture to such an extent that it no longer even existed; who'd helped to create a soft, fat people whose poor were more interested in claiming benefits and watching reality TV than in doing anything to stop the rot all around them; and whose rich just wanted to make themselves ever richer. Fox wanted to wake the people up. He wanted to cause chaos and terror, to smash the old established order and pave the way for a new, more honourable society. It was this desire that had pushed him into extremism, and into the arms of others who shared his views.

From there it had been only a small step to the position he found himself in today. An introduction from one of his extremist contacts had put him in touch with Ahmed Jarrod, aka Wolf, a man with rich backers, and an exciting and lucrative proposition. Wolf wanted Fox to set up a small, hand-picked team of mercenaries to assist him in carrying out a devastating terrorist attack on the UK. It would be an opportunity for Wolf's backers (who Fox had always assumed were an Arab government) to get revenge on the UK for its perceived interference in their affairs. For Fox, who knew that Muslim extremists would get the blame for this, it was the perfect opportunity to divide and infuriate the British people, and give the establishment the bloody nose it so richly deserved. The irony of fighting alongside the type of people he despised in a battle against his own people was not lost on him. But in common with all other extremists, he was convinced his actions were necessary, and served a greater good.

He stopped outside the Deco suite, while Wolf stopped outside the Garden.

They nodded at each other, and Fox raised his rifle and opened the door, excited by the shock he was about to deliver.

The music got louder as he walked through a foyer with high ceilings and expensive-looking art on the walls, and into the bedroom.

They were on the bed. Three of them. All naked. A middle-aged Arab with a pot belly and a flaccid penis flanked by two much younger women, a Thai and a long-legged blonde, both of whom were clearly pros. The Thai had a tightly rolled fifty-pound note in her hand and looked like she was just about to snort one of two long lines of coke that ran from the Arab's dick almost to his belly button.

For a moment Fox felt as shocked seeing them as they obviously were to see him. Then he moved the rifle round and put a bullet through the iPod speaker system.

The room fell silent.

'Please,' the man on the bed said, trying to cover himself up, 'take whatever you want.'

Fox shot him once in the forehead, then turned the gun on the two women. But he didn't fire. The rich Arab deserved his fate, they didn't. Like him, they were only doing their jobs. He gestured to them to get out of bed and get dressed. They both stood and, trying hard not to look at their client, who lay motionless on the bed in a rapidly spreading halo of blood, started pulling on their clothes.

Fox lowered the gun and walked over to the bedside table where a half-full bottle of Johnnie Walker Black Label sat next to an open wrap of coke and two full ones. He'd never understood the allure of hard liquor and drugs. All they did was addle your brain and make you weak physically. There were plenty more enjoyable ways of having a thrill.

Like taking over a hotel in the middle of a big city in front of the whole world.

With a flick of his hand, Fox scattered the coke on to the floor. Then he walked over to the window, pulled back the curtain and looked out across Hyde Park, where the emergency vehicles and news crews were beginning to gather in numbers. In the sky above he could see two police helicopters circling. Fox knew that in a situation like this the authorities would set up an exclusion zone round the building as soon as possible, and do everything they could to keep the media at a safe distance where they could do no harm. They would have learned the lesson of Mumbai, where the terrorists had been able to check the movements of the police outside the hotel just by watching the TV. Fox was expecting a far more sophisticated approach tonight. The problem for their adversaries was that he and the others were ready for it.

He let the curtain fall back into place and turned away. The girls were dressed and looking at him expectantly. He was about to tell them to follow him out when Wolf came into the room.

'We have a problem,' he told Fox.

'What is it?'

'Not something I can talk about in front of these two.'

He produced a pistol from his overalls and shot the Thai girl in the face. Then, as the blonde tried to turn and make a dash for it, he put a bullet in the back of her skull, sending her sprawling on to the bed.

Wolf looked at the Arab. 'Is this man a Saudi?'

Fox shrugged. 'I don't know.'

Wolf glared at him. 'We don't kill Saudis, understand? It's not good public relations. Who do you think is bankrolling this whole thing?'

Fox shrugged again. 'Fair enough. So, what's the problem?'

Wolf led him out into the corridor and unlocked the Garden Suite. 'This,' he said simply, and opened the door.

35

As Wolf moved to one side, Fox saw it immediately. An outstretched arm, hanging out from behind one of the interior doors. It belonged to a man, and it looked like there was a small patch of blood on his sleeve.

'Go inside,' Wolf told him.

Wrinkling his nose against the stale smell, Fox entered the suite. Keeping his gun pointed in front of him, he walked slowly through the foyer, and into the sitting room, stepping over the arm. It was then that he saw the full extent of the carnage.

There were three men in the room and they were all sprawled out on the shag-pile carpet. The one in the doorway, a well-built, well-dressed man in his early thirties, had had his throat cut, as had another guy, bigger, black, with a bald head and a sharp suit, who was lying on his back ten feet away. The third one looked Greek. He was older, with a thick head of dyed-black curly hair and an open-necked shirt and medallion combination that would have gone down a storm in 1987, when everyone got their fashion tips from *Miami Vice*, but now, frankly, looked ridiculous. He was propped up against a tan leather armchair with his head bowed, and Fox could see he'd been stabbed a number of times in the upper body. He took a deep breath. It reminded him of what Panther had looked like downstairs.

He lifted the man's head up and saw that he too had a neck wound, although it was not as clean-cut or as deep as those on the others. The blood had stopped flowing from it, but it hadn't yet coagulated, meaning he hadn't been dead long.

He dropped the head and stood up, puzzled. It looked like Jack the Ripper had set to work in this room, yet he knew for a fact that none of his people had been up here, and even if they had, they would have used guns rather than knives. There were also very few signs of a struggle. The room was spacious, with exotic houseplants in pots at regular intervals along the walls, yet only one of them had been knocked over. It looked to Fox like all the men had been caught by surprise, and had died within seconds and feet of each other. It meant that whoever had killed them was good.

'Well?' said Wolf, coming into the room behind him.

Fox looked round the room one more time. 'This is the work of the man who killed Leopard and Panther, I'm sure of it. And he's a pro.'

He walked through to the bedroom and looked around. The bed was made and there didn't appear to be anything out of place. 'We need to ask the manager who it was who was staying here. That might give us some indication as to who we're dealing with.'

Closing the doors of both suites, they made their way back to the emergency staircase. Wolf waited while Fox set a grenade booby-trap behind the door. If Special Forces landed on the roof and came in through the undefended top-floor windows, their arrival would be announced with a loud bang.

'Don't say anything about what's happened up here,' said Wolf as they headed down the stairs. 'We don't want to panic the men.'

Fox nodded. For once he agreed with him. They were unlucky to have attacked the hotel on the day that it contained a man who should have been working for, not against, them, but he knew there was no point in dwelling on this. In battle, events can conspire against you at every turn. The solution was to ride with them and make new plans.

As they walked back into the Park View Restaurant, Wolf nodded curtly at Dragon and Tiger, then called the hotel manager over.

She stood up reluctantly, and Wolf and Fox moved her to one side so that the other two couldn't hear what was being said.

'Do you have any soldiers staying here?' Wolf whispered.

The manager frowned. 'Not that I know of, but I don't always know the details of the guest lists.'

'Do any of your staff have military training?'

'I don't think so.'

Fox could see that her curiosity was piqued. 'Who's staying upstairs in the Garden Suite?' he asked.

'Mr Miller. He's had the suite for most of the last two months. I think he's going through a divorce.'

'What does he do for a living?'

'I think he's some sort of businessman, but he keeps himself to himself.'

'And does he have bodyguards?'

She nodded. 'Yes, I believe he does. But that's not unusual. We have a number of clients—'

'Has he got any enemies?'

The manager looked puzzled. 'No, why? Has anything happened?'

'All right,' snapped Wolf, pushing her away. 'Sit back down, and don't say a word to anyone.'

'We need to make a change of plan,' said Fox when she'd returned to where she'd been sitting. 'We've lost two men, which leaves us with six. It's not enough to hold hostages securely in three separate locations. We should keep the MI6 man apart, but we need to take the ones in here down to the ballroom.'

'But the whole point is to keep them in different places. That way it's far harder for the security forces to launch an assault.'

'I know all that,' said Fox, working hard to keep his

voice quiet. 'But if we keep the hostages up here we're splitting our resources too much. In fact, it actually makes it *easier* for them to launch an assault. By now they'll know we've brought people up here – it'll have been caught on the TV cameras. But with the blinds down, they won't know we've moved them, so they'll still think we've got them in separate places.'

Wolf shook his head emphatically. 'No,' he said. 'We stick to the plan.'

His pigheadedness irritated Fox, but he could hear the stubbornness in his voice, and knew he wouldn't change his mind.

'I'm doing the right thing,' said Wolf. 'You'll see that. We'll keep Dragon and Tiger up here, and Cat and Bear in the ballroom.' He stopped and looked at his watch, his eyes lighting up. 'It's nearly twenty past,' he said. 'Time we began negotiations.'

36

The helicopter followed the trajectory of Oxford Street, flying five hundred feet above the gridlocked roads, going as far as Lancaster Gate before banking over Hyde Park and landing on a hastily assembled landing pad three hundred yards directly north of the Stanhope Hotel.

Arley was talking to Chief Inspector Chris Matthews outside the command centre – which consisted of two mobile incident rooms side by side, surrounded by a cluster of police vehicles – trying to organize an HQ for the hundred or so Special Forces and their support teams, whose arrival was imminent, when she saw the helicopter coming in. She immediately excused herself and started across the park towards the landing pad, lighting her first cigarette since the crisis had broken nearly two hours ago, and savouring the acrid hit of smoke in her

200

throat. It was pretty much her first moment alone, when she hadn't been talking to someone about something.

On the ground, all three cordons were now in place around the Stanhope. In total there were about three hundred police officers on the scene, with more arriving all the time, but Arley was pretty sure that there were none more important than the man she was going to see now.

Riz Mohammed was one of the most successful negotiators in the Met. He had the right mix of hardness and empathy to get under the skin of hostage-takers, and it was well known that in ten years in the job he'd never lost a hostage. He also had the priceless asset of being a Muslim, his Jamaican-born parents having converted from Christianity before he was born. Three months earlier, two Algerian terror suspects wanted for the attempted murder of a police officer had taken their neighbours – a family of four, including two young children – hostage in their Brixton flat. They'd been armed with handguns and a very unstable homemade bomb (which, according to Counter Terrorism Command, they'd been planning to use in a suicide bomb attack) and were demanding their freedom and safe passage to Ankara in Turkey, as well as £50,000 in cash, otherwise they'd start killing the hostages one by one. Riz had been given the task of negotiating with the two men, who'd been desperate, angry and hopelessly unrealistic in their demands. Yet over the next excruciating twenty-two hours he'd coaxed, empathized with, listened to, and finally persuaded them both to release the four hostages, before surrendering peacefully.

Arley took three rapid puffs on the cigarette, taking in as much nicotine as possible, before stubbing it underfoot at the edge of the landing pad. She watched as Riz emerged from the cockpit door, covering his ample head of hair from the updraft of the rotor blades.

'Hello, ma'am, how are you?' he said, shaking her hand with a firm grip.

As the head of Specialist Operations, the Met's Kidnap Unit fell under Arley's overall control, and she'd worked with Riz several times before.

'I've been better. Thanks for coming, Riz. I appreciate it. I know it's your day off.'

They walked in the direction of the command centre, which sat just inside the central cordon, Arley having to increase her pace to keep up with him. Riz Mohammed was a big man with a big presence.

Up ahead the Stanhope loomed from behind the trees that bordered the park, illuminated by the many lights across its façade. It was a grand Georgian structure, and showed no obvious signs of being the location of a violent attack. There were no fires, no other unusual activity. If it hadn't been for the flashing lights of the many emergency services vehicles surrounding the hotel on three sides, and the noise of the helicopters overhead, it would have made for a perfectly ordinary night-time scene.

'Can you give me a rundown of what's happening?' Riz asked her as they walked.

'Things are still sketchy, but we've definitely got multiple gunmen, large numbers of hostages in at least two different areas of the building, a lot of people trapped in their rooms, and there've been reports of sporadic shooting inside the hotel for the last forty-five minutes. What makes it even more critical is that one of the hostages is the Head of the Directorate of Requirements and Production at MI6 and one of its top people.'

'You're joking. What the hell's he doing in there?'

'We don't know yet. The hostage-takers have released a film of him tied up in one of the hotel's rooms. It's been picked up by Al-Jazeera and a number of Islamist websites. On the film, one of the hostage-takers is holding a gun to his head and saying that if their demands aren't met they'll execute him at midnight. All this is confidential, of course.'

'Of course. What are their demands?'

'The broadcast called for all British operations against Muslim and Arab countries to stop, but they haven't made direct contact yet. We've tried calling the hotel on the external lines but there's been no response. To be honest, we don't know if they actually want to negotiate. From what we can gather they're holding hostages rather than conducting a massacre. Having said that, though, the military are being put on standby and my guess is responsibility for the operation will get turned over to them sooner rather than later if we can't make contact.'

Riz nodded. 'I'm assuming this is connected with the bomb attacks at the Westfield and Paddington.'

'We think so, so it's obvious they're not too worried about taking human life. Also, when they attacked the hotel, which happened at just before five o'clock, they killed several people in the kitchen, and opened fire on the first officers at the scene.'

'That's not going to help the negotiations. I was told they're from an organization called the Pan-Arab Army of God. Does that mean they're Islamic extremists?'

'We don't know anything about them yet but, given what we've got so far, we've got to assume that, yes.'

She saw the concern on his face when she said this. Islamic extremists were notoriously tricky to negotiate with because they were unpredictable and far less concerned with staying alive than the average hostage-taker.

'I'm sorry to put this on you, Riz. But if anyone's got a chance of turning this round, it's you.'

He sighed. 'I'll do my absolute best, but I'm no miracle worker.'

'I know,' she said. 'None of us are. We've just got to

hope we can conjure up something.'

By now they were approaching the command centre. Groups of officers and assorted emergency services personnel were milling about, talking in low voices, as they waited in the cold night air for instructions. Most of them looked nervous, but then, thought Arley, that was to be expected. Their home city was under attack from a group who'd already caused carnage and chaos at two separate locations, and who now controlled one of the most prestigious hotels in London. And right now it looked like the bad guys were winning.

Arley took a deep breath. One thing she'd learned in the best part of a quarter of a century in the force was that criminals, however well organized, had weaknesses that could be exploited. The key to success was locating those weaknesses.

Her mobile rang in her trouser pocket. It was Gold Commander, Commissioner Phillips – the first time she'd heard from him for over half an hour.

'Has your negotiator turned up yet?' he asked, trying to sound calm and collected but falling just that little bit short.

'I've just collected him. We're outside the incident room.'

'You need to hurry. We've had contact. A man with a Middle Eastern accent has just phoned, saying he's the commander of the Pan-Arab Army of God forces in the Stanhope Hotel. He's demanded to speak to me

personally in the next fifteen minutes, or his men are
going to kill a hostage.'

'You haven't spoken to him, sir, have you?' she
asked, thinking it would be a complete breach of
procedure if he had.

'Of course not,' he answered gruffly. 'That's your
negotiator's job. The call was made from a landline in
the kitchen on the mezzanine floor, and it was logged
at 18.20. That's six minutes ago.'

'What instructions shall I give our negotiator?'

Phillips paused. 'That's the thing, Arley. They're
very specific. I've just been on the phone to the Prime
Minister, and he's very concerned.'

'We all are, sir.'

'Not just about the situation with the civilian
hostages.' Phillips spoke slowly and carefully, the
concern in his voice becoming steadily more obvious.
'Can you move away, so there's no risk you're being
overheard?'

'Of course.' She excused herself from Riz and
walked a few yards away.

'Apparently the MI6 man Michael Prior has some
information that, should it fall into the wrong hands,
would be disastrous for the country. There's no reason
to believe that the terrorists know he has this
information – only a handful of people do know
about it – but it's absolutely essential your negotiator
speaks to him. He's got to insist on it.'

'But how are we going to find out whether Prior's

given away information without alerting the people holding him?' she asked.

'Prior has two pre-arranged codewords. He'll use one if he has been compromised, and the other if he hasn't. They're both on your desk in the incident room. As far as anyone else is concerned, the code-words are simply to find out if he's been mistreated or not. Is all that clear?'

'It's clear,' she said, not liking the sound of his voice at all.

'Good. Then get your man on the phone to the hostage-taker right away. We need this cleared up fast.'

37

Fox slipped into room 316, shutting the door quietly behind him and bolting it from the inside.

Michael Prior, the director of MI6 and their VIP prisoner, was still in the tub chair where they'd left him earlier, and he was staring cautiously at Fox from behind the gag. He seemed to be quite calm for a man who had a bomb strapped to him.

'You know they wanted to kill you on film,' said Fox, reverting to his normal accent as he threw his rifle on the bed and pulled off his backpack. He leaned round behind Prior's head and unstrapped the ball gag, letting it fall to the floor.

'If you let me go, I'll do everything I can to minimize your prison sentence.' Prior's voice was deep and authoritative, his expression stern and unwavering. It was obvious that he was accustomed to giving orders and being obeyed.

Fox ignored him. He was just another public-school establishment man used to getting his own way. Perhaps he thought that because Fox spoke with a local accent and was clearly English, he could be reasoned with. 'They wanted to shoot you dead as a show of strength to the UK government. I stopped them.'

'Thank you. You don't sound very much like a member of the Pan-Arab Front, or whatever you people are calling yourselves. So, why are you involved?'

Fox sat down on the bed, facing him. Even trussed up like a chicken, Michael Prior exuded a certain gravitas. With his silver hair and finely delineated features, he had the distinguished, well-fed look of confidence backed by old money. 'I told the man who was holding the gun to your head that you were much more useful to them alive.'

'You keep saying "them" and "they". If you're not a part of them, then who are you?'

'That doesn't really matter right now. What matters is that you have information that I need.'

Prior's eyes widened just a little. 'I know a lot less than you think.'

'Don't try to bullshit me. We haven't got time. I need a name. A name that only you and a handful of other people know.'

Prior swallowed, and Fox could tell that he knew exactly who he was referring to. 'I thought this was a terrorist attack.'

Fox stood up. 'It is. Now, we can do this the hard way, or we can do it the easy way, but the result's going to be the same. You're going to give up that name, and if you do it quickly, then it'll be a lot less painful.'

'Please, if you have any decency or patriotism . . .'

He stopped talking as Fox produced a scalpel and a small container of liquid from the backpack.

'Give me the name and as soon as I've verified it I'll unstrap the bomb, untie you, and let you go. You'll have to take your chances, but you'll probably make it out alive.'

'I can't. Please. I'll give you any information you want, but not that.'

'Last chance,' said Fox. 'Then I'll have to replace the gag while I go to work on you.'

He lifted the scalpel, and Michael Prior's eyes grew wide with fear.

38

The interior of the mobile incident room was long, narrow and windowless, like the inside of a shipping container. A bank of TV screens – some blank, others showing rolling news footage of the Stanhope Hotel – lined one side, beneath which were a half dozen work stations.

There were three other people in the room when Arley and Riz Mohammed walked in. Will Verran and Janine Sabbagh were both police technicians whom Arley had only just met. Janine was a petite blonde-haired South African in her mid thirties with very dark eyes and a friendly smile, while Will was a tall, lanky twenty-something with a boyish face and sandy hair that was thinning fast. Their responsibility was to keep open the channels of communication between Arley and all the other people and agencies involved in the operation.

The third person was John Cheney. He'd removed his jacket and was down to his shirtsleeves as he stood talking on one of the phones. He gave them a nod as they walked in, sizing up Riz with watchful eyes. So far, Cheney and Arley hadn't had much to do with each other, which suited her just fine. Even after all these years, she didn't feel entirely comfortable around him, although she wasn't exactly sure why.

Arley saw the surprised look cross Riz's face when he saw the three of them. It was clear he thought there'd be more people inside the police's forward control room.

'We've got officers in the incident room next door but most of our non-frontline resources are remaining off-site,' she explained as she introduced him to the others. 'Mainly because it's so difficult to get down here with the traffic, and' – she swept an arm round – 'obviously there's not a great deal of room. But we're in touch with everyone we need to be, and we have video conferencing facilities set up. Right, Janine?'

'We've got a video link to the Scotland Yard control room, which means they'll be able to see and hear us in here,' said Janine, pressing a couple of buttons on her keyboard. 'And we're just establishing one to the chief commissioner's office so he can listen in on the call.'

Arley turned to Riz. She'd already briefed him on her call with Commissioner Phillips, and knew that time was short. 'Don't forget, you've got to insist on speaking to Prior. The codewords he'll use are written down there. Anything else you need before you make the call?'

'The most important thing for me is to know who I'm dealing with,' said Riz, addressing the room. 'If we can ID any of the hostage-takers, particularly those in charge, it'll be a huge help.'

'We've got MI5 and CTC checking the voice records from the calls to see if they match any known suspects,' said Arley, 'and GCHQ are listening in on all the mobile phone conversations taking place inside the building. Any new developments we should know about?' she asked Cheney.

'We haven't had any matches yet,' he answered in that deep, gruff voice of his. 'GCHQ also haven't been able to pick up any mobile phone conversations between the terrorists in the building, which suggests they're not communicating by phone. They're also checking for use of short-wave radios and the internet, but apart from the uploading of the earlier video showing the Director, there's been nothing.'

'And the people calling out from the hotel. What are they saying about the hostage-takers? Are they speaking English? If so, with local or foreign accents?'

'The leader's speaking with an Arab accent,' said Cheney, 'and we've got phonetics experts trying to place it to a specific locality, but they haven't come back to us yet. As to the rest of the hostage-takers, we've had surprisingly few reports, although we

Simon Kernick

believe they're a mixture of Middle Eastern and eastern European accents.'

'OK,' said Will Verran, interrupting proceedings, 'we've got live feed to the commissioner's office.'

One of the blank screens lit up, showing Derek Phillips sitting at his desk, watching them. 'Are we ready to make the call?' he asked the assembled room, checking his watch. 'We're only two minutes off the hostage-taker's deadline.'

'We're ready now, sir,' Arley answered, feeling a rush of excitement, before turning to Riz. 'It's all yours.' She pointed at a handset on the desk in front of him. 'That's the phone to use. It's a secure landline. Press one and it'll get you straight through to the phone the terrorist leader made his original call from.'

'Remember,' said Phillips, 'we have to insist on speaking to Michael Prior.'

'I'll do everything I can.'

Riz squeezed his bulk into the seat, picked up the phone and held it in his hand for a few moments, looking pensive but calm. Everyone in the room was watching him. Arley knew he was under a lot of pressure, but then they all were. She recalled his performance in Brixton and was confident she'd made the right decision in picking him for this, probably the biggest job of his life.

Finally, he pressed 1 and put the phone to his ear.

39

The phone rang six times before it was picked up.

'Who am I speaking to?' The voice at the other end of the phone sounded clear in the confines of the office.

'My name's Rizwan Mohammed. I work for the Metropolitan Police's Kidnap Unit. Is this the commander of the Pan-Arab Army of God at the Stanhope Hotel?'

'I said I wanted to speak to the chief commissioner of the Metropolitan Police. The organ grinder, not one of the monkeys. Get him on the phone in the next five minutes or a hostage dies.'

'I'm afraid I can't do that. I'm the representative of the police and security forces. You're going to have to talk to me.'

'Then a hostage dies, and one will die every five minutes until he comes on the line.'

'That's not going to help you get what you want,' Riz said calmly, but the line had already gone dead.

Arley looked up at the screen showing Phillips' desk, and was surprised to see he was no longer sitting in it, and the audio feed was turned off.

'Do you think he'll carry out his threat?' Arley asked Riz.

He shook his head. 'I don't think so, but in any case we can't give in to him. Not at this stage. Otherwise he'll be running rings round us. The hostage-taker always wants to establish control, and every negotiator knows that you can't let him, however high the stakes are. We have to be the ones calling the shots.'

Arley knew this, but like most police officers who'd got as far as she had, she was a political animal with big ambitions, and she was aware that her actions tonight would put her in the spotlight. 'But if he starts killing hostages and it comes out that it was because we wouldn't let him speak to Commissioner Phillips, it won't look good.'

She looked back at the screen. He still wasn't at his desk.

'And if we start letting him order us around this early in the negotiations then the chances are there'll be more people dead later on.'

There was silence as they both weighed up their options.

'Let me try him again,' Riz said at last.

Arley sighed, knowing that whatever happened tonight, the buck would end up stopping with her. 'OK. It's your call.'

This time the phone was picked up straight away. 'Yes?'

'It's Rizwan Mohammed again. Look, I know we can resolve this peacefully. Why don't you tell me what you want?'

'I want to talk to the man in charge.'

'And I want you to know that if you talk to me, your message will be responded to at the highest level. Do you mind if I ask your name?'

'You may call me Wolf.'

'OK, Wolf. Are you the leader of the hostage-takers?'

'I am,' he said, and Arley could hear the pride in his voice.

'And what is it that you want?'

There was a pause and what sounded like the rumpling of paper at the other end of the phone before Wolf started speaking again. He was clearly reading from a prepared text. 'We want a commitment from the British government that British crusader forces will cease their hostilities against all Arab and Muslim lands, and remove their representatives from Arab and all Islamic soil within sixty days. We want a public statement from the Prime Minister promising that Britain will not use its influence in the United Nations Security Council to pursue Arab leaders for so-called crimes against humanity, and that it will henceforth keep out of Arab and Islamic affairs, and end its involvement in the so-called War on Terror.'

There was another silence.

'Those are very ambitious demands,' Riz said at last.

'We are very ambitious people. And we also have a hotel full of prisoners, including a director of MI6. This puts us in a position of strength. Not you.'

'Before we go forward, I need to speak to Michael Prior to ensure that he's in good health.'

'You and your government do not make demands of me. I make demands of you.'

'And I will definitely do all I can to meet those demands. But I do need to speak to him now.'

'We'll consider it.'

'It's going to be extremely difficult to get my government to move on your demands if you don't let me talk to him.'

'I told you: we'll consider it.'

'Please do. It'll be seen as a real gesture of goodwill by the British government.'

Riz looked up at Arley. His expression said: what more can I do? On the screen, she saw that Phillips had returned to his desk and was now listening intently. He made no move to speak, so Arley mouthed the words 'leave it' to Riz.

'Also, we want the internet kept on,' Wolf continued. 'If you take away our access, a hostage will die every five minutes until you reinstate it. Do you understand that?'

'Yes, but it's not going to help our negotiations if you start killing people.'

'Then do as I say and no one will get hurt. You have until midnight to meet all our demands. If they haven't been met by then, we will execute your MI6 man and then one hostage every five minutes until they are. And for your information, we have rigged the building, including the areas where we're holding the prisoners, with explosive devices, none of which needs to be detonated by mobile phone. If your forces make any attempt to storm the building in the meantime, we will detonate all the devices, and kill the hostages, and ourselves if necessary. We are warriors, and we are prepared to die.'

Arley saw the way Riz tensed at these words. It was exactly what they'd all feared. She tried to catch his eye, but he was hunched over his phone. Instead, she caught the eye of John Cheney. He raised an eyebrow but otherwise seemed unfazed by the way the conversation was going.

'We understand there are wounded people inside,' Riz said at last. 'We'd like to send ambulance crews in to bring them out.'

'There are no wounded people here.'

'That's not our understanding. We'd also like the release of all the children too. It will do your cause no good at all if any of them get killed. I'm sure you remember what happened in Beslan. All those children dying did untold damage to the Chechen cause.'

'What do you know about the Chechen cause?'

'Enough to know that the Chechen leadership acknowledged that Beslan was a failure. I'm sure the Pan-Arab Army of God don't want that to happen.'

'Don't lecture me.'

'I'm not,' said Riz, and Arley could tell he was struggling to keep his voice conciliatory yet firm. 'But it will help your cause if you're shown to be merciful.'

'We will consider your request,' said Wolf impatiently. 'And we have one final demand. Do not make contact unless you have good news. I'm well aware of the kinds of stalling tactics negotiators use, and we're not going to tolerate them.'

The line went dead.

Arley took a deep breath as the tension slowly seeped out of the room, and put a supportive hand on Riz Mohammed's shoulder. 'You handled that well.'

Riz sat back in his seat and stretched. 'That wasn't easy.'

On the screen, Arley saw Commissioner Phillips talking to someone off camera. The audio feed was again turned off. Then he turned back and addressed the room. 'I've just received word from the PM's office that all mobile phone coverage and internet access is to be switched off inside the Stanhope with immediate effect.'

'What?' asked Riz, sounding startled. 'They specifically demanded the internet be kept on.'

'I know they did,' said Phillips. 'But these are the PM's direct orders. He's not prepared to let them make propaganda videos or communicate with the outside world from inside the hotel without us knowing about it. He's currently hosting a meeting of COBRA, so it's likely to be a group decision.' He addressed Riz directly. 'You can tell them we'll restore the internet as soon as we speak to Prior.'

Riz looked concerned. 'It's a very risky course of action we're taking. Their commander is not talking like a desperate man. He's talking like a man who's holding lots of cards. He's part of a well-organized team. The way they got into the building, the way they booby-trapped the place – it all means that they know exactly what they're doing. And we already know they're quite prepared to kill innocent people. My feeling is that if we push them, they'll react violently.'

Phillips' sigh was loud in the room. 'We have to make a stand and face the consequences.'

'We have another major problem as well,' said Arley. 'We can't actually meet any of their demands. The British government doesn't negotiate with terrorists. And it would be political suicide to make a public statement effectively surrendering the UK's foreign policy because we were being held to ransom.'

Riz nodded. 'I believe the hostage-takers know that.'

Arley frowned. 'So, why make the demands in the first place?'

'Because they've planned this very carefully. First of all, by making demands, it extends the publicity they and their organization can get out of their operation. Also, it helps to shift the onus of blame on to the British government, because if we refuse to negotiate and turn down every demand flat, we're going to end up catching a lot of the flak if things go wrong.'

'For what it's worth, I agree,' said John Cheney. 'They're expecting an assault, which is why they've split up the hostages, and set such a short deadline. It's all designed to make things harder for us to retake the hotel without mass casualties.'

'There must be a way of bringing this to a peaceful conclusion,' Arley objected.

'Anyone can be negotiated with,' Riz replied. 'The fact is he's already backed down a little by speaking to me. The key is to keep pushing him. One thing I know about Islamic culture, being a Muslim myself, is the importance of family. I know it's a long shot, but if we can ID him and get members of his family involved in the negotiations, then we might be able to sway him from the present course.'

'We're doing everything we can to ID him,' said Cheney. 'But even if we do manage it, there's a small something that we seem to have overlooked.'

Arley turned his way. 'What's that, John?'

Cheney moved away from the desk so that Commissioner Phillips could see him as he spoke. 'The man we're speaking to made some pretty major demands, and was obviously reading from something he'd prepared earlier, but at no point did he do what almost all hijackers and hostages do when they're trapped. He didn't ask for safe passage out. Not for himself or any of his men.' He paused, and Arley felt the tension in the room cranking up again. 'Which suggests to me that neither he, nor they, have any intention of leaving that place alive.'

40

As soon as Fox had the information he needed from Michael Prior, he used the laptop from his backpack to log into a hotmail account that only he and one other person had access to, where he left a simple three-word message in the drafts section: *I have it*. Leaving a message in the drafts folder was an old anti-surveillance trick. It meant that the content couldn't be monitored or read by the security forces, since no message was ever actually sent over the internet.

He knew he had to move fast. Leaving Prior behind, he exited room 316 and took the emergency stairs to the second floor, where he stopped at room 202. Before he'd tampered with the guest reservation database, 202 had been empty. Now it was registered to Mr Robert Durran, a freelance architect who was on the first night of a two-night stay.

Using the master key card, Fox let himself into the room. The lights were off and the curtains open, letting in the flashing lights of all the emergency services vehicles gathered across the street. The bed was made and the room still had a fresh, unoccupied smell.

Fox unzipped the rucksack and removed the clothes and shoes he'd been wearing when he arrived at the Park Royal rendezvous earlier that afternoon. Next he pulled out a wallet containing a driving licence, passport and credit cards in the name of Robert Durran, as well as several hundred pounds in cash, from an internal pocket. He slipped the wallet into the front pocket of the trousers, then carefully placed the whole bundle under the bed, pushing it in so that it was well out of sight.

Finally, he looked round the room and, satisfied that his contingency plan was in place, headed back to join the others.

In the ballroom, Bear and Cat were sitting on hard-backed plastic chairs a few yards apart, watching the hostages. Both of them turned round as he entered the room. Cat gave him a bored, vaguely dismissive look, which meant that Wolf had yet to tell her about the death of her brother, while Bear, the 'man with the face' who'd saved Fox's neck in Iraq all those years ago by pushing him out of the way of an IED, gave him a nod, which he returned.

Only a handful of the hostages looked up. There

were seventy-seven of them in all, forty-six men and thirty-one women, and Fox had to admit they were an acquiescent bunch. Seated quietly at the far end of the room, their heads were down and they were behaving exactly as they'd been ordered. Either sensible or cowardly, depending on which way you chose to look at it.

To Fox, they were cowardly, and he walked past them and into the satellite kitchen.

Wolf was sitting alone at the far end next to the phone in the kitchen drinking a coffee and smoking one of his foul-smelling cigarettes. He turned round as Fox entered. 'I've spoken to the negotiator and given him our demands. They want to speak to Prior. In fact, they are insistent.'

'We need to be careful about that,' said Fox. 'They'll be trying to pinpoint his location in the building. If you let them speak to him, they'll know exactly where he is.'

'We can always move him.'

'True. But we're already two men down so we can't just shift him from room to room. It means manpower and logistics, not to mention risk.'

Wolf frowned. 'So you think we shouldn't?'

'We don't have anything to gain from it. Let them sweat a little. And in the meantime, let's release the children. That'll give them something to work with, and help to stave off any chance of an early assault.'

'OK,' said Wolf slowly. 'That's what we'll do. But

I'm not releasing any of their parents. I don't want them giving anything away about us.'

Fox agreed with him. The minute any hostages were released, the police would be on them like a shot, trying to extract any information they could about what was going on inside the Stanhope – information that would later be handed over to the military for when they staged their inevitable assault. Children, however, would be of only limited help.

He rubbed his face beneath the balaclava. His skin felt itchy and sweaty, and he wished he could take the damn thing off, but there was no way he could risk anyone seeing his face tonight.

'I'm guessing you haven't told Cat about her brother yet?' he asked.

'Not yet, no.'

'She's not going to take it well.'

'Of course she isn't, you fool.' Wolf looked agitated. 'I'll handle her. She listens to me. Take over out there and send her in.'

He turned away and Fox left the kitchen, thinking that not only was Wolf an arsehole, he was a weak one too. He looked at his watch. 18.50. The siege was two hours old. A little more than four more and it would all be over. And he'd be a rich man.

It was well worth putting up with a few insults in the meantime.

41

Clinton Bonner was dying to urinate. A weak bladder had been a constant companion ever since he'd hit his fifties, over a decade before, and right now it was tormenting him with a vengeance.

He was in the walk-in cupboard of the ballroom's satellite kitchen, lying in the same spot he'd been in for more than three hours now – the crawlspace beneath the left-hand bottom shelf. When he'd sneaked in there to have a quick nap towards the end of his second double-shift of the week, it was 3.30 on a normal November afternoon. He hadn't bothered to set the alarm on his phone because he usually only shut his eyes for twenty minutes, but this time, bizarrely, he'd slept for well over an hour, and when he'd woken up at ten to five, already needing the loo, his whole world had changed.

The first thing he remembered was the faint but

unmistakeable rat-a-tat-tat of automatic gunfire coming from downstairs, then lots and lots of shouting and screaming. He had no idea what was happening, but his instincts had told him to stay put until it stopped, and being far past the age where curiosity would get the better of him, he'd obeyed them.

The shooting had finally stopped, but the shouting hadn't. It had got closer until it seemed to be coming from the ballroom, barely ten yards from where he was lying. Totally confused, his need to pee temporarily forgotten amid the drama, Clinton had lain there until he'd heard voices, quieter and calmer now, inside the satellite kitchen. He'd always had good hearing. 'Ears like a fruit bat's' his mother used to claim when he was growing up in Trinidad, as she boxed them for listening in on conversations that didn't concern him. And what he'd heard in that room had been truly terrifying. It was obvious armed men had taken over the Stanhope, men who'd made Elena Serenko, the pretty young duty manager who was always so friendly to him (unlike some), tell them the locations of the master key cards to the rooms, as well as the mains sprinkler system.

That had been some time ago now. Clinton sneaked a peek at his watch, sheltering the fluorescent green light with his hand, and saw that it was five to seven, almost an hour and a half since the official end of his shift. His wife, Nancy, would be home from work herself by now and would have heard about what was happening at the hotel. She'd be worried sick – she was a worrier at the best of times – which was why he'd sent her a text earlier, telling her he was safe and hidden away, but couldn't talk. He'd then immediately switched off the phone, not prepared to risk the fact that it might make any kind of noise and betray his location to the men who'd taken over the hotel.

His bladder felt like it was bursting. He tried to think of something else, anything that might provide some temporary relief, but nothing seemed to work, and it was taking all his willpower to hold it in. He considered wetting his pants. Almost did it. But the fear that the odour might give him away held him back.

But he wasn't going to be able to hold out for much longer.

The talking outside had stopped but he could still hear movement. Someone was there, just beyond the door. Someone prepared to kill him.

He heard footsteps approaching, and he felt the fear rise in his chest as they stopped immediately outside.

And then the door opened and light flooded in.

The fear seemed to squeeze Clinton's bladder so hard that it felt like it would explode at any second, and he held his breath, pushing himself as far into the crawlspace as possible, silently praying to the Good Lord that whoever the intruder was, he wouldn't look down.

The intruder was inside the store cupboard now, rummaging around on the shelves, probably looking for something to eat, his booted feet only inches from Clinton's face, the barrel of a wicked-looking rifle dangling down by the side of one leg.

Clinton desperately wanted to breathe. To breathe and to pee. Terror coursed through him as he realized that he could be just seconds from the end of his life and meeting a God he'd genuinely not expected to see for many years yet, because no one thinks this sort of thing will happen to them, do they?

Please, God. Don't let me be discovered.

Which was when Clinton felt the wetness running down his leg as his bladder finally gave way.

Oh God, no. Please.

His eyes filled with tears as he tried to stop himself. But he couldn't seem to manage it, and now he could hear the urine dripping on to the floor beneath him, forming a puddle that any second now was going to be discovered, because the boots were only inches away. And still he couldn't stop himself.

The man grunted as he dropped a can of something on to the floor. It rolled towards Clinton and he reached out a finger and rolled it back out, away from the crawlspace, praying the man wouldn't look down and see the growing puddle, or pick up the strong odour of urine that seemed to Clinton to be overwhelming.

The seconds crawled by like days in the hot,

claustrophobic silence. At last, Clinton managed to stop the flow of urine, but still he didn't dare breathe, even though his lungs were close to bursting.

Finally, the man turned and walked out of the store cupboard, carrying a case of bottled mineral water under one arm. He didn't shut the door, allowing Clinton to catch a look at him for the first time as he placed it down on one of the worktops, and pulled one of the bottles free. He was short and squat, with a wide frog-like face peppered with acne scars. What truly scared Clinton, though, was the fact that if he could see the man, then the man could surely see him.

Feeling utterly exposed, Clinton lay still, conscious of the pooled urine on the floor beside him, at least part of which was clearly visible from outside the door.

Then he heard the kitchen door open more widely and a moment later a woman came into view, pulling off a black balaclava. Clinton could only just see her because the other man was in the way, but she was dark-haired and pretty, and wearing a surprisingly sexy black dress underneath a thick bomber jacket. She had a handgun down by her side.

The man said something in Arabic, his tone subdued, and walked over to her.

Clinton couldn't hear the remainder of their conversation because a few seconds later the woman let out a wild animal howl that filled the room before storming into view, a hand covering her face. The man pulled her back and they continued to talk in hushed voices for several minutes more before she broke free from him and paced the room in ferocious, intense silence, while he watched her, making no move to intervene. On three separate occasions she passed just in front of the open store cupboard door, but was thankfully too preoccupied to look inside.

Finally, she stopped. 'I want him alive,' she hissed to the man, speaking in English for the first time. 'And I want to be the one who slices his balls off.'

'You shall have him, I promise you that.'

'When?'

'Later. There are things we need to do first.'

'Like what?'

'We have to release the children.'

'That is more important than finding the man who murdered my brother? Your fellow countryman and soldier?'

'We need to give a sign of goodwill. When we have done that, we will look for this man. Remember, this whole building will burn tonight, and he will burn with it.'

'I want them all to burn,' she said, walking into view and putting a manicured hand on one of the worktops. Her face was no longer pretty but set hard and merciless, and her dark eyes blazed with a terrible anger. 'I want to kill as many of these dogs as possible.' She was looking past the man now, right towards where Clinton was lying.

'Something smells strange in here,' she said, wrinkling her nose.

Clinton almost cried out with fear as he heard those words.

The man turned round, and now he too was looking straight at Clinton. He frowned. 'It's something in there.'

Clinton didn't move. It was over. He was going to die here in this hot, windowless place, away from the family he loved so much.

The man was walking towards him, his rifle dangling from his arm. Getting closer and closer.

And then, in one single terrifying movement, he slammed the door shut, plunging Clinton back into welcome darkness.

42

Arley Dale was drinking from a huge cup of Starbucks coffee and thinking about having a cigarette. In the last few minutes, things in the mobile incident room had quietened right down, and the phones had stopped ringing. Will and Janine, the two technicians who'd also been acting as coordinators and receptionists, were still tapping away on their computers while Riz Mohammed and John Cheney were leant over another desktop going through lists of terror organizations and their various front companies, searching for anything that might provide a link to the Pan-Arab Army of God. Their body language suggested they hadn't found anything of use yet.

So far, Arley was reasonably satisfied with the way she was handling her end of the operation. The situation was contained; there'd been no further reports of shooting in the previous half hour, or threats made by the hostage-takers; and it seemed they hadn't noticed that the hotel's internet access had been switched off. Riz might not have been able to make contact with Michael Prior, but Arley wasn't so worried about that. There was no point forcing the issue and running the risk of antagonizing the terrorist who called himself Wolf. In the end, he'd call them. Like most sieges, it was a waiting game, each side hoping that the other would crack.

The orders from Commissioner Phillips, and from the Prime Minister himself, who as Platinum Commander was in overall charge of the operation, were to attempt a negotiated settlement, but they were also hedging their bets. A full squadron of SAS troops and support staff had arrived on the scene a few minutes earlier, ready to stage a rapid assault on the hotel if the situation suddenly deteriorated. They were being billeted in an office building behind the hotel that had been requisitioned by Chris Matthews, on Arley's orders, and which was well away from the dozens of camera crews.

Arley was going to need to call the SAS leader and give him a briefing, but she decided to have that cigarette first, figuring she'd earned it. 'Anyone fancy joining me for a smoke?' she asked the room.

'Sorry,' said Will, still tapping away on his PC and pulling a face like he'd just smelled something bad. 'I've never smoked.'

'I've quit,' said Janine ruefully, 'and it was so bloody hard, I don't dare go back to it.'

Apparently, smoking was against Riz's religion, or so he said, and Cheney only smoked these days when he had a drink. 'Although if things deteriorate too much I might end up doing both,' he added, giving her one of his winning smiles, which she made a point of ignoring, so as not to give him the wrong idea.

Thinking that she really ought to quit herself, and that the youth of today were turning into lightweights, Arley went outside, walking away from the office and the police vehicles as she lit up.

In the near distance, the Stanhope rose high above the other buildings, with lights on on every floor, and Arley thanked God neither she nor her loved ones were trapped in there. She was hopeful that a Mumbai-style massacre might still be averted, particularly if negotiations continued, but even so, she couldn't begin to imagine the terror the hostages were feeling. It was her job to get them out of the hotel safely. It was, she thought, as she took a long draw on the cigarette, a daunting responsibility.

Her mobile rang, and she sighed. Back to work, she thought, wondering what had happened now.

It was Howard, her husband. She'd left a message on his phone close to two hours back now to let him know that she was involved in the siege at the Stanhope, and it had taken him this long to get back to her. Doubtless he'd been busy getting supper ready and hadn't wanted to disturb her. He was good like that, and she realized, almost with surprise, that she was pleased to be hearing from him.

But the voice at the other end wasn't Howard's. It belonged to a man with a foreign accent.

'We have your family,' he told her.

43

Arley felt a physical lurch of terror that almost knocked her over. 'Hold on,' she said, moving further away from the police vehicles towards a nearby oak tree.

'Your au pair is dead,' continued the caller, his tone matter of fact, 'and your husband, son and daughter are being held in a secure location a long way from where I'm calling now.'

'What do you want?' Arley whispered into the phone.

'I'm going to send you a short video of your children with the au pair. Then I'm going to call you back. In the meantime, do not try to trace me. I am in contact every fifteen minutes with the man holding your family. If he doesn't hear from me for more than half an hour he has strict instructions to execute all of them.'

'I'm not going to do anything stupid, I promise,' she said, angered at the note of pleading that had crept into her voice. But she was already talking into a dead phone.

For perhaps the longest few minutes of her life she stood in the cold staring at the phone, ignoring everything around her, before it bleeped to say she'd received a text message from Howard with a video attached. Taking a deep breath, she opened the message and pressed play on the video.

It lasted barely thirty seconds but it was enough to confirm that the people holding her family were utterly ruthless. The frightened expressions on the faces of her children as they were forced to sit either side of Magda's dead body made her want to throw up.

Don't panic, she told herself. Think.

The phone rang again, Howard's name and a photo of him pulling one of his stupid faces coming up on the screen.

'You've seen the video?' asked the caller.

'Yes. What do you want?'

'I understand you are in charge of the police operation at the Stanhope Hotel.' It was a statement, not a question. 'You're going to find out the SAS's plan of attack, and when they're aiming to penetrate the building. If your information is correct, your family will be released unharmed.'

'There is no plan of attack,' she whispered urgently

into the phone, stepping even further into the shadows of the oak tree. 'We're still at the negotiating stage.'

'There will be an attack,' said the man with a confidence that scared her. 'And you will find out the details of it.'

'I don't think you understand. Even if some kind of attack did go ahead – and there is no guarantee that it will – it would be a military operation, and under military jurisdiction, which means I won't be party to any of their plans.'

'Then you will need to find a way, Mrs Dale. This phone is now going to be switched off. I will call you again when the time is right. If you ever want to see your family again, you'll tell us everything we need to know.'

44

19.12

The Park View Restaurant, usually a busy yet relaxed place full of the buzz of conversation, was hot and silent, and the exotic smells of Asia and the East had been replaced with the stench of fear, human sweat and, in the last few minutes, urine.

Elena glanced up at the two guards. The taller of the two was sitting down with his foot dangling above the detonation pedal for the bomb that had been placed in the middle of the group, only a few feet from where Elena herself sat. He hadn't said a word the whole time they'd been here, but was still watching them carefully, while occasionally checking the TV screen on the table next to him, which appeared to be showing news coverage from outside the hotel. The other guard was smaller and wiry. He had a pronounced limp and he spoke with a Scandinavian accent. He seemed more agitated and unpleasant, and was often limping up and down the far end of the room. When the mother of the youngest child had requested permission to take her to the toilet, the Scandinavian had refused, saying that no one was allowed to go to the toilet. The mother had started to plead, looking over at Elena for support, but the Scandinavian had marched over to where the family were sitting and pointed the gun at the child. 'Keep arguing and I shoot her dead right here,' he spat. His words had been delivered like a boast, as if he was proud of his cruelty, and when the poor child started to sob Elena had so, so wanted to stand up and say something.

But she hadn't. She'd stayed silent. And so had the mother. For the last few minutes Elena had watched as she comforted the child, whispering soothing words to her.

At least now everyone was calm again, and the Scandinavian guard had left the room, which had eased the tense atmosphere a little. Elena was thankful that the blinds were pulled down on the windows so that the world's TV cameras couldn't see them. She wondered how many people were right now looking at the normally beautiful image of the Stanhope Hotel at night. There would be millions of them. Hundreds of millions. They would probably include her own family. And Rod. God alone knew how worried they'd all be, although it would be nothing to the fear she was experiencing. Because the thing was, the people holding them were killers. Most worrying of all, Elena could see no joy or hope in any of their eyes, only the cold certainty that they were prepared to die. Possibly even looking forward to it.

She shifted position on the floor so that she was sitting with her arms clasped round her knees. She was trying to get comfortable, and ignoring the thirst that was beginning to gnaw at her, the result of dehydration from the previous night's drinking session. God, how long ago that seemed now.

The man next to Elena, the one who'd come to the hotel to commit suicide and who'd fashioned a noose in his room, caught her eye and gave her a reassuring smile. They'd barely looked at each other this past hour, and hadn't exchanged as much as a word. All that time he'd sat unmoving with his head bowed.

She smiled back, curiosity getting the better of her. Here was a normal-looking, quite attractive middle-aged man and he'd come here to die a lonely, bleak death.

'Are you here alone?' she whispered to him, even though she knew the answer. She glanced up as she spoke to make sure the tall guard hadn't heard her. It didn't look like he had.

He nodded, looking ashamed. 'Yes, I am.'

They were silent for a few moments after that, then he sighed, clearly wanting to unburden himself. 'I have to admit, I came here to die,' he whispered. 'But not like this.'

'Forgive me for asking, but why do you want to die?'

'Because I'm going to die soon anyway. I've got cancer.'

Elena's jaw tightened. 'I'm sorry. I shouldn't have asked.'

'It's OK,' he said, and they both fell silent.

'What's your name?' she asked him eventually, wanting to keep the conversation going, if only to take her mind off everything else.

'Martin.'

'I'm Elena.'

'So I see,' he said, pointing at her nametag. 'I'm sorry about choosing your hotel to finish things in,' he continued. 'I didn't want to inconvenience anyone, but the Stanhope has a very special place in my heart.'

Elena was curious. 'Why?'

He paused. 'I came here with a girl once. Twenty-two years ago now. Her name was Carrie. She was the love of my life.' He shook his head sadly. 'Christ, I should have stayed with her. I know it sounds clichéd, but don't ever let anything get in the way of love, Elena. It's the most important thing there is.'

She thought of Rod, and it made her feel happy for the first time since this had begun. 'I know.'

'You're engaged?' he whispered, looking down at her new ring.

'Yes. He proposed last night.'

'God, I'm sorry. Not that you got engaged, but ...' He looked around. 'Because of all this. You don't deserve it.'

'None of us do.'

'What's going on over there?' The voice cut through the quiet of the room like a knife. 'You were told to keep your mouths shut.' It was the Scandinavian guard. He'd come back into the room and was limping over to them, the rifle out in front of him, his eyes blazing with anger beneath the balaclava.

Elena felt a flash of sheer terror and bowed her head, hoping he would go away.

He didn't. He stopped in front of them, the rifle pointing down at her. 'What were you talking about?'

'I was just asking if she was OK,' said Martin, who'd bowed his head too. 'That's all.'

'What did I tell you, shithead? No talking.' He kicked Martin hard in the chest, knocking him backwards. Martin went down hard on to his side, gasping for air, and the Scandinavian immediately kicked him again. 'Talk again and I'll really make you suffer,' he sneered, before turning away.

'You coward,' said Elena, unable to stop the words coming out of her mouth.

The Scandinavian stopped. Then, very slowly, turned round. 'What did you say?' he hissed, raising the rifle and pushing the end of the barrel against her forehead.

Elena swallowed. 'He's ill. And he can't fight back.'

'Please, leave her,' she heard Martin say, his voice full of tension. 'She didn't mean it.'

For several seconds, nothing happened. The Scandinavian didn't move, and Elena realized with a growing dread that he was debating whether or not to pull the trigger. She closed her eyes. If the end was about to come, then she prayed it would be quick. In the background, she could hear one of the children sobbing again.

Then she heard the ding of the kitchen lift, and the door from the kitchen opening. Instinctively she opened her eyes and saw the terrorist leader, Wolf, walk into the room accompanied by the woman from downstairs. Both of them were masked and armed – he with an assault rifle, she with a handgun – and right then, Elena was hugely relieved to see them, because the Scandinavian immediately lowered his gun and retreated as Wolf beckoned him over.

There followed a hushed debate in the corner involving the four hostage-takers. While this was going on, Elena leaned down and helped Martin back up. His face was twisted in pain, and he'd gone so pale that she thought he might vomit.

Still struggling for breath, he gestured for her to come closer. 'You shouldn't have done that,' he whispered. 'You could have been killed.'

'I hate bullies,' she whispered back, putting a hand on his arm.

Wolf came forward so that he was standing in front

of the hostages. It was clear he was about to make an announcement. 'As a gesture of goodwill, and in an effort to help with negotiations, we're going to release the children.'

The mother with the little girl who'd wanted to go to the toilet gasped, and clutched her child even closer.

'They are to come with us now. They will not be harmed and they will be released through the front doors of the hotel within the next fifteen minutes.'

For a few seconds, nobody moved.

'Do you not want them to be released?' Wolf shouted. 'Would you rather they stayed here?'

The mother who'd gasped raised a hand. 'Are parents able to go with their children? My daughter needs me.'

'No. They go alone. But we will release them safely. You have our word.'

The mother started to say something else, then thought better of it. Holding her daughter close, she whispered something in her ear, tears streaming down her face. The daughter immediately tightened her grip, but the mother pushed her away, promising that they'd be together again very soon. Across the room, three other sets of parents said goodbye to their children: the eight-year-old girl, the boy of about twelve in his school uniform, and a Japanese boy closer to sixteen.

'He's not going,' said Wolf, pointing to the Japanese boy as he got up.

The boy stopped, looking unsure what to do, and both his parents got to their feet.

'Please, sir,' said his mother, 'let him go. He's very young.'

'Not young enough. In my country, he'd be considered a man. Sit down, all of you. Now.'

The mother kept pleading, holding on to her son, her manner bordering on the hysterical, but Wolf stared at her coldly and told her that he'd shoot them unless they did as they'd been instructed. The husband gently took hold of his wife and son, a sorrowful expression on his face, and they sat down slowly, the mother's sobs quickly subsiding.

It was a heartrending scene, and one that affected all of the hostages, many of whom had tears in their eyes, but it seemed to make no difference to the terrorists. What shocked Elena the most was the expression on the face of the female terrorist as she viewed the pathetic group of frightened children as they clustered together, the two little girls holding the hands of the older boy. It was as if she had a heart made entirely from stone, and it made Elena wonder what could possibly have made someone so pretty on the outside become so ugly within.

And then they were all gone, leaving behind only a hot, frightened silence.

45

Arley Dale stood in the cold night air of Hyde Park, still stunned by the phone call she'd just received. In the space of a few cruel minutes her whole world had become a nightmare from which it seemed there was no escape.

If she told the man holding her children the details and timing of any SAS entry into the Stanhope she would be betraying them, perhaps even sending the soldiers to their deaths. She would effectively be committing treason. She would also almost certainly be found out, which would mean losing her career, her life as she knew it, and her liberty. Even if a judge took into account the extenuating circumstances behind her betrayal, she could still spend the next ten years of her life in prison.

But if she didn't do what the caller wanted, what then? There was, of course, the possibility that if she told her bosses they could keep things under wraps while the full resources of the Met were thrown into the hunt for Howard and the children. But the problem was, her family could be anywhere. The only thing she knew for certain was the people they were dealing with were highly organized and utterly ruthless. They'd planted bombs in civilian areas; they'd gunned down members of the public at the Stanhope; they'd even murdered her own au pair, Magda, and forced the children to pose with her corpse. There was therefore absolutely nothing to suggest that they wouldn't do the same to Howard, Oliver and India if it suited them. And as soon as they realized that she'd given them false information about any planned attack (which she'd have to do if she confided in Commissioner Phillips) they would take their revenge.

She also knew that, even if she did cooperate, there was absolutely no guarantee that her loved ones would be released. In fact, it would be far simpler for the terrorists to kill them, and perhaps even bury them somewhere they'd never be discovered.

She couldn't believe what was happening to her. It all seemed so bloody surreal. How on earth had they got to her family? How did they even know she'd be involved with the Stanhope Hotel siege? It wasn't as if the Met's major incident command structure was decided in advance. It simply depended on who was available and on duty when an incident actually happened. But they had known. Just as they seemed to know that the SAS would be launching a rescue operation later that night.

Arley felt physically sick as she lit another cigarette with shaking hands, and looked over towards the incident room. She was going to have to go back there soon, act as if nothing had happened and run a huge and stressful operation.

She pictured Oliver and India. How would she ever live with herself if they died? She thought of Howard too. She loved him too, of course, but not in the same desperate, all-encompassing way she loved her children.

She dragged hard on the cigarette. Thinking. Weighing up her options.

What fucking options?

Unless . . .

She looked down at the phone in her gloved hand. There was one person who might be able to help her; one person she felt she could trust with this, the darkest of secrets.

It was a hard call to make, but as Arley flicked through her contacts until she found the number she was looking for, she knew it was worth the risk.

In the end, she'd destroy anyone, whoever it was, to save her children.

46

Tina Boyd had never been a conventional police officer. In a career of sailing close to the wind she'd been shot twice, kidnapped once, involved in cases that had led to the murders of both a colleague and a lover, and even killed violent murderers herself on two occasions (one case had officially been deemed an accident; the other, nobody but her knew about – although both men had deserved what they got in her opinion). She'd also knowingly planted evidence on suspects, had assaulted quite a few, been suspended twice, and had finally been unceremoniously fired earlier in the year after an unofficial case she was working on in the Philippines had ended with a lot of dead bodies, and even more unanswered questions. In short, Tina Boyd was trouble to anyone mad enough to get involved with her.

But she had one unique selling point, which was

the reason she'd lasted as long as she had in the Met: she got results. Not necessarily by the book. Often not even within the boundaries of the law. But the statistics didn't lie. Of the thirty-nine major investigations she'd been a part of, or had led, including several involving multiple counts of murder, her clear-up rate was one hundred per cent. Even the most cock-eyed commentator couldn't argue with that.

Ultimately, though, nothing had been able to stand in the way of her own volatility and lack of discipline, and now, nine months on from parting acrimoniously with the Met, she was scraping by doing unofficial private detective work, and the occasional bit of consultancy for film companies looking for her 'unique' take on life as a police officer. But ask her if she regretted anything and her answer would always be the same.

Everything I did, I did for the right reasons.

Although, as she sat in her living room watching events unfold at the Stanhope Hotel on the TV, Tina realized how much she missed her old life.

She'd been planning on making dinner, but found it impossible to drag herself away from the rolling coverage of the siege and bomb attacks. The speed with which things were happening was addictive. Tina had taken part in a few sieges in her time, and for the most part it was simply a matter of waiting until the hostage-takers got bored, hungry, or too depressed to carry on. But this was different. These people really knew what they were doing, taking advantage of the lax security in the capital to launch a series of spectacular attacks. So far no one seemed to know very much about them, although, as usual, there was no shortage of talking heads popping up to offer theories. The consensus seemed to be that they were foreign extremists taking revenge on the innocent in retaliation for British involvement in foreign wars.

Tina's mobile rang just as the PM appeared on the screen for a news conference, adopting a suitably Churchillian pose for the cameras but not quite managing to hide the strain on his face.

She picked it up and frowned at the screen.

Arley Dale.

They'd been friends once – or perhaps acquaintances was a better word for it. Tina didn't have many friends. In fact, she was actually surprised she still had Arley's number stored. They hadn't spoken in months.

She was just about to click on the answer button when the call ended, leaving Tina wondering whether Arley had called her by mistake. They'd met a few years earlier at a function honouring special achievements by women and had spent much of the evening standing outside smoking, hitting it off straight away. Tina liked Arley's bluntness and confidence, and the fact that she didn't take crap from anyone. They'd kept in touch, gone out for the occasional drink, including one night when they both got so hammered neither of them could remember how they'd got home.

When she'd been suspended eighteen months earlier, Arley had stood up and supported her, saying that the Met needed more strong women like Tina Boyd. But she'd been noticeable by her absence back in February when Tina had finally got the push, which was fair enough. You can only stick your neck out so far when the other person insists on hanging one-handed from the parapet. Especially when you're a high-flying DAC in the Met, with the job of being the force's first female commissioner in your sights.

And now here was Arley calling her, out of the blue, and just as suddenly hanging up. Tina was surprised she wasn't involved in dealing with today's attacks. She was the kind of high-profile copper who was always in the midst of the action.

Like Tina had once been.

The phone rang again, and Arley's name flashed across the screen for a second time.

Tina picked up. 'Arley? How are you?'

There was a pause. Three seconds. The sound of breathing down the other end of the line. Then five words, laced with quiet desperation.

'You've got to help me.'

47

Arley took a deep breath. She was taking an immense risk confiding in someone like Tina Boyd, a woman for whom the term 'loose cannon' might as well have been invented; but she knew too that she was running extremely short on alternatives. 'I'm in real trouble,' she whispered into the phone, keeping one eye on the incident room, twenty yards away, 'and I don't know where else to turn.'

'What is it?'

There was no sarcasm in Tina's voice, even though she and Arley hadn't spoken for a long time. Just genuine interest.

So Arley told her everything that had happened, keeping it as brief and businesslike as possible.

'Jesus,' said Tina when she'd finished. 'You've got to tell your superiors. You can't deal with something like this on your own.'

'I can't, Tina. The government will sacrifice my family if they have to. They won't let their safety stand in the way of an assault on the hotel.'

'But why are you calling me?'

'I want you to find them. I want you to find my husband and children. I know it's a long shot—'

'It's more than a long shot, Arley. It's a physical impossibility. I'm one woman. One woman who no longer has a warrant card or access to any police resources.'

'I've got access to resources.' Arley could hear the desperation in her own voice. 'I'll give you every assistance I can.'

'We haven't spoken for nearly a year.'

'I know we haven't. And I know I should have helped you over that Philippines thing. But you're a bloody good detective, Tina. One of the best I've ever come across. And you get things done. Where are you now?'

'I'm at home.'

'That's near Ridge, isn't it?'

'That's right.'

'Well, that's only twenty minutes away from me. I'm in Mill Hill.'

'I know where you are. You could have called, or visited, or something, couldn't you? In an unofficial capacity, so that it wouldn't have affected your career.'

'I'm sorry. I truly am.' Arley looked towards the

incident room door, knowing she was going to have to go back soon. 'But they have my family. Can you imagine what that must feel like?'

'I still don't see what I can do.'

'I know I'm putting you on the spot, Tina. I know I'm asking you to risk everything. But I'm completely trapped here, and you're the only person I could think of to ask. The only one I know who might just be able to find them.'

There was a silence at the other end.

Arley waited, not knowing what else she could say.

'When did you last have contact with them?' Tina asked eventually.

'This morning. I left the house at seven thirty. They were all there then.'

'Nothing suspicious? No unfamiliar vehicles? Anything like that?'

Arley wrenched her mind back to earlier that morning. 'No. Nothing.'

Tina was silent again. 'I'll go over there. But listen, Arley. I would think really carefully about telling your bosses about this because the chances are I'll turn up nothing. You have to understand that.'

'I do. Just please, please, do what you can. And call me, will you? As soon as you find out anything at all.'

Arley ended the call, dabbed the corners of her eyes with her sleeves, pulled some more cold air through her nose into her lungs, and turned back towards the incident room.

48

Scope sat on the floor against the bed, Ethan beside him. Abby had drifted off to sleep, and after checking that she was all right, Scope had let her be. Although it was clear she was still in a lot of pain, the bleeding had stopped and it seemed she'd stabilized.

'When are the police coming?' Ethan asked for the hundredth time.

Scope knew how he felt. The slow turn of the minutes was hugely frustrating. 'They'll come as soon as they can,' he answered, yet again. 'They just need to find out where the bad guys are so they can come in here and save us.'

'They need to hurry up. Mom's really sick.' Ethan's face was white and strained. He took her hand and tried to wake her.

'Leave her now, Ethan,' said Scope gently. 'She's resting.'

Ethan looked at him, his gaze imploring. 'She can't die, though. She can't.'

'She won't.'

'I wish my dad was here.'

'Where is he?'

'He left home. Last year.'

'Do you still see him?'

Ethan shook his head. 'No. Mom says he still loves me, but he's very busy. She says when he's less busy, he'll come and see me. He calls me sometimes, though.'

'I'm sure he misses you.'

'I miss him.'

Scope wished he'd seen more of his own daughter when he'd had the chance. And yet, like Ethan's dad, he'd left home and his family, and since then he'd lost count of the number of times he'd wondered how different things might have been if they'd all stayed together. He remembered Mary Ann as a laughing two-year-old running round the back garden on tiny legs while he and Jennifer looked on with the broad, dopey smiles of new parents full of love for the beautiful creature they'd created.

'Are you OK?' asked Ethan.

Scope smiled down at him. 'Yeah, I'm fine. I was just thinking.'

'What about?'

For a moment, Scope considered telling him. It was almost like he wanted to unburden himself, which came as a surprise to him. He'd never been much of a talker. 'Nothing much,' he answered.

Silence.

'Grandpa brought us here as a treat. I've never been to London before. And I don't want to come again now. Never.'

'Where are you from?'

'America.'

'I guessed that. Whereabouts in America?'

'Florida.' Ethan looked at Scope again, his face calmer. 'Near Disneyworld. Have you ever been to Disneyworld?'

'No, can't say I ever have.'

'Where are you from? You've got a funny accent.'

'A place called Manchester, and it's not funny.'

'What are you doing here?'

Scope thought of the three men upstairs. 'Visiting friends.'

Ethan was silent a moment, his face scrunched up in thought. 'Why are those men killing people?' he said at last. 'They killed Grandpa. And the man in the mask wanted to kill Mom and me too. Why?'

'Some people like hurting other people for no reason. There aren't very many of them, and you were very unlucky to have run into some today. I'm sorry for you.'

Ethan's eyes flashed. 'I'm glad you killed them,' he said defiantly.

Scope nodded. So was he.

'Are you a policeman?'

'No.'

'A soldier?'

'You ask a lot of questions.'

'I think you're a soldier,' said Ethan knowingly. 'Thank you for helping us.'

Scope shrugged. 'You should never walk by and leave people who are in trouble.'

But even as he said this, he wasn't sure he believed it. Helping Abby and Ethan had already caused him a hell of a lot of grief. Quite how much depended on what happened when – or, of course, if – they got out.

Scope's attention was caught by something on the TV. The camera had suddenly panned from a reporter to the front entrance of the hotel. As Scope watched, the far left door was slowly opened and a masked terrorist in navy overalls appeared in the doorway with a small group of children. The terrorist then disappeared back inside, locking the door and leaving the kids standing on the front step, holding hands and looking confused.

As the camera panned back to reveal more of the scene, two armed police officers, accompanied by a pair of paramedics, rushed over, and led the children away from the hotel entrance, the camera following the group as they went behind the cordon before disappearing into a mêlée of emergency services people.

'What's happening?' asked Ethan, who was also watching the TV.

Scope got to his feet and stretched his legs. 'I think they might be releasing some of the hostages.'

'Can we go too?' For the first time, there was excitement in Ethan's voice.

'I'm not sure,' said Scope, trying to figure out a plan of action, knowing that there was no guarantee they would let Ethan go. But knowing too that he couldn't simply sit here waiting for events to unfold, not with Abby injured and in need of insulin.

Scope sighed. The last thing he wanted to do was draw more attention to himself, not after what had gone on upstairs. But it looked as though he didn't have much choice.

49

In the incident room, Riz Mohammed was grinning as he and the others watched the screen which showed the three children being released.

'Well done, Riz,' said John Cheney, patting him on the back. 'That was some good negotiating.'

The two technicians, Janine and Will, were both on their feet, smiling and adding their own words of encouragement, and Arley had to force herself to do the same, even though she was finding it almost impossible to concentrate.

'The children are going to need debriefing as soon as they've been checked out at St Mary's,' she said. 'John, can you call your people at CTC and get them to send their people over there, and then let us know what, if anything, they find out?'

Cheney nodded and picked up one of the phones, and Arley was amazed at her own capacity for carrying on in the midst of this, the worst personal crisis of her life.

One of the secure phones rang in the incident room and Janine picked it up. 'Gold for you, ma'am.'

Decision time.

Arley picked up the phone at the far end of the office and got Janine to patch him through, turning her back on the others in an effort to get some sort of privacy.

'It's good news about the children being released,' said Commissioner Phillips without preamble. 'Congratulations are in order to you and your negotiator.'

Tell him. Tell him now.

'Thank you, sir,' she replied, her voice sounding hollow.

'But the PM and I are still very concerned that your negotiator hasn't yet been able to speak to Michael Prior. We need to find out urgently whether he's been compromised.'

They've got my husband and children. What do I care about that?

'I can understand that, sir, but if we insist, we risk antagonizing them or, worse still, letting them know that we're really worried about what he might say.'

'Which is why we're preparing for a possible armed intervention.'

Oh Jesus. The assault the caller was talking about.

'Are we handing over control of the scene to the

military?' she asked, unable to keep the undercurrent of fear out of her voice.

'Not yet. The PM's very keen for a negotiated settlement.'

'So am I. Especially now that we've secured the release of some of the hostages peacefully.'

'But we're also going to have to review our options if Michael Prior remains unaccounted for. Do we have any news on where he might be in the building?'

'According to calls made to his phone, he was initially being held in one of the guest rooms somewhere on the third floor, but the phone signal was last picked up on the ground floor. We don't know where the phone is now, because we no longer have coverage within the building. And, of course, there's no guarantee it's with him anyway.'

'So, we don't have a clue, basically,' said Phillips, sounding irritated.

'No,' she responded tightly, 'I'm afraid we don't, sir.'

A silence stretched between them. 'Are you all right, Arley? You sound very tense.'

Last chance. Tell him.

'It's a tense situation, sir.'

'Well, you were picked because you're calm and level-headed, and it would be a great help to all of us if you didn't forget that.'

'I won't.'

Phillips sighed. 'Carry on doing what you can to

locate Prior, and keep me informed of any progress, however small. No one wants a bloodbath, which may well happen if the SAS are sent in, but if the terrorists don't let us talk to Prior, then I'm afraid it may become inevitable.'

50

Tina Boyd drove her car past the Dale family home as slowly as she could. There were no lights on inside, but that was to be expected. If the kidnappers were holding the family there, they wouldn't want to advertise their presence, although Tina didn't think they'd risk staying put with three hostages. It would be far easier to move them to an undisclosed location, just in case Arley didn't choose to cooperate, or came here looking for them herself. She also noticed something else. None of the curtains at the front of the house had been drawn, which was the first thing you'd do if you were a kidnapper and didn't want anyone seeing inside.

An Audi estate, which Tina presumed belonged to Arley's husband Howard, was the only car parked in the driveway. She continued driving, checking to see if any of the cars parked on either side of the road were occupied. She didn't think the kidnappers had the necessary resources to be keeping a watch on the house, but it paid to be thorough.

When Tina was satisfied that the street was clear, she found a parking space about thirty yards further on and got out, shivering in the cold night air. She walked back towards the Dales' house, trying to look as natural as possible – just another commuter coming home after a late night at the office – but instead of turning into their drive, she turned into the one next door. She crept by the side of the house, ignoring the lights in the window, and tried the side gate, which was locked. Hoping there wasn't a dog on the other side, she clambered over it and into the back garden, thankfully without the accompaniment of angry barking.

A high evergreen hedge separated the two properties, and Tina had to force her way through it like some kind of rainforest explorer, before emerging on the other side at the back of the Dales' house. There were no curtains closed on this side either. She stayed in the shadows of the hedge for a full minute, watching for any signs of life.

Nothing and no one moved. There were no lights coming from inside to signify someone watching the TV. No sounds either. Just the distant hum of traffic and the occasional plane rumbling through the clouds overhead. Tina had been on enough surveillance jobs in her life to know when a place was empty. Human beings can't stay still for long, even when they're trying to.

She gave it another thirty seconds, then slowly approached the nearest window, which looked straight into an expansive kitchen diner.

Straight away she saw the body lying there. Or, more accurately, she saw a pair of legs, a pair of forearms, and half a torso lying across the chequered floor, the remainder hidden by the kitchen sink unit. A dark pool of blood had formed round the upper part of the body and the hands were dipped in it, the fingers outstretched. Tina had never seen a photo of Howard but she was certain it was him. And it was clear from the amount of blood that he'd been lying there some time.

She took a step back. This was the time to call the police. If she went inside, she'd be contaminating a crime scene, and giving herself a whole lot of trouble. It was also possible that the kids were still in the house – and if they were, they were almost certainly dead too. She could feel her mobile in her pocket, and she almost took it out to make the call, but stopped herself.

With a long sigh, she put on her gloves and retrieved the spare keys from the potting shed, where Arley had said they'd be, trying them one after the other in the kitchen door until it finally opened. As she stepped inside, she was greeted by an empty, all-pervading silence and the telltale sour smell of death

– something she'd experienced too many times before, and which she'd never managed to get used to. Holding her breath, she crouched down beside the body, avoiding stepping in the blood, and felt for a pulse as a simple formality. She wasn't surprised when there was no sign of one.

To make absolutely sure this was Arley's husband, Tina crept into the hallway looking for family photos, which was when she saw the second body, propped up against the wall. This would be Magda, the Dale family au pair. Arley had told Tina that she'd been killed by the kidnappers, although she hadn't mentioned that her body had been left here.

There was a professional family portrait on the opposite wall. Arley, her two teenage children, and Howard, a big bluff smiling man standing a good head taller than the others, and without doubt the corpse she'd just seen in the kitchen.

'Jesus,' whispered Tina in the gloom, wondering what the hell she was getting involved with here, but also feeling the kind of intense righteous anger she hadn't experienced in a long, long time. She wanted to get the people responsible for this. She wanted to make them pay.

With a renewed sense of purpose, she searched the rest of the house, but there was no sign of the two children. Both they and the kidnappers were gone, just as she'd expected. She checked for anything that might give her some clue as to the kidnappers' identity, or their final destination, but nothing sprang out at her.

All of which left Tina with a stark choice. The chances of her finding Arley's children were slim in the extreme. The best course of action was to persuade Arley to tell her colleagues what was going on. But she wasn't at all sure that Arley would. And Tina knew she was almost certainly right not to. Neither the Met nor the government would put her two children before the lives of the hostages in the Stanhope.

Tina let herself out of the house, pulling from the pocket of her jeans a fake warrant card she used sometimes for PI work.

She'd made her decision.

51

This was the dead time. The time in the middle of the operation when they were simply waiting around and guarding the hostages, counting down the hours until they were ready to make their next move.

In the ballroom, Fox was back on guard duty with Bear. They'd both just eaten some pot noodles in the satellite kitchen, during which time Bear had complained more than once about Cat's volatility. The whole room had heard her scream when she was told what had happened to her brother, and since then the rage had been coming off her in waves, and she'd hardly spoken a word. Fox had told Bear not to worry, that as long as she didn't go off on a one-woman hunt for the man responsible and get herself killed, everything would be OK. Bear had calmed down, but he still seemed spooked, as he had been ever since he'd found out about what happened to Leopard and

Panther. Fox was more sanguine. The man responsible for their deaths was certainly dangerous but the chances were that he was hiding out in one of the rooms and would stay out of their way.

Fox was more worried about the atmosphere in the ballroom, which was tense. He could see that some of the hostages were agitated, while others seemed to be looking around for ways to escape. Clearly they were beginning to forget what had happened to some of their fellow hostages earlier when they'd made their bids for freedom.

He and Bear were sitting on chairs twenty feet apart, and well back from the hostages. Bear's foot rested on the detonation pedal for the bomb that sat in the middle of the hostages, and Fox hoped that none of them would work out that there was no way he or Bear would detonate it, given that they were sat right in the path of any shrapnel. In fact, the bomb, like all but two of the others, was set to timer and would explode at 23.00 hours, not before. Both the pedal and the det cords were there for show only.

One of the more troublesome-looking hostages, a young stocky guy dressed like an American high school jock, caught Fox's eye, and started to stand up.

Fox shouted at him to sit down.

The guy went down on one knee. 'I need the toilet, badly,' he said, his accent public school.

'I don't care.'

'Come on. Cut me some slack. Please.' There was a

confidence to his voice that made some of the hostages take notice.

Fox knew a show of weakness or indecision here would be fatal. He took his time getting to his feet, then took two steps forward and very slowly put the AK-47 to his shoulder, pointing it at the young man's head. When he spoke, his words cut across the room like a knife. 'I've already shot two people downstairs. Do you think it'll bother me if I shoot a third? Your life means absolutely nothing to me. If it means anything to you, then keep still and shut up. Understand?'

The hostage nodded, every ounce of confidence now gone.

'Good. That goes for the rest of you too. Stay silent and you stay alive.'

As Fox sat down, Bear gave him a supportive nod. Bear had always looked to Fox for leadership, ever since he'd served under him in the army. Not for the first time, Fox wondered whether Bear ever resented the fact that he'd been disfigured for life while Fox – who should, by rights, have been blown to pieces – had escaped the IED largely unscathed. If he did, then he hid it very well.

Fox took a brief look over his shoulder towards the kitchen where Wolf and Cat were. God knows what they were doing in there, but as long as it wasn't anything stupid, like starting a hunt for their fugitive, he didn't mind. In the meantime, he had something else he had to do.

Still keeping a firm grip on his rifle, he slid the pack from his back and, as casually as possible, removed his laptop. He wanted to check that the individual he'd left a message for earlier in the drafts section of the hotmail account had received it and responded with a message of his own.

But when he tried to go online, the computer didn't respond. He tried again, keeping his face impassive, but it definitely wasn't working.

The bastards had cut them off.

This was a real problem. He wasn't so worried about his own private message. He knew it was there, so a response was less important. However, one of the key components of their plan was knowing where and when the security forces would launch their attack. This information was also going to be provided through the drafts section of a separate hotmail account so that it couldn't be read by the authorities. But if they didn't have an internet connection, they wouldn't get it, and they'd lose a key advantage.

He tried one more time, got the same result, and replaced the laptop in the backpack as he got to his feet.

Bear gave him a questioning look. 'Is there a problem?' he whispered as Fox crouched down next to him.

Fox knew there was no point spooking him further. 'I just need to see Wolf quickly. I'll be back in a minute.' And then louder, so the hostages could hear, he said: 'Anyone moves, put a hole in them.'

He turned and walked quickly towards the kitchen, knowing that they had to get the internet back on, and fast.

Even if it meant killing a hostage in front of the world's cameras to make the authorities act.

52

'Did you manage to get the insulin pens?' Abby asked groggily. She looked tired but in OK shape, and was drinking from a bottle of water while Ethan knelt beside her, holding her hand.

'I'm afraid they weren't there,' said Scope, shutting the door behind him and putting the chair back against it.

'But they were in my black handbag by the side of the bed. I'm sure of it.'

'Your handbag was on the floor, and it looked like someone had been through it.'

'Who?'

'I'm guessing one of the terrorists. He was probably looking for clues about who killed his friends.'

A wave of panic crossed Abby's face, and Scope could see that Ethan was scared too.

'Don't worry,' he said. 'We'll sort something out.'

'What, though? This siege looks like it's going to go on a ways longer yet, and I'm going to need that insulin soon, as well as something to eat, otherwise my blood sugar levels are going to start getting way too high.'

'What happens then?'

Abby looked down at Ethan. It was clear she didn't want to worry him. 'If they keep going up, then it could be a problem, but I should be good for a few hours yet.' She squeezed her son's hand and forced a smile.

'Mom, you'll be OK,' said Ethan quietly, before turning to Scope. 'Won't she?'

Scope nodded, but something in Abby's expression worried him. He didn't know a lot about Type One diabetes, but he was pretty sure the consequences would be serious if she didn't get her insulin soon. 'Leave it with me,' he said. 'I'll sort it.'

He grabbed the hotel phone, walked it as far as possible from the bed, and dialled the emergency services.

As soon as the operator picked up, Scope asked to speak to a paramedic. At first, the guy on the other end was reluctant to put him through, but Scope wasn't taking no for an answer. 'This is a matter of life and death,' he hissed into the phone. 'If this woman dies because you wouldn't help, then I'm going to come looking for you, and you're going to pay, do you understand that?'

'There's no need for that kind of attitude, sir,' said the operator indignantly, but clearly there was, because two minutes later he was through to a male paramedic who identified himself as Steve.

Scope briefly explained the situation, keeping his voice low. 'We need that insulin fast. She told me she thinks she's good until about ten, so we've got an hour and a half maximum.' This was a lie, but he knew he needed to inject a sense of urgency into the situation.

'Where's the patient's supply?'

'She dropped her bag when she was shot,' answered Scope, avoiding telling the truth, 'and it's not there any more.'

'How much blood has she lost?'

'I don't know, but I got the bleeding under control fast, and I've only had to change the dressing once, so I don't think she's lost that much. Will the blood loss affect how soon she needs her next dose?'

'I honestly don't know, but it might have some effect.'

'So we need to move fast. In a hotel this size they must keep medical supplies somewhere on-site. I just need to find out where.'

'I can't help you there,' responded Steve.

'That's where you're wrong. You can find out for me.'

'But I'm nowhere near the Stanhope.'

'One thing I can guarantee about this siege is that

someone in the emergency services will be in touch with the hotel's owners, and they'll know. You've got to ask to be put through to someone at the scene.'

'It'll take time.'

Scope looked over his shoulder and saw mother and son staring up at him expectantly. Abby still looked OK, but for how much longer was anyone's guess. He gave them both a reassuring smile before turning away. 'We haven't got time, Steve,' he whispered. 'There's a woman in here who's going to die if she doesn't get her insulin, and her eight-year-old son's going to have to witness it.'

Steve sighed. 'I'll see what I can do, but it's not going to happen just like that. This whole thing is bedlam at the moment, and I'm only a lowly paramedic.'

'Just do what you can, and do it fast. Have you got a number I can get you on?'

Steve hesitated for a moment, then gave Scope his mobile phone number.

'I'll call you in fifteen minutes,' Scope told him, hanging up the phone before Steve had a chance to protest.

53

The SAS team had been billeted two streets south of Park Lane, well away from the TV cameras, which had been placed almost exclusively around the perimeter of Hyde Park from where they had a clear, if distant, shot of the front of the Stanhope.

It was a six-minute walk to the team's temporary base from the mobile incident room but Arley Dale did it in four. It wasn't official protocol for the head of the emergency services to meet face to face with her military counterparts. It would have been far easier to give their leader a briefing on one of the secure phones. But Arley couldn't afford to do it that way. She needed to find out as much information as she could. The lives of her husband and children depended on it.

The office was large and open plan and full of casually dressed men unpacking kit, which included an impressive arsenal of weapons. There must have been a good thirty of them in all that she could see, and they didn't look to her like soldiers. A few of them were talking and joking among themselves, but there was an air of studied concentration about them as they worked, and not one of them glanced up as she walked into the room, even though she was in full dress uniform.

In one corner, a table had been set up and three men, again all casually dressed, were bent over one of three laptops that had been lined up in a row, along with several telephones. One of them was older than the others – probably about forty-five, with greying hair and a lined, weather-beaten face that suggested he spent a lot of time outside. He was dressed in jeans and an open-necked shirt, and there was no sign that he was carrying a weapon.

'Major Standard?'

He looked up and gave her an appraising look.

'I'm DAC Arley Dale,' she said, forcing a smile. 'I'm in charge of the emergency services on the ground.'

'And I'm the man in charge of this lot.' He put out a hand. 'Good to meet you, DAC Dale.'

'Please, call me Arley.'

'Well, Arley, I'd offer you a cup of tea but, as you can see, our kettle hasn't arrived yet. Nor have the chairs.'

'I can't stop. I just wanted to give you a brief face-to-face rundown of what we've got so far.'

Standard nodded, and Arley thought he seemed a

nice guy, which somehow made what she was about to do worse.

'We've had some information,' he said, 'but not a great deal.'

'There isn't a great deal to be had. We've got a previously unknown group of men of Middle Eastern and possibly eastern European origin who are making some very ambitious demands, and who we believe are linked to the bombs at the Westfield and Paddington.'

'Were they suicide bombs?'

'We think one of the two at Paddington was.'

'That makes things a little tricky,' said Standard with admirable understatement. 'Our understanding is that they're holding one group of hostages in a restaurant on the ninth floor.'

'That's right. They've released a handful of children, and we've managed to get some limited information from the oldest of them, a boy of twelve. He says there are about thirty hostages in the restaurant guarded by two terrorists armed with assault rifles. The terrorists are situated near the restaurant entrance, and they have access to a TV showing the news, so they can see what's going on outside. Because they keep the blinds down the whole time, we can't see their exact locations.'

Standard nodded thoughtfully and, though he was trying to hide it, Arley could see he wasn't liking the information he was receiving.

'They also have a rucksack that they claim contains a bomb which they've placed in the middle of the hostages, and one of them always keeps his foot close to the detonator.'

Standard nodded again. 'And there's another group being held in the ballroom on the mezzanine floor. Is that right?'

'That's what we believe, yes, but we have no idea of numbers, of the hostages or the hostage-takers. According to GCHQ, the hostage-takers aren't communicating by radio, and there's no mobile phone signal inside the hotel, so it's impossible to track them. Our negotiations are being held on the telephone in the kitchen next door to the ballroom, so we think that's the terrorist's command centre.'

'And what about our VIP hostage, Michael Prior? Do we have any idea where he's being held?'

Arley shook her head, conscious of how limited their information was. 'All I can tell you is that as of five p.m. he was being held in one of the guest rooms on the third floor at the front of the hotel, but we haven't been able to find out which one because he wasn't booked into the hotel under his own name, and neither his wife nor his office knew he was there. Since then his mobile phone's moved within the building, and it's now been switched off. We've asked the lead hostage-taker for permission to speak to him, but so far it hasn't been forthcoming.'

Standard sighed. 'It sounds like these gentlemen

are very well organized. Not your usual Angry Brigade bunch of extremists. It's clear they've been studying how we operate in these kinds of situations. What about their state of mind? Do they come across as agitated, or desperate?'

'We've been dealing with one man, who calls himself Wolf, and he seems remarkably calm under the circumstances. I'm hoping we can negotiate a peaceful solution.'

'We're all hoping that.'

'We've got the TV cameras well back from the scene and we're operating a complete no-fly zone in central London, but if you go in from the roof or the front, your actions will be seen live on TV. With the technology they've got these days, there's no way round that.'

'I'm aware of that,' said Standard with a frown.

'Right now, the situation's calm, but if things deteriorate rapidly, what's your plan for penetrating the building?'

There it was. The life-or-death question. She asked it calmly enough, but all the time she was thinking of Howard, Oliver and India. Wondering if they were even still alive. Just as she had been ever since she'd received that phone call.

Standard looked at her, and the lines on his face seemed deeper than before. 'If things go totally awry and we have to go in at a moment's notice, our IA – the immediate action plan – is a multi-entry assault via the roof and neighbouring buildings. But I have to tell you, it's a very risky strategy, given the way the terrorists have split the hostages, and our lack of knowledge of their numbers. Or what booby-traps, if any, they've laid.'

'We can't afford large numbers of civilian casualties.'

'We know that,' said Standard. 'Which is why we're currently in the process of formulating a more subtle surprise attack. But we only received the digital plans for the building in the last ten minutes, and we're still waiting for the guest lists from the Stanhope's owner, so it's going to take time.'

Arley needed more than this. Much more. 'The hostage-takers claim to have booby-trapped the whole building,' she said, 'including the ground floor entrances. And we know they've got ready access to explosives.'

'In that case, we'd be looking at a silent entry through windows on the mezzanine floor into guest rooms on either side of the ballroom. That way we're almost certain to bypass any booby-traps they've set. The idea would be to take out the terrorists in the ballroom, then continue through the building, securing it floor by floor, before engaging the hostage-takers in the restaurant. The terrorists think they're being clever by not communicating by radio, but in a surprise attack like this it would actually count against them.'

Arley smiled, trying hard to look impressed. 'What

about Michael Prior? How do you intend to find him?'

'We're still working on that, but if you can get a location for him, it would be a huge step forward.'

'We'll do everything we can,' Arley replied, feeling a knot in her stomach. Somehow they had to find a way to end the siege without the SAS having to go in. Somehow, too, Tina Boyd – a disgraced detective, with virtually no leads to work on – had to find her family and bring them home safely. Both things were still possible. They had to be. Hostages had been released, and right now, at least, the situation was calm inside the Stanhope.

Allowing herself to see the tiniest chink of hope, she stepped out of the office and into the street as her mobile rang.

'Are you on your own?' asked Tina.

'Yes. What have you got?'

'I've got bad news, and I've got good news. The bad news is bad, and there's no easy way to say it.'

Arley felt her stomach lurch. 'Go on.'

'Your husband's dead. I found his body in your house.'

The news was a terrible shock, but Arley didn't have time to process it. 'What about the twins?'

'There's no sign of them. I think they must have been taken this morning, not long after you left. Your husband's been dead quite a long time.'

'Christ . . .'

'The better news is I've just come from one of your neighbours, a Mrs Thompson. She saw two men in a red van leaving your house just before eight o'clock this morning. She noted the registration number.'

Arley felt a rush of hope that seemed to lift her off her feet. As a senior police officer, she knew how much useful information you could glean from a simple registration plate. 'Give me the number,' she said, pulling a notebook and pen from her pocket. 'I'll get on to the ANPR guys.'

'Arley, you know as well as I do that as soon as you make the request there'll be a paper trail leading back to you, and you might have to answer some very awkward questions later.'

'Right now, that's the least of my worries.'

'Have the kidnappers been back in contact?'

'Not yet, no.'

'They will be,' said Tina emphatically. 'You know, we shouldn't be doing this alone, Arley. A single registration number isn't going to lead us straight to your kids.'

'Look, Tina, I really appreciate everything you're doing for me but I can't afford to tell anyone else what's going on.' She paused, wondering whether she should put her concern into words. 'These people know so much I'm beginning to wonder if it's an inside job. The thing is, I don't know who I can trust.'

'You're going to have to put your trust in somebody.'

'And I have done. You.'

'I'm not enough, Arley. If the SAS go in and you give their plans to the terrorists, you'll have a lot of blood on your hands. And so will I.'

'I know, but just let me see what this registration number gives us. Where are you now?'

'Just down the road from your house.'

'Can you stay there for the moment? I'll call back as soon as I can.'

'OK. And while you're at it, try and get a trace on your husband's mobile too. It might help me pin down a location for your children.'

Arley hesitated. The man who'd called her on Howard's phone had told her that if anything happened to him, the twins would be killed by the man who was actually holding them. But she also knew that Tina needed as much information as possible. 'OK, I'll do it. And, Tina?'

'What?'

'Thank you.' She felt herself beginning to well up as the emotions of the evening fought to get the better of her.

Tina sighed. 'Just get on with it, Arley. Time's not on our side.'

54

As soon as Arley stepped back inside the mobile incident room, she knew that something was wrong.

'I've just tried calling you, ma'am,' said Riz Mohammed. Like everyone else in the room, his expression was tense.

'What's happened?' she asked, shutting the door behind her and telling herself to remain calm. Tina was looking for the twins. She had a lead. It might still turn out all right.

'I've just had a call from the man called Wolf. Either we switch the internet service back on inside the hotel or they kill a hostage publicly. They've given us fifteen minutes to comply. And the call came in at 20.35.'

'We've got a tape of the call if you want to listen to it, ma'am,' said Will Verran.

Arley shook her head. 'Have either Gold or Silver been informed?'

'I relayed the message to Gold,' said Riz. 'We're waiting for him to come back to us.'

'What's your assessment, Riz?'

'Wolf sounded a lot more stressed than he did when we first talked to him. Given their propensity to violence, I'd say we've got to take this threat very seriously.'

Arley's gaze found Cheney, the most senior person in the room after her. 'What's your take, John?'

'I agree with Riz. It's serious. Are the SAS ready to go in yet?'

Arley felt her guts clench. 'I don't believe so, no.'

'Then we should let them have their internet connection back. They probably only want to bang out one of their propaganda videos, and it's not worth sacrificing a life not to let them. Not if we're not ready for an assault.'

'I think it would do a lot to help calm the situation,' added Riz.

Arley was wholeheartedly in agreement, but what she knew and the other two didn't was that Michael Prior possessed highly sensitive information that the government were desperate to keep inside the building.

At that moment, Commissioner Phillips appeared on one of the screens as he sat back down at his desk in his office at Scotland Yard. 'Can you hear me?' he said, his voice booming through the incident room.

'Loud and clear, sir,' answered Arley.

'I've just spoken with the PM, and it's been agreed that internet access can be restored to the hotel as the terrorists have requested, as long as we are able to speak to Michael Prior and ascertain that he's in good health.'

Arley felt a rush of relief. 'We'll get on to them straight away, sir.'

Riz picked up the secure phone and the incident room fell silent. The mood was tense for everyone, but for Arley it was almost unbearable, and she had to make a conscious effort not to drum her fingers against her cheek, a nervous habit of hers that was capable of driving others to distraction.

The phone rang twice before being picked up.

'We still haven't got internet access,' said Wolf angrily. 'Don't you care about your hostages?'

'Of course we do,' said Riz, his tone firm yet conciliatory. 'But we need something in return.'

'What?'

'We need to speak to Michael Prior.'

'He's not available.'

'Is there a specific reason why we can't talk to him?'

'Yes. Because we don't take orders from you.'

'But I'm not ordering, Wolf. I'm asking you to allow us to talk to him. If you do that, we'll restore the internet immediately. I promise you that.'

'Just turn the damn thing on. Understand me? Now. I gave you an ultimatum, and you're ignoring it. Your deadline runs out in ten minutes. After that, a hostage dies. And then one dies every five minutes until you reconnect us.'

'This is not going to help anyone,' Riz said, working hard to keep his voice calm, but Wolf had already hung up on him. He exhaled loudly, and looked at Arley, and then at the screen where Phillips still sat impassively at his desk. 'Do you want me to call back?'

Arley wanted to shout: yes, call back, do whatever you can to delay things. If a hostage was executed then the SAS would go in and that would be the end of everything.

But it was Phillips who answered him. 'No. We can't show weakness here. We have to call his bluff.'

'I'm pretty certain he's going to do it, sir,' said Riz, and for the first time there was a definite quiver in his voice. 'And it's very likely he'll kill other hostages until he gets what he wants.'

'And I have orders from the Prime Minister not to restore access until we speak to Prior.'

Arley's body was rigid with tension. She desperately wanted to throw up. 'Doesn't the PM realize the kind of flak he's going to get if the family of the hostage find out that he or she died because we wouldn't let the man holding them have a bloody internet connection?'

'This is a matter of national security, DAC Dale,' the commissioner said coldly. 'You of all people should know that. I'm sorry, but on this we're going to have to stand firm.'

55

20.50

You're never so alive as when you're on the verge of death. Martin Dalston remembered reading that somewhere once. And the thing was, it was true. He felt more alive than he'd felt in years. Probably since those heady days with Carrie, almost a quarter of a century ago now. He wanted to survive this night. He wanted to tell his friends all about it over a pint and a decent Italian meal.

It was quiet in the restaurant. The thirty or so hostages looked tired and drawn, but an uneasy calm seemed to have descended on everyone. For the last hour there'd been no threats or angry scenes. The guards had become visibly more relaxed, and occasionally one would disappear into the kitchen for a few minutes, leaving the other on guard alone. At the moment, the cruel Scandinavian with the limp was the one in there, which made Martin feel a little better.

He was thirsty, but knew better than to ask either of the men for a drink. Best just to keep his head down and count the hours, because at some point this ordeal had to end. Either way, he'd decided that he wasn't going to carry out his plan for a quiet, dignified departure from the world. He wasn't usually superstitious, but he took the day's events as a sign that perhaps he should make the best of his last few months rather than throw away what little time he had left.

Still keeping his head down, he looked over and caught Elena's eye. They hadn't spoken since the incident earlier, when the Scandinavian guard had threatened her with death, but they'd exchanged the occasional smile, and he'd mouthed more than one 'thank you' at her for sticking up for him when he was being beaten.

He smiled at her again now, and she smiled back. 'Tell me something,' she whispered, stealing a glance towards the guard to check that he wasn't looking at them. 'I've been wanting to ask. What happened to Carrie? If she was the love of your life, why did it end?'

Martin never spoke about Carrie, not to anyone. She'd always been the guilty secret he'd carried with him all his adult life, but now he was suddenly keen to talk. 'Because I was a fool.'

'Tell me about her.'

He leaned closer, keeping his voice low as he

pictured Carrie Wilson as she was more than twenty years ago. 'She was beautiful. We met in Australia when I was travelling after university. That's where she was from.'

Elena's eyes lit up. 'That's where my fiancé Rod's from too. We're going to move there at Christmas.'

Martin grinned. 'You'll love it. I loved it. Carrie and I bought a clapped-out Beetle and travelled the whole country. It was the best time of my life. I still dream about it at night.' For a few seconds he took himself back to those wild, carefree days, with the heat and the sun and the azure sea. 'When my visa ran out I had to come back here. But we were still together, and we kept in touch, and we talked about all the things we were going to do. She was going to move to the UK for a couple of years, and a few months later she came over on business. She added a week to her stay and we spent it driving all over England. That's when we came here for a romantic weekend.' He smiled to himself. 'I don't think we left the room once.'

'It sounds lovely,' whispered Elena.

Martin sighed. 'It was, and I really thought it was all going to work, but she had to go back to Oz, and although she applied for jobs over here, it was in the midst of a recession and there wasn't anything. She didn't want to come without a job so she asked me to go over there. I was working as an accountant and I think I probably could have got something over there, but I dithered, and I made the mistake of listening to my dad, who kept telling me I had a good job, with good prospects, and shouldn't even think about leaving it. And in the end, I didn't. Our conversations got fewer, I kept delaying a decision even though I was desperate to go, and finally the conversations stopped altogether. She stopped taking my calls, and then eventually she sent me a letter. It said that she'd met someone else.' He paused. 'That was twenty-two years and two months ago, and we haven't spoken since.'

Elena put a hand on his arm. 'Sometimes things just aren't meant to be.'

Martin felt tears well up and forced them back down. He looked away, which was when he caught the eye of a well-built man in his mid-twenties who was sitting on his own a few feet away. He was dressed in a crumpled suit and had the lived-in, slightly puffy face of a rugby player. The man looked at him and gave a very small nod. There was a grim determination in his face, as if he'd recently come to an important decision, and Martin noticed that he was inching closer to him across the floor.

Martin looked away quickly. He knew the man was thinking about some kind of escape attempt, and he wanted no part in it. It was far too dangerous, and he didn't think he had the physical strength or the necessary speed to take on the guards. Deliberately, he lowered his head and stared at the floor, telling himself he wasn't a coward, that under the circumstances he was simply being rational.

The sound of a lift door opening, followed by purposeful footsteps, interrupted his thoughts, and he looked up to see the leader of the hostage-takers march into the room through the kitchen door followed by the female terrorist in the black dress and jacket. They were both holding handguns with silencers attached, and the Scandinavian was just behind them.

Something about their demeanour told Martin that their presence meant bad news.

They stopped and conversed with the other guard in hushed tones, occasionally looking over at the assembled hostages; then, as Martin watched, the leader handed the woman a balaclava, which she quickly pulled over her head.

The tension in the room seemed to mount substantially. Something was about to happen. Everyone could feel it. Martin and Elena exchanged glances but neither spoke.

The woman broke away from the others and skirted the floor and the hostages before leaning over the furniture and pulling up one of the six blinds that covered the restaurant's viewing window. She secured the drawstring then stepped to one side, facing the hostages again, the gun pointed at a forty-five-degree angle in front of her – a pose that, with the balaclava, gave her the appearance of an executioner.

'Your government, the people you voted for in your precious elections, do not want to help you,' announced the terrorist leader, stepping forward, his tone angry. 'You are not important to them. None of us here wants violence, but we have to make your government listen to us.' He paused. 'And for that reason, one of you has to die.'

A collective gasp went up. Someone cried out, a strangled 'oh God', but otherwise there were no hysterics. Just a cold, silent sense of shock. Two young women to Martin's right, still in their work clothes, probably no older than he had been when he came here with Carrie, clung to each other, shaking with fear.

Keeping his gun in front of him, the leader walked out among them, his eyes scanning the group as he hunted for a victim.

Martin stared at the floor, every nerve in his body taut, every sense heightened, more alive than he'd ever been. More terrified too.

I don't want to die. Not any more. Not yet. I want to see Robert, my only son, one more time. I want to phone Carrie and tell her that I've never stopped loving her, that my greatest regret in life is that I didn't follow her to Australia when I had the chance.

He could sense rather than hear the footfalls as they came closer, and he bent his head down even lower, as if this would somehow make him invisible.

I know it should be me. I've probably got the least

amount of time of anyone here. But I just want one more chance at life.

He could hear breathing right above him, knew that the leader was there. Only inches from him. He didn't move. Didn't breathe. Just waited. Praying.

'You,' said the leader, and Martin felt a hand grip him firmly by the shoulder.

His prayers, it seemed, hadn't been answered.

56

Arley Dale stared at the ops room screens. Three of them were showing close-ups of the Park View Restaurant, where the recently opened blind was giving the whole world a narrow view inside. Behind the piled-up tables and chairs, Arley could clearly see hostages sitting on the bare floor, and a masked gunman moving among them. As she watched, the gunman leaned down, pulled a middle-aged man to his feet, and put a gun to his temple. The man looked pale and terrified as the Sky News camera panned in on him, and Arley felt her mouth go dry.

'CO19 have a moving target inside the building,' said Chief Inspector Chris Matthews, speaking from the incident room next door, his voice reverberating loud and clear through the loudspeaker in the incident room. 'They have a clear shot at him, ma'am. They can take him down now.'

Everyone in the room was looking at Arley. Waiting for her to say something. Rather than leading from the front, Gold and Silver – Commissioner Phillips and Assistant Commissioner Jacobs – were nowhere to be seen. Doubtless keeping their heads down, leaving the hard decision for her. Bastards.

The gunman was leading the hostage towards the window now. On the TV screen Arley could see resignation in the hostage's demeanour. So could five hundred million other people. He was about to die, and only she could stop it. She could give the order for CO19 to fire and save his life, even if the respite was only temporary. She had that power in her hands.

'Ma'am?'

She thought of her children, thought of everything she had to lose personally, and knew there was only one decision she could make.

'Tell them to keep their guns trained, but not to fire,' she said. 'We can't risk the gunmen shooting other hostages as well. I'm sorry.'

57

Martin didn't resist when he was hauled to his feet and felt the pressure of the gun barrel against his head. In fact, a strange calm descended upon him. The leader wasn't gripping him roughly, rather there was an almost respectful manner in the way he led him towards the window.

In a few seconds' time it would all be over. One loud bang and all the stress, the sadness and the regrets would be gone. He would leave his life, and his cancer, behind. He would finally be free. He closed his eyes, shutting out the world, as he allowed himself to be guided towards the place where he knew he would die.

And then there was a sudden commotion, and he was pitched forward.

Martin's eyes flew open and he saw the young rugby player who'd looked at him a few minutes earlier struggling violently with the terrorist leader as he wrestled to get his gun.

'Help me!' he yelled, a desperation in his voice, as he, Martin and the terrorist stumbled around together. The rugby player was holding on to the terrorist's wrist, forcing his gun up in the air. The gun went off with a loud pop, and someone screamed.

'Help me!'

Martin knew that this was it – his chance to do something, even if it meant dying a hero's death – but everything was happening so fast that he didn't have time to react before the woman took three quick steps forward, calmly took aim, and shot the rugby player in the upper body, the force of the bullet knocking them all backwards.

'Everyone stay down!' she screamed. 'Move and you die!'

No one moved except the rugby player, who let out a tortured gasp as if he'd been winded, and fell to his knees, clutching at his arm.

The terrorist leader threw Martin to the floor, then swung round and kicked the rugby player hard in the chest. 'You want to die, uh? You want to die? You *can* fucking die!' He grabbed him round his neck, dragging him to his feet. Still cursing him, he drove a path through the hostages before slamming him up against one of the restaurant tables in front of the uncovered window and forcing the gun into the base of his skull. The rugby player cried out, but Martin could see it was too late, much too late. The next second, there was another loud pop, and blood splattered against the window.

Immediately he stopped struggling and, as the leader let go of him and stepped aside, Martin could clearly see the wound in the back of his head. Slowly and silently, the dead man slipped from the table and fell to the floor.

'That's what happens when you try to escape!' the leader shouted, turning on the rest of them, the barrel of his gun still smoking. 'Do you understand?' He was shaking with rage and spraying spittle as he talked, his grip too tight on the trigger – a stark contrast to the woman, who stood calmly alongside him. 'He stays here as a warning to the rest of you.'

He looked down at Martin, who looked back steadily. For three seconds they stared at each other, and Martin could hear his heart beating in his chest. Then the leader turned away and he and the woman strode past the two guards and out of the room, leaving the rest of them in stunned silence.

58

Cat and Wolf left the restaurant in silence, and travelled in the lift back down to the satellite kitchen adjacent to the ballroom. Cat noticed that Wolf was shaking, although whether it was due to excitement, anger or shock, she couldn't tell.

The lift door opened and they walked back out into the kitchen. Wolf immediately went over and checked the laptop. 'They still haven't turned it back on, the bastards. I'll phone the negotiator and let him know another will die.'

'If they're so desperate to speak to Prior, let them.'

'We don't want to give away his location.'

'Then let me record a message from him and we'll play it down the phone to the negotiator. That way they will realize he's still alive but they won't know where he is.'

Wolf looked surprised. It was clear to Cat that he

hadn't thought of this, which concerned her. Before tonight, she'd respected him, but she was far less sure now, and wondered whether his reputation as a strong soldier and leader had been inflated. He was too much in thrall to the mercenary, Fox, for her liking – a man she wouldn't trust an inch herself.

'That's a good idea,' he said. 'Do it now and I'll tell the negotiator that we'll let them hear from him soon, as long as they put the internet back on.'

With a nod of acknowledgement, Cat left the room. She was looking forward to seeing Michael Prior again. She'd extract a message from him, of course, but she'd also make him suffer a little as well, to ease the rage that was coursing through her heart at the thought that her brother's killer was still alive and somewhere in the hotel.

Fox spotted her walking towards the ballroom door and beckoned her over. Although officially Cat was below him in rank for this operation, in practice they were equals. It was she whom Wolf had chosen to accompany him to the restaurant earlier, not Fox, something that she was sure rankled with the other man.

'Did you kill someone up there?' he whispered as she stopped in front of him.

She nodded, making no attempt to disguise her disdain for this mercenary.

'And are we back online?'

'Not yet. We'll let you know when we are.'

They were silent for a few seconds as they appraised each other coldly, like two dogs sizing each other up, hunting for weaknesses. Cat sensed he wanted to say something else, but she didn't give him the opportunity and instead turned her back on him.

When she was out in the silence of the corridor, her grip tightened on the gun. She kept it down by her side and out of sight, in case she ran into one of the guests, or, if she was really lucky, the man who'd killed her brother. Her frustration at not knowing how to find him in this maze of rooms was increasing the more time went on, and her rage meant she would take it out on whoever crossed her path. As far as she was concerned, all the people in this hotel were the enemy, and deserved whatever fate God chose to dish out to them. In two hours' time, the Stanhope would go up in flames, and Cat would go up with it, dying a martyr's death, taking as many of the enemy with her as possible.

It was a prospect that excited her.

Pausing outside the room where they were holding Prior, she imagined the terror he must be experiencing, bound up and alone inside. Slowly, she opened the door, bringing the gun up from her side so its suppressor would be the first thing he saw.

And then she saw him, and stopped.

Michael Prior sat dead in his chair. But it wasn't so much that which grabbed Cat's attention.

It was the fact that his left eye had been gouged out.

59

Arley felt sick. Events were now running completely out of her control, and the control of everyone else on the scene. Watching the hostage die onscreen had given her a terrible premonition of what might be happening right now to her children. She was dealing with people more ruthless than she'd ever come across before.

'We don't want anyone else dying, Wolf,' Riz Mohammed was saying. 'It will only hurt your cause.'

But Wolf was shouting down the phone. 'Then turn the internet back on!'

'I'll do everything I can, I promise, but in the meantime, don't hurt anyone else.'

'You have five minutes. Five minutes, do you hear?'

'And you'll let us speak to Michael Prior?'

'If you put the internet back on, yes.'

'I'll see what I can do. Give me ten minutes. Can you do that?'

'OK. You have ten minutes. But after that, another hostage dies in full view of the world.'

The line went dead, and the incident room fell silent.

On the screen, Commissioner Phillips' seat in his office was still empty, although Arley had heard from her immediate superior, AC Jacobs. He'd told her to stall the terrorists while Phillips talked to the Prime Minister about their next course of action. Jacobs had sounded shocked by what had happened with the hostage, as if he hadn't expected the terrorists to carry out their threat. Everyone in the incident room had expected it, but maybe that was because they were right there at the scene, rather than over at Scotland Yard. And now that it had happened, Arley knew it meant the end of any possibility of a peaceful solution to the crisis.

Riz turned to Arley. 'We're going to have to give in and buy ourselves some time. He's said we can speak to Prior so at least we're making some kind of progress.'

'I agree,' said Arley. She took a deep breath, trying to hold things together.

'For what it's worth, you did the right thing earlier,' said John Cheney. 'With the hostage. There was nothing else you could have done.'

The others in the room murmured their agreement.

Arley nodded, acknowledging Cheney's comments. Her face, she knew, said it all. She might have been doing everything she could to hide her torment, but there was no way she could disguise it completely. She was glad that he thought it was the dead hostage that was bothering her.

Say something. Speak to Phillips. Tell him what's happening. Get him to look for Oliver and India. You're running out of time.

She sat down as Phillips reappeared at his desk. He looked grim-faced and pale.

'I've just been told by Silver that the lead terrorist has given permission for us to speak to Michael Prior,' he said, addressing the room in formal businesslike tones. 'Because of this, the Prime Minister has given permission to re-establish the internet connection inside the hotel with immediate effect. Like the rest of us, he doesn't want to see any more needless loss of life.'

Arley flinched as relief, however temporary, flooded through her.

'However, the PM also believes there's now no alternative to a rescue mission to free the hostages. Responsibility for this has now officially been passed to the military. Arley, you and your colleagues need to continue doing everything you can to keep the terrorists from killing any more hostages, while the SAS planthe logistics of their operation.'

Arley nodded slowly, accepting the inevitable,

conscious that the phone in her pocket was ringing. She pulled it out and saw Howard's grinning face filling the screen, which meant only one thing.

Her family's kidnappers were calling.

60

'Are you in the control room?' asked the man on the other end of the phone, his voice calm.

Arley walked across the grass, away from the incident room, glancing over her shoulder to check she wasn't being followed. 'Not any more.'

'Is the internet coming back on?'

'You need that, don't you? For your plans to work.'

'That doesn't concern you. What should concern you are your husband and children. Have you spoken to anyone about our discussions?'

She thought of Tina, and wondered if she'd made a terrible mistake involving someone like her. 'Of course I haven't. I need to know my family are alive, though.'

'All in good time, DAC Dale,' he said, with a hint of a smile in his voice. 'Now please answer *my* question.'

Arley wondered what this man looked like. He

sounded middle-aged. She wondered if he had children of his own. She desperately wanted to reason with him, to tell him to please release her children, but she'd been around long enough to know that pleading wasn't going to work. 'The internet should have come back on by now.'

'And what are the plans for an assault?'

'I don't know. All I know is that the military have taken control of the operation.'

'Does this mean it's imminent?'

She knew there was no point lying. 'Not necessarily, no.'

'The phrase "not necessarily" is of no use to us. We need to know what's being planned. So do you, if you ever want to see your family again.'

Arley took a deep breath. Jesus, she had to hold herself together. 'The military have only just taken control, and it'll take them some time to organize a rescue operation. I'll make sure I know their plans.' She considered adding that she'd already had a meeting with the SAS commander, but held back. There was no point giving this man anything until it became absolutely necessary.

'I'm going to keep this phone on for the next fifteen minutes. The moment you have an update, call me. Do you understand?'

'I do.'

'If you try to trick us in any way, your family will die. Remember that.'

Arley slowly removed the phone from her ear and looked back towards the incident room, wondering if her absence, and the manner in which she'd taken it, was arousing suspicion among her colleagues.

A group of uniformed officers were in conversation next to an armed response vehicle parked nearby, too far away for Arley to hear what they were saying. One of them laughed, and Arley felt an overwhelming jealousy. For him, this was just another night on the job. For her, though, it was a matter of life and death. She could lose the two people she loved most in the world in one bloody moment, and what frightened her above all was that there was no guarantee she hadn't already done so.

Her phone bleeped. She had a message from the people running the ANPR database at Hendon, and she felt a surge of hope mixed with dread. Had they been able to get a location for the van that was parked in the driveway of her home that morning, the one that had almost certainly been used to abduct her children?

Taking a deep breath, she returned the call.

61

21.12

Tina lit a cigarette and turned on the car's engine to stay warm. A chill wind blew down the street making the foliage shiver, and it had started to rain.

Sitting there in the dim light of the streetlight, with the BBC news on the radio, she wondered what the hell she was doing, risking her neck to help a woman she hadn't spoken to in months, and who was an acquaintance at best.

And yet somehow she was here in the cold, having been dragged into the middle of a case that had global implications. So far tonight she'd impersonated a police officer, interfered with a crime scene, and withheld vital information in what was shaping up to be one of the biggest single crimes in modern policing history.

But that was Tina. She never did anything by halves. And so far she still believed that she was doing the right thing, although the more she thought about it, the more the doubts gnawed away at her. She understood why Arley hadn't wanted to say anything to her bosses, but at the same time Tina herself didn't want to be responsible for the deaths of any SAS men. After all, they had families too.

Her phone rang. It was Arley.

'What have you got?' Tina asked her.

'The vehicle with the registration you gave me was last picked up on the ANPR cameras in Willesden,' stated Arley. Her voice was calm, but only just, as if she was only a wrong word away from hysteria. 'That was at eight twenty-seven a.m. this morning, and it hasn't moved within camera-range since. And it's definitely the same vehicle because it was caught on camera a few hundred metres from our house at five to eight.'

'How big's the area it could be in?'

'About four hundred metres by six hundred. And it's high-density residential. The Hendon guys are contacting the local council to see if there are any other cameras that might narrow it down, but that's going to take time, and it's unlikely.'

'Driving there's going to take time too, and unless I strike bloody lucky, I could still be looking round for it tomorrow morning.'

'It doesn't look like there's much off-road parking or garages,' said Arley hopefully.

Tina didn't share her optimism. 'Any news on the location of your husband's phone?'

'It's been switched off most of the day, but on those occasions it has been on, it's been nowhere near Willesden.'

'Have any calls been made on it today?'

'Only the ones to my mobile.'

Tina suppressed a frustrated sigh. The man dealing with Arley was a canny operator with a thorough knowledge of police tactics, and he was being careful to give away as little information as possible. 'You need to get me a map of the area where the van could be. I've just set up an anonymous hotmail account. Send it to me there.' Tina gave her the address.

'Will you be able to go over there right away?'

'Yes, but it still might take me time when I get there. And I'm guessing that now they've killed a hostage, that's something we haven't got a lot of.'

'You know about that?' Arley sounded surprised.

'The whole world knows about it, Arley.' She thought for a moment. 'Listen, I've got an idea. The next time you speak to the kidnapper, demand proof of life. Demand to speak to your family. Say that if you don't, you won't cooperate.'

'What if he doesn't go for it?'

'Make him go for it. Put him on the back foot for once. You haven't got anything to lose.'

'I've got everything to lose, Tina. My children, for God's sake.'

'But you need to know they're still alive. And you need to make him want to keep them alive so that you do what he wants. And the only way you're going to do that is by being firm. It's the only way.'

'OK,' said Arley uncertainly. 'But wait, he doesn't have the children. He told me he was in contact every fifteen minutes with the man holding them.'

'That doesn't change anything. Insist on speaking to your family – not just the children, or he'll know you know that Howard's dead. And if he won't go with that – which I suspect he won't – demand that he send a video message from them, and insist that one of the children says a certain word or phrase, something that tells you that the footage has been taken after you demanded it.'

'But how will that help us locate them? He's obviously using a different phone to stay in touch with the man holding the twins.'

'The man who makes the video will send it via a phone to the man you're in contact with. He won't have time to do it all through email. I reckon your man will get him to send the video to Howard's phone so that he can send it straight on to you, and as soon as he does that we've got the other guy's number, and we'll be able to track his location.'

'But he'll see through it, surely? It seems too obvious.'

'Not if you sound frightened enough. He'll think you genuinely want to hear from them, which of course you do. And remember, he'll be under pressure himself by now, and people under pressure make mistakes.'

There was a silence on the other end of the line. 'Unless, of course, they're already dead,' said Arley at last. 'They killed Howard easily enough.'

'We can't think like that,' Tina told her firmly. 'I'm on my way to Willesden.'

Tina ended the call and pulled the car away from the kerb. For the first time that evening she felt in control, now that she was actually doing something rather than sitting around watching events unfold without her.

62

Graham Jones should have been home for dinner at eight at the absolute latest. He'd told his wife that morning before he left for work that he had a business meeting in Birmingham which was why he'd be home at eight rather than the usual time of six.

In truth, since 1.30 that afternoon Graham Jones had been in the Stanhope Hotel, ensconced in a room on the fifth floor with his lover of more than two years. Like Graham, Victor Grayson was married with children and couldn't afford for his secret to come out – at least not until his children had grown up and left home. Perhaps then the two of them could live together in peace and quiet. But until that time they had to make do with clandestine meetings at anonymous London hotels where no one would give them a second glance. And today they'd chosen the worst venue possible.

For the last four hours they'd been trapped in their room as the dramatic events of a full-blown siege played out around them. Victor had stayed remarkably calm, saying that they should stay in the room and wait for help to arrive, which it surely had to do eventually. But then Victor had the advantage of not being expected home until much later. His wife seemed to be a lot more laid back than Graham's wife Carol, who these days acted as if she was permanently suspicious of him, even though he was sure she had no idea about Victor. Carol would have a heart attack if she knew he had a male lover, and who could blame her? It was bad enough losing your husband of more than fifteen years to a woman, but for a conservative, middle-class woman like Carol, who liked to keep up appearances, losing him to a man would be too much to bear. Graham kidded himself that this was the reason he didn't want her to find out, but deep down he knew it was far more than that. He didn't want the embarrassment of being outed as a gay man in front of his parents and brother, and he didn't want a messy divorce while the kids were still young.

But as time kept ticking by, so the chances of his secret being exposed to the world grew greater. Surprisingly, it was this, rather than being caught by the terrorists who'd taken over the hotel, that scared him the most. He was sure Victor was right when he said that they should stay put, but he also knew how long sieges could last. Days in some cases. He'd read once about one in Hackney that had lasted three bloody weeks. He couldn't have that. He had to get out. Make a break for it somehow.

Victor had told him not to be so stupid. That he'd be risking his neck for no good reason. 'Text her,' he'd suggested. 'Say you're stuck on the train.'

But when he'd tried to text, the message had bounced back. He'd tried again every fifteen minutes until eventually he'd realized that the signal had been cut deliberately, leaving him with no means of communication with the outside world, other than the hotel phone, and if he used that he'd have to whisper and the stress he was suffering from would be obvious. Also, Carol was technically minded and suspicious enough that she'd be able to trace where the call had come from.

Which was how Graham now found himself alone in the hotel lobby, having walked all the way down the emergency staircase from the fifth floor. It had been the most terrifying journey of his life, and Victor had begged him not to make it. At one point he'd even tried to physically prevent Graham from leaving the room, grabbing him in a bear hug. 'I can't lose you,' he'd whispered, tears in his eyes.

But Graham had made his mind up. 'I'll be all right,' he'd answered. 'I promise.' And with that he'd broken free and gone, with barely a goodbye, still hoping that he could come up with a reason Carol would believe as to why he was so late.

Keeping close to the side of the main staircase for cover, he looked over towards the hotel's front doors, wondering if there was someone guarding them. He couldn't see anyone, but that didn't necessarily mean no one was there. One of the glass panes was cracked and it looked as if someone had fired shots through it.

Thirty yards separated him from freedom, and the heavy silence gave him confidence that no one would try to stop him if he made a dash for it.

But there was another problem. He was pretty sure Carol would be watching events on the TV. Since she'd got made redundant earlier in the year, she'd become something of a newshound with an addiction to Al-Jazeera, of all channels. If he went out the front of the hotel, she might see him on TV, and even if she didn't, someone would, and his secret would be out. It seemed so stupid under the circumstances to worry about something like this, but he couldn't help it. So much of his life was based on this one major lie that if it were to be discovered, everything else would come crashing down around him. Right then, he'd rather die than face that happening.

He'd go out the back. That would be easier. He knew that the Stanhope backed on to narrow streets where TV cameras would almost certainly be prohibited. He could get out without being seen, at least in public. Then one quick call to Carol, apologizing and bemoaning the state of the British railway system – a perfectly plausible explanation given how appalling it usually was – and everything would be fine. The strange and terrible events of this night would be his and Victor's secret for ever.

From somewhere up the top of the stairs he thought he heard a moan. It was followed immediately by a barked, unintelligible order. Turning away quickly, Graham made his way across the floor and through a door marked STAFF ONLY.

Straight away his nostrils were assailed by an appalling stench. Holding his breath, he made his way down a narrow, dark corridor, then through another door, and into the hotel kitchens. The smell was far worse in there and it took him only seconds to realize why, as his eyes became accustomed to the gloom. There were bodies, three of them as far as he could see, dressed in chef's whites and lying on the floor in pools of blood. A wave of nausea overcame him and he had to put his hand on one of the work-tops to steady himself. Graham Jones had never seen a dead body before, and to see three in such appalling circumstances was a nightmare come true.

Plucking up the necessary courage, he skirted around them and tried the windows that led out on to an empty courtyard behind the building, only to find them all locked. He needed to get away from the stench of death and breathe some fresh air. After hours trapped in the hotel room, freedom was finally so close.

Making a conscious effort not to look down,

Graham stepped over a body and went through another door. He almost tripped over another corpse blocking the way, but managed to stop himself. To his right was a fire door with a push-lever handle. It had to lead outside, and it wouldn't be locked. It might be alarmed, but right then that was the least of Graham's worries. He hurried over to it, forcing down the lever and pushing it open in one movement, immediately feeling a welcome slap of frigid air against his face, hardly hearing the clunk as the fully primed grenade dropped to the floor.

63

Fox stood in the ballroom satellite kitchen, waiting impassively while Wolf ranted and raved.

'You were the last person to see him alive, Fox. If it wasn't you who killed him, who was it?'

'I have no idea. And why on earth would I want to gouge his eye out?'

'I don't know, but it was your idea for us to kidnap him in the first place—' Wolf stopped in mid flow, interrupted by a dull boom coming from below. 'What was that?'

'It sounded like a grenade,' said Fox, immediately tensing. 'I set a couple of them as booby-traps on the exit doors to the kitchen.'

Wolf checked the portable TV, then leaned over the laptop. 'Are we under attack already? You said it would take them time to strike.'

'What's the TV showing?'

'Just the front of the hotel. It all looks the same.'

'Is there any email message on the laptop?'

'No, nothing.'

There was an edge of panic to Wolf's voice, and Fox knew he was going to have to take charge.

'If they've come in via the kitchen, then they're on their way up now. Come with me.'

Fox walked rapidly out of the kitchen with Wolf behind him. Cat and Bear were guarding the increasingly restless-looking hostages, and they both turned round when they heard the door open.

'Everything's all right,' Fox called out, more for the benefit of the hostages than anyone else. 'One of the booby-traps went off accidentally.'

Keeping a firm grip on his AK-47, he opened the ballroom doors and went over to the top of the main mezzanine floor staircase, leaning back against the wall to give himself cover as he looked down into the empty hotel lobby. If this was an attack the SAS would have been slowed down by the booby-trapped grenade. There was no sign of them yet.

He heard Wolf come up behind him.

'Is anything happening?' he whispered.

Fox pointed his AK-47 down the stairs, finger on the trigger. 'Nothing yet.'

They waited a full minute. In the background, Fox could hear the faint ringing of the phone in the satellite kitchen. It seemed the negotiators were trying to make contact. If this was a surprise attack, then the element of surprise had long gone. And if it was a full-scale, multi-entry attack, then where the hell was everybody?

'I don't think that was the SAS,' said Fox at last, still watching the lobby.

'Then what was it?'

'I'm not sure. We need to investigate.'

'Are you going to go downstairs?' asked Wolf.

Fox turned round. 'I've got a better idea. Send Cat. She looks like a civilian, so if it is the military, or the police – and I'm pretty damn sure it's neither of them – they won't open fire on her.'

Wolf's eyes narrowed and he looked at Fox suspiciously. Fox knew that, after the discovery of Michael Prior's body, Wolf no longer trusted him. He'd spent a good five minutes interrogating him about Prior, and it was clear that Cat had stirred matters as well. In this paranoid place, with the tension mounting, Fox's suggestion could easily be construed as a plan to get rid of Cat, yet it wasn't. Sending her down seemed to him the logical thing to do. She was relatively inconspicuous, unlike the rest of them.

Wolf looked past Fox into the silence of the lobby. 'All right,' he said with a sigh. 'We'll send Cat down.'

64

In the incident room, events had taken a sudden and unexpected turn. Officers inside the inner cordon had heard the explosion at the rear of the Stanhope, its exact location obscured by the high wall bordering the courtyard, but the officer who'd called it in said he could see a thin plume of smoke rising up.

Arley glanced at her watch. Her fifteen-minute deadline for calling the kidnappers was up, and she was going to have to make contact again. But she needed more time.

Tina needed more time.

One of the secure phones started ringing and Will Verran, the young police technician, who seemed to be looking younger as the night progressed, picked up. 'It's Major Standard for you, ma'am.'

She took the receiver, conscious of the sound of her heart beating in her chest. 'Major Standard.'

'Hello, Arley,' said the major, sounding so calm it made her almost physically sick with jealousy. 'Our spotters tell me there's been an explosion at the back of the Stanhope on the ground floor. My understanding is its some kind of ordnance, possibly a booby-trap of some kind. Have you had any explanation for it from the terrorists?'

'Not yet, sir. But it only happened a few minutes ago, and we're going to keep trying them. It seems it might be some kind of one-off incident.'

'Perhaps,' said Standard, his tone noncommittal. 'And you've got nothing new on Prior's location?'

'Nothing yet, but as I mentioned earlier, the lead terrorist calling himself Wolf has promised we can speak to him. As soon as we do, I'll let you know immediately.'

'Good. We're ready to go in at short notice now.'

'It may be worth waiting until we can speak to Prior.'

'Keep trying to talk to him, but if you're still having no joy in fifteen minutes, let me know. We may have to reassess.'

She handed the phone back to Will and left the incident room without a word, knowing that her actions were beginning to look odd, but no longer caring.

She'd got barely ten feet from the building when she dialled Howard's number.

'I said fifteen minutes,' snapped the kidnapper, picking up on the first ring. 'Not twenty.'

'I was on the phone to the man in charge of the SAS operation,' she whispered into the phone. 'It was a long conversation.'

'And you have the details of their assault, yes?'

'I do.'

'When will it be happening?'

'Not yet. At the moment they're waiting until we can find a location inside the building for Prior.'

'That seems reasonable. Tell me the plan for the assault.'

'Not until I get visual proof that my family are still alive. Right now. Otherwise I give you nothing.'

'You're not in a position to make threats,' he hissed into the phone.

'It's not a threat. I just need to see my family.'

'I'm not with your family, so it won't be possible.'

'Then speak to whoever is and sort something out fast, because otherwise I'm not going to go through with this.'

'I hope this isn't some sort of trick to determine their whereabouts. Because if it is—'

'It isn't, I promise. I just need to see that they're still alive. And to prove it, I want to hear my daughter say the name of her former primary school.'

'Impossible. You'll do as you're told.'

'No,' she said firmly, remembering Tina's advice to establish some kind of control. 'I won't. Not unless I hear from them.'

There was a pause at the other end of the phone.

'I'll see what I can do,' the man said at last, and the line went dead.

Arley took a deep breath, turning round, and almost jumped out of her skin. John Cheney was standing right behind her, and immediately she wondered what he'd heard of her conversation.

But it seemed he hadn't heard much. 'Is everything OK, Arley?' he asked her, using her Christian name for the first time that night.

She stared at him for a long moment, trying to pull herself together, wondering whether she should tell him everything. He'd always had a solid, reliable air about him – the result of his size, and an expressiveness in his eyes that suggested a real sensitivity. She almost said something, then remembered that the sensitivity and reliability hadn't stopped him cheating on her. It was just too risky to let another person in on her dark secret.

'Everything's fine, thanks, John.'

'You seem to be going in and out a few times.'

'I've got a personal issue I've been having to deal with.'

He thrust his hands in his trouser pockets, shivering against the cold. 'It's not like you to let the personal get in the way of business, Arley. Is it anything I can help with?'

She shook her head, suddenly wanting this conversation to end. 'No, but thanks for your concern. Give me a moment and I'll be back in.'

Cheney nodded. 'Of course,' he said, giving her an appraising look that lasted a second too long, before starting back towards the incident room.

She watched him go, paranoid thoughts flying crazily through her mind. How much had he heard? Was he going to say something to Commissioner Phillips about her ability as a boss?

And most prevalent of all: *how long have I got left to save my children?*

65

Scope cursed as he slammed down the phone receiver.

'Still no luck?' asked Abby.

He sighed. 'No. The lines out are all still busy.'

This had been the problem for more than half an hour now, ever since the terrorists had killed a hostage in the upstairs restaurant, in full view of the TV cameras. It seemed that plenty of the guests trapped in their rooms had seen it too and were panicking and phoning out. Luckily, Ethan wasn't one of those to witness the killing. He'd fallen asleep beside his mother just before it happened, and had been sleeping ever since.

Scope had last spoken to Steve at a quarter to nine, but at that point the paramedic was still trying to find out where the hotel kept the insulin, and was sounding stressed. He dialled Steve's number again, but got the engaged tone. Jesus, how many people were blathering on the phone? And who the hell were they talking to?

He turned back to Abby. She was sitting up on the bed, her leg still propped up on the pillow, as it had been all evening, but she looked awful. Her face was thin and drawn, its complexion fish-grey, and he could see that her hands were shaking.

He asked her if she was all right.

'I'm going to need my next dose and some food soon. I'm feeling pretty weak.'

'Tell me honestly,' said Scope, checking that Ethan was still asleep. 'What happens if you don't get it?'

'At some point, my blood sugar will get so high that I'll start fitting. If it's still untreated, then eventually I could die.' She smiled tightly, wiping sweat from her brow. 'But that's a ways off yet, I promise. Do you think they're going to have insulin here on the premises?'

He nodded. 'I'm sure of it. It's a big hotel.'

'If you can't get through to the man you need to talk to, and something happens to me, please will you promise me that you'll get Ethan out of here safely?'

Scope stopped in front of the bed, looking down at her, touched by her vulnerability. 'Nothing's going to happen to you, I promise. If I have to, I'll go out there and find the insulin myself.'

'No,' she said emphatically. 'I want you to look after Ethan.'

Scope wondered how much time she had left until she started to deteriorate seriously. She looked bad already. He could also see that she was beginning to panic, although she was trying hard to hide it, and for the first time it struck him that he might not be able to save her. It angered him that the authorities hadn't made any attempt to save the hostages. He was as aware as anyone of the logistical difficulties involved, but it was also abundantly clear to him that the terrorists were going to have to be confronted at some point. Delaying the inevitable only risked more lives.

'You know,' continued Abby, 'we know almost nothing about you, but I can tell by your eyes that things have happened to you. Bad things.'

'Bad things happen to everyone,' said Scope, not liking her gaze, or the questions it seemed to want to pose. Questions to which he didn't dare give an answer.

'I don't feel so great.' She slurred the words, and as Scope hurried over to her, she closed her eyes and fell sideways on to the bed.

Cursing silently, he leaned over and checked her breathing. Shallow, but enough.

'Abby?' he said quietly, giving her cheek a gentle tap. 'Abby?'

There was no response, so he laid her gently on her side. He stood back up and immediately dialled Steve's number again, willing it to ring.

It did.

And kept ringing.

'Answer, you bastard,' he hissed, through gritted teeth. 'Answer.'

'Steve Grantham.'

Thank God.

'Steve, I've been trying to reach you. Have you found out where the insulin is in here?'

'Yes. There's a medical station behind the reception area, but it's kept locked. The keys are in a strongbox, also behind reception, but only the duty manager has the key to it.'

It wasn't what Scope had wanted to hear, but it was no less than he'd expected. 'But they have insulin, right?'

'Yes, they do. In standard pen form.'

'Thanks, Steve. I appreciate your help.'

'Listen, it sounds extremely risky going down there. It might be best to stay where you are. I'm sure this situation will be resolved soon.'

'Are you? I'm not.'

Steve sighed. 'You're not going to be any help to anyone if you're hurt.'

'I'll take my chances,' said Scope, and hung up.

Ethan lay fast asleep beside his mother. He looked so peaceful that Scope wondered whether he should wake him or not. But if Ethan woke up and saw Scope gone, that would panic him even more.

He checked Abby's breathing and pulse,

wondering if she'd gone into some kind of coma, then put a hand on Ethan's shoulder and roused him.

Ethan looked up at Scope groggily, and smiled. 'I was asleep.'

Scope smiled back, suddenly seeing an image of Mary Ann as a young girl, with her button nose and curly blonde hair. Remembering those days when she was little and he'd put her to bed with a story. 'I'm going downstairs to get the insulin. I know where it is now.'

'Is Mom OK? It's getting late, isn't it?' He sat up and put a hand on her shoulder.

'She's asleep, and she needs it soon. That's why I'm going to get it.'

'What if something happens to you?'

'It won't.'

'How do you know?'

'I'm a soldier. And I've been a soldier a long time. I'm good at what I do. Nothing will happen to me.'

Ethan looked relieved. 'Good.'

'When I come back, it'll be like the last time I left the room. I'll knock on the door five times: bang, bang, bang, bang, bang. Nice and slow. That'll tell you it's me. Then I'm going to let myself in, and I'll put my arm round the door first, very slowly, so again you know who it is. In the meantime, you do like I told you. Anyone knocks on the door that doesn't use the code, ignore them and don't say a word, even if they beg to come in. Do you understand?'

He nodded. 'What if they force their way in, like before?'

'I'm pretty sure they won't, but if anyone does, hide behind the bed. But I won't be long. I promise.'

Ethan looked scared but determined. 'Do you promise you'll be back?'

'Yeah,' said Scope, meaning it. 'I promise.'

66

The shuffling sound was coming from beyond one of the doors.

Cat stopped and listened.

The sound came again, followed by a low moan. Someone was still alive.

She smiled and moved through the gloom of the hotel's main ground floor kitchen, keeping her gun hidden under her jacket, and out of sight, just in case it was a trap. The smell of spent explosives and smoke was strong in her nostrils. Combined with the stench of corpses, it reminded her all too vividly of times gone by.

Stepping over the body of a young man with curly hair and a beard, she looked through the window to the rear courtyard, being careful to stay well back, but couldn't see anyone. However, whether they were planning an imminent assault or not, there would be

Special Forces spotters round here somewhere, and she hoped it was one of them who'd blown himself up, although somehow she doubted it. If he had, he wouldn't still be here.

The moaning grew louder as she opened the door, and stepped into a narrow corridor that led through to the delivery entrance.

A badly burned man was lying on his back on the floor, his clothes in shreds and his face blackened. Beyond him was what was left of the fire door, little more than a shredded piece of wood hanging off one of its hinges. It was obvious that he'd been trying to leave the hotel and been caught in one of Fox's booby-traps. A cold wind blew through the gap in the door, and Cat scanned the courtyard through it. It still looked empty, but she felt exposed and uneasy standing so close to the outside world.

The man had heard her approach, and with a huge effort he managed to lift one of his arms a few inches. 'Help me,' he whispered, his voice a hoarse rattle.

Removing the gun from where she'd hidden it, Cat stopped next to him and pointed it at his head.

The stench of burnt flesh coming off him was intense, and there was a huge hole in his stomach that was exposing intestines. But his eyes were bright and alert, and they moved round wildly as he saw the gun. 'Don't shoot me,' he whispered weakly. 'I've got children.'

Cat stared down at him dispassionately. Then,

without a word, or even a change in expression, she pulled the trigger, the bullet passing directly through one eye.

Having found no one else in the kitchen, Cat crept back, listening out just in case there was anyone else for her to deal with. But the silence was perfect and total.

And then, as she opened the door leading back into the main part of the hotel, she saw the man on the other side of the lobby, beyond the central staircase, heading towards the reception counter. Even though he had his back to her, and the lighting was fairly dim, she could see that he was holding a gun. She could also see that he was dressed in a suit, which meant he wasn't one of their group.

Which could only mean one thing: this was the man who'd murdered her brother.

A burst of intense rage shot through her veins and she raised her gun once again, aiming down the sights towards the back of his head, following him as he walked, and wondering why he wasn't trying to break out of the main doors. Then she lowered it. He was at least thirty yards away – too far to guarantee a direct hit. And anyway, a bullet in the back was far too easy a death for a man like him.

No, this one was going to die slowly, and at her pleasure.

67

Scope was ten feet from the reception area when he heard a door close behind him.

He swung round fast, conscious of the fact that he was away from immediate cover, automatically crouching down and holding the pistol two-handed in a classic shooting position, and saw a young woman standing at the other end of the lobby. Her hands were thrust high in the air and she looked scared stiff.

'Please,' she said in a loud whisper. 'You're not one of the gunmen, are you?'

Scope let her come towards him. She was young. Late twenties, thirty at most, very attractive, and would have looked faintly vampish in her black dress and stockings if it wasn't for the bomber jacket she was wearing over the top.

'Stop right there,' he said when she was ten feet away. 'Where have you come from?'

346

'I was hiding in the kitchen,' she answered, still keeping her hands firmly in the air. 'I heard a noise in the lobby, looked round from behind the door, and saw you. Are you a police officer?'

Scope shook his head, beginning to relax, although he still pointed the gun at her. 'I'm not, but my advice is get out now.' He motioned towards the hotel's front doors. 'Quickly.'

'I can't,' she whispered. 'The doors are locked, and I think they may have booby-trapped them. Look.'

He looked back quickly and, in the reflected light of the emergency vehicles beyond the entrance, saw a holdall tucked away next to the leftmost door. It had two command wires attached that ran across the floor and up the main staircase. 'Then you need to get back to your hiding place. It'll be safer there.'

'I can't stay in the kitchen. There are bodies everywhere. Can't I come with you?'

Having someone else to look after was the last thing Scope needed, but it seemed he had little choice. 'OK,' he sighed. 'Follow me.'

'Where are we going?'

'I've got someone upstairs who needs insulin urgently. I'm looking for the room where they're storing it.' He went over and opened the door next to the reception area. 'Are you coming?'

She nodded, dropped her arms by her side, and followed him inside as he walked through a corridor that ran past the reception bay and into a small foyer with doors going off on three sides. The nearest one had a sign on it identifying it as the medical room. There was no key in the door, but luckily it was unlocked. He stepped inside, flicking on the lights and glancing back briefly to check that the girl was still following him. She gave him a small smile and, in spite of himself, his eyes drifted down towards her ring finger. There was nothing there, and for an indulgent moment he imagined what she'd be like as a girlfriend, then banished the thought. The last thing he should be contemplating when stuck in the middle of a situation like this was a young woman's marital status. Clearly, he needed to get out more.

The medical room was small and cramped, with a treatment area consisting of a bed and chair, which took up most of the floor space, and a set of locked glass cupboards filled with various substances lining the upper walls.

Scope smiled when he saw the set of keys sitting on the room's only worktop next to a couple of boxes of pills. This was going to be easier than he'd thought.

He slipped the gun into the waistband of his suit, but as he went to pick up the keys, a worrying thought struck him. For someone as scared as the woman behind him should be, she'd seemed extraordinarily calm and together.

Which was the moment when he saw her reflection in one of the glass cabinets. She was standing in the doorway, pulling a pistol with suppressor attached from beneath her jacket, her teeth bared in a snarl.

Scope dived to the floor in one rapid movement, just at the moment the girl fired, her bullet shattering the glass on one of the cabinets and immediately setting off a piercing alarm. Twisting his body round as he fell and ignoring the pain as his head struck a cupboard door, he yanked out his own gun and let off a single round in her general direction in a desperate effort to prevent her getting an accurate shot at him.

But she was quick too and she'd already jumped out of sight behind the door, firing off two more rounds that ricocheted off a cupboard door, narrowly missing his head.

He leaped to his feet, charged forward, and came out of the room in a roll, keeping the gun out in front of him, just in time to see the girl vault over the reception counter. Tightening his finger on the trigger, he took aim from the hip. But he was too late. She was gone.

For a few seconds he didn't move, waiting to see if she'd reappear. But he also knew that the shots would have alerted the other terrorists so he couldn't afford to hang around. He got slowly to his feet, assessing the situation. He'd come close to making a fatal mistake by being way too careless, which wasn't like him. If he'd given her a cursory search, he would have found the gun. But he genuinely hadn't expected a pretty girl in western clothes to be part of a group of extremists. It was bizarre. But then everything about this whole day had been bizarre, including the fact that he'd already killed five men – two more than he'd planned to.

His problem now was that not only was he trapped, he'd also given away his position. He went back into the medical room and took a quick look round, scanning the glass cabinets for insulin pens, but there was too much stuff in them. It was going to take a good five minutes to find what he was looking for, and right now he simply didn't have the time.

Putting the keys from the worktop in his back pocket, Scope crept towards the reception counter, keeping low, knowing that the woman would be waiting for him to reappear. He had two shots left. He was going to have to make them count.

The reception counter was maybe fifteen feet long, and the door they'd come in another five feet further on. This meant that she had quite a large area to watch, and she was likely to be using one of the lobby sofas as cover, so she was going to be a good few yards away, which would make it difficult to get an accurate shot in.

He jumped up fast from behind the counter and saw her straight away behind a leather tub chair, resting her pistol against the arm. Swinging his gun arm round, he fired a single shot at her position, keeping his gun arm steady and making no attempt to duck back down, even though all his instincts were telling him to get out of the way of her aim.

The girl fired back, but she was already ducking down behind the chair to give herself better cover, and Scope took the tiny respite this offered to jump over the counter, taking off at a run down the lobby towards the back of the hotel, still keeping his gun pointing in the girl's general direction.

She was up fast, cracking off three quick shots that were pretty damn close to him given the fact that he was a fast-moving target and she wasn't getting a lot of time to aim, and he fired his last bullet back, aiming from the hip, not expecting to hit anything but hoping just to buy himself a little time.

It worked. She ducked again, and by the time she was back up he was almost level with the central staircase, running in a zigzag and keeping low, putting some much-needed distance between them.

Which was the moment when he glanced up and saw the masked gunman at the top of the staircase, aiming his AK-47 down at him.

The wall just above Scope's head erupted as the bullets stitched across it, sending clouds of dust and pieces of plaster flying in all directions, and from somewhere behind him he heard more shooting as the girl tried to take him out. Adrenalin surged through him and he put his head down and kept running, knowing that the gunman's angle was extremely tight.

More shots ricocheted off the carpet just beside him but he ignored them, kept going, and a second later he was past the staircase and out of range and sight of the gunman on the stairs.

He managed the briefest of glances over his shoulder, saw that the girl had broken out of her hiding place and was now standing twenty yards back, behind one of the sofas, legs apart and slightly bent, both hands on the gun. He dived to the floor and rolled as she fired, then scrambled to his feet, turned a hard left and ran across the lobby floor, aiming for the cover provided by the back of the staircase.

She tried to bring him down with more shots, but he was moving too fast, and two seconds later he was out of sight and charging down the hallway in the direction of the restaurants and the emergency staircase, knowing that he had only just escaped death and that he'd failed Ethan and Abby.

He might have been unarmed and running for his life, but he couldn't go back yet.

Not until he'd got the drugs.

68

From his vantage point at the top of the main staircase, Fox saw Cat race after the fugitive, her face a mask of fury.

He yelled at her to come back but she'd already disappeared from view. Knowing she'd almost certainly get herself killed, he ran down the stairs, taking them three at a time, annoyed with himself for missing the guy when he'd opened up on him with the AK-47.

He raced round the corner, reloading the rifle as he went, catching up with Cat in the main restaurant. She was standing near the bar, gun outstretched, looking round for her quarry. It was clear she'd lost him.

'We need to get back upstairs quickly,' he told her, conscious of the fact that all the gunfire would have spooked the hostages in the ballroom.

'But he's here somewhere,' she hissed. 'He must be. I'm going to find him.'

'He could have made for the emergency stairs or one of the ground floor rooms.'

'Why didn't you hit him when you had the chance?' she snapped.

'For the same reason you didn't,' he snapped back, pulling off his balaclava and wiping his brow. 'Because he was too fast. And if he has gone somewhere through that door, you could be walking straight into a trap.'

She turned on him, her dark eyes radiating fury. 'He murdered my brother. I owe him. But someone like you ... a *mercenary*' – she spat out the word – 'wouldn't understand that, would you?'

'What I understand is that all this gunfire's going to bring the SAS down on us fast. We need to defend our positions, which means sticking together, not chasing guests round the hotel, whatever they've done. Was he the one who caused the explosion in the kitchen?'

'No. That was someone else trying to escape.'

'So what was this guy doing in reception?'

'He was trying to find some medicine for another guest.'

'Insulin?'

She frowned. 'How do you know?'

'I found some in the room where your brother and Leopard were killed. I took it with me. It means he'll have to break cover again soon. Come on.'

Fox gestured for Cat to follow him, and reluctantly she did so, but they'd only gone a matter of yards when he heard a burst of automatic gunfire from the mezzanine floor, followed by shouts.

'Jesus,' he grunted. 'This is all we need.'

Knowing it was essential he stay calm, Fox pulled on his balaclava and took off up the stairs at a run, charging into the ballroom and what appeared to be a full-scale rebellion in progress. At least a dozen of the hostages were on their feet shouting, while Bear retreated slowly in front of them. From the way brick dust was floating down from the ceiling it was clear he'd fired into it as a warning, and it hadn't worked. Far more worrying was the sight of Wolf struggling on the floor with a male hostage in a suit who was trying to wrestle the AK-47 out of his hands, and looking like he was getting the better of him.

As Fox strode across the floor, all the hostages looked at him and the fight went out of most of them. But not all. Bear also turned his way, and the hostage closest to him – a middle-aged member of the kitchen staff – seeing that he was momentarily distracted, went for him.

It was a brave move. But stupid, too. He had a distance of twenty feet to cover and he'd covered less than half of it when Fox put the rifle to his shoulder and put a burst of gunfire into the man's upper body, sending him sprawling backwards until he fell over one of the seated hostages.

'Sit down now,' Fox yelled, 'or you die!'

Everyone hit the floor, except the man fighting Wolf, who'd now yanked the weapon from Wolf and was in the process of getting to his feet, while Wolf held on to one of his legs like an annoying dog, all the trappings of leadership gone from him now.

The hostage pulled away from his grip, turning the weapon round in his hands.

Behind him, Fox could hear Cat firing at him with her pistol and missing. He and Bear then turned their weapons on him and opened up at the same time.

The hostage's head snapped back as he was hit, and he dropped the AK, doing a kind of manic dance as the bullets tore him apart. Then, finally, he fell heavily to the floor, and all was silent in the room, except for the sound of the ringing telephone coming from the satellite kitchen next door.

Fox stood in front of the hostages, noticing with interest that nobody had attempted to move the rucksack bomb. 'Anyone else try anything like that again, and ten of you will die as punishment,' he shouted above the ringing in his ears. 'Do you understand?'

No one spoke. The hostages sat hunched and motionless, their heads down, subservient once again.

Angry, and still short of breath, Fox looked across at Bear. This was why he'd been anxious about using him for the operation. He was a good, solid soldier, but he simply didn't have the necessary ruthless streak to kill without question, and it had almost cost him, and them all, everything. 'You messed up,' Fox told him, loud enough so that everyone else in the room could hear. 'The next time someone gets to their feet, kill them. OK?'

Bear answered with a respectful 'Yes, sir' and settled back to watching the hostages, while Fox went over to Wolf and pulled him to his feet.

Wolf looked furious, but there was shame in his eyes too, as there should have been. He'd been made to look a fool, and Fox could see that he knew it.

'You need to check the laptop for any messages, Fox told him, then answer the phone. You'll need to calm the negotiator and get things back on track.'

Wolf nodded, and a silent message passed between them. Whatever the situation had been a few minutes earlier, Fox was now the leader.

69

Arley Dale stood in the middle of the cramped incident room desperately waiting for proof that her son and daughter were still alive, while all around her was chaos. The phones inside the room were ringing off the hook with reports from senior officers stationed at various points inside the inner cordon about the sudden and prolonged eruption of gunfire coming from various points inside the hotel. On the screens in front of them, the TV cameras were panning round the front of the building, searching for any sign of activity behind the curtains and blinds. And all the time, its sound like a death knell, the incessant ringing of the terrorist's phone over the loudspeaker, as Riz Mohammed waited for Wolf to give them some kind of explanation of exactly what was going on in there. Something that might just delay an assault and give Arley breathing space.

She was already late in calling back Major Standard to give him an update on their failed attempts to speak to Michael Prior, and she was dreading making the call now. With the deadline looming, and still no sign of Prior, Arley was sure that Standard would decide enough was enough, and begin the assault.

She looked across at Riz.

Just pick up the phone and let us speak to Prior, she thought. That's all I need.

The ringing stopped and Wolf's voice filled the room. He sounded agitated. 'Everything is fine in here,' he said, before Riz had a chance to speak. 'We had some problems with a couple of the hostages, but all is back under control.'

'Has anyone been hurt?'

'No. They were warning shots only. Everything is fine.' As he spoke, he began to sound calmer.

'You promised me we could speak to Michael Prior. Is he there?'

Wolf hesitated. 'Not at the moment.'

'Why not?'

'Because we haven't had time to get him. You can talk to him soon.'

'You said that over half an hour ago. We need to speak to him now.'

'And I need you to meet our demands. How is that going, uh?'

'All your demands are currently under discussion. I believe we have until midnight to meet them.'

Wolf hesitated again, clearly thinking. As he did so, Arley felt the mobile in her pocket vibrate with the arrival of a text. She desperately wanted to look at it, but knew that to do so at this juncture would raise all kinds of suspicions among the other people in the room, especially Cheney, who she'd caught looking at her strangely several times since they'd talked outside.

'I will let you speak to Prior in the next half an hour,' said Wolf finally. 'You have my word on it.'

The line went dead.

Commander Phillips, sitting back at his desk on one of the screens and patched into the incident room, took a very deep and very loud breath. 'Mr Mohammed, you're an experienced negotiator. Tell me frankly, do you think this man Wolf is going to let us speak to Prior?'

Riz sat back in his seat, making it creak under his bulk, and ran a hand through his thick head of hair. 'No, I don't. For some reason, he seems to be stalling.'

'Why might that be?'

'I honestly don't know, but the only reason I can think of is that Prior's been incapacitated.'

'You mean he's dead?'

'It's certainly possible.'

'We don't think he's been compromised, sir,' said John Cheney. 'GCHQ haven't picked up any coded messages being sent out of the Stanhope containing classified information.'

'That's one thing, I suppose,' said Phillips grudgingly. 'But the fact remains that because we can't get hold of him, we can't get a location for him inside the building, which was the reason for holding up the assault. I'm also keenly aware that the terrorists' deadline is only just over two hours away. Therefore, we need to get on to the military and tell them that there's no longer any point waiting to go in.'

Arley felt her heart sink, but she stood up straight. 'I'll call Major Standard and inform him, sir. Janine, can you get him for me?' she added, before Phillips had a chance to interrupt. If anyone was going to speak to Standard, it was her.

She was aware of the mobile ringing in her pocket, but flicked it on to silent.

'You're through to Major Standard on line four, ma'am,' said Janine.

Arley picked up the receiver, conscious that all eyes on the room were on her. Briefly she explained the situation, and the fact that they'd all but discounted making contact with Prior.

'Thank you for keeping me informed, Arley,' said Major Standard, with a warmth that pained her. He was a good man, and she was going to betray his trust and help send his men to their deaths. She knew this was her last chance to say something. To take this terrible burden and its consequences away.

But they have your children.

'Are you sticking to your original plan of attack?' she asked, trying to sound as casual as possible, knowing he was under no obligation to tell her.

'Yes, we are. We haven't had enough time or information to formulate anything substantial, so we'll be going in round the back, out of the glare of the cameras, and making a silent entry. It's now exactly 21.49 according to my watch. At 22.05, I want your negotiator to call the lead hostage-taker, Wolf, and tell him that the British government will be making an announcement to the world's media at 23.00 hours tonight, and that it's a potential breakthrough. Are you clear on that?'

'Absolutely.'

'And make sure he keeps Wolf talking, without it looking suspicious. After that, I'll contact you the moment we need your police, and the emergency medical back-up.'

'Of course. I'll have everyone on full standby.'

She put down the phone and looked round the room. On the screen, Commissioner Phillips was no longer patched into the incident room, and instead was talking silently on his phone.

Sixteen minutes. She had sixteen minutes.

'Well,' she said evenly. 'It's out of our hands now. I need another cigarette.'

Trying to be as casual as possible, Arley went outside, lighting a cigarette with fumbling hands as she checked her mobile.

She'd received a text from Howard's phone containing a video attachment, plus two missed calls.

She took a deep breath and opened the attachment. It lasted barely ten seconds but it was enough to make her stomach churn. Oliver and India were sitting on the floor side by side, their hands bound behind their backs. Oliver's mouth and eyes were bound with grey duct tape, while India's eyes were covered, but a piece of duct tape hung down from her cheek where it had been torn away from her mouth, leaving behind a strip of red skin. It was obvious by the slight shaking of the camera and the picture quality that it was being taken on a mobile phone.

'Go on,' prompted an unseen, muffled voice.

'My primary school was St Mary's,' said India, looking round uncertainly as she uttered the response Arley had insisted upon. 'And I really want to come home, Mum. So does Olly.'

Oliver made a noise behind his gag but then the film ended, leaving Arley staring at the screen, trying to control her breathing, wanting to throw up from the terrible stress of seeing her two children being treated like this.

But there was hope. Jesus, there was hope. They were still alive.

The screen lit up with Howard's face and Arley pressed the answer button before it even started to ring.

'Your turn,' said her tormentor. 'Tell me the assault plan.'

The time for doubts about her course of action was gone. Now all that mattered was keeping her children alive until Tina could locate them. Speaking as quietly as she could, she began to give him the details of Major Standard's plan.

'When are they going in?' he demanded.

She kept walking further from the incident room, ignoring the icy rain that had started to fall. 'Our negotiator's going to make a call to Wolf at 22.05. This'll be a decoy, so I believe the attack will be starting then.'

'Thank you. We will talk again soon.'

'Hold on, I haven't finished yet—' But she was talking to a dead phone. 'Shit,' she cursed, taking a hard drag on her cigarette, suddenly feeling the terrible vulnerability that comes when you've played all your cards. She'd betrayed her colleagues and her country, and at that moment she had nothing to show for it.

And only one hope. That Tina's hunch was right and the man who'd filmed her children had sent the footage directly to Howard's phone, because if he had, then she could get a location for him.

The only person who could trace the calls was Phil Rochelle, the police coordinator at Hendon whose job it was to speak to the mobile phone companies on behalf of the Met. Arley had already spoken to him earlier that evening and got him to run a continuous trace on Howard's number. She dialled his number, praying that he had something useful for her.

He answered on the second ring, with his nasal, slightly pompous greeting, and Arley started speaking immediately, trying to keep the fear out of her voice. 'Hello, Phil. Have you had any phone traffic to the mobile you're tracking for us?'

'Your husband's. Yes, I have. Two calls were made on it to your phone in the last few minutes. And a call was received on it a few minutes before that from another mobile phone.'

Arley felt her heart lurch into her throat. 'Do you have the number of that other mobile phone?'

'Yes, I do.'

'Good,' she said, trying to stay calm. 'We need a current location on it.'

'I'm going to need to know what this is about, DAC Dale. We're talking about your husband's mobile here, and there is the very real matter of protocol.'

'I'm afraid the matter is top secret, but I can tell you it's to do with the current situation at the Stanhope Hotel and the earlier bomb attacks.'

'With all due respect, I'm still not sure what this has to do with your husband's mobile phone.'

'And I can't give you the answers right now because we're in the middle of an ongoing and fluid situation.'

'Then I'm going to need authorization from the

Home Secretary, or the chief commissioner at the very least.'

This was what Arley had most feared. Being found out by pushing too hard. It was always going to be a huge gamble trying to convince someone like Rochelle, a by-the-book man if ever there was one, that her husband's mobile records were essential to the Stanhope siege. But it was also too late to stop now. 'Neither the Home Secretary nor Chief Commissioner Phillips is available right now, Phil. Believe it or not, they're bunkered up in the Cabinet briefing room with the Prime Minister and the heads of the security services trying to deal with this crisis. And with all due respect, as Bronze Commander I am the person in charge of the situation on the ground, and I am requesting immediate assistance from you. If you refuse to give it, you may well find yourself having to explain why to the inevitable public inquiry into the events of today. So, are you going to risk lives, or are you going to help us save them?'

She could hear her heart thumping in her chest as she waited for his response. If he didn't go with it, she was finished.

You're finished anyway.

He sighed. 'I'll have the latest location of the phone in the next few minutes.'

'Thank you. Please make it top priority.'

Arley ended the call and took a deep breath, fighting down a wave of nausea. It occurred to her for the thousandth time that she should talk to her bosses and tell them what was going on. With Phil Rochelle's information, they could use armed police to free the twins rather than having to rely on an alcoholic female ex-cop. They could even probably delay any assault on the hotel while they secured the area where the twins were being held and took down the bastard holding them.

But once again she stopped herself. Because, in the end, there was every chance that they wouldn't delay the assault. Or that they'd try to negotiate with the kidnapper rather than make an immediate arrest. Whichever way Arley cared to look at it, her children were expendable to the authorities, and she couldn't allow that.

She had to do this her way, whatever the consequences might be.

70

'We've got less than ten minutes,' said Fox, standing alongside Wolf and staring down at the laptop screen.

'And you think this is the true plan?'

Fox looked at him. 'We've got this woman's kids at gunpoint. It'll be the true plan.'

'I want you and Bear to organize the first line of defence against our attackers,' said Wolf. 'You both have the most recent military experience. Cat and I will remain here guarding the hostages. What about your two operatives in the restaurant upstairs? Do they need informing of what's going on?'

'No. They'll have seen the message so they'll know what's happening. And they'll hold their positions.'

'You're going to need to be able to hold off the attacking forces at least until I can get through to the negotiator and tell him that unless the assault stops, we will blow up the building. Do you think that will be enough to make them pull back?'

'If they lose the element of surprise and the authorities realize we're still in control of the situation, they'll have to stop the assault.'

Wolf's breathing had quickened, and he suddenly looked excited. 'Which will leave them totally humiliated. We are doing good work here, Fox. The British government will fall over this.'

'Let's hope so,' said Fox, although right then he was far more interested in getting out of the building alive, which was no sure thing.

As they hurried from the kitchen, Fox felt the adrenalin pumping through him. Zero hour was approaching – the time when he'd finally earn his money.

The plan had always been to trigger an assault on the building. It was why they'd set a midnight deadline while timing the bombs inside the hotel to detonate an hour earlier. They'd never expected to last until midnight. Ideally, the assault would have come just before 23.00. That way they could repel the SAS forces, thus heaping public humiliation on the British government, and use the subsequent timed explosions (which could also be blamed on the government) as cover to escape from the building.

Instead, they were going to have to put up with the assault coming nearly an hour earlier, which, Fox knew, would mean a nerve-jangling climax to the siege as they tried to keep the security forces at bay.

But it was still manageable, as was the fact that they were operating two men short. The most important thing was that, unlike the SAS, they still possessed the element of surprise.

The ballroom was quiet. The bodies of the two hostages who'd dared to resist their captors were still propped up against the wall in full view of the others as a warning. As far as Fox could see, it was proving effective, but then it needed to. The next hour was going to be extremely challenging.

He motioned Bear over and, ignoring Cat's glare, and Wolf's comradely pat on the shoulder, led his old army buddy towards the ballroom door.

It was time to prepare their reception.

71

Scope worked as quietly and methodically as he could under the circumstances, going through each of the cupboards one at a time, amazed that they had such an array of medicines on-site.

He'd taken a huge risk coming back as he knew the terrorists were aware how much he needed the insulin. He'd been only feet away from them, hidden behind the bar in the ground floor restaurant, while they'd discussed the fact that they could take him out when he emerged from cover to find it. He'd even seen the face of one of them in the bar mirror as he'd temporarily removed his balaclava, and was surprised to see that it belonged to an ordinary-looking white man in his thirties.

Right now, Scope was relying on the fact that the terrorists were too busy upstairs, and too short of numbers, to send someone down here. But if he was wrong then he was trapped, and almost certainly dead. Strangely, though, it wasn't death he was scared of. He'd faced that on many occasions in his time as a soldier fighting other men's wars. And in truth, since Mary Ann, probably the only truly important person in his life, had gone, life had ceased to be anything other than a simple mission for revenge.

No, he didn't fear death. What he feared was failure. He had to save Abby and her son. He cared about them now, had bonded with them, which was something he hadn't done with anyone in a long time. The world was a hard, brutal place; it had destroyed his daughter, and it had come close to destroying him. But so far it hadn't, and right then he was determined to keep it that way.

He found the insulin pens in a box at the back of the middle cupboard.

Feeling a sudden burst of elation, he ripped open the box and pulled out a handful of the pens, shoving them in his trouser pocket.

Then, holding his knife by the blade, in case he ran into one of the terrorists, he exited the room at a run, praying he wasn't too late.

72

'What the hell was that?' Bear had stopped in the middle of the lobby and turned his head.

'What the hell was what?' demanded Fox.

'I thought I heard a noise behind reception.'

Fox briefly wondered if it was the man he and Cat had just had a firefight with. He stopped too, but couldn't hear anything.

'It's nothing,' he said, although he tightened his grip on the gun. 'Come on. We need to hurry.' He had no desire to help Cat avenge her brother, and if this guy, whoever he was, was out the back trying to find insulin, then that was fine too, because it kept him out of their hair. 'Just keep down,' he hissed as they moved through the STAFF ONLY doors and into the gloom of the main kitchen, before stopping at the windows looking out on to the courtyard, where the van they'd arrived in was still parked with the rear doors open. It was raining outside and the cobble-stones were shiny and wet.

The two men crouched low and Fox scanned the area, squinting in the darkness. When he was satisfied that the courtyard was empty he reached down and carefully retrieved the button detonator he'd left underneath the worktop earlier, and held it in the palm of his hand, button up. 'In a few minutes the military will come through there,' he said, pointing towards the archway they'd driven through earlier, where the body of the security guard still lay. 'They'll head over to the wall here and rendezvous under-neath the mezzanine floor windows. What they don't know is there's a bomb hidden in one of the wheelie bins just outside the delivery entrance. You can't see it now, but it's about twenty feet to the left of us. It's a simple low-tech command wire device so any radio jamming gear they've got won't be able to stop it from detonating. Your job's to man this position. You don't move, you don't turn away, you don't lose con-centration. Do any of those things and we're all dead.'

'Jesus, you don't have to tell me that, Fox. How long have we worked together?'

'I know. But we're up against the best in the world here. We can't afford to make even the smallest mistake.'

'Sure. I know.'

'When you see movement through the arch, and you've confirmed it's enemy forces, you get down, count to twenty, so they've got time to come into the courtyard in numbers, then press the button. And make sure you're behind the kitchen units, because it's going to be a big bang.'

'Won't they have recced this place already? I mean, like you say, these guys are the best in the world. What if they've already located and disabled the bomb?'

'They haven't.'

'You're very confident.'

'First off, the bomb's hidden underneath a load of rubbish in an area where the bins are meant to be. Secondly, Dragon cut a hole in the back of the bin and ran the wires through there and under the delivery room door, so they'd be impossible to spot without moving the bin.'

'They could have moved the bin.'

Fox smiled. 'We'd have heard them. Dragon also taped a grenade between the bin and the one next to it, on the underside where you can't see it. If anyone moved anything, it would have come free and blown.' He gave the detonator to Bear, telling him to handle it carefully, then pulled a pair of noise-suppressing headphones from his backpack. 'You might want to wear these when you set off the bomb. I'm going to be upstairs in one of the function rooms. As soon as I hear it go off, I'll open up with the AK and chuck out a couple of grenades. If you get the chance, unload a few rounds yourself, but then make your way back to the mezzanine floor using the emergency staircase. We'll rendezvous there.'

'What if they keep coming? They're not going to want to give up just like that.'

'They'll be sitting ducks out there so they're going to want to get back and regroup. Also, as soon as Wolf hears all the commotion, he's going to get on to the negotiator and threaten to kill all the hostages unless they pull back.' He patted Bear on the shoulder. 'They'll pull back. Remember, they've had hardly any time to prepare for this and we're forcing their hand. They'll be making mistakes too.'

Bear shook his head slowly. 'I never thought I'd end up killing fellow British soldiers.'

'They're unavoidable casualties,' said Fox, who had no desire to get into a debate about the morality of what they were doing. It was way too late for that. 'You want to make the government fall, you want to make the people angry, this is the way you do it. Plus, you've got the best motivation of all: if you don't kill them, you can bet your life that they'll kill you.'

Bear nodded slowly as he thought this through, then grinned. 'Reminds me of the old days,' he whispered, peering out into the gloom. 'Waiting for the enemy to appear.'

'And we got out of that OK, didn't we? We'll get out of this too. Then we can all retire.' Fox got to his feet, keeping low. 'Rendezvous back in the mezzanine foyer. I'll be waiting for you there. Good luck.'

Keeping to the shadows, he slipped back through the kitchen and headed upstairs.

Barely a minute later he was inside the Meadow Room on the mezzanine floor, a mid-sized function room with a long boardroom table and chairs and an electronic whiteboard taking up one wall. He stood in the corner of the room, the AK-47 in his hands, and looked round the edge of the curtain, into the courtyard below.

This was it. The culmination of months of training and planning. He slowed his breathing, knowing how important it was to remain calm as he prepared for the coming onslaught. One more hour and he'd either be a very rich man or a dead one.

He looked at his watch. 22.01.

73

Tina was driving round the maze of rain-soaked residential streets where the van she was looking for was supposed to be parked, as she had been for over twenty minutes now, when her phone rang.

'They sent me a video from Howard's phone,' Arley announced breathlessly. 'My children were alive ten minutes ago.'

'That's brilliant news.' Tina had thought they would be, but she still felt a rush of relief. 'Were there details in the video that could be of any use to us?'

'Only that it was shot inside a house.'

'And a location?'

'I've just emailed it to you. It's not exact, but it's down to a twenty- or thirty-metre area around Pride Street, within the same wider location as the van.'

'I drove down Pride Street two minutes ago and I

378

didn't see a van, but I'll have another look now. But listen, Arley, I'm not risking my neck here. I'm unarmed. I'll see if I can find the house, but that's it.'

'If you can find proof that the kids are there, that's all I need. Then the security forces can deal with it. But I need to know for sure. Please. We're so close.' The desperation was clear in her voice.

'Have the SAS made the decision to go into the hotel yet?' asked Tina, knowing that if they had, she was going to have to make this thing public.

'Not yet, but it's going to come soon.'

'OK. Leave things with me, and make sure you get the ANPR people to get in touch with you if that van starts moving. I'll call you the moment I have something.'

Tina ended the call and shook her head. She shouldn't be doing this. Yet she couldn't help feeling an excitement she hadn't experienced in many months. In fact, not since the last time she'd found herself acting totally illegally by teaming up with a wanted killer in order to bring an even worse one to justice. Tina had always attracted trouble. It was in her nature. But she also prided herself on always doing what she thought was the right thing.

Except this time she wasn't at all sure she *was* doing the right thing. There were too many other lives at stake. Not just her own.

She pulled over. Her laptop was open on the seat

next to her and she picked it up and checked the hotmail account, opening the attachment from Arley's email of three minutes earlier.

It showed a small-scale street map of the area she was in with an irregular red circle over a section of Pride Street that was about two hundred yards west of her current location. Pride Street backed on to a railway track, and as Tina looked at the map more closely, she could see that there was a track running behind the houses with another house at the end of it, next to the railway line – one she hadn't seen earlier on the bigger map. The house was just inside the red circle, and it struck Tina that it was isolated enough for the kidnappers to have got the children out of the back of the van without attracting attention.

There was no time to check whether or not it had been rented recently, so she pulled back out again and accelerated towards the railway line.

She almost missed the narrow turning with the dead end sign that, according to the map, led down to the house she was interested in. Slowing up, she caught a glimpse of a high-wire fence about thirty yards distant just as a train passed on the other side of it with a steady rumble.

Straight away she knew that it was too risky to drive down there, in case someone was watching. Instead she continued further down the street, still checking the parked cars just in case she was wrong and the children were being kept somewhere else, but after thirty yards and no sign of any red van, she found a spot and parked.

Taking a deep breath, she grabbed the can of pepper spray she'd bought in France from the glove compartment, as well as an eight-inch piece of lead piping – both totally illegal for a civilian to be in possession of, but small beer in comparison to the crimes she'd already committed that night. She slipped the pepper spray into her coat pocket and the lead piping into the back of her jeans, and then got out and hurried along the street, keeping her head down against the rain and the cold.

The turning down to the house was little more than a muddy track, with overgrown brambles and scrub on either side. There were tyre tracks in the mud but it was difficult to tell whether they were recent or not.

Keeping to the side of the track, Tina followed it as it turned at a narrow angle in front of the barbed-wire fence before ending at the entrance to a small rundown cottage that was almost entirely obscured by high vegetation and an unsteady-looking brick wall. Parked in the narrow carport in front of the cottage, beyond two ancient wrought-iron gates, was the red van they were looking for.

Tina stopped. There were lights on in the ground floor of the cottage and all the curtains, upstairs and downstairs, were drawn. This was the place, she knew it.

She should have got straight back on the phone to

Simon Kernick

Arley and told her that she'd done as much as she could. But she didn't. Instead she switched her phone to vibrate and climbed over the gates, tiptoeing across the gravel until she was level with the driver's window of the van. She peered inside. The front was empty, while the rear was hidden by a makeshift curtain, and she couldn't see or hear anything. Satisfied it was empty, she approached the cottage along the edge of the driveway, keeping close to the undergrowth before stopping outside the first of the ground floor windows. She put her ear to the glass and heard the sound of a TV.

Slowly, carefully, Tina made her way round the back of the cottage. A back door led into an unlit utility room with washing machine and sink, and beyond that Tina could see a narrow hallway with a staircase and the glow of lights at one end. Nothing moved inside, but there was definitely someone in there.

Putting on her gloves, Tina tried the back door and wasn't surprised to find it locked. It didn't matter. The lock looked as ancient as everything else about the cottage. She'd been trained in covert entry years before when she was in SOCA, and she'd brought a set of picks with her tonight.

Even so, she paused. The man who'd kidnapped Arley's children was armed and extremely dangerous. He'd already killed her husband, and Tina knew he wouldn't hesitate to do the same to her. Far better just to call the police, or better still Arley herself.

Except she hadn't found the kids. Not yet.

Tina felt her whole body tense. She was going in. It was just the way she was. All her instincts told her to hold back, but in the end it made no difference. She wanted to find those kids and make them safe. If anything happened to them because she hadn't done all she could . . . Well, she found it hard enough to live with herself anyway.

Reaching into her jacket pocket, she pulled out the picks and set to work, and in thirty seconds she had the door unlocked. It would have been twenty, but she was out of practice.

Slowly, she turned the handle and crept inside.

74

Liam Roy Shetland, codenamed Bull, had been buzzing all day. He'd finally killed a man. Put a gun against his head and pulled the trigger.

It was one of the most amazing things he'd ever experienced. Better even than sex, and similar too, in a weird way. There'd been this incredible rush as the bloke died – like having a really big orgasm. He'd been reliving every detail in his head ever since – the way the blood had splattered on the floor; the funny little grunt the bloke had made. Which was just as well really, because otherwise the day would have been shit boring, hanging round on his own in a house that reeked of mould, babysitting a couple of brats, and without even a Playstation or the net to keep him occupied. Just a tiny little telly with nothing but Freeview.

But the time was fast approaching when he would

achieve the kind of notoriety he'd been dreaming of all his life, and he could feel the anticipation building. This was his chance to prove wrong all the bastards who'd ever doubted him. His mum. His teachers. The Paki at the Job Centre who always used to look down his nose at him. All of them.

The handler should be calling him any time now, telling him he could leave. There wasn't a lot of time left if he was going to get to the rendezvous in time. His instructions were simple. He was to drive the van as close as he could to the Stanhope Hotel, and park it in as public a place as possible. There was a bomb in the back, set to go off at eleven p.m., and he needed to be well away from it when it blew. Fox had given him a rucksack containing a smaller bomb, and his job was to take this and continue towards the Stanhope on foot. When he got to the outer cordon where the crowds and TV cameras were gathered, he'd been told to get rid of the bag somewhere among them, without making it look too obvious, and then get the hell out, because the rucksack bomb was timed to go off at 11.15.

Liam was pleased he'd been given such responsibility by Fox, who was a bloke he seriously admired. Fox was the kind of soldier Liam wanted to be, and he was jealous of him in that hotel with the others, holding the whole world at bay. He'd been watching what was happening on the telly for most of the day, proud that he was a part of it all, although he still couldn't quite understand why they had to work with Arabs and Muslims, the very people he most hated, even though Fox had explained it to him several times.

His mobile bleeped and he checked the screen. It was a text from the handler. All it said was WE'RE READY.

Liam smiled, leaning over and picking up the gun from the table next to him.

It was time to do the kids.

75

Tina was halfway up the staircase when she heard what she was sure was the bleep of a phone coming from beyond the half-open door that led into the living room – the only room downstairs she hadn't yet checked for signs of the children. A couple of seconds later, it was followed by the sound of someone – a man, from the noise he was making – clearing his throat loudly and moving around.

It was too late to go back downstairs now. She was trapped in no-man's land, and the weapons she was carrying – a piece of lead piping in one hand, a can of pepper spray in the other – were no use from a distance.

Making a snap decision, she continued up the last few stairs as quickly as she could, gritting her teeth when one of them creaked loudly, and darted behind the wall at the top just as the living room door opened with a loud squeak, and the man cleared his throat again.

There were three doors up here, two on her side of the landing, one on the other. Tiptoeing across the carpet, she opened the nearest one and stepped inside, and was immediately assailed by the smell of urine.

They were both on the floor in the middle of the empty room, lying on their fronts, trussed up from head to foot with duct tape like caterpillar larvae. As she gently closed the door behind her, they both started wriggling and making moaning noises beneath their gags.

'It's OK,' Tina whispered, coming closer and feeling a huge sense of relief. 'I'm here to help. Your mum sent me. You've just got to stay quiet for a second.'

They both fell silent and stopped moving. Tina crouched down beside the girl, whose name she'd forgotten, and, after putting down the weapons, removed the duct tape covering her mouth as gently as she could, before doing the same with the tape covering her eyes. This way the girl could see who she was dealing with. She blinked up at Tina with wide, frightened eyes, and Tina smiled back at her reassuringly, putting a finger to her lips.

'Do you know how many men are holding you here?' she whispered.

'Two came to our house this morning,' the girl whispered back. 'They both had guns. I haven't heard any talking down there, so I don't know if they're both still here, but one definitely is. He was up here a little while ago.'

'OK. Now, I'm going to untie you both and then we're going to go out of the window as quietly as possible. Understand?'

The girl nodded. She looked incredibly relieved that Tina was there. Next to her, the boy, who Tina remembered was called Oliver, rolled on to his side to face her and made a noise behind his gag.

She immediately leaned over and began to remove the tape round his eyes, at the same time pulling out her phone so she could text Arley the news.

And then she heard it. The stair that had creaked earlier when she'd been coming up had creaked again. Even louder this time. Another stair creaked, and she stopped.

The man was on his way up.

76

390

22.05

Arley watched as Riz Mohammed picked up the phone and put it to his ear. A second later he was connected to Wolf's phone in the satellite kitchen on the mezzanine floor, the sound of it ringing over the loudspeaker, filling the tense silence in the room.

This was it. The decoy call. The police's only part in the operation to free the hostages.

No one spoke as they waited. They all knew what none of the pundits on the news channels on the screens in front of them knew. That an unseen assault was about to take place.

And yet what no one in this room knew, aside from Arley, was that the terrorists were ready and waiting for it. She stood in her customary position in the middle of the room, wearing a mike and earpiece connecting her to the mobile in her pocket. The moment it rang with news from Tina she'd call Major

390

Standard in the SAS control room and tell him what she'd done. It would mean the immediate loss of her job, and the possibility of a whole raft of criminal charges, but in truth she didn't give a hoot about any of that. All she wanted was her children back with her safe and sound, and to stop the assault on the hotel. Everything else was irrelevant.

'We've got some movement in Worth Street at the back of the hotel,' said Will Verran. A few minutes earlier he'd connected the incident room to a police camera that had been set up on Worth Street, just inside the inner cordon, and he was watching the screen that showed it.

Arley peered over his shoulder at the screen. Sure enough, she could see a line of dark figures moving through the shadows on the pavement towards the Stanhope's delivery entrance, before stopping behind a parked lorry, where they were hidden from view. She tensed. This was the assault force. She'd run out of time.

Instinctively she took out her mobile and stared at the blank screen.

Call me, Tina. Please, just call.

It was all over. For the first time in this whole crisis, she was simply unable to speak. DAC Arley Dale, a high-flying career cop and only a few hours earlier a potential future Chief Commissioner of the Metropolitan Police, was now knowingly sending a group of men to their certain deaths, and she knew it was something that would haunt her dreams for ever.

In the background, the phone in the Stanhope's satellite kitchen continued to ring.

77

Tina stood back against the bedroom wall, just behind the door, wondering what the hell the guy who kept clearing his throat was doing. He'd been up here close to two minutes now, yet he hadn't come in. She'd got the two kids lying back on their fronts so that he wouldn't notice anything amiss when he eventually came in, but now she was wondering whether she should have tried to get them out of the window and to safety, or at the very least texted Arley to let her know she'd found them and they were OK. But then she heard the flushing of a toilet and knew she'd made the right decision. He was coming.

She could hear his heavy footfalls on the landing, stopping directly outside the door. The boy made a moaning noise beneath the gag as the door opened and the light was switched on.

Tina held her breath, blinking against the light, her

hand tight on the pepper spray canister. She'd replaced the lead piping in the back of her jeans because she needed a free hand in case the guy was armed. It was a great weapon if she scored a direct hit on his head, but if she didn't, it would be next to useless. She needed to blind him, and for that, the spray was perfect.

Her heart hammered as he moved through the open door. She knew she had to be quick. She was only going to get one chance.

And then he was in the room, a huge hulk of a man holding a pistol with a suppressor attached. He turned to shut the door and Tina charged straight into him sideways on, her free hand grabbing his gun arm by the wrist as the force of her attack knocked him back against the wall. She thrust the pepper spray into his face and pressed the button, sending clouds of chilli powder straight into his eyes.

He screamed in pain, and she tried to drive her forehead into his nose, but he was already turning his head, and she only caught his cheek. It didn't stop her. She butted him again and again, desperately trying to press her advantage and disorient him as she reached into the back of her jeans, yanking out the lead piping.

But then with a roar he ripped his gun hand free of hers, grabbed her by the throat in an iron grip that cut her breath like a knife, before literally throwing her across the room.

As she careered backwards, she stumbled over the

legs of one of the kids and her head slammed into the wall with a dizzying thud and then she was on her back on the floor.

'Bitch!' he howled, swinging the gun round in a jerky arc as he pawed at his eyes. A shot rang out, the bullet ricocheting off the floor and into the ceiling. He fired again and again, trying to pinpoint Tina without the aid of vision, one bullet passing so close to her head she could see the dust spray from the wall out of the corner of her eye.

And then he was blinking and staggering away from the wall, his gun hand jerking crazily as he searched for a target. The kids were wriggling about wildly, trying to get out of the line of fire, the girl crying openly, and suddenly the weapon was pointing at a spot right between Oliver's shoulder blades.

Tina's head was spinning and she felt like throwing up but she knew she had to act, because it looked like the guy was going to pull the trigger, even though it was clear he couldn't see who he was aiming at.

She still had hold of the lead piping, and using her free hand to propel herself off the floor, she leaped to her feet.

Catching the movement, he swung round to face her, still blinking wildly but managing to take aim. His finger tightened on the trigger at just the moment she threw the lead piping.

It struck him full in the face and his nose erupted, sending blood squirting all over his mouth. Crying out, he lost his footing, his shot going high and wide, and, as he tried to right himself, Tina charged, taking full advantage of his lack of defence to drive a knee into his groin, and her head into his ruined nose.

This time he screamed. Not just in pain, but also in fear, and she sensed him weakening under the ferocity of her assault. Blood was pouring from his nose and he looked dazed, and still unable to see properly.

But he still had a gun, and as he brought it up to aim it at her she grabbed desperately for the barrel, managed to get a grip on the suppressor, ignoring the stinging heat pulsing out of it, and yanked with all the strength she had.

The gun came free and flew across the room, clattering into the corner without discharging, and Tina pressed her advantage, kicking, punching and butting her adversary in a bid to beat him into submission. But he was a big man, probably twice her weight, and though she'd hurt him, he wasn't finished yet. With an angry roar, he literally lifted her up and threw her off him, and as she tried to right her footing, he backhanded her across the side of the head and sent her crashing to the floor. He aimed a kick at her head but she'd already brought her arms up to protect her face and they deflected much of the force of the blow.

She wrapped herself into a ball as he kicked her a second time, shrieking out an angry curse, his breathing coming in ruined gasps. Now she was hurt too, but as long as she kept her position and he kept aimlessly kicking her, she'd be all right.

Except he didn't keep kicking her. Instead, he stamped hard on her arms as they protected her head, and then she heard him loping and stumbling across the room in the direction of the gun.

She had to get up. To keep fighting. If she gave up now, he'd put a bullet in her while she lay there. Then do the same to the kids.

Rolling over, she jumped to her feet and was immediately assailed by an intense dizziness. Her vision darkened and blurred, and she almost fell back down again, but she held herself together, and as it cleared she saw him bending over to pick up the gun, his back to her. His movements were slow and clumsy, but he could afford that, now that he almost had hold of it.

Tina saw the lead piping on the floor. Operating entirely on instinct and adrenalin, she grabbed it and ran at her adversary, lifting the weapon above her head.

He could hear her coming, and he straightened with the gun in his hand, already turning towards her.

But it was too late. She brought the lead piping down with a roar of her own, driving it into his temple with all the force she could muster.

He went down heavily, making no sound at all, and Tina fell over him, putting a hand out to stop herself colliding with the wall, before landing on her side on the carpet, noticing with a bloody exhaustion that the room had suddenly fallen utterly silent.

For a good ten seconds she didn't move as she fought to get her breath back. Then slowly, in great pain, she got to her feet, feeling in her pocket for her phone.

78

Arley felt her personal mobile vibrate as she watched the black-clad men on the TV screen disappearing one by one into the archway leading to the back of the Stanhope. She pulled it out of her pocket and her heart immediately skipped a beat. It was Tina.

'What's happening?' she demanded, concerned only for news.

Tina's voice was full of exhaustion, and there was a distant quality to it. 'I've got your kids. They're safe.'

Arley wanted to faint with the sudden burst of euphoria she experienced at that moment, but there was no time for that. 'Thank you,' she said simply. 'I'll call you back in five minutes.' She pocketed her mobile and grabbed one of the secure phones, speed-dialling through to the SAS control room.

An unfamiliar voice picked up, introducing himself as Captain Hunter, and Arley spoke rapidly. 'This is

DAC Arley Dale, Bronze Commander. Stop the attack now. I have reliable information that your men are walking into an ambush.'

'It's too late,' said the other man. 'They're going in.'

'They can't. Get them back.'

'I'm not going to do that. This is a military operation. You have no jurisdiction.'

'Then let me speak to Major Standard. Please. This will only take seconds.'

'He can't speak to you. He's controlling the assault.'

'If he's controlling the assault, then he has to speak to me. It's a matter of life and death.'

The captain told her to hold on, and Arley was conscious of the expressions on the faces of her colleagues as they stood or sat watching her in shocked silence, but she was beyond caring now.

She could only pray that she wasn't too late.

79

From his position in the Meadow Room on the mezzanine floor, Fox saw them as they emerged one by one from the darkness under the arch, fanning out into the courtyard, their guns trained on the rear of the building as they checked the windows for any sign of ambush.

The enemy.

He slipped back out of sight, his AK-47 down by his side as he counted to twenty in his head, waiting for Bear to detonate the bomb. Willing him not to weaken.

Seventeen, eighteen, nineteen . . .

Even though he'd braced himself for the impact, Fox jumped when the bomb exploded, the force of the blast shaking the windows. But his reactions were still lightning fast. Taking advantage of the seconds of chaos and disorientation that always follow an explosion, he looked out of the window and opened fire on fully automatic into the thick cloud of rapidly rising smoke.

As the glass exploded, he leaned further forward, strafing the courtyard with bullets, not sure who he was hitting through the smoke, before he was forced to leap back out of sight to avoid a burst of returning fire from somewhere near the courtyard entrance. More of the window glass shattered, spraying shards into the room, but Fox was already rolling away and pulling a grenade from his belt. He yanked out the pin, counted to three and lobbed it out of the window, hearing it explode just as it hit the ground. At the same time, amid the wild ringing in his ears, he heard Bear's AK-47 open up from the ground floor – a single long burst followed by the angry crackle of returning fire and the whump of a stun grenade.

Fox didn't know if Bear was going to get out in one piece or not, but he knew that he couldn't hang around where he was any more. Bullets were flying into the room. The SAS might have been badly surprised and taken casualties, but they were still professional enough to react to the attack, and they'd be concentrating at least part of their fire on him.

It was essential for Fox to keep the momentum of the ambush going. If the SAS thought they'd snuffed out the initial resistance they'd keep coming, and Fox couldn't afford to have that. They needed to be made to retreat.

Jumping to his feet, he reloaded his AK with the spare magazine and went into the next-door function room, pulling a second grenade from his belt. He strode over to the window and, keeping out of sight, unleashed a burst of gunfire into the glass, before pulling the pin and flinging the grenade out through the hole he'd created.

As it exploded, he let loose another burst of fire through the window, unable to resist taking a quick look at the carnage he'd caused as the smoke cleared.

He stiffened, confused. Unable to believe what he was seeing. Because what he was seeing was nothing. Other than a few small fires and the remnants of the smoke, the courtyard was empty. There were no bodies at all.

The ambush had failed.

80

'How on earth did you know that was going to happen, Arley?' asked Major Standard.

'I had good information,' said Arley into the phone. 'The point is, did it work? Did you pull your men out in time? It sounded like there was quite a firefight over there.' From their position in the mobile incident room two hundred yards away, they were unable to see what was happening, and the Worth Street camera wasn't showing them much, but they'd all heard the explosions interspersed with the automatic gunfire easily enough.

'Yes. Every man's been accounted for. We had to return fire to cover the retreat, but I don't know if we hit any of the terrorists or not. I need to speak to your source urgently. I want to know how he knew about our movements, and what he can tell us about the terrorists inside the building. Do you have a name and number for him?'

'No,' lied Arley, improvising as she went along. 'He called from a callbox.'

'Then who is he? And why did he call you?'

'He's an informant through an MI5 source. He was put on to me because I'm the police commander on the scene. I'll try to get through to him right now.'

'Do that. It's urgent I speak to him. We can't make another move on the building until we've got some idea what we're up against.'

'I've still got our negotiator trying to get hold of Wolf,' said Arley. 'He hasn't been answering. What do you want our man to say if he does?'

'Get him to tell Wolf it was a mistake and there was no attack. And get me that contact now, Arley. That's an order.'

'Yes sir,' she said, hanging up and repeating Standard's instruction to Riz Mohammed.

It was just in time, because barely twenty seconds later the phone in the hotel's satellite kitchen, which had been ringing off the hook for close to ten minutes, was finally picked up, and Wolf was on the line. 'Stop the attack now!' he was shouting, his voice filled with a volatile mix of fear and anger as it reverberated round the room. 'If you don't, we will detonate the bomb in the ballroom and kill all the hostages. You have one minute to comply. Do you understand?'

'Yes, I do,' answered Riz, who seemed as shocked as anybody that Wolf had actually answered his call.

'But there's been some mistake because there hasn't been an attack.'

'What are you talking about? What were the explosions and all the shooting, then?'

Riz raised his eyebrows at Arley. Whatever was happening in there, it was clear Wolf wasn't at the cutting edge of it. 'I don't know, but my understanding is that two members of the SAS were watching the rear of the hotel when some of your operatives opened fire on them. They then immediately retreated.'

'Bullshit. That can't be right. They were attacking us.' But there was the first hint of doubt in his voice.

'It wasn't an attack, Wolf,' said Riz, the calmness in his own voice a clear contrast to the terrorist's. 'I can promise you that. We genuinely want to negotiate.'

'Your men shouldn't have been round the back of here anyway. What were they doing there?'

'They were simply keeping an eye on things.'

'Tell them to stay away. Do you understand that? If we see any more of them again, we kill ten hostages.'

The line went dead, and Riz Mohammed took a deep breath. 'Bloody hell, that was close. He's not happy.'

'It could have been one hell of a lot worse,' murmured Arley.

'So, who's this contact of yours?' asked John Cheney, frowning as he posed the question everyone in the room wanted an answer to.

They all looked at her.

'I can't talk about it right now,' she said dismissively. 'It's classified.'

'That's ridiculous,' complained Cheney.

Arley gave him a look that cut him dead. 'That's the way it is. No more discussion.'

But even as she spoke the words, she knew she was on the verge of being found out.

81

'What's happening?' asked Ethan, his face etched with fear, as he sat on the bed next to his mother.

'It's all right,' Scope told him, putting a protective arm round his shoulder as the last of the explosions and gunfire from down below faded away. 'We're safe here.'

'What about Mom?'

'Your mum's going to be all right too.'

But as they looked down at her, Scope wasn't at all sure he was right. It had been five minutes since he'd roused her and injected the insulin. He'd managed to get her to take a few sips from a Lucozade bottle he'd found in the minibar, but she'd almost immediately thrown it up, and she was barely conscious. She needed proper medical treatment urgently, and as long as they were trapped in here, she wasn't going to get it.

He looked over at the TV, wondering what on earth all the fighting had signified. If it was an assault by the SAS, there was no sign of them yet. If they were coming, they were taking their time.

The TV was showing the front of the hotel, as it had done through most of the evening, and the rolling headline at the bottom of the screen said that explosions and gunfire had been heard inside.

Tell me something I don't know, he thought.

Another rolling headline appeared: UNOFFICIAL SOURCE SAYS SAS STAGING A HOSTAGE RESCUE AND MEETING STIFF RESISTANCE.

'Are the cops coming now?' asked Ethan, pushing up closer to Scope for protection. 'Is that them doing all that shooting downstairs?'

'It looks like it.'

'So will they be here soon to help Mom?'

'Shit,' Scope said aloud before he could stop himself. A third headline was now rolling along the bottom of the screen: UNOFFICIAL SOURCE SAYS NO ASSAULT TAKING PLACE, NEGOTIATIONS CONTINUING.

This was bad. More than that, it was almost unheard of. There'd definitely been some kind of attack, but it seemed it had been abandoned, which put him, Ethan, and especially Abby in a dangerous position.

'Why are you saying bad words?' asked Ethan. 'What's going on?'

Scope did something that had always served him

well in his military career. He made a big decision under adverse circumstances.

'We're getting out of here,' he said. 'Right now.'

82

'What the hell happened?' demanded Fox as he and Bear came together at the top of the central staircase, a few yards from the ballroom door. 'We didn't get any of them.'

'I saw them come in,' said Bear breathlessly. 'There were loads of them. I kept my head down and counted to twenty, then blew the thing. Just like you said.'

'Well, it didn't work.'

'They must have been pulled back. If they'd been within twenty yards of that bomb, they'd have been blown to pieces. Are you sure none of them were killed?'

'Well, there aren't any bodies out there,' snapped Fox. 'Come on, we'd better give Wolf the good news.'

As they went through the doors, Fox could see that the hostages were looking extremely agitated, the noise of the attempted ambush having clearly spooked them, while both Wolf and Cat kept watch on them, weapons at the ready.

Hearing their return, Wolf stepped back, still keeping his gun trained on the hostages, until he was level with Fox and Bear. He looked furious. 'I called the negotiator. He says there was no attack.'

'There was. At least one person fired at me. And they threw a stun grenade.'

'Someone fired at me as well,' added Bear.

'Did you get any of them?'

Fox shook his head. 'No. They were definitely ordered back.'

'So someone told them about our ambush. Your plan failed, Fox. You've made us look like fools.'

'No, I haven't. They came in. We fired at them. They left. Which meant it was a victory to us.'

'But you didn't kill any of them.'

'It doesn't matter,' said Fox, who was beginning to get heartily sick of Wolf. 'The point is, we're still in control, and holding the military at bay. All we have to do is keep this up for another three quarters of an hour and then the hotel goes up in flames and we make our escape. Just as we've always planned. We can still say we repulsed their attack. It's still a victory.'

'Except we didn't humiliate them. That's what we always wanted. To make the great SAS look like amateurs.'

Fox noticed Bear bristling as Wolf said this. For all his anger with the government and the establishment, Bear was still a patriot at heart, a man who'd been disfigured for life fighting on behalf of his country, and he didn't like the British Army being disrespected. Fox didn't either, but he was sensible enough not to react and he needed to make sure that his old army buddy kept his cool as well. 'I think they've been pretty badly humiliated already,' he said, meeting Wolf's hard stare with a far harder one of his own. 'And right now, it's the best you're going to get.'

Wolf grunted. 'All right. You and Bear watch the hostages. I need to speak to the negotiator again.' He turned away, motioning for Cat to follow, while Fox and Bear took up positions standing twenty feet apart.

'Can you tell us what's going on?' one of the younger female hostages asked Fox. 'Please.' She fixed him with a vulnerable, doe-eyed gaze.

'No,' said Fox, loud enough for the whole group to hear. He pointed his AK-47 at the girl, and made a play of putting his finger on the trigger. She immediately looked away while Fox scanned the rest of the hostages, knowing that it was essential they were kept under control. Their plans had been thrown off course, but if he kept calm, soon most of these people would be dead, and he'd be on his way to a new life.

83

Tina had wrapped the children in blankets she'd found in one of the cupboards and they were now sitting at the kitchen table taking it in turns to speak to their mother on her mobile. They were both in tears, and by the sounds of things, Arley was too. Tina couldn't blame any of them.

She left them in there, putting up a finger to say she'd be back in one minute, then returned to the bedroom where the kidnapper lay face down on the carpet. Crouching down, she felt for a pulse, but there was nothing. He was dead.

Jesus, thought Tina, standing back up, I've killed again. She might have taken a pretty bad beating herself, but she was still standing, whereas the last blow she'd laid on the kidnapper had been to the side of his head with a piece of lead piping. But as far as she was concerned, he'd deserved what he got. There were some people out there whose crimes were so terrible they didn't deserve life and, in her opinion, this man was one of them. What did bother her, though, was being on the receiving end of a manslaughter charge; she still had enough enemies in the Met to make this a definite possibility. Either way, she was in a lot of trouble.

She went back downstairs and made her way into the living room, where the kidnapper had been sitting when she arrived. A rucksack was on the sofa and she went over to it, wondering if there'd be a clue to his identity in there. The news had been saying for most of the day that the prime suspects in the bombings and the subsequent siege were Islamic fundamentalists, but the man she'd killed was white, and the single curse word he'd uttered when they were fighting sounded like it belonged to someone with a local accent.

She pulled open the rucksack and stopped dead when she saw the battery pack and wires, realizing she was staring at a bomb.

Slowly, very carefully, she stepped away from the device, knowing she had to get the kids out of there. As she turned towards the door, she glanced briefly at the TV, which was showing live footage from the Stanhope, and saw the rolling headlines saying that explosions and gunfire were audible from the back of the hotel and that unofficial sources suggested a rescue attempt by Special Forces was being repelled.

Simon Kernick

The nausea Tina was already experiencing suddenly grew a whole lot worse. So there *had* been an assault on the building by the SAS, and it seemed that things had gone badly wrong, which meant only one thing: Arley must have told the terrorists of their plans, despite Tina's warning to her about having blood on their hands as a result.

Oliver was speaking on the phone when Tina came back into the kitchen. 'I need to speak to your mum urgently,' she said, taking the phone from him. 'And we need to get out of here right now.'

'What's going on, Tina?' asked Arley.

'Give me a minute,' she answered, pushing the kids out of the front door and on to the driveway, ignoring their questions. It occurred to her that there might be further devices in the house, and that the van might contain some kind of bomb too. 'I've just seen the news on the TV. So the SAS went in. You all but promised me you wouldn't let that happen.'

'They did go in, but I managed to get a message to them to abort the attack. They pulled back just in time, and although there was some shooting and a couple of explosions, none of them were hurt.'

'Are you sure? Because there's no point lying to me now, Arley.'

'I swear it, Tina. There were no casualties.'

'Surely they must want to know how you came by the information.'

416

'They do. It's one more thing I'm going to have to deal with when this is over.'

'Where are you now? It sounds like you're in a cupboard.'

'I'm in the mobile toilet. Listen, Tina, I won't implicate you, I promise.'

'It's too late. You already have. And I've killed a man here. I can hardly try to hide it. That just implicates me more.'

'God, I don't know what to say, I really don't.'

Nor did Tina. She could hardly scream and yell at a woman who in the last few hours had lost her husband, her career, and so nearly her children.

There was a long silence while both women processed the events of the night and their inevitable repercussions.

'It's all over for me, Tina,' said Arley quietly.

'I know it is.'

'And I know how this must sound, but can I ask you one final favour?'

Tina almost laughed. 'Jesus, Arley. You've got chutzpah, I'll give you that.'

'I need to see my children while I'm still free. I need to tell them about their father. And I want to do it face to face.'

'I don't see how that's going to be possible,' said Tina as she ushered Oliver and India down the muddy track outside the cottage.

'My mother lives in Pinner. If I text you the address,

417

please can you take them there? I know I've asked a lot of you.'

'You've asked everything of me.'

'I know. And I'm begging you . . . please.'

'I need to phone the police. There are bombs in the house where I found your kids, as well as a body, and we need to get the area sealed off.' Tina sighed, looking in turn at Arley's children, shivering under their blankets. 'Then I'll take them to your mother.'

84

Martin Dalston was feeling nauseous and tense, although he wasn't sure how much of this was due to his illness and how much to the atmosphere inside the Park View Restaurant, which had deteriorated steadily ever since the execution of the hostage more than an hour earlier.

And then ten or so minutes ago they'd heard explosions and shooting coming from somewhere far below in the building. The taller of the two terrorists, the one Martin had overheard being referred to as Dragon, had told them in advance to expect some gunfire, but that the situation was under control.

But it seemed it wasn't fully, because both terrorists were now on their feet, their body language riddled with tension as they kept their assault rifles trained on the hostages, screaming threats the moment someone so much as changed position on the floor. Dragon had his foot on the detonator pedal, and he kept exchanging nervous glances with the other guard, the one with the Scandinavian accent and the limp. Both were checking their watches every few seconds, as if they were waiting for something.

Their erratic behaviour, and the uncertainty of the situation, was also affecting the hostages, whose expressions were becoming more and more panic-stricken. One person in particular, a white-haired businessman in his sixties, only a few feet away from Martin, had started to breathe very heavily in the last few minutes, and it looked like he might be having a panic attack. People were ignoring him, and several had turned away, as if, like prey animals in the wild, they'd sensed his weakness and were abandoning him to the predators. Martin gave him a reassuring look, but the man either didn't see him or chose not to meet his gaze.

Strangely, Martin himself was feeling less scared than he had done all night. Or maybe it wasn't strange. Maybe it was because, having been so close to death earlier on, and realizing that at the last second he'd actually been ready for it, he felt there was little else they could threaten him with. There was also something comforting in being back among the group rather than being singled out and alone. He wondered what the bombs and shooting had been about. At first he'd thought it was an Iranian Embassy-style attack on the building by the SAS, but that didn't make sense, because the two terrorists guarding them had known what was going to happen beforehand.

Martin caught Elena's eye and they gave each other the kind of supportive look they'd been exchanging all night. Something had changed between them, though. Elena looked more self-conscious under his gaze, embarrassed even, and he guessed it was because she hadn't intervened earlier, when he was about to be shot. Not that he blamed her. Ultimately, there was nothing she could have done. He wanted to explain this to her but he wasn't sure how he could do so without it sounding like he *did* actually blame her; and anyway, since the killing of the hostage, everyone had been taking seriously the warnings not to speak to each other. Nobody wanted to be the next to die.

A few feet away, the businessman's breathing was getting louder and more laboured, and he was now bent forward, one hand on his chest, the other holding a handkerchief to his forehead. Martin could see he was in a bad way, and he wanted to do something to help. Too many people had died needlessly already that day.

Elena was looking over at him now, a concerned yet helpless expression on her face. She wanted to help too. Martin could see that. But she wasn't going to. None of them was, including Martin himself.

He suddenly felt a terrible anger, not just towards the terrorists, but towards himself, for not doing something. He might be unarmed, physically weak, and desperately thirsty, but he had one huge advantage over all the hostages: he had nothing left to live for. He was already a dead man. It was just that his body hadn't yet realized it.

The businessman suddenly cried out in pain and fell over, clutching at his chest with both hands as he began to hyperventilate.

Several people gasped, but no one moved.

Martin knew that for once in his life he had to stand up and be counted. 'This man needs help urgently,' he shouted at the two terrorists, who were both looking over but making no move to do anything. 'Please. You've got to help him.'

Other hostages murmured in agreement, their confidence boosted by Martin's actions.

'Leave him, he'll be all right,' said Dragon dismissively.

'He won't be all right unless he gets some kind of medical attention.'

Martin crawled over to the man on his hands and knees, feeling liberated now that he was actually doing something, and put a steadying hand on his arm. The man stared up at him with wide, frightened eyes, but he was still conscious, and Martin had no idea whether he was experiencing a panic attack or something more serious.

He looked round at the other hostages. 'Does anyone have any first aid experience?'

'Get back!' yelled the Scandinavian, the crueller of the two terrorists. 'You were told to leave him alone. Get back now.'

But Martin was defiant, the fact that he was finally doing something worthwhile empowering him. 'He needs some water. Come on. Please. Have some kind of humanity.'

The man's gasps were coming thick and fast now, and Martin feared some kind of heart attack.

'I'm a retired doctor,' someone called out from behind him, but before Martin could turn round to see who it was, the Scandinavian marched over.

'You want to see my humanity?' he sneered. 'Yeah? I'll show you my fucking humanity.'

He grabbed Martin by the shirt and yanked him out of the way. Then, with barely a moment's hesitation, he took a step back, pointed his assault rifle down at the businessman's chest, and pulled the trigger, shooting him three times in rapid succession.

The man's desperate, rasping breathing suddenly stopped, just like that, and he lay still.

The Scandinavian turned to Martin, his bright blue eyes alive with excitement. 'There. That's my humanity. Anyone else move, and they get the same. And that includes you, big man.' He aimed the rifle at Martin's head. 'Get it?'

Martin looked down. Said nothing.

'Good. Now shut up. All of you.'

The gunman turned away, walking back towards his colleague.

Which was when Martin Dalston leaped to his feet, fury sweeping through him in a physical wave that gave him a strength he'd never experienced before. He charged at the Scandinavian, grabbing him in a bear hug and biting him as hard as he could in the exposed flesh of his neck, almost immediately tasting blood.

The Scandinavian let out a startled yelp and tried to throw him off, but the adrenalin was pumping through Martin and he held on tight. He knew that the moment he fell off, he was dead.

Then, out of the corner of his eye, he saw a flash of blonde. Elena was on her feet and leaping towards him too, her momentum knocking all three of them to the floor.

A burst of gunfire filled the room as the assault rifle discharged, but Martin had no time to see who, if anyone, had been hit. The Scandinavian had rolled on to him as he struggled to break free from his two attackers, and Martin was no longer biting him. Instead, he was gouging at his eyes and face, while Elena fought with him from the front, the weight of their two bodies crushing down on him.

Another burst of gunfire filled the room, as Dragon fired into the air. He was shouting for people to sit down. 'Get back, or I'll blow the bomb!' he screamed.

It was difficult to see from Martin's position on the

floor, but it looked like more people had got to their feet to join in the resistance, but even as he watched, he could see Dragon looking more confident, as if he could see that his orders were being obeyed.

Above him, the Scandinavian threw off Elena, and tried once again to wrench himself away from Martin's grip, but still Martin held on like grim death, even though he could feel his strength fading.

And now Dragon was coming over, his rifle pointed at Elena, who was on her hands and knees looking terrified.

Which was the moment when a figure appeared out of the corner door behind Dragon and charged him.

85

Scope had never intended to be a hero.

His plan had been to try to get on to the hotel roof from where he hoped to be able to summon some kind of help, but as he, Abby and Ethan had reached the ninth floor on the emergency staircase, with its sign for the Park View Restaurant, he'd heard the sound of shouting and gunfire, and reassessed. He could have carried on going but he remembered from the news that the terrorists had been holding hostages in the restaurant, and that the restaurant itself led out on to a flat roof terrace, which probably represented a better escape route.

Having sat Abby down and instructed Ethan to look after her, he'd made his way along the corridor towards the restaurant, and through the glass in the door had witnessed a scene of chaos. One gunman was struggling on the floor with several hostages, while another had his back to Scope and was shouting at the remainder of the group – twenty-five or so people of varying ages, some of whom were on their feet. This gunman had his foot resting on a pedal detonator and was threatening to use it.

As Scope watched, the gunman on the floor threw off one of the people he was struggling with, a blonde-haired woman in a business suit, while the second one took his foot off the detonator and started walking into the crowd.

Immediately, Scope saw his chance. Pulling out his knife, he threw open the door and ran into the room.

At the last second, the second gunman – a big guy with broad, muscular shoulders, and a good four inches taller than Scope – heard him and swung round fast, finger tensing on the trigger.

But he was too late. Still sprinting, Scope dived at him, using one hand to knock the rifle to one side, and the other to ram the knife into his neck.

Momentum sent them both hurtling through the crowd, the blood spurting from the gunman's severed jugular vein, the life literally emptying out of him. But even as he died, his finger pressed down hard on the trigger, sending more shots into the ceiling, and scattering hostages in every direction.

They hit the floor hard, with Scope on top, and as the gunman made a final grunt as the last of the air escaped his lungs, Scope turned round, just in time to see the other one hauling himself heavily to his feet, kicking off a smaller man who was trying to drag him back down.

The blonde woman jumped up and made a lunge at the gunman, grabbing for his weapon, but this one's reactions were quick and he slammed the barrel into her face, knocking her backwards to the floor, before swinging the rifle round towards Scope.

Scope yanked the AK-47 from the dead man's hands and rolled round to face him, but even as he did so he knew he was too late. The gunman had already steadied his aim and was ready to fire. For a split second, their eyes met, and Scope could see him grinning beneath the balaclava as his finger tensed on the trigger.

But the smaller guy grabbed him round the legs again, knocking him slightly off balance, just as he fired a burst of shots. Scope felt them pass close to the left side of his face, but he didn't even have time to think about how close he'd come to being hit, because he was already firing himself. The AK was set to single shot, and he put two into the gunman's torso, knocking him backwards at just the moment he let loose another burst of gunfire. Then, remembering that one of the terrorists he'd taken out earlier had been wearing a bulletproof vest, Scope adjusted his aim and shot at the gunman's head. One round missed and a second hit him in the shoulder, spinning him round, before the third took him through the cheekbone.

Unable to stagger because the smaller guy was still holding on to his legs as if his life depended on it, the gunman began to sway like a tree in the wind, a thin line of blood running down his face, before toppling to the carpet with a loud thud.

Scope could hear his own breathing, even though he'd been partially deafened by the gunshots. His back felt wet, and he realized he was lying in a pool of the other gunman's blood. He clambered to his feet, knowing that they all had to get out of there before the other terrorists arrived. The hostages were scattered all over the place and they were all looking at him, including the blonde girl who'd helped save his life, and who was now holding her nose as blood poured out of it. Some looked elated; some looked awed; a few just looked plain shocked. Scope looked at the smaller guy – the other person who'd helped save his life. He was panting hard and his face was pale. Scope nodded at him, and mouthed the word 'thanks'.

'All right, we've got to leave now,' he shouted.

'What about that rucksack?' one of the hostages shouted back. 'It's got a bomb in it.'

'I'll deal with it,' said Scope. 'The rest of you, get the hell out.'

The blonde woman got to her feet. 'Follow me,' she said through her fingers. 'We can go on to the roof terrace outside. The doors should be unlocked.'

No one needed asking twice. As they scattered the

Simon Kernick

tables and chairs piled up against the windows and pulled up the blinds, Scope picked up the rucksack, knowing there was no time for caution, and placed it round the other side of the restaurant, out of sight of the windows. Then, slinging the AK-47 over his shoulder, he ran back towards the staircase.

It was time to get Abby and Ethan.

86

Cat heard the shots as she was drinking the contents of a bottle of water in the satellite kitchen next to the ballroom. Beside her, Wolf was on the phone talking loudly to the negotiator. 'We have waited hours for the British government to come back to us on our demands, and all you have done is send SAS men sneaking round the rear of the building, shooting at us, rather than trying to negotiate in good faith.'

There was a second burst of gunfire from high up in the hotel, faint but definitely distinguishable in the silence, and Wolf stopped talking and cocked his head.

'I thought you said there was no attack!' he shouted down the phone. 'What is all that shooting?' Then his face broke into a frown. 'What do you mean it's not you?'

The noise of more shooting tore down the staircase,

and Cat glanced over at the TV on the worktop. It was showing live news footage of the Park View Restaurant on the ninth floor. A number of the blinds had been pulled up and people were pouring through the open French windows that led out on to the roof terrace. The two men supposed to be guarding them, Dragon and Tiger, were nowhere to be seen.

When Wolf saw what was happening on the TV, his face darkened. 'Keep your people back!' he shouted at the negotiator. 'Do you understand?' Then he slammed down the phone and turned to Cat. 'What's going on up there?'

'I don't know,' she said coldly. 'But we have to stop them. It'll be the work of the bastard who killed my brother.' Even as she spoke the words, she felt a rush of frustration and anger that made her face flush, and her grip on the pistol tightened. She had to find him.

Wolf shook his head angrily. 'It doesn't matter now. They'll be sending the SAS in again. We need to get out of here.'

'How? We're half an hour early. The bombs won't blow, and we'll be caught. This wasn't part of the plan.'

'We have to try.'

Cat was annoyed by his weakness. 'Be a man, Wolf. It's time for us to make a last stand. Let's go up there and fight.'

'I *am* a man,' he said indignantly. 'But the plan was to escape.'

'Mine wasn't. I never expected to leave alive, and I'm surprised you did. We must kill as many of the enemy as possible. For our country. For our leader. For our religion.' She lifted her pistol in a defiant gesture, and patted the pockets of her jacket. 'We have the weapons. Let us make them pay.'

87

Fox was in the ballroom when he heard the gunfire.

'What the hell's going on up there?' hissed Bear.

Whatever it was, it had to be serious. Their hostages had heard it too, and their tension levels were rising once again. The problem was they numbered close to eighty, and with only him and Bear guarding them, all it took was a concerted effort and they'd be overrun in seconds.

'Do you think the SAS are attacking again?'

Fox shook his head. 'I don't think so. Let's just stay calm. I don't want this lot to know you're worried.'

The shooting stopped, but it didn't make Fox feel any better. It had almost certainly come from the Park View Restaurant. Either Dragon and Tiger had sorted whatever it was and had the situation back under control, or they were dead.

At that moment, the door to the satellite kitchen

opened and Cat marched out, with Wolf following. But they didn't come over. Instead, they made straight for the ballroom door.

'Shit,' cursed Bear. 'Now what are they doing?'

'Watch the hostages,' snapped Fox as he caught Wolf's eye.

Wolf put up two fingers to suggest he and Cat would be back in a couple of minutes, and then they were out of the door.

Fox knew instantly they weren't coming back. There was something too purposeful in their manner. Which meant it was time to make a quick decision. If they stayed put, they risked being trapped there. If they abandoned their stations, they ran the risk of not being paid the balance of the money for the job. But with the information he had, Fox didn't actually need that money. Also, he knew that the only way Wolf could stop either him or Bear being paid was by sending a message to the clients claiming they hadn't done their job properly, but it didn't look like that was top of his priorities right then.

Bear was standing a few feet away, looking at Fox expectantly.

Fox made his decision. 'All right. Let's go.'

Before anyone could react, he fired a burst of shots over the top of the hostages, and as they cried out and covered their heads, he and Bear turned and ran for the door.

It took a few seconds for the hostages to realize

what was happening, but when they did, some jumped to their feet. Someone shouted that they were going to detonate the rucksack bomb that was still right in the middle of them, causing a panicked rush after Fox and Bear.

As Fox reached the door, he turned round and unleashed another burst of fire, scattering the hostages as he tried to buy himself and Bear a few extra seconds, not really worried who or what the bullets hit. Then they were through the door and out into the corridor.

Fox couldn't hear any movement coming from the ground floor but it wouldn't be long before the SAS came blasting through the doors. Yanking a grenade from his belt, he pulled the pin and rolled it down the central staircase, keen to cause as much mayhem and noise as possible, then he and Bear sprinted through the double doors in the direction of the emergency staircase.

Ahead of them, the corridor was empty, but behind he could hear the panicked shouts of the hostages as they fought their way through the door, followed by the loud blast of the grenade. In a few minutes, this whole place was going to be a screaming mass of people trying to get out, and SAS men trying to get in, which was exactly what Fox had planned. It would have been helpful if the bombs they'd set on timer had accompanied their escape, but in the end it probably wouldn't matter.

There was just one more thing to do.

As they ran up the emergency staircase to the second floor, where they'd stashed their civilian clothes and fake IDs in separate rooms, Fox pulled out his pistol, and in one swift movement shot Bear twice in the face, not even stopping to watch as the other man grunted and fell back down the steps. He didn't feel bad about killing the man who'd saved his life in Iraq all those years before, and who'd got his face ripped to pieces in the process. For Fox, it was all business. The fewer people who knew about him the better. Especially ones with big mouths like Bear.

Fox had already stopped thinking about him as he used his master key card to open room 202, from where he would shortly emerge as Robert Durran, freelance architect and guest in the hotel, and join all the other fleeing guests unlucky enough to have been caught up in the terrible events of that day.

88

As Scope gently laid Abby down on the roof terrace, helped by Ethan, she was beginning to come round again and blinking against the search beam of the police helicopter circling overhead.

'You're still at the hotel, but you're going to be OK,' Scope told her, putting the bottle of Lucozade to her lips. 'There are people coming to help you.'

So far, though, with the exception of the helicopter, the cavalry hadn't actually arrived. The twenty-five or so hostages mingled uncertainly on the terrace, some of them standing at the far end, signalling to the people below to send assistance, nobody really sure what was going on. Scope wasn't too worried. This was just the chaos of battle – all delays and confusion. The rescuers would be here soon enough, and now that Abby was awake, there was less urgency. It was cold and wet out there on the terrace, but he'd wrapped her in the duvet from the room, so she was protected from the worst of it.

He grinned at Ethan. 'See? Your mum's going to be all right.'

But as Ethan grinned back, a long burst of gunfire came from somewhere in the building, followed by a loud explosion, and a few seconds later a couple carrying two young children, who must have come from one of the guest rooms, hurried through the double doors on to the terrace.

'There are terrorists coming!' said the woman breathlessly.

'They've got guns and grenades,' added her husband. 'They're shooting at everyone and everything.'

Scope stood up. 'How many of them are there?'

'I don't know, but they're not far away.'

A worried murmur went up among the crowd, and they immediately moved further away from the double doors. Scope picked up Abby and took her over to the far end of the terrace, where she'd be seen and dealt with by the rescuers when they finally arrived.

Another burst of gunfire rang out, closer this time, and people started crying out.

'Stay here with your mum, Ethan. I'm going back inside.'

Ethan looked scared. 'But you might get hurt. Don't leave us. You keep leaving.'

Scope smiled. 'And I keep coming back. Remember that.'

He looked around for the blonde manager and saw her holding a bloodied tissue to her nose as she directed people back from the edge of the terrace. 'I'm going to try and hold them back,' he told her, 'but can you look after those two over there and make sure they get to safety?'

'Of course. But be careful.'

'And you.'

Turning away, he ran back into the restaurant. He'd stashed the AK-47 under a chair to avoid getting mistaken for one of the terrorists by the security forces, and he grabbed it now, keeping it down by his side as he strode over to the doors leading back to the emergency staircase. He peered through the glass and immediately saw a young man in bare feet sprinting along the corridor towards him, as if the devil himself was on his heels. He stepped aside as the guy came charging through without even slowing down and ran towards the open terrace doors.

More gunfire rang out, and this time it was really close. As Scope peered through the glass, he saw a man stagger out of the emergency staircase door, about halfway along the corridor. He'd clearly been shot and was clutching at his side, his shirt already stained with blood. Unable to keep his balance, he fell into the opposite wall and went down on his knees.

Holding the rifle out in front of him, Scope kicked open the door and went out to help him.

At exactly the same moment, the side door flew open again, and a man in a balaclava and boiler suit came storming through, already firing into the injured man, who pitched forward with a strangled scream.

The man turned Scope's way. He was short and well-built, moving with a confidence that came when you had a gun in your hand and the people you were hunting didn't. But the moment he saw Scope he took an instinctive, startled step back, and hesitated for just half a second too long.

In one fluid movement, Scope put the rifle to his shoulder and opened up on fully automatic.

The masked gunman flew backwards, firing from the hip, his bullets ricocheting off the ceiling, and Scope charged him, wanting to get in close for a headshot. The gunman went down on his back and lay still, but Scope knew there was a good chance he was wearing a flak jacket, and faking it. He'd been hit in the chest, and was still holding on to his weapon with one hand.

Scope stopped ten feet short of him and took aim at his head.

The gunman realized at the last second that he'd miscalculated and brought round his weapon to fire, but he was too late. Scope shot him twice in the face and the rifle dropped out of his hand as he died.

For a few moments Scope stood staring down at his

corpse, then slowly he opened the door to the emergency staircase. There was no longer any shooting, just a lot of shouting, and doors slamming coming from further down the steps, coupled with a pungent smell of smoke and ordnance. It was obvious that those guests who'd barricaded themselves into their rooms had seen images on the TV of their fellow guests escaping and were following suit.

He turned to go, eager to leave himself.

And then he heard a pained cry coming from the next floor down.

'Is anyone down there?' Scope called out, still keeping his finger tight on the trigger, knowing it could easily be a trick.

'Help me,' came the voice. It was young and female. English accent. 'I've been hurt.'

Knowing he couldn't just leave her, Scope started down the staircase. 'Stay there,' he said. 'I'm coming.'

He saw her as he came round the corner on to the next set of steps. She was about twenty, no more, a pretty Asian girl in a waitress's uniform, standing in the middle of the stairwell with her arms down by her side. She was shaking, although Scope couldn't see any sign of injury. There was another girl, partially obscured, lying in a foetal position behind her.

Scope frowned. He couldn't see the face of the girl lying down, but she was wearing a black dress.

The Asian girl opened her mouth to say something, her eyes wide with fear, and then her face seemed to explode in a shower of blood and gore as the stairwell erupted in the noise of gunfire.

Scope tried to jump out of the way as the girl pitched forward, landing heavily on the stairs, but he was too late. He just had time to register the pretty dark-haired woman who'd tried to kill him earlier, sitting up in the corner of the stairwell and firing at him with her silenced pistol, before a bullet struck him in the shoulder, spinning him round. One more caught him somewhere in the back, and he was slammed hard into the staircase face first. He felt his own rifle clatter down the steps as he instinctively released it.

There was no pain, just a massive sense of shock. He tried to move, but couldn't.

Then he felt a hand on his suit jacket, pulling him over, and he was looking into a pair of dark, hate-filled eyes.

'Good,' hissed the woman with a cruel smile. 'You're still alive.' She lifted the knife, holding it only millimetres from his right eye. 'Now you're all mine.'

89

Martin Dalston knew he should have stayed with the others out on the roof terrace, but when he saw the man who'd saved them all earlier run back inside the hotel to try to keep the remaining terrorists at bay, he wanted to help him. He'd had no idea what he could possibly do that would be of any use given that, with the exception of a day's paintballing near High Wycombe, he'd never had any kind of military training or experience whatsoever, but the way the man was risking his life inspired him. He wanted to do something valuable before he died, something that would make his son proud of him, and now he had an opportunity.

No one noticed him run back into the restaurant. He heard gunfire coming from the corridor, but Martin didn't hesitate. He ran through the doors into the corridor, not really sure what on earth he thought he was doing.

Two bodies lay on the floor about halfway down. One, by his outfit, was clearly a terrorist, while the other was a guest, lying on his front in a pool of blood.

The shooting had stopped now. There was just silence, and Martin wondered where the man had disappeared to, and whether he was the one who'd shot the terrorist. He walked towards the bodies, remembering that this was the way to the emergency staircase – the route he and the other hostages had taken when they were led up here after the hotel was taken over.

He looked down at the dead terrorist, wondered briefly what he'd hoped to achieve by murdering so many innocent people, and whether he'd died satisfied. Somehow Martin doubted it. It was all such a terrible, terrible waste of life.

But at least, he thought as he opened the door to the emergency staircase, he could try to save some others.

He heard the words straight away. Spat out of her mouth and dripping with hate: 'Does that hurt, yes? Does it?'

Martin froze. He recognized that voice. It belonged to the cruellest terrorist of them all. The beautiful dark-haired woman who had seemed to care not one iota for any of them.

'Fuck you,' came the grunted reply.

It was the man from the restaurant. The one Martin

had been looking for. He was clearly in immense pain, the defiance in his voice tinged with resignation.

'I can make you scream. Perhaps if I cut this eye out, just—'

And then Martin was running down the stairs, letting out some kind of weird battle cry. He came sprinting round the corner, saw the man lying on his back, bleeding badly, unable to move, while she crouched over him, a knife in her hand. She was looking up, having heard his approach, but he was so quick that she hadn't had time to grab her gun, which he could see was lying on the stairs next to her.

He had two choices: hesitate and die, or keep going and probably die. He chose the latter, diving straight into the woman, his momentum making up for his lack of weight and power, and the two of them crashed down the stairs and into the stairwell, landing on the body of a young woman which, grotesquely, still felt warm.

As they rolled on to the floor, Martin kept her in a tight bear hug so that she couldn't use her knife. But she was stronger than he was and she wriggled ferociously in his grip, screaming and cursing into his face, her eyes black as coals.

And then they were rolling down the next set of steps and Martin could feel the wind being taken out of him. As they hit the bottom, she pulled her knife hand free, rolled on top of him, and thrust the blade at his chest. He put out a hand to stop her, grabbed the knife by the blade, and screamed in pain as it tore open his flesh.

The knife caught him somewhere in the upper body – he couldn't see where. He felt a tremendous shock, and then the whole world seemed to slow right down. He felt his head fall back against the floor and his hands slip to his sides. Almost immediately his vision began to darken, as if he was entering a tunnel, and the woman became hazy in appearance as she got to her feet, turning away from him, still holding the bloodied knife in her hand.

And then he heard the sound of bullets echoing round the stairwell and the woman cried out and crashed backwards into the wall. She writhed against it for a moment, and more shots rang out. The woman appeared to perform a juddering little dance before sliding down the wall, leaving a long dark stain behind.

Everything was now utterly silent, and Martin began to feel very, very tired.

A face appeared in his fading vision. He thought it was the man he'd just rescued, but he couldn't be sure. The man was saying something to him, but Martin couldn't hear what it was.

Nor, it had to be said, did he care. All he wanted to do was sleep.

He closed his eyes and felt himself letting go, pulling away like a boat from a harbour, heading slowly out to sea.

His last thoughts as he died were not of Carrie, or what could have been. They were of his son, and his wife. Of what was.

90

Elena stood in the wind and the rain at the edge of the roof terrace, looking across a Hyde Park dominated by the lights of emergency vehicles. The fire brigade had put up two ladders and a cherry picker, and were in the process of evacuating the hostages. Behind her, the first thin plumes of smoke were drifting out through the restaurant double doors, but nothing moved in there, and the shooting had stopped.

She'd seen Martin go running in there a few minutes ago, after the other man – the one who looked like a soldier – but neither of them had emerged, and she was beginning to fear the worst. She didn't want to leave without them, but at the same time she desperately wanted to get back to Rod. And she needed to have her nose looked at. For the last few minutes the extent of the pain had been disguised by the adrenalin coursing through her system, but now it was beginning to make her feel nauseous.

A steadily growing roar filled the air and, as Elena watched, a huge military helicopter came into view, blocking everything else out as it stopped just metres above her, dropping down long rope lines. A few seconds later, two dozen armed men dressed completely in black abseiled down on to the terrace, pausing only to gather together in groups of four.

And then, beyond them, Elena saw a figure stumbling through the restaurant in the direction of the French windows. He was wearing a suit, and she immediately recognized him as the man Martin had gone in after.

The armed men in black saw him too, and one group of four approached him, weapons outstretched, the search beams attached to the sights homing in on his face.

The man stopped in the doorway, shielding his eyes with his hand as the men in black barked orders at him. Then he appeared to totter and fell on to one knee.

'He's hurt!' shouted one of the men in black, and they descended on him quickly, moving him rapidly to one side as their colleagues poured through the French windows and into the restaurant.

Elena ran over and saw that they'd laid him out on his back. Two of them were frisking him for weapons, even though his shirt was stained with blood, and it was clear that he was badly injured. 'Please,' she said as one of the soldiers peeled off and blocked her view, 'he's not a terrorist. He attacked the terrorists in the restaurant. He saved our lives.'

'Get back, ma'am, please,' said the man in black, giving her a none too gentle push.

Behind him, his colleagues had finished their frisking and two of them had lifted the man to his feet. As they led him past Elena, her eyes met his.

'Where's Martin?' she asked him. 'I saw him go down to look for you.'

'He didn't make it,' said the man in the suit. 'I'm very sorry.'

And then he was being helped into the cherry picker, where two firemen waited to take him.

'Come on, ma'am, you need to come to.'

Elena looked up towards the sky, and for a long moment she forgot everything and simply savoured the feel of the rain on her face.

The nightmare had ended. She was free.

91

As they emerged from the front of the hotel, the hostages were searched individually by SAS teams stationed just outside. The injured were moved to one side to be treated by paramedics, the remainder were funnelled into a narrow corridor formed by two lines of police tape, and flanked by armed officers, that ended in a large tent that had been erected earlier in the middle of Park Lane. The tent was a processing centre where the hostages would need to provide ID and an explanation of what they were doing in the hotel, in order to sift out anyone who might have been involved in the terrorist attack.

Fox wasn't unduly nervous as he joined one of the queues that led down to four desks at the far end where officers with laptops were processing individuals, even though armed CO19 cops and at least one team of black-clad SAS men were positioned around the interior to make sure no one tried to make a break for it. He was dressed in a crumpled suit, with smoke marks on his face, and he looked just like any other civilian.

There were only a couple of people in front of him, and as he waited, he checked his new civilian phone, which had been registered in the name Robert Durran two weeks earlier. There was reception, and he felt confident enough to send a text to a number he'd memorized earlier. The content was innocent enough: HAVE MADE IT OUT! TOMORROW AT 10. I HAVE GREAT NEWS. RD XXX. Fox didn't think anyone would bother checking his phone, but if they did he would tell them that, having made it out of the hotel in one piece, he now wanted to propose to his fiancée.

In reality, TOMORROW AT 10 represented his payday, the time when he would hand over to his contact the information given to him under torture by Michael Prior, in exchange for five million dollars. The information was simply a name, nothing more. But it happened to be the name of a very senior member of the Chinese government who was providing high-level intelligence to MI6, and very likely the CIA. This man's identity was so secret that, including Fox himself, probably no more than half a dozen people knew it, which made the information very valuable indeed. Fox suspected his contact, the same right-wing extremist who'd put him in touch with Wolf all those months ago, was selling it on for far more money, but that wasn't his concern. He'd be rich enough after this to retire to the home he was having built for himself in the tropics, and never be seen or heard from again, which was just the way he liked it.

It was his turn at the desk. Two officious-looking uniformed cops sat there, while a CO19 with an MP5 stood behind them.

'Name please, sir,' said the first one.

'Robert Durran.'

'Were you a guest in the Stanhope?'

'Yes. Room 202.'

The second one typed something on the laptop, and nodded to the first, who asked Fox if he had any ID.

'Yes, I do.'

But as he reached into his pocket for the wallet, he heard a commotion behind him.

'I know him,' said an older-looking black man in dungaree overalls who was standing a couple of people back in the next line. 'He's one of them,' he continued, pointing at Fox. 'He's one of the terrorists. I was hiding in the crawlspace in the ballroom kitchen. I heard him speaking in there loads of times. It's him. I'm sure of it.'

Everyone was looking at Fox now. He could have tried to brazen things out, but it wouldn't take the authorities long to work out the truth if they delved any deeper into his background. Which left him with only one option.

In one movement he turned and bolted for the exit,

knowing he was never going to make it. He was trapped and unarmed, but he knew he couldn't surrender and face the rest of his days behind bars. That would be too much.

He heard the angry shouts of armed officers screaming at everyone to get down, saw people hitting the deck like a falling line of dominoes, saw the guns pointing at him from every direction.

And then someone in one of the lines threw out a leg and Fox pitched forward over it, his mobile clattering across the tarmac.

In the next second, he felt someone jump on his back, knees first, screaming and shouting. Fox gasped in pain as the wind was taken out of him. It was one of the hostages. As Fox tried to struggle free from his grip, a great shout rose up from the other hostages, and they fell upon him, tearing at his hair and face and screaming abuse as they dragged him to his feet.

He felt a surge of panic as he was kicked and punched and scratched. These people were going to tear him apart limb from limb – he could hear the bloodlust in their voices. They weren't going to stop. Someone spat in his face; someone else was trying to ram fingers into his eyes; another tugged savagely at his hair.

But then the people moved away, and once again he was being slammed back to the ground, except this time he felt the cold metal of gun barrels being pushed against his head, and gloved hands roughly searching him. Unable to stop himself, he threw up, just as someone took a photo of him lying with his face in the dirt, completing his humiliation.

With his vision blurred from the attempt to gouge out his eyes, he heard rather than saw someone pick up his mobile from the ground, and shout something about the text he'd just sent.

It didn't matter. None of it mattered any more.

He was caught.

92

The moment Arley walked back in the room, everyone turned her way.

'Ma'am, where the hell have you been?' John Cheney asked incredulously. He was down to his shirtsleeves and looked more stressed than she'd seen him all night. 'The SAS have gone in and we've got hostages coming out.'

'Silver Commander's on the line from 1600, ma'am,' said Janine.

Riz Mohammed had the phone to his ear, but he was shaking his head. 'I'm getting no answer at all. Right now, I have no idea what's going on in the hotel.'

Arley looked around. She felt numb. She had her children back, and for that she was truly thankful in a way she couldn't describe, but now that they were safe the enormity of her losses bore down on her like a lead weight.

She turned to Janine. 'Can you tell Silver that I wish to be relieved of my post. I'd recommend that Chris Matthews take over for the duration. Thanks to each and every one of you for all your efforts tonight.'

There was a stunned silence lasting a good three seconds, before Cheney finally broke it. 'Arley? Ma'am? You can't just leave in the middle of a crisis like this. It's bloody madness.'

Arley fixed him with a hard stare. 'I'm sorry. There's nothing else I can do.'

Cheney started to say something else, but she'd already turned her back and was walking out the door, knowing it was only a matter of time before her colleagues realized what she'd done, but knowing too that she had to see Oliver and India before she was arrested. Only then would she be able to prepare herself to face the consequences of her actions.

But she'd barely gone ten yards across the grass in the direction of the outer cordon when she heard footsteps behind her.

It was Cheney.

She stopped, facing him. 'Leave me alone, John.'

'At least tell me what's going on, Arley. You've been behaving strangely all night. And who exactly was your mysterious source who knew that the SAS were walking into an ambush?'

'You'll find out soon enough.'

He took a step forward. 'Come on. We go back a

long way. I may be able to help.'

She didn't know if he could or not, but before she had time to think about it, she was talking. 'My children were kidnapped by the terrorists who organized this siege. They used me to tell them the plans for an assault on the building. I almost sent those SAS men to their deaths.'

'Jesus. What stopped you?'

'The kids escaped,' lied Arley, knowing she had to be careful to protect Tina's role.

'So, there was no informant?'

'No, there wasn't.'

'I'm sorry. If there's anything I can do.'

'You can cover my tracks, and give me some time. I need to go and see my children. I need to tell them about Howard.'

Cheney nodded. 'I understand. And I'll do what I can.'

Arley managed a tight smile. 'Thanks, John.'

'Good luck, Arley.'

They looked at each other for a long moment, and she wondered if he still felt something for her after all these years. If he did, it was way too late.

She turned away and started walking, her pace quickening on the wet grass.

And then, just as suddenly, she stopped, feeling a growing sense of dread.

She turned round and watched John Cheney walk back towards the incident room.

Which as far as Arley was concerned could only mean one thing.

He already knew.

93

'How the hell did you know about Howard?'

They were just a few yards from the mobile office, the area around them almost deserted now that all the available officers had gone forward to deal with the hostages as they came out of the hotel. Fires burned in some of the Stanhope's upstairs windows, lighting up the night sky, but Arley hardly noticed them. She was too busy confronting the man she was now convinced had something to do with the kidnapping of her children.

When he turned round, Cheney looked so shocked and confused that a part of her doubted the accusation she was throwing at him. 'I don't understand what you're talking about,' he said.

'I told you that I had to tell my children what had happened to him, and you said you understood. You didn't ask what happened to him. That means you must have known he was dead.'

'Arley, I think all this stress is getting to you.'

'It's not. You know something.'

But did he? Or was she imagining it?

No, she couldn't be. All night she'd wondered how the terrorists had known so much about the police operation. It stood to reason that they had an inside man. Cheney wouldn't have been able to get hold of the SAS plans himself. Nor would he have wanted to when he could use Arley to do it for him, and therefore keep suspicion firmly away from himself.

Her mind was a maelstrom as she stood glaring at the man who'd once, many years ago, been her lover. Now she was accusing him of complicity in mass murder, including that of her husband. It all seemed so surreal.

'I ought to have you arrested right now,' said Cheney angrily. 'And if there was anyone round here, I would. But right now, someone's got to take responsibility for the operation now that it's been compromised. Just go and see your children while you still can.'

He turned away from her.

'You'll get found out,' she called after him. 'When they arrest me, I'll tell them to investigate you. And they will. They'll want to know how the terrorists knew I was going to be a commander today.'

'Anyone could have guessed it if they'd known you were on duty. It's not rocket science.'

'You won't have been that good at covering your tracks, John,' she continued, ignoring his protests.

'Come on, Arley,' Cheney sighed, turning back round and walking up to her. 'This is ridiculous.'

At the last second, she saw him glance out of the corner of his eye to check that there was still no one around, and knew immediately what was going to happen next.

His hands shot up and he grabbed her roughly by the throat, squeezing as hard as he could as he tried to drag her behind one of the empty squad cars. But Arley reacted fast, grabbing his crotch and twisting with all the strength she had. His grip loosened and they both fell over, Cheney on top. They struggled violently on the ground, Arley driven on by anger as she scratched and kicked him, but Cheney was a big man and his hands were still round her throat, applying more and more pressure, and Arley began to feel herself passing out.

'What's going on?'

It was Janine Sabbagh, standing over them.

Cheney immediately released his grip and Arley gasped for air.

'It's not what it looks like, Janine,' said Cheney, rolling off her. 'DAC Dale was resisting arrest.'

'It seemed like you were trying to strangle her,' said Janine, looking totally shocked.

'He was trying to kill me,' Arley gasped, getting shakily to her feet.

'Don't be stupid,' snapped Cheney. 'Get back inside, Janine. I'll handle this.'

'No, stay here, please.'

'Look, I don't know what's going on here,' Janine said uncertainly.

There was a shout from behind her and Chief Inspector Chris Matthews came running into view, accompanied by three CO19 officers. 'I need to see both your phones,' he said, addressing Arley and Cheney. 'In fact I need to see the phones of everyone here. We've just traced a mobile phone contacted a few minutes ago by one of the terrorists to this exact area.'

'It'll belong to him,' said Arley, recovering herself now.

'I don't know what you're talking about,' spat Cheney, but there was the first sign of doubt in his voice.

Matthews put out a hand, and one of the CO19s raised his MP5. 'I need to see the phones now.'

Arley saw Cheney tense just before he made a run for it. As he took off into the darkness away from Matthews and the others, she leaped forward and rugby-tackled him, sending him to the ground with a hugely satisfying thud.

Matthews was on him like a whippet, followed by the CO19 officers, and Cheney's struggles ceased as his hands were cuffed behind his back.

'Do me a favour, ma'am,' said Matthews, turning to

Arley, 'and tell me what's going on here.'

'This man's working with the terrorists,' she answered, standing up and brushing herself down. 'I discovered his identity and he tried to kill me. Get him into the incident room and we'll organize a vehicle to take him down to Paddington Green for questioning.'

Matthews and the others hauled Cheney to his feet, and Cheney pointedly ignored Arley's gaze as he was led back to the incident room. Only Janine lingered. She looked at Arley strangely, as if there were still a lot of unanswered questions, which there were. Then she too turned away.

Arley pulled out her phone, putting it to her ear as if about to make a call, then she started walking briskly across Hyde Park towards the outer cordon, before finally breaking into a run.

It was time to see her children.

94

Tina stood on the doorstep of Arley Dale's mother's attractive modern townhouse, looking out on to the empty wet street. Lights were on in all the houses, and Tina was pretty sure that behind every curtain people were watching the events continue to unfold at the Stanhope.

On the way over here in the car, she'd heard the news that all the gunmen were supposedly now dead and Special Forces were in the building, clearing it room by room, floor by floor, while bomb disposal teams had dealt with a number of suspect devices. Tina knew that her actions had almost certainly saved the lives of SAS operatives, but it had been a close-run thing, and, given everything else she'd done, including killing a man, it might not be enough to save her from prison.

For the past few months, at the back of her mind

she'd toyed with the idea of appealing against her dismissal from the Met and trying to resurrect her career as a police officer. But this had scuppered any such ambitions completely. There was no way on earth they could let her back in now.

But Tina didn't regret what she'd done. A man had once told her that you should judge your actions by how much good they do; if the good outweighed the bad, then those actions were worth it. The man who'd said it might have been a killer many times over, but even so Tina felt he had a valid point. And tonight, the good she'd done far outweighed the bad.

She stubbed her cigarette out on a waist-high stone flowerpot, and rubbed her hands against the cold. She could do with warming up but she had no desire to go back inside, where Arley's mum would only keep bombarding her with questions. And to be fair, who could blame her? But right now she wasn't interested in answering them.

A black cab turned into the street, stopping directly outside. It was Arley, still in her DAC finery, although it was looking somewhat dishevelled. Tina had always thought there was something pompous about the uniform of the senior officers in the Met, and she wondered what the taxi driver must have thought when Arley had hailed him.

After paying him, Arley walked up the steps to where Tina was standing, stopping in front of her. She took a deep breath, and threw her arms round Tina.

'Thank you so much for what you've done. I don't know how I can ever repay you.'

Tina pulled away gently. 'Save the hugs for the children, Arley. You haven't got much time.'

Arley took a step back. 'Have you called the police?'

'I have, but I haven't told them where to find us. I'm going to need to call them again now and tell them to come here.'

'Can't you leave it for a little while?'

Tina shook her head. 'I left a crime scene containing the body of the man I killed. I can't afford to avoid them. Neither can you right now.'

Arley gave an understanding nod. 'Then I guess I'd better hurry up.'

Tina stepped aside to let her past. She didn't envy Arley, having to tell her children that they'd lost their father. It was going to be a hard conversation, especially after all they'd been through. But they were good, brave kids and they would have family around them. And at least, unlike many of the victims of that day, they still had their lives in front of them.

Lighting another cigarette, she put up her collar against the cold and walked slowly up the street, waiting until she finished it before making the call.

Then she walked back down to the house and sat down on the bottom of the steps to wait.

Sixteen Days Later

95

It was a mild afternoon for December, but raining steadily, as it had been for days, and already very dark, as the mourners filed slowly out of the ancient church. Beyond the wall stood a very wet-looking camera crew – the only sign that the funeral of Martin Geoffrey Dalston was any more than just a run-of-the-mill event. Dalston was by no means the first victim of the terrorist attack on the Stanhope to be buried, but there was a rumour that he was in line for a posthumous bravery award, which probably explained the presence of the camera crew.

Scope had stood at the back of the church, keeping well out of sight, and consequently he was one of the first people out. He wore a beanie hat with a scarf pulled up over half his face, so that no one would recognize him, but unfortunately the walking stick he was having to use, courtesy of the bullet in his arse, was a bit of a giveaway. During the week he'd spent in hospital the police and the staff had kept the media at bay, but since then everyone had been trying to get some sort of comment from him. Scope knew he was a big story – the guy who'd taken on the terrorists and saved the lives of dozens of hostages. They'd dug up and picked over his past. His eighteen-year military service, including two tours each in Iraq and Afghanistan; marriage to his childhood sweetheart, and fatherhood at nineteen; the affairs; the messy divorce; and, most poignant of all, the tragedy of his daughter.

That was the part Scope hated about it the most. Dredging up what had happened to Mary Ann for the entertainment of the masses. He didn't want anyone knowing about her. It was none of their business, and never would be. He was surprised, though, that the media hadn't delved further into what had happened after her death. If they had, they'd have discovered an explosive story that would have satisfied even the most jaded reader. Maybe one day they would, and he'd be found out. But there was no point in him worrying about that now. He'd done what he had to do.

It was a two-hundred-yard walk back to where he'd parked his car, and since he was still out of practice at walking with pins in his leg, his progress was slow. He kept his head down as other mourners overtook him, and was relieved that he wasn't seen by the camera crew. He'd looked for Abby and Ethan in the church but didn't think they'd been there, which was probably for the best, although he'd've liked to see Ethan again one more time. He'd received a card from them when he was in hospital, thanking him for all he'd done. It had had a Florida postmark, and Ethan had enclosed a picture he'd drawn of Scope as an action man with immense biceps, an ill-fitting suit, and a very big gun. Scope had put it on the table by his hospital bed, and he had it now, packed up among his belongings.

As he reached the car and felt in his pocket for the keys, someone tapped him on the shoulder. He turned round and saw that it was the blonde manager from the hotel whose name, he'd found out afterwards, was Elena Serenko. She was wearing a black dress underneath a long dark raincoat and black headscarf, and she reminded Scope of a young Bette Davis.

'Hello,' she said, with a shy smile. 'I thought I saw you inside the church.'

'I was trying to keep a low profile. I guess it didn't work.'

'The cane doesn't help. How are your injuries?'

'I'm on the mend. I was very lucky. I got hit twice and no major internal damage, but I'm going to be walking with this for a while yet.'

'I wanted to say thank you again for what you did for us in the hotel.'

'Thank you too. You helped save my life.'

There was an awkward silence, and Scope had the idea that she wanted to say something else.

'Are you going back to the wake?' she asked.

Scope shook his head. 'No. I only came to pay my respects. He was a good man.'

'Do you know I only knew him for a few hours but I feel like I found out so much about him. Does that make sense?'

'You can find out a lot about someone in that time. Especially in difficult circumstances.'

'Martin told me he had a girlfriend once. Someone he'd stayed with in the hotel many years ago, who was the love of his life, and who he hadn't seen in more than twenty years. It's mad, I know, but I kept looking for her today. I wanted to talk to her.' Elena suddenly looked embarrassed. 'I'm sorry. I don't know why I'm standing here in the pouring rain telling you all this.'

'It's OK.'

There was another awkward silence, this one longer. Scope was about to say something when Elena started speaking again. 'We had a guest in one of the suites at the Stanhope called Mr Miller. He'd been there for a while, and I have to admit, I didn't like him very much. On the day of the terrorist attack, he was killed, along with his two bodyguards. But the thing is, the terrorists didn't kill them. I know that because I heard them talking about it.' She frowned. 'I don't know how to say this,' she continued, looking embarrassed again, 'but did you know anything about him?'

For a moment, Scope wanted to tell her everything. But he knew it would put Elena in a terrible position. He smiled. 'I'm sorry, I can't help you with that one. I don't know how I'd have fitted it in.' He looked at her steadily, and he could tell she knew he was lying. 'Have you told the police about it?'

She looked down. 'No. The police have plenty to keep them busy as it is, and anyway, I'm off to Australia with my fiancé very soon.' She smiled, and looked him in the eye. 'We're about to start a new life.'

He smiled back. 'Good luck. If I had my time again, I think I'd do the same thing.'

This time there were no awkward pauses. She thanked him almost formally, and said goodbye.

Scope watched her go, suddenly feeling very lonely. He thought of Mary Ann and the trail of revenge that had led to that fateful day at the Stanhope Hotel.

When she'd died of an overdose of unusually pure heroin aged barely eighteen, the news had devastated him. His ex-wife had died six months later in a car accident, hitting a tree on a country road late at night. Scope had often wondered whether it was suicide, and concluded that it probably had been. He could easily have gone the same way too, almost did on more than one occasion when the pain and the loneliness had got too much.

But slowly he'd pulled himself together, and as

he'd done so, he'd begun to feel a new emotion. Anger. He realized, almost with surprise, that he wanted to make those who'd contributed to Mary Ann's death pay, and he'd set about planning how to make this happen.

It was two years from the moment he put a bullet in the man who sold the fatal dose to when he finally got to the individual at the top of the pile.

Frank Miller was running his business from a suite in the Stanhope, ever since a messy divorce of his own. Miller didn't get his hands dirty. A middle-aged businessman and entrepreneur, he had a colourful background, which included prison for fraud in his youth, but he'd pulled himself up by his bootstraps and become a multi-millionaire with interests in construction, retail and property. He was also one of the biggest importers of heroin into the UK, and dealt directly with contacts in Turkey and Afghanistan.

Scope had spent months planning that particular killing, and it had all gone incredibly smoothly. Neither Miller nor his bodyguards had been expecting a thing, and they'd died within seconds of each other. Even so, Scope had still expected to get caught for this particular crime. His luck had held well for a long time, but three killings in a big London hotel was always going to be a risk too far. And yet, because of everything else that had happened in the Stanhope that day, their deaths were being treated as directly connected to the terrorist attack.

So now, three years after her own death, Mary Ann could finally rest in peace.

He took a last look up and down the road, shivering against the cold, wondering whether he would ever be brought to book for what he'd done. In the end, it was out of his hands, and therefore not something worth spending too much time contemplating. Instead, he slowly got back into his car, threw his stick on the seat and, with a deep breath, drove away from the church, and the mourners, and the past.

The Inspiration for *Siege*

Like everyone else, I was shocked by the brutality of the Mumbai attacks of November 2008, and the utter ruthlessness of the men who took over the hotels, indiscriminately slaughtering the guests. I remember trying to imagine how terrifying it would be to be one of those guests trapped inside the building, knowing that there were people in there with them who actively wanted to kill.

At the time, though, it didn't make me want to write a book about a hotel siege. I think it all seemed too raw for that. However, in the summer of 2010 I was staying in a big old hotel in Taba Heights, Egypt, very close to the Israeli border, and the idea for *Siege* hit me. There was a large raised sundeck twenty feet above the pool, from where I had a panoramic view of all the hotel grounds and the Red Sea beyond, and it occurred to me that if a group of terrorists were to storm through the hotel entrance, where two bored and not very efficient-looking security staff stood guard, we'd all be caught like rats in a trap, since there was no way out of the hotel except through the front. Almost immediately after that, I had a vision of a man, possibly a criminal, who was already inside the hotel and up to no good when the terrorists struck – someone who'd be prepared and able to fight back. I knew then I had a story.

The whole burst of inspiration lasted barely thirty seconds, but sometimes it just happens like that.

To be honest, I thought long and hard before putting pen to paper. I think most writers are nervous about creating any story with a strong terrorist connection because of the possibility of being overtaken by real events. I wanted to set the book in London, using a fictional West End hotel, but I was mindful of the fact that the UK's been on heightened alert for most of the past decade, and that only a year ago intelligence came out of Pakistan warning of a plot to carry out a Mumbai-style attack in London.

In the end, I decided it was worth taking the risk.

However, I wanted to avoid taking the obvious Islamic extremist angle. At the time I was planning the details of *Siege*, the Arab Spring had just begun, and the call across the Muslim world seemed to be for democracy rather than fundamentalism, making it feel almost out of date to be writing about al-Qaeda-inspired violence. So I decided to make my terrorists extreme right-wing mercenaries allied with agents of an unnamed Arab government who were looking to wreak revenge on the UK for its support of the Arab Spring. To me, that felt like a plausible scenario. It also meant that the terrorists could be well organized, with highly focused goals and ready access to weapons, making them a potentially greater challenge for the authorities than any group they'd dealt with before. Most importantly, some of them planned to get out of the building alive – something which I felt added to the tension of the book.

It took me months to plot *Siege*. I was keenly aware that a 'siege' scenario isn't necessarily a good format for a book, because after the big bang opening there's often plenty of time in the middle when very little happens, as both the hostage-takers and the police get down to negotiations. That was why I added the Arley Dale subplot. It helped to keep things moving, so that you, the reader, never had time to get bored. Originally, I wasn't going to use Tina Boyd in the story, and in the first draft her part was actually taken by an ex-lover of Arley's called Ray Mason. Ray was also a maverick cop, with an interesting back story, and I liked him enough that I'm definitely going to use him again – possibly even in the next book. But for some reason, Tina worked better. She's one of those characters who keeps bouncing back into my writing, even though I'd always fully intended to rest her for *Siege*.

Finally, in March 2011, I was ready to start writing the first draft. It should have been pretty straight-forward. I'd created this huge, forty-page, chapter-by-chapter synopsis which told the whole story from start to finish, and I honestly thought I'd have the whole thing done and dusted by the summer.

But as I've discovered more than once in my writing career, what looks like a straightforward story doesn't always turn out that way. Almost as soon as I started writing, I ran into complications. Because of the sheer number of characters and the limited physical area in which they were operating, coupled with the short chapters (most of which had to end in cliffhangers), the logistics of the plot – choreo-graphing where people were so that they ended up in the right places during the climactic scenes – became a bit of a nightmare. Also, trying to make the police response realistic was a challenge. I had visions before I started the book of the police HQ at the scene being like something out of 24, with scores of highly co-ordinated officers armed with laptops and high-tech comms devices. But when I talked to one senior officer in Counter Terrorism Command, he said that, although the Met trained regularly for these sorts of scenarios, in reality, the initial couple of hours would be pretty chaotic as officers, acting on sketchy and sometimes conflicting information, battled to get to the scene through gridlocked traffic, while those already there were forced to operate pretty much 'on the hoof'. I wanted to capture this sense of confusion and fear, as well as the coming together of the police response as the lines of command were established. I did take a couple of liberties to ensure the story worked smoothly (most obviously, largely ditching Silver Commander, and having Gold liaise directly with Arley, the Bronze Commander, which wouldn't usually happen), but I hope I gave an approximate impression of what things might be like in such a tense and fast-moving situation.

Strangely, some characters worked far better than others. The guests in the hotel, and Elena the manager, came quite easily to me – probably because, as a pretty ordinary person myself, I was able to identify with them. More worryingly, though, so did the terrorists, especially Fox, whose character I really enjoyed writing. I was even intending for him to escape at the end of the book, but because he was such a horrible piece of work, with so few redeeming features, I ended up changing my mind.

Scope, though, was a problem from the start. Originally, I didn't want him to be a good guy. I wrote him as an American hitman carrying out a hit on an American businessman in the Stanhope, but that didn't work. Then I wrote him as a British drug dealer, who was at the Stanhope to make a major deal, which ended in bloodshed. But the problem was, there were already too many bad guys in the script. So, in the end, I compromised and made Scope a mysterious killer, one who turned out to be a basically good man who'd done some bad things, but only in a bid to avenge the death of his daughter.

Changes were made constantly to the script as I wrote. In one draft, Abby and Ethan were captured, and Scope gave himself up to the terrorists so that they could be freed. He was then tortured for several hours before finally making an escape, helped by Clinton. I later changed this because it seemed implausible that the terrorists would keep Scope alive if they captured him. Elena, too, nearly didn't make it to the end. In an early draft, she was executed by Cat about halfway through, but I liked her too much, so she came back. That's one of the fun things about being a writer – being able to commute people's death sentences.

Even the ending changed pretty dramatically, after I got some negative feedback from my editor (which proved bang on target). Unfortunately, this was only three weeks before the book was due, which meant a whole load of rewriting, so it was all 'skin of your teeth' stuff.

Incredibly, I didn't read it the whole way through until two days before the 21 October deadline, and I was terrified that it would be a load of crap, given how many changes had been made. That's one of the less fun things about being a writer. You're so close to the work that it's very difficult to be objective about how good it is.

Thankfully, when I did read it, I was pretty pleased (and mightily relieved) with the result. More importantly, I hope you were too.

Either way, I'm praying the next one's easier.

Simon Kernick
November 2011

Acknowledgements

There are plenty of people who provided me with information to help write this book. Most of them, as always, have to remain nameless, but I am allowed to say a big thank you to Siobhan Thomasson, the General Manager of the Holiday Inn in Winchester, who was kind enough to give me an insight into the workings of the hospitality industry. Thanks, too, to my editor, Selina Walker, and agent, Amanda Preston, who, as usual, made some great suggestions to help improve the story.

Without all of you, it would have been a far lesser piece of work.